ALL THINGS BROKEN
DAVID JAMES LYNCH

Western Cahruia

ALL THINGS BROKEN
THE EGIMIAN CHRONICLES

Published in Canada by Engen Books, St. John's, NL.

Library and Archives Canada Cataloguing in Publication information for this title can be accessed via the CIP website.

ISBN: 978-1-77478-113-5

Distributed by:
Engen Books
www.engenbooks.com
submissions@engenbooks.com

First mass market paperback printing: December 2022
Second mass market paperback printing: March 2026

Cover Design: Ellen Curtis

For Norah and James.
Sometimes, it's just magic...

At the fount you well may stare,
But nought save pebbles smooth is there,
And small straws twirling one and all,
Hie thee home, and be thy pray'r
Save us all from Fairy thrall…

Samuel Ferguson
The Fairy Well of Lagnanay

PROLOGUE

She walks in dry sand.

Her feet sink into its grasp as she breathes the forgotten sweetness of sea air. With each step she is held for one warm moment until the bond is broken, leaving behind a print that is both shapeless and enigmatic to those who would follow. Tiny grains fall from her feet as she moves; the sand's desperate attempt to hold her, to keep her from reaching an unknown destination.

Yet, she must do this. She tells herself this, repeating it in an attempt to soothe her mind as the waves soothe the shore. The sun, in the midst of its descent, sears the sand beneath her. Foamy waves disintegrate beside her, their journey complete, and she can almost convince herself that she hears their sigh of relief. Though her feet burn, she does not think of walking in the cool, clear water.

Her path is not meant to be easy.

She watches the waves slide across the shore, causing the sands to sparkle – each grain a diamond that would disappear before ever it could be grasped. Sea birds call in the distance, and she looks up. The sun has turned the sky a brilliant orange, and the chest of the ocean rises and falls, reflecting light in infinite directions.

A single tear shines on her cheek.

She has set herself on this path, and there is no turning back. She has felt the darkness, the sickness growing within her.

She was told it may return in time, and now, she knows she must leave. She stops and looks back, scanning her past through a shimmering haze of memory above her footprints.

It is then that she sees him; distant, but moving with purpose.

He is coming.

She knows he has seen her; his pace has quickened. There is no mistaking his stride or the aged brown cloak which flows behind him. A glint of sunshine catches upon the long, cold weapon in his hand. A moment later, he begins to run.

She turns and runs as well, setting her sight on the trickling brook that emerges from the forest ahead. It is here she must go. She can almost hear the stream now, descending from the hills to rejoin its source. Its sound is one of anticipation, one of completion. It has come full circle.

Now, so must she.

She hears him calling to her, and a hint of panic enters her heart. The stream meanders just ahead of her and she listens to its voice, wishing that it would rage and wash him fully from her memory and sight. She looks around the stream nervously, her eyes darting left and right. She stops.

There is no one here. *Why is there no one here?*

She doesn't understand. Her breath burns in her throat as she moves a hand to the sharp pain in her side. His voice is screaming behind her. He was not supposed to find her. Not here.

She reaches the stream and with a tiny gasp wades into its cool flow as it carves its path through the sand-swept beach. A slight chill runs up the sides of her legs. She swings around, her thin, pale dress, not worn in years, clinging to the surface of the water.

There is no one here.

She lifts the hem of her dress and moves up the stream, carefully in her bare feet. Looking left she sees him running, sand flying from his feet. He is closing the space between them, and in short moments, panic sets in fully.

She splashes through the water to the place where the stream leaves the wooded hills. Tall grasses protrude and brush her skin. Just a few paces beyond the fringe of trees, the water deepens. The air darkens and grows heavy. She enters the forest and slows, surveying the area around her as she moves. She feels foreign in this place, mesmerized, unable to shake the feeling that she is an intruder here even after all these years. Overhead, thin rays of sunlight force their way through the branches in an attempt to reach the forest floor below, flickering on her worried face.

There is a presence in this place that she can neither see or explain. She wades further along the stream, which grows deeper the further she goes. She realizes suddenly that her pace has slowed, and she steps onto the soft riverbank to run beneath the birch that have just begun to shed their leaves. The branches surrounding her soon blur into flickering arms, and she briefly considers whether their embrace might be preferable to that of the one who chases her.

She looks over her shoulder, wondering if he will appear again before she reaches her destination. He is a good tracker, and she has no doubt that he will catch her.

Then she sees it.

Before her, the stream has slowed and widened beneath a tall ash tree to form a pool. Moving slowly despite her fear, she approaches and steps into the dark water which swirls, enthralling her weary mind. She steps further into its depth, and gasps again as the water reaches her hips.

Faintly, she hears his voice, screaming as he tears through the thick of the forest. In moments, he will arrive. But all pain and worry has left her now. Standing in this pool, she is at peace.

Yet, somewhere deep within the far recesses of her heart she feels sorrow for the man – this man, whose roar now scatters the birds from the limbs above.

"Forgive me…" she whispers, as thin hands burst from the water and pull her below.

1

THE TRENOC AND THE BOY

Cold water lapped the feet of the boy.

The water caused no discomfort. In truth, there was very little he noticed when he sat beside the mighty current, save the low, static roar of its movement. The sound, as well as the sight of the water, transfixed him, and he lost himself here on many an occasion. *Too many*, some would say.

For Sivino Spallic, the River Andel was a sanctuary. It was here that he came to find peace, to find the quiet – of a sort – that he needed now more than ever. That fluid roar seemed to dull the jagged thoughts that troubled his mind.

His head tilted slightly as he studied the river's motion, its erratic flow seemed rehearsed, no movement random. Waves broke against immovable rocks, over and over in a battle that frothed for months until the approach of autumn calmed its current. The river was a living creature, its roar a language of its own, communicating emotion in the only way it knew.

And Sivino seemed to understand.

He snapped a branch from a tree that had fallen nearby, and tossed it into the flow. It was snatched hungrily and swept downriver, tossed by the water, beaten against rocks, submerging, reappearing. Broken.

His father had used such demonstrations on a number of occasions to illustrate the power and danger of the Andel when Sivino was a young boy. Dels Spallic's lessons were quiet and to the point, but they held as much hidden meaning as the Nucono Forest held birch.

We don't always see the strength, the power *of that river,* Dels had said to his son several seasons prior as the two watched chunks of ice float by on the spring thaw. There had been talk in town that some of the older boys had been attempting to ride the large pans of ice, making a precarious game of how far they could float downstream. Dels had been leaning on a pale walking stick, a stick that he'd shaped over a number of weeks and into which he'd meticulously carved the likeness of three trees; an amilliat for himself, an oak for Sivino's brother Leath, and an ash for Sivino himself. His father worked wood as deftly as he etched lessons into the malleable minds of his sons. He'd turned from Sivino as he continued. *But never doubt that such strength is there…*

With no warning, his face void of emotion, Dels had turned and flung the stick high over the waters of the Andel. Sivino had gasped, watching in disbelief as the beautiful staff landed and was swept up in the current.

"Father! What a waste!" Sivino had shaken his head as the heavy river carried the stick. Moments later, it caught on a cluster of rocks near the centre of the Andel. A large chuck of ice followed the same path and crushed the stick upon the rocks, leaving broken pieces to float away and out of sight.

Dismayed, Sivino had turned to his father. "You spent weeks shaping that stick!"

Dels smiled, though it was one without joy. "Imagine I'd spent years shaping it." He turned and walked past Sivino, ruffling the boy's hair gently. "And imagine it couldn't be replaced. *That* would be a loss."

Now, as Sivino sat on a log that had fallen at the river's edge, his father's lesson remained firm in his mind. *Such strength is there*, Sivino thought. *And sometimes, we don't see tha—*

The creature fell from the trees, a blur of dark brown fur that hit the ground directly in front of him. Sivino had no time to react before the creature was upon him. It swung a long, muscular arm, striking him across the shoulder with the back of its hand. Sivino fell backward over the log, landing painfully on his back in a shallow pool of water. He tried to gasp, his breath knocked from his body. Above him, the creature stood on the log, looking down on him. It snarled and panted in equal measure. It pointed a long, gnarled finger at Sivino.

"Home! *Now!*"

Slowly, Sivino felt his breath come back to him. He turned himself over and stood slowly, his shirt wet and clinging to his slender body.

"*Creation*, Drip!" Sivino gasped as he wiped dirt and twigs from his clothing. "Are you unhinged? Can I not have an hour's peace?"

"Peace?" The trenoc repeated with the word with disgust, the furry face contorted. "Yes, certainly, *certainly*! Shall I tell the cattle to herd themselves as you splash the waters like a fool?"

Sivino opened his mouth to protest the scowling trenoc, but stopped as the realization washed over him. It was his turn to herd the cattle. Before the sun set, he was supposed to relieve his brother Leath. His eyes fell shut, and he silently berated himself as he pulled on his shoes. *Mist-headed fool!*

They set off for the Spallic homestead at breakneck speed, though the trenoc's continued mumbling suggested that he felt such speed was decidedly lacking. Their home, situated southwest of the village of Egim, was but a ten minute walk from the Andel, which lay to the south. Too often, Sivino wandered through the vegetable gardens and fields of wheat that surrounded the home, only to find himself within the familiar shade of the Nucono Forest. No sooner would he enter the forest than the river's roar beckoned him and, while time often stood still for the boy, his feet did not.

Drip kept mainly to the trees as they returned. A trenoc moved with more agility when able to use all four limbs and, if necessary, the long, hooked tail that gripped with the strength of a fist. They were creatures of unique disposition, whose determination to accomplish every task was rivalled only by their determination to be miserable while doing so. Fast though Sivino might be, he could not outrun the incessant muttering and curses that were hurled from the branches above.

Forty years ago, the race of trenoc had been driven

from their native realm of Jhora, northeast of the Cudgel Mountains. The people of Jhora – from what little Sivino knew of such a distant population – were not known to be particularly *inclusive* in their thinking or governmental policies. It was said that a sense of superiority permeated the Jhoran culture, and nowhere was this more apparent than in the capital city of Corapall. When rule of the realm fell to Eral Thoccien, a young man who epitomized this hubris, the days of the trenoc were numbered. Thoccien had long despised everything about trenocs, from their hunched stances and furry bodies to the rags they used to cover themselves. As the population of their settlements grew on the outskirts of Corapall, so too did their presence within the city walls. Short time passed in Thoccien's reign before he initiated the *Great Purge*, which sought to 'relocate' the race of trenoc to more suitable regions. Jhoran politicians put their full support behind Thoccien's initiative, which was touted as a catalyst for the rejuvenation of the realm. In the new Jhora, Thoccien stated, there simply wasn't a place for trenoc. Law was passed, and the trenocs were told to move on to neighbouring realms. When they refused, the Jhorans quickly utilized the armed forces of the realm to further *encourage* the marginalized group. Hundreds of trenocs fell, and those that survived crossed the border with the tips of sword and arrowhead close behind them.

It was but one of many dark events that smeared the history of the realms of western Cahruia, Sivino knew. He, like most eastern Embarrians, did not harbour ill will toward the trenocs. Indeed, the Spallic family, like many, had engaged in partnership with the race; a partnership that, while productive, could be most infuriating at times.

As Sivino ran through the forest, he could neither see nor hear Drip. He couldn't help but glance toward the trees, watching for the bothersome trenoc. The creature was more irritable of late, if that was possible, and he seemed to take every opportunity to share his misery with those around him. Sivino took the brunt of the foul-tempered behaviour. A dreamer by nature, Sivino knew that his reflective demeanour was repulsive to the practical trenoc. It was not that he was lazy; rather, his inquisitive mind and deep thoughts often led him down a path quite opposite the one he was expected to follow. The trenoc felt it was his duty to keep Sivino in line, and doing so required him to be a constant, unwelcome presence in the life of the boy.

He did not see Drip fall from the trees. The trenoc landed roughly before him and raised a quick hand to stop him in his tracks. Sivino jerked sideways and fell sprawling into a redhollor bush. He jumped up instantly, an instinct set into him from years of clumsy falls.

"For the love of *Dahnu*, Drip!" he swore as he stood and wiped the redhollor berry juice from his arms. "What are you *doing*?" He stopped, however, when he saw the eyes of the trenoc. His voice lowered. "Drip? What is it?"

The trenoc was silent for long moments before he replied. "Nothing, boy."

"Drip?" Sivino looked past the trenoc, trying to see what had caused that look of fear in his eyes. "Is there something out there?

"Yes, there's something! Cattle that need herding." He

glanced upward before turning to Sivino. "Come – the sky darkens."

"I'm moving as fast as I can," Sivino replied.

The trenoc opened his mouth, surely to comment upon the boy's stamina, but closed it again, narrow eyes turning to the north.

"Come, Sivino. *Now*."

Sivino nodded his head, pushing his long brown hair from his eyes. Short for his sixteen years – he stood but a couple of feet above the perpetually hunched trenoc – his lanky frame gave a false impression of height. He watched as the creature gave one more look to the sky, sniffing softly at the air in a manner that he likely assumed Sivino would miss. The boy saw all of this, and shivered. Trenocs were not given to fear. The look on Drip's face was quite unfamiliar to Sivino. Drip blinked the look away and set to walking once more, and with a quick tilt of his head indicated that Sivino was to do likewise.

Under a quickly setting sun the trenoc and the boy set out for home, both of them eager to be free of the forest's darkening embrace, and the shadow of unease that neither could shake.

2

IN THE DYING LIGHT

Leath's backhand was as quick as it was heavy.

The vicious blow landed just above the strike received from Drip, which still ached. This one, however, took Sivino back a couple of steps.

"How *hard*, Sivino, to remember your duties?" His teeth were clenched, such was his anger. "Perhaps we should tether you like an untrained foal?"

"Sorry Leath, I– It's just–"

Just what? he thought. He knew that any truthful answer would bring nothing but disdain from the young man he considered a brother. His thoughts ran to the river again, lost in its movement, its language. Leath, least among those of Egim, would understand or care.

Leath's wavy blond hair dripped with sweat from his day's work. His narrowed green eyes made Sivino lower his own, as they always did.

"In the Andel again!" spat Drip. "The *Andel*! Should have been a *merrow*, splashing around like a fool."

Sivino shot a look at Drip, who knew how much the boy hated the name. Referring to Sivino as a merrow – the half-man, half-fish creature of myth – was a common slur in Drip's arsenal of insults.

"Again," Leath said, his voice low and cold. "Must I remind you, *again*, that you have responsibilities that lie within the posts of your home, Sivino, not between the banks of a river? Have you such disregard for the well-being of the herd, as well as those who depend on them, that you would neglect their care *again*?"

"My apologies, Leath. Please, go and rest, and tell Father I am here."

"Tell him yourself." He nodded over Sivino's shoulder to Dels Spallic, who walked slowly through a meadow, golden beneath the fading sun.

"Come Drip, let's find a more productive use of our time." Leath sighed as he walked away. "I waste my breath on the little one."

"How well do *merrow* swim in excuses?" Drip asked as he turned away. The trenoc shook his head; shaggy hair waving before his eyes. As he strode off behind Leath, Sivino could not help but notice the look of concern which hung still upon the trenoc's face as he glanced toward the forest.

As the two departed, Sivino put his hands on his hips. He kicked aside a dry piece of bull dung and exhaled slowly, his thin shoulders hanging low. He lifted his gaze and watched his father move across the field. It was not a backhanded strike that he feared receiving from Dels. The big man did not believe in using physical force to instruct his sons. *Hard fists*, he'd say, *are usually as effective as loose tongues. You'll learn very little from either*. Dels preferred to make his sons think. *Think before you act, keep your wits about you, and face every difficult situation head on.*

Recalling these words, Sivino took a deep breath and set off toward his father.

Dels Spallic stood well above six feet tall. His black hair, slightly tinged with silver, hung to his shoulders, which were impressively broad. He walked slowly, though with purpose, and his face held a contemplative look as he scanned the meadowside. The slightest furrow of his brow indicated that his mind was troubled. It was a look that over the years seemed to have ingrained itself in his strong face.

Dels Spallic was no stranger to sorrow.

Looking at his smooth hands as he walked, Sivino thought on those of his father; large and scarred, the hands of a hero. For years, a young Dels Spallic had been a respected member of the *Ryndarra* – the Embarrian men and women charged with the safety and protection of the citizens of the realm. He'd served loyally until the fateful day that fire had stolen the lives of his brother Talen and Talen's young wife Jola. Sivino had never been told what had happened by Dels himself. His knowledge of that dark day came solely from what he'd overheard from the hushed conversations of relatives and townsfolk. A house in flames, screams from an upstairs room as the fire rose, devouring the dwelling room by room. Through a tiny window, young Leath had been dropped into the arms of Dels Spallic. As he'd moved his tiny nephew away from the house, Jola's screams - interspersed with rough coughing - had intensified as Talen continued to shout encouragement and reassurance. So confident was Talen's voice that Dels had been sure they would emerge from the home. He'd laid Leath on the grass and circled the house, looking for some way to help. Tongues of fire darted from every door and window. He'd shouted to the couple, trying to ascertain their location. Again and again he'd circled the home, until he realized that the only screams he now heard were coming from Leath.

The heart wrenching cries within the house had fallen silent.

As he'd knelt by the conflagration, Dels and the child had wept alike. Turning his tear-streaked face to the sky, the young man had screamed his curse at the Goddess Dahnu as he held the child close. By the time his tears had dried, he'd forsaken the life of the Ryndarra.

He'd become a father.

Some years later, the cold hands of Grim would steal another love from Dels. Sivino pushed these thoughts aside. It seemed that memories of his mother Rhenna arose most often when he was at his most vulnerable, times when he was most uncertain of himself. *Which*, he conceded to himself, *seemed to be most days of late.*

"Sivino," Dels said, calm and sure.

"Father, I—"

"Wait, Sivino. Hold your apologies. I'm sure they hang upon your lips like freshly washed trousers, eager to fly." The smallest smile.

"They do," he replied. He lowered his head.

"Hold your head up, Sivino." Dels' voice was firm. "Never defer to others that way. There is no one who can cause you to look to the dirt."

The boy looked up.

"I don't make light of the situation. It is time for you to act as the man you're becoming. Solitude and reflection are fine, even necessary, but there's a time for these things, and that time mustn't conflict with your duties. Leath has worked hard today, and should not be expected to herd the cattle to the lower field during your watch."

"Sorry, Father. I assure you it won't happen again."

"Drip found you at the Andel?" He breathed deeply as Sivino nodded. "Your mother was fond of the river. On occasion, she would walk with our clothing for half an hour to reach its wildest parts. The crashing foam, she'd say, could remove any stain." His smile reflected the memory.

Sivino smiled as well, and remembered how his mother's hair had smelled of lavender. *You smell like a flower*, he'd often told her, to which she'd reply, *And you grow like a weed*.

"Be mindful now, Sivi. We work together to make things work. Losing track of time on the river is a poor excuse when you're needed in the fields. Get the animals rounded up, and see them secured. That gate latch needs fixing as well. Although," he nodded over Sivino's shoulder, "even the best of fences won't keep out every wild creature that roams the night."

Sivino turned to see his friend walking through the neighbouring herd, smacking a cow playfully on the rump before jumping the fence. Ston Tros had become Sivino's best friend before either could see above the meadowgrass. Broad and strong, Ston could easily overpower the slender Sivino. They were opposites in most things;

Ston was quick with his tongue, where Sivino was contemplative. Ston was slow-footed against Sivino's agility. Despite their differences, one would face certain death for the other at a moment's notice. Upon seeing Sivino, Ston snapped his fingers and pointed at the lad as he swaggered toward him.

Dels shook his head, rolling his eyes gently. He patted Sivino on the shoulder. "I'll see you in a bit, Sivi. Remember what I said."

"I will, Father. Find a little rest."

The look on his father's face told Sivino that rest was the farthest thing from Dels' mind. It seemed he never stopped, moving from one task to another without pause. *Idle hands won't tend the lands*, he'd say. The big man nodded, and turned back toward their home. He retraced his steps through the fields, his eyes on the distant forest.

Sivino turned to greet his friend, who walked with the casual gait of one unburdened by worries. A long piece of straw dangled from a wry smile.

"Look who lowers himself to rejoin us humble folk. My dear Siv, I'd thought you up and left to join the Ryndarra!"

"A merry evening to you likewise, Ston. I was but minutes late."

"Yes, from the cursing of Leath, I'm sure you were in just beneath the grains of the hourglass. I was watching when you arrived. I figured Leath would throttle you. Count yourself lucky you received but one hit."

"Two," Sivino replied, rubbing his arm. "Drip is not a creature to waste time with words."

"Nonetheless, perhaps you've learned your lesson?"

"If the lesson includes how to tolerate meddlesome neighbours, I've not learned enough."

"Oh, the *wit* of this one! Unfortunate that this wit leaves you in the presence of certain Rallo damsels... abandoning you to stumble on your words as if they were gnarled tree roots."

Sivino turned to the north, hoping the shadows of the setting sun would hide his flushing cheeks. Torla Rallo and her brother Kef completed their companion group, and as the years continued to pass, Sivino found his evolving relationship with Torla to be rather... *perplexing*.

"Roots?" Sivino continued with a smile. "I should think my words were the apples of the upper branches."

"Well, perhaps you should pick a couple of ripe ones right about now, my friend." Sivino turned to see him nodding in the direction of Leath, who rode toward them with two horses and a scowl.

"Damnation," Sivino muttered.

Leath rode high upon a steed and trailed a mare close behind. When he reached the pair, he shoved the mare's reins roughly toward Sivino.

"Evening, Leath." Ston's tone was laden with whimsy, the hint of mockery unmistakable. "Doesn't that sunset just take your breath away?"

Leath spat to his side. "If you enjoy losing your breath, Tros, I'll gladly assist. Have you finished delaying Sivino?"

"Not quite. We were just discussing the progression of trenoc table etiquette in recent years. If you'd like to join us, we'd be more than hap–" Ston jumped aside as Leath kicked the steed into motion.

"I've come to help you round up the cattle, Sivino. Left on your own, I'm sure you'll end up looking for cows well after nightfall. Tros, have you no beasts of your own to attend to? Get to it."

"Very well." He turned, and bowed toward Sivino. "Master Spallic, good luck in your cattle rounding and your apple picking. We'll chat on the morrow."

Leath shook his head and muttered a curse as the Tros boy departed. "Take the eastern fields, Sivino. I'll take the west." Sivino nodded quietly and mounted the mare.

He pushed the cattle hard. There had been enough cause for criticism today, and the last thing Sivino wanted was to prove unable to round the herd up quickly. The animals voiced their deep-throated complaints as they were forced to abandon the grassy meadows located near the wheat fields, but Sivino ignored them. He tried to shake the thoughts of inadequacy, but again and again, the faces of Leath and his father came to the forefront of his mind. Closing his eyes, he tried to replace them with a face more given to acceptance. Torla Rallo. Feelings for the young girl were complicated, and much as he tried to deny it, there was truth in Ston's comments.

The sudden moaning of the cattle shook him from his reverie, and he gave the mare a small kick to speed her up. The cows, which had been moving obediently toward the southern field, now began to separate, their heads turning as though they were uncertain of where to go.

"Come on you laggards. The light is dying and–" He stopped. A sound drifted toward him from beyond a rise in the land, distant but unmistakable. A cry. He strained to hear it, difficult with the noise of the cattle, but there it was again. Distinct, and full of pain. It came once more, louder, and he knew there was trouble. Forgetting the herd, he moved up the incline, looking to his right for Leath. As he saw the young man, an agonizing cry reached them both, one that suggested a torture Sivino could not imagine. He saw Leath's head whip around, and then they were both racing across the field. He crested the slope first, and was almost overrun by the cattle which ran in the opposite direction. He'd never seen the animals move so quickly. He skirted around them, and then gave a great tug on his reins, causing the mare to momentarily stand on her hind legs.

Blood. So much blood. And a destroyed cow that sucked at her last ragged breaths. He looked around. For Leath. For anyone. A movement near the forest caught his eye, and he had just enough time to see the figure before it disappeared into the shadows of the Nucono.

"Dahnu save us," he whispered. There was a pounding of the earth, and moments later Leath pulled up his steed and dismounted. He whispered a curse that was uncharacteristically profane, even for him.

"Sivino?"

"Leath. How? What could–" He stopped as Leath drew his knife, his narrow eyes never leaving the forest.

"Sivino. Get Father. *Now*."

The group stood in a quiet circle around the ruined beast. Drip and the Spallics had been joined by neighbour Stellen Tros, who shook his head. The two older men spoke in hushed tones to the side of the group, their eyes repeatedly darting to the trees.

"Damned fool, I was," muttered Drip. "I sensed something in the forest, sensed it and said *nothing*. Should have trusted my instincts. And now, this."

"You couldn't have predicted this, Drip," Leath said, continuing to watch the men. Stellen moved in closer to scrutinize the cow once more. He crouched by the animal.

"Brudogs aren't known to come this far north. They never have." He turned to Dels. "Though, that's not to say they couldn't. Two brudogs, working together, could have done this rather quickly." He stood and folded his arms. "I can think of nothing else that would be capable of inflicting this damage."

"I can."

The group turned instantly to Sivino, their eyes shocked and questioning. Dels moved forward.

"Sivino."

"Father, I saw something. When I reached the animal."

"I saw nothing," Leath interjected.

"Before you arrived. Just– Just for a moment. By the trees. It was running."

Dels reached out and put a hand on Sivino's shoulders. "What did you see, Son?"

Sivino hesitated. "Father, it ran upon two legs."

"You can't mean to suggest that this atrocity was committed by one of our own."

"No, not our own. Two legs, Father. Yet, the way it ran – it was the movement of no humanfolk, be sure of it. It was huge, and hunched as it ran, and Father, the light was failing, but it looked to be covered in fur." He paused, considering his words and how they would sound to the man he so respected. "I think it had horns."

Leath closed his eyes and rubbed the bridge of his nose slowly. "Two legs? And horns? You fool, are the shadows of the trees so fearsome to you that they create monsters where n–"

"Leath, please," Dels interjected. He paused, then forced a smile. "The shadows of the dying light are deceiving, especially those cast by the amilliat trees. Indeed, something escaped into the forest, but I'm inclined to agree with Stellen. This appears to be the work of brudogs. We need to get the rest of the herd secured. Come. I've a feeling this night will be more wakeful than most."

Sivino watched as Leath and the men began walking, their voices hushed and their eyes laden with worry. It was a look that was reflected in Drip's face also.

And on the face of the dead cow, there hung still the pure, abject terror that it must have felt when the better portion of its hind leg was so brutally ripped from its body.

3

SHADOWS AND SECRETS

The path home narrowed steadily.

The full foliage of the summer forest blocked the early morning sun as the ragged man raced to the east. His aging, faithful steed ran the Westroad as best he could, given that he'd been running for days and the road gradually deteriorated the further east one travelled. The ruts deepened as the road narrowed, now of a size that would scarcely allow sufficient room for a wide cart. Had he not known the lands as well as he did, he'd still be able to gauge the distance to Egim by the width of the Westroad. *Westroad*. Even the naming of the artery of Embarria suggested an imbalance, the man thought. It was a road meant for venturing west, for who in their right mind would find reason to journey into the eastern lands? Naught but villages and hamlets, the westerners would say. It was a land of rough living and few comforts – scarcely preferable to the colder, more barren climes of the north – a land void of the material riches and haughty indulgences of those who lived upon the Embarrian coast.

And that suited Lomin Lailoken just fine.

His shoulder-length of greasy hair whipped behind him as he rode. Once as auburn as an Embarrian acorn, it was now streaked with a grey that showed his sixty years nearly as much as the deep crow's feet that ran in rivulets from his eyes. He'd never been one to care for outward appearances, even in the time he'd spent living in the west, but his recent trip of a few short days was enough to remind him how shallow people could be when it came to the appreciation of others. He'd been shunned like a common beggar, though in his cloak he'd carried enough iron crendiscs to more than pay for his meagre needs while in the city of Torg. At one point, a Quiet Sister of Dahnu's Order had actually offered him a dozen nickel rings. When he'd politely refused the well-intentioned alms, she'd silently insisted and forced the coins into his hand. He'd relented, and had given the money to the first beggar he encountered at a nearby market.

He smiled as he remembered looking into a mirrored glass in the city market. So long had it been since he'd seen his reflection in anything but a pool of water, the man looking back at him had been admittedly frightful. Despite this, he'd grunted a *hmph* at the reflected man and smiled; a severe smile that showed teeth less straight than most, and with marginally wider spaces between those of the bottom row. He'd looked up to see the vendor staring at him, her raised eyebrows had suggested that her appraisal of him would be less than flattering, should he care to hear it. He had not. He'd given a second *hmph*, and slipped away quietly.

The wolf, the young ones called him. It was a name that he'd introduced to them in a long-ago lesson, telling them of the magnificent sandy grey dogs that could, on rare occasion, be spotted in the mountains near Forachia where he'd grown up. *They live in packs*, he'd told them. *Lean grey face. Beautifully furred. Fairly wary of the world of men.*

Aside from the pack bit, they sound much like yourself, Sivino had noted.

Uncanny resemblance, it sounds to me, Ston had added. *Lomin, old boy, are you certain you don't share a bloodline?*

He'd pointed a warning finger at the lad and, feigning anger, opened his mouth to retort. As he did so, he looked down at his tattered, chestnut-coloured pants. Slowly, he rubbed the greying scruff of his thin face.

Hmph, he'd said.

The young ones were in fact the reason that he now raced back to Egim. In recent days, there had been disturbing talk in the taverns of Torg; traders who'd returned from the east with stories that had caught the attention of the old wolf as he sipped a quiet ale in a dark corner. Strange sightings, it was said. Men, apparently dressed in the fur of beasts, who had attacked the livestock of several homesteads. Some of these were reported to be around the town of Rovil, and, of more concern, the eastern village of Stallion's Cross. There were few real details, and those stories that Lomin heard could have very well been inflated for the benefit of the inebriated audience, but what he'd heard had been enough to convince him that it was time to return home.

He'd planned on spending another couple of days

in the city, in part to settle the family business that had brought him there. A letter had been sent several weeks prior, stating that his brother Andreis, twelve years his elder, was deathly ill and not expected to last a fortnight. The death of a family member is never easy, but in the Lailoken clan, it was more complicated than most. The final rites to be performed required all living siblings to be present at the moment of death, and so, he and his younger sisters, Loanna and Aleisse had made their way to Andreis' bedside to bear witness to his passing into the Land of Ever. Things, however, did not transpire according to plan.

They rarely do where magic is involved.

Lomin tried to shake the thought from his head, and with a shout to Sleipnir he urged the steed to pick up the pace. Coming out of a particularly thick patch of forest, the sight of the rising sun provided some distraction. The giant orb turned the entire sky a deep shade of red as it rose from behind the distant hills before him. Running upon the grassy median between the road's ruts, he watched the sunrise, and recalled the day that the young ones had discovered the long-kept secret that none but his family knew.

It had happened innocently enough, upon a similar morning five years prior. The four young friends had been roaming the forest, tree branch swords held aloft as they saved the world from unseen foes. When they'd noticed Sleipnir grazing in a distant grove, they knew the wolf was near. Torla, the lone female of the group, had felt it would be a good opportunity to sharpen their skills of stealth. Creeping through the underbrush, they'd gotten close enough to hear Lomin muttering unintelligible words. As the boys prepared to scare their old friend, Torla had turned quickly with a finger raised. *Wait*, she'd mouthed silently. The group watched as Lomin stood in the centre of the clearing, his eyes following a rather large bumbled bee that buzzed around him. Suddenly, he'd pulled a small white branch from his side pocket, and pointed it at the insect. The bee seemed frozen in place, though by its nature it often appeared this way. Slowly, however, Lomin had begun to push the stick he held back and forth – subtle movements to be sure, but the bee followed. He pushed forward and pulled back repeatedly, as the bee and branch moved in synchronicity. Then, he'd moved left to right, gradually increasing the speed. The bee was whipped from side to side, and it was obvious to the young ones that Lomin was controlling its flight.

Kef gasped, and Lomin spun.

"Show yourselves!" he'd bellowed.

Silently, the group had come out of the bushes, and stood before him. His face, sharp with anger, looked at each of them before softening. He'd closed his eyes and sighed.

"Come," he'd said quietly. He'd indicated a patch of grass beside him, and sat with the children. He'd looked at them for a long time before he spoke. When he did, his voice was gentle but serious. Laying the small branch on the ground between them, he'd looked to the trees and breathed deeply.

"So," he began, his voice little more than a whisper. "Who can keep a secret?"

Shadows and secrets. He sometimes wondered if the world were made of anything but these things. *Yet, there was brightness,* he conceded. The young ones were proof of this.

It was to them that he now raced. For something had stirred in him upon hearing the drunken talk of the western taverns; a terrible, unsettling feeling that he could not shake. The young ones were fine children, but reckless at times, and there was no telling when they might find themselves in a dire situation. If the dark talk he'd overheard held any merit, his assistance might be required sooner rather than later.

He needed to protect them, for many reasons; not least of which was the promise he'd made to the ancient creature sixteen years ago. A promise that could never be broken.

Shadows and secrets, he muttered to his steed as he raced into the sunrise.

4

THE UTTERANCE OF A LIE

The Embarrian sun rose with the swiftness of a young child, eager to enjoy the day that would be of its own creation. Its beams climbed steadily up the sill of Sivino's window, and leapt in to play upon his face.

Metal pans clattered in the adjacent room. Sivino sighed. Leath would likely be finishing breakfast preparations, no doubt muttering a stream of oaths toward his *lazy slug* of a brother. For his part, Sivino *had* helped to keep an extra eye on the herd until shortly after midnight, when Dels had relieved him and suggested he get some rest.

Rising from his bed, he wiped sleep from his eyes and stretched his neck. He threw aside his hemp blanket and watched as a thousand brilliant specks of dust danced in the sun. Moving to the window, Sivino looked at the forest beyond. Dark images from last night's dreams raced through his head. Quickly, he splashed cold water from the basin onto his face, dressed, and left the room.

The home was modest. The floor, like the walls and roof, were built from the common but strong amilliat wood. Wide windows gave the home light through mildly distorted glass. Higher quality panes might be found in Levebule and other fair cities, but in Egim, folk settled for what was available. The shutters had rarely been used since the winter passed. Woven rugs, one of his mother's many talents, graced each room. Sivino walked over and took his seat at the oak table – it was round, a departure from traditional Egimian design. Rhenna had asked that it be so when Sivino was born. *We are all one,* she had said. *There should be no sides.* As always, Dels had agreed with a smile, and removed the rectangular table.

"Fine morning," Sivino said to Leath.

"Indeed, when you spend most of it asleep after a short watch. When did Father head back out last night?"

"Just past midnight, perhaps," Sivino replied. He knew better than to show offence at his brother's words. "Things remain quiet?"

"From what I hear. Or, more rightly, from what I don't. Could you not have–"

"He did but what he was asked, and I'd expect the same from you, Son."

Dels stood in the doorway holding half a bucket of fresh milk. He wiped his feet on the mat woven by his late wife; *Let Sunshine Enter*, she had stitched into the intricate design. The perfectly curved words weaved above a beautiful sunrise. Sivino had believed that it was her subtle way of informing guests and family alike that within her home, there was no room for darkness of any kind.

"Yes, Sivino. Things are quiet. The cattle graze peacefully, but I think we'll keep them in the lower fields today. That being the case, duties are lessened for *both* of you." As he spoke these last words he turned to Leath, though his older son did not acknowledge hearing them. Forcing a smile, he laid a strong hand on Sivino's shoulder as he walked past the boy to see what Leath was cooking on the woodstove.

Sivino smiled, glad of the extra freedom for one reason in particular. Today was fishing day, a day of relative leisure. He fished often with Ston Tros, usually near the Falls. The local landmark was a waterfall in the Andel on its journey from the Cudgel Mountains. Though it stretched less than fifty feet above the pool below, there was something majestic about the waterfall and the large boulders that embraced it. For this reason it was the preferred location for sport and fun during the warmer days of Embarrian summer. Few excursions could offer more enjoyment than a day fishing near the top of the Falls.

As Leath and Dels discussed a plan to reinforce the two weak fence posts, Sivino slipped away unnoticed to find his fishing line and gear. Breakfast would wait and he didn't want to think about carpentry or cattle on the one day given to adventure.

Rich green grass covered every inch of the Spallic property not used for growing crops. Rhenna's flower beds bordered the home, and spread to the small vernal pool that collected by the trees in the wetter months. The cows kept the grass neatly trimmed, feasting on it for most of their waking hours. Several amilliat trees grew throughout the meadow, as well as oak, vennar and Whispering Leah. The Leah, planted by Sivino's mother, formed a walkway to the little pond. Though they were spread apart widely upon planting, their limbs had reached for each other as they grew and the distance between them closed. *Like children*, Sivino had often heard her say to Dels. He thought of his mother each time he walked beneath the pink and purple leaves that whispered secrets to anyone who took the time to listen.

Slowly, he made his way to the storage hut at the back of the house, located a hundred feet from Drip's tiny, humble dwelling. Entering the hut, he tried to recall where he had placed his fishing hooks after his last trip. *Cursed mess*, he thought. Though Dels swore that he would soon clean out the hut, or ask Drip to do so, it remained in shambles. Sivino sorted through the disorder: axes, shovels and various tools used on a daily basis; watering cans for the garden, harnesses for the bulls when they were required to pull a plow; unfinished weavings of his mother's; and two wooden blades he and Leath had once used to practice their swordsmanship. As children, they had aspired to be the greatest soldiers to ever join the ranks of the Ryndarra. Sivino smiled as he looked at the two sticks, recognizing his own immediately as the one in far worse shape. Their mother had incessantly warned them to take care as they played, as Dels looked on with a smile. The former Ryndarra saw the value in such skill.

Laying down his battered blade, Sivino looked up at the wooden box located on the highest shelf of the furthest corner. His father's Ryndarran gear; the garb and sword of the realm's protectors. He walked over and ran a hand across the rough wood of the box, allowing images of glory to play on his young mind.

"So," came the rasp behind him. "Does the little mer-row hope to be a mighty warrior?"

"Morning, Drip," Sivino sighed, not turning around. The trenoc was always about at an early hour. "I was beginning to miss you."

"Planning a journey south?" Drip ignoring Sivino's sarcasm. "The sword of the Ryndarra is not so needed in this realm, but I'm sure the soldiers of the southern conflict would be pleased to have you lend your mighty blade to the cause."

Sivino looked down at the blade that hung at his side, much shorter than those wielded by the Ryndarra who now fought in the south. For the better part of a year, the southern realm of Rentorria had been engaged in a bitter struggle against the neighbouring Isror. Angered by the injustice of the Isrorian invasion of Rentorria, and concerned about what an Isrorian victory would mean for her people, Inlonia Talchol, queen of Embarria, had sent a host of the Ryndarra to aid King Dunarrk in his defence of the Rentorrian homeland. Though it had evened the playing field somewhat, the addition of the Ryndarra had not brought about the resolution that many had hoped for. The fighting had grown more intense, and the death toll continued to climb.

Sivino secured his shortsword in its battered scabbard. Not much longer than the commonly used long-knife, it served as a useful tool in hunting and other daily activities. Dels had given it to him several months ago, on his sixteenth birthday. He had finished his breakfast and gone in search of his father. He'd found him in the storage hut, sitting on the old rectangular table Rhenna had want-

ed replaced. On his lap lay a sword, small but polished
to a shine. With a wood carving chisel, Dels was etching
the rough wooden hilt. He hadn't looked up as Sivino
entered, but smiled sadly as he continued his work. *It's
heavier than a wooden one, Sivi,* he'd said in a soft voice. Sivino had stood by his father and watched as he completed
his work on the hilt. Though he hadn't the artistic skill of
his wife, the big man's hands were more creatively adept
than most people knew. The carving was that of a rising
sun, an image already etched in Sivino's mind, burning
with all the brilliance of the woman who'd first created it
on a woven mat.

Small though it was, Sivino had taken great care of his
weapon, sharpening and cleaning it regularly, applying
oil as Dels had instructed. Its small size was in no way a
reflection of the pride he felt in wearing it. Its pale leather
scabbard was softened by age, and was worn through in
several places. *Better we be worn through than run through*, his
father had said as he gave him the scabbard. With painful
ease, Sivino had seen the aching heart behind his father's
smile. The big man handled the sword deftly, spinning it
in his scarred hands almost without thought. Sivino had
watched as Dels' thick fingers gripped the weapon; fingers covered in scars which, like the memories of blood
and battle, would never entirely fade.

"Where does the little warrior intend to spend his
day?" Drip asked.

"I'll be fishing, Drip. With Ston."

"Terrible surprise, going to the Andel again." Drip
shook his head, turned and walked toward the house,
muttering under his breath.

Sivino found his fishing hooks and line, and left the hut to grab breakfast and pack some food for the trip. If memory served, there was still an ample supply of hard-tack bread in the larder, as well as a few biscuits – Torla's favourite – and an apple or two that would sate his appetite throughout the day. The others, he knew, would bring along something as well – especially Ston, whose hunger was a constant.

As he secured the hut door, Sivino could see his friend approaching with his father. Ston, infamous for sleeping well past the second hour of daylight, would not do so on a fishing day. He was nearly the height of his father, whereas Sivino stood at least a foot shorter than Dels, and Leath as well, for that matter. Leath, it was said by most Egimians, would surely grow to be the image of Dels despite the fact that the man was not his bodily father. Leath would listen to the words of the villagers with pride, stealing satisfied glances at Sivino all the while. Inwardly, Sivino would remind himself of his mother's contention that there was inherent strength that did not equate with size.

"Morning, young Spallic," Stellen Tros smiled, smacking Sivino on his shoulder as he moved toward the house.

"Morning, Sir," Sivino replied, smiling to hide the grimace of pain.

The big man leaned in and whispered to Sivino. "Be sure to outshine this one today," he said, nodding playfully at Ston. "He's beginning to fancy himself the best fisher in all of Egim."

"He *is* quite good," Sivino answered in a likewise

whisper. "Almost as good as Drip."

This brought a rough guffaw from Stellen, who slapped Sivino again on the back. Drip, who lingered nearby, never missed a word of the conversation, quiet though it was. As he lurked, he glared at Sivino through narrow eyes, muttering something about fools and merrows. It was no secret that the trenoc race had no affinity for water. They could not swim and hated getting wet. A light drizzle was enough to dampen the already cantankerous mood of a trenoc.

"Where's your father, Sivino?" Stellen asked, the smile fading slightly.

"Morning, Stellen," came the reply from the doorway. "About to pour a cup of tea. Come in."

The group moved into the Spallic home. As the men sat and spoke about the previous night's events on the far side of the room, Ston leaned in close to Sivino at the table.

"We're not going fishing today," he said quietly. "Torla has other plans."

"She was along? When?"

"I'd hate to say. You may think me meddlesome." A small smile.

Torla Rallo was, by Egimian standards, a wild child. Free with her words and actions, she lived in the moment and dared to hope for things of which most Egimians would only dream. *Our world is much too small,* she'd told Sivino on many occasions. Whether she spoke of Egim or the whole of Embarria, Sivino was uncertain. It was possible, he thought, that she was referring to the very ends of Cahruia or beyond.

"What did she have to say?" he asked in his most unconcerned tone.

"She came by late last evening. I told her about that brudog that killed your cow." He shook his head in confusion. "Despite this, the girl wonders if we are interested in venturing to Levebar."

"Levebar?" Sivino spoke quietly as he poured two cups of milk from the bucket his father had brought in earlier. "Bit of a hike, Ston. Especially with Kef's leg. We don't know what killed that cow. Maybe brudogs… Maybe something else." He very nearly knocked his cup over as he recalled the creature he'd seen disappear into the forest. "I don't know. A trek that far west, after what happened last night? It could be dangerous."

"I assume," Ston replied, "that this is precisely why she wishes to go."

Sivino's eagerness faded slightly as he thought of lying to his father. He knew that Dels would consider such a journey reckless and likely forbid it. *Taking unnecessary risks is the habit of a fool*, he'd said so often. Yet, they could easily be back before sunset if they travelled with haste, so journeying in the darkness was not a fear. *And surely, a day as brilliant as this one couldn't hold encounters with dark creatures. And the journey would be made upon the banks of the Andel, where the trees were not quite so dense*. Having convinced himself with these reasons, he turned and looked at his father.

Having finished their conversation, the men moved to sit at the table with the boys. Dels' wooden cup was barely visible in his large hand.

"So, what adventure will your longknives carve today, lads?" He laid his cup on the table, eager to speak of things of a lighter nature.

Sivino questioned whether he would, or even could, lie to his father. *A lie is a grievous wound that the giver and the recipient must forever bear*, his mother had once said. She'd been referring to a dishonest trader that had given the family seeds in exchange for a mat Rhenna had woven. The seeds, it turned out, were from the pod of a tangly foreign weed, and not those of a lush purple flower that would draw the bumbled bees to their garden. *There is nothing more despicable than the utterance of a lie*, she'd muttered.

"Sivi?"

He jerked his head up, and saw the confused look on his father's face.

"Just the fishing." Without hesitation the response leapt from his tongue, though he knew it was false. He put his head down and focused on the fried dough before him. "Near the Falls."

"Be sure to make your day of leisure worthwhile," Leath replied, his back to Sivino and the others as he looked out the window at the rear of their home. "We've not had a good meal of fin in weeks. And there's some in town who'd pay three nickel rings for a small basket, if they're fresh."

"I hear some will pay a crendisc for two full baskets," Ston added.

Leath scoffed. "I hear there are fools who believe everything they hear."

"Don't wander too far, Sivi," Dels continued, ignoring the exchange. "I'm serious. Given what happened last night, I'd prefer you stayed closer to home than usual.

Drip tells me that you were quite a ways up the Andel yesterday. *Alone.* If you'd met a brudog up there–" He stopped, letting Sivino consider the possibilities of such an encounter.

"I know," Sivino replied. "I lost track of distance as well as time, I guess. It won't happen again."

Leath grunted from the basin where he was now washing dishes. Sivino knew full well that his brother considered him a dreamer; careless and absent-minded. In Leath's eyes, Sivino would always be a child. Sivino's efforts to change his brother's perception failed, no matter how hard he tried. His ability to make Sivino feel all the significance of a grain of sand was staggering. He did so with a look, a gesture, or simply by ignoring his young brother outright. Dels of course noted the strained relationship of his sons, but was unable to mend the rift that existed and apparently widened as they aged.

They will sort it out themselves, Rhenna had always assured him, *when the time is right.* Though it pained him to feel this way, Dels was doubtful.

Thanking his brother for the meal, Sivino rose from the table, leaving Ston to finish his fried dough.

By the door, he picked up his burlap bag and began to pack the day's necessities – a short knife, extra hooks and bait, a water-skin, food and flint, should a fire be needed. Ston had left a similar, if slightly larger bag next to the door when he'd arrived.

"Ston, help Sivino pack up," said Stellen. Sivino, being used to such comments given his smaller stature, ignored the big man's implication that he needed help.

Ston drained his cup, nodding to his father as he rose from the table.

"I hope Torla doesn't push us too hard this morning," Ston said through a yawn as the two boys stepped outside. "Though," he continued, looking to the west, "the day has the feel of one with promise."

"And what does it promise, great seer?" asked Sivino.

"A break in the tedium, perhaps."

Sivino smiled as he tightened the straps on the bag. "Where are we meeting them?"

"On the edge of the wood, near Lomin's hut."

Sivino turned quickly. "Has he returned?"

"Not sure," he replied, stifling another yawn. "Elusive, that one. Though I thought I spotted smoke rising from his grove yesterday evening. Torla was anxious to see if he was back. Wanting stories, I presume. She'll likely be there soon. Could you hasten the progress a little, my boy?"

Sivino finished securing the straps of his pack. He heard concerned voices from the house. The men were talking of the brudogs again. He closed his eyes, and tried to dismiss the fear he felt for the day's journey.

Quickly, he composed himself and moved toward his waiting friend. He was practiced in the art of hiding fear, having done so his entire life. As he glanced down at his short blade, he wondered what good it would do if he ever encountered a foe that posed a real threat. He thought once more on the creature he thought he'd seen stalking away through the field last night, and almost laughed. Given the greatest sword in the *world*, what could a boy like him possibly do in the face of such a creature?

As the pair jogged across the meadow and fell under the shadow of the Nucono, Sivino silently hoped he'd never find out.

5

AN OLD FRIEND

The boys had not been gone half an hour when Dels heard the beating of hooves.

His ear was trained to hear all, and he was instantly on his feet. He looked first in the direction that the boys had headed, knowing that they were well into the forest by now. He then glanced toward the path to the Tros homestead, but Stellen had only left fifteen minutes prior and rarely came to the Spallic house on horseback.

The rider, unfortunately, came from the northwest. Leath joined Dels beside the well as the rider came into view. "Father? Is that one of the Ryndarra?"

"It is." It was rare for Ryndarra to be seen in the region. Those not fighting in the south were stationed in Levebule, Torg, and Vor primarily, though many could now be found in cities throughout Rentorria. Those that made their way this far east of Rovil were generally unwelcome. Either they were engaging in recruitment efforts, or carrying news of soldiers who'd lost their lives in the conflict.

Most often, it was the latter reason that brought them to rural doorsteps.

Too often these days, they were seen as messengers of death.

The sight of the approaching rider took Dels back many years, to days of swords and sacrifice. Having climbed quickly through the ranks of the Ryndarra, Dels had been greatly respected for his skill and intelligence, and subsequently, was offered the role of commander. It was, however, a position he did not care to accept. He enjoyed the wide-ranging patrols that were the charge of more experienced Ryndarra, travelling from town to town to keep the peace, settle disputes, and help wherever needed. The one role that rivalled the enjoyment he took from the patrol was that of training the new recruits. Dels had always maintained that the minimum age for recruitment should be raised from eighteen to twenty years. And then, he'd suggested, these youth should be trained as intensely as possible, for at least two years. His commander had scoffed at this, but the Egimian held firm to his principles. *Young men and women need to be trained well*, Dels had said, *or they will die quickly. They need lessons in the sword, but also in reasoning, mediating, empathy and patience.*

And so, Dels Spallic split his time between patrolling the lands and training the recruits. On his patrols, he took the recruits that were in the advanced stages of their training as apprentices. *You have to experience conflict to be able to understand it,* he'd said. *And you have to understand conflict if you are to prevent it.* He looked now at the man who approached, a man to whom he'd said those words, many years ago.

"Son of a brudog," he whispered.

"Dels Spallic," the rider said as he slowed near the Whispering Leah closest to the house. He dismounted quickly, and tossed the steed's reins over a nearby water pump. "It's been a long time my friend." He removed his tight-fitting helmet and extended a hand, which the Egimian shook vigorously.

"Harcole Cross." Dels' disbelief was evident on his face. He turned then from the man and indicated the young lad beside him. "I'd like you to meet my son, Leath. Leath, Harcole is an old friend from my days in the northern regiment."

"And your finest recruit, as well." Cross shook Leath's hand with a smile and a nod, though Dels' keen eyes saw a small shadow move over the Ryndarra's rough, tanned face.

"Leath. The last time I saw you, you were a swaddling baby. Has it been so long?"

"It has," Dels replied, his voice a little lower. He glanced over his shoulder to see if Drip was nearby, but the trenoc kept a comfortable distance, satisfied to avoid introductions as he watched from the periphery with narrowed eyes.

Cross turned to survey the property, his eyes resting on the rolling fields of wheat that swayed in the morning breeze. "The farming life has been kind to you, my friend."

"It has," Dels said again. "It's a good life. A peaceful life."

"Ah, peace. Would that I could say the same. I've

known little peace these past years, the last couple especially. This ride to Levebule has been the most peace I've had in recent memory." He laughed bitterly. "Imagine, a peaceful trip to Levebule! I've done a bit of recruiting on my way back – Rovil, Stallion's Cross, most recently in Slattenton." He looked toward the fields of wheat, then back at his friend. "I envy you, Dels. Your hands pull life from the earth. Mine bury it beneath. I accepted the role of messenger a year ago, thinking that I could escape the agony of the field." Again, that sardonic smile moved his lips. "I tell you, it doesn't compare to the agony of telling a mother that her seventeen year old son has been killed." He shook his head slowly. "Doesn't compare."

"How do we fare in Rentorria?" Leath asked, steering the subject in another direction.

"The changes are slow, and not in our favour. The Isrorians move certainly to the west. The Rentorrian Guard are well trained, as are we, but the training and weaponry of Isror is fierce. Their numbers seem without limit, and ours insufficient to push them back."

Dels did not miss the look that Cross gave Leath as he said this. Quickly, he turned the conversation. "How are things in the fair city? I assume that Inlonia Talchol grows more comfortable on the throne?"

Cross was silent for a moment. "She rarely sits upon it. Our queen does what she can. Does what she must. I do not envy her position."

A young woman of rare intelligence, Inlonia Talchol was a queen bound by obligation, by the blood that ran within her veins; a woman who had recently and reluctantly accepted the unwanted position. The Talchol family tree was thinner than most, Dels knew, and Inlonia had become the branch that would bear the weight of responsibility in the absence of a traditional male heir. As well, she knew better than any what a reign as Embarrian ruler would entail in these days – sending her people into a bleak war whose outcome would be horrific, no matter which side emerged as victor. Two years prior, the death of her father Intraal had caused a stirring among the Embarrian population. Speculation and suspicions, whispers of fell deeds and dark motivation rose like a river after rain, overrunning the banks and meandering among the cities and settlements. She saw her ascension as more burden than blessing, but had set about the work with the same ethic and dedication as her father.

"The city has accepted her, generally." Cross scoffed. "It's funny, no? For over twenty years, we've seen fit to train women as Ryndarra. They've helped keep the peace, and now, with this bloody conflict, they fight beside us. They die beside us." Dels noted the sadness that crept into Cross' face as he continued. "They *kill* when they must, as we all do." He shook his head, as if to right himself. "But Levebule – and much of Embarria for that matter – is still wary of their *leadership*. Some old fools would call me mad, but I think it's high time that women had the opportunity to try to set things right in these lands. My Goddess, Dels, I can't imagine what my homestead would look like without Jennie keeping it all together." Dels knew his friend's meaning, but an unwelcomed pang of loss hit him in the chest nevertheless. Cross seemed to notice this, and he quickly made a clumsy attempt to steer the conversation elsewhere.

"But you know how the city works, Dels. Change comes so slowly. The merchants fight the commoners, the Ryndarra fight the criminals and the Royal Council fights amongst themselves. Incessantly." He turned and smiled toward Leath, who seemed intrigued by talk of the city. "Aside from the people," he laughed, "it's a beautiful place." He turned again to Dels. "Most realize that the queen's edicts are necessary, and are done in the interest of keeping the realm safe. Though it pains her, she realizes that she has to send additional Ryndarra south. It's a tough trade, as the crime rates continue to rise in the cities where patrols are scarce. And changing the recruiting age to fifteen – that was difficult for her. Granted, those young men and women are spared the horrors of direct conflict initially. But still, it's difficult. For everyone. There've been extensive debates around conscription within the Royal Council. To this point, she's been able to dissuade the councillors, but that's a battle in itself, you can be sure. She believes that Idach Garron will not be satisfied with the taking of Rentorria. He would see the Three Realms become one. He'd look north before the blood dried."

"I've had my fill of blood, even here on my own land," Dels muttered. Seeing Harcole's inquisitive look, he continued. "A cow, last night. Looks to be a brudog attack. It was rather brutal."

"Really?"

Dels realized that to the soldier, brutal must be a relative term. In their years patrolling together, they'd seen more bloodshed than he cared to recall. And that was before the war.

"Damnation." Cross looked at the Egimians. "Not the

first such incident I've heard of in recent weeks. I spoke with a man in Slattenton, north of Stallion's Cross, a couple of days ago. He'd travelled to Ras, trying to trade leathers for the stoneware of the Drales, those big buggers. I told him that he should have tried to recruit a few of the giants for the Ryndarra. Their sheer size would turn the tide of the war inside a month."

"Harcole," Dels interrupted gently. "The attacks?" Dels recalled his former comrade's propensity for digression, a habit that no amount of training had been able to eliminate. When they'd served together, Dels had used a subtle throat-clearing noise to remind Harcole to focus on the task at hand, especially during mediations.

"Yes, sorry, sorry," he said, shaking his head. "Anyway, the fellow said that he'd heard of such attacks on three separate occasions, three separate homesteads. In each case, the victim was an animal. Two cows and a goat."

"And it happened at the homesteads?" Leath asked.

"On the doorsteps," Cross replied. "He said the families were quite shaken. In each case, a leg snapped, partially removed, leaving only a bloody trail."

"Hellfire," Dels whispered.

"Dels, I don't know if these incidents are related, but you'd be well advised to be on alert these days. One can't be too careful."

"True enough." Dels glanced to the forest where Sivino and Ston had gone, and then turned quickly, as if trying to dismiss his thoughts. "Harcole, join us for a bite. I'm sure the road has made you hungry."

"Hungry and weary, to be sure. But I cannot. My

thanks, but I need to get back on the road south. Every hour counts." Cross looked once more toward Leath, who now filled the skins hanging from the saddlebags of Cross' steed. "This war won't fight itself." When he turned, he saw equal parts hurt and anger in Dels' eyes. "No, Dels, don't take offence. It's just–" He thought on the right words, taking Dels by the shoulders in his strong hands. "You'd have been twice the commander of most I met on the fields of battle. You are missed, my friend. Your skills would have been invaluable in this conflict, I'm certain. Our soldiers follow Commander Tyon, but you, Dels, you would have *led* them. Tyon is heavy on procedure, but light on charisma. The Ryndarra need leadership; commanders that are respected, commanders that inspire their troops. Unfortunately, such commanders are scarcer than an honest merchant." He sighed, realizing that he was on the verge of a lengthy rant. "Suffice it to say, you are missed."

Dels laid his hands on Cross' shoulders in a likewise fashion. "Once, maybe, my friend. But fate seems to have chosen my path for me. Now, I live for my boys. I wish you could have met Sivino. He's gone to do a bit of river fishing."

Cross nodded. "One day, perhaps. Let us hope that such a long time does not lapse between our next meeting."

After shaking Dels' hand, Cross approached his horse and noted that Leath had filled the skins, oiled the stirrup leathers, and brought a few apples for the steed. Cross thanked him, smacking a big hand on the young man's shoulder.

"You are indeed your father's son."

Dels nodded. "Stay safe, Harcole."

His friend laughed as though he'd been asked the impossible. "Safe as can be," he replied.

The smile faded however as he turned his horse to the south. With a quick kick, the steed broke into a gallop. Dels sighed, knowing full well that he'd likely never see the man again.

"Well," said Dels as he laid a hand on Leath's shoulder. "Let us hope this day holds no more surprises.

"There's work to be done."

The work, Dels soon realized, was the furthest thing from his mind.

After striking his hand for the second time with his hammer, he tossed the tool aside and called to the trenoc. He simply couldn't shake the thoughts of last night's attack, or the tidings brought by Cross.

"Drip. Would you care for a break from the garden?"

The trenoc sucked a thorn from his thumb, and spat it away. "The merrow?"

"*Sivino*," Dels corrected him, "should be fine." He looked toward the western forest with hands on his hips. "However, I'm troubled by what happened last night, and by Harcole's report. Perhaps a little scout work by one as skilled as yourself would help ease my mind." He turned to the trenoc, his eyes serious. "But while you're at it, would you look in on the lad?"

6

WITHIN THE FOREST

The meadow hung low with morning dew. As the sun continued to climb the orange purple sky, so too did the grass rise upward, giving up the moisture to the early morning heat.

Sivino wished he could so easily shed his worries, allowing them to evaporate and take their weight from his shoulders. Yet, troubled though his mind was, he could not help but enjoy the walk through the deep grasses. There was something magical about this time of day. It seemed the sun caught every droplet that clung to the delicate stalks, and the land sparkled for acres.

They walked a path that had been beaten down by the many trips made from the Spallic home to the Nucono Forest. Throughout the meadow, Sivino saw the movement of smaller animals; jack-hares and birds that broke their fast on the unseen bounty that lay hidden in the undergrowth. Berries of myriad varieties grew on parts of the property that were not currently used for grazing cattle, and flowers of yellow and white added a touch of colour to the natural masterpiece. Sivino recalled a morning that he and his father had watched Rhenna walk through a similar sunrise. Her dress had been blowing to the side, and Dels had lamented the fact that the artists of Levebule were not present to paint the scene. Smiling, he'd laid an arm across Sivino's shoulders. *I guess it doesn't really matter,* he'd said. *Images etched in our memories last just as well.*

He'd had no idea how right he was.

Sivino walked for some time with his eyes closed. He could walk this trail in his sleep. He enjoyed how the sounds of the land became all the more distinct without vision. He could hear the birds twitter back and forth, both in the field and the trees that lay in the distance. A woodpecker drummed against a tree, content to work for its morning meal. In another part of the forest, this rapid hammering was answered by the ridiculous squawk of the dokka-bird, whose unmistakable call might have told the woodpecker it was offended by the early morning noise.

Behind all these sounds lay the whisper of the Andel, meandering powerfully beyond the trees. As the fluid sound reached his ears, Sivino picked up his pace.

"Slow yourself a little, Siv. Are you so anxious to see Torla?"

"I'm more anxious to see Lomin. He may have outside news."

"Of course the old wolf will have a story to tell. Otherwise, he wouldn't bother venturing out in the first place. You know what he says…" Sivino smiled as Ston subtly transformed before him, his back hunching ever so slightly, his eyes narrowing as his brow furrowed and his upper lip curled. He looked to the ground as if searching for berries, one hand on his hip and the other pointing a shaky hand at Sivino as he spoke in an excessively deep voice. "It's not the destination, young ones, it's the story of the journey."

Sivino could not help but laugh. So accurately was Ston able to imitate Lomin that at times, Lomin himself would spin around as if expecting to encounter his double.

"Still, I hope he doesn't find himself in harm's way," said Ston, turning more serious for a moment.

"He has an impressive knowledge of most of the creatures that roam his land." Sivino looked at his friend, his voice lowered. "And those that don't." He recalled the stories Lomin had shared over the years, strange tales of mythical creatures. So detailed was his knowledge that Sivino often wondered if Lomin had actually encountered such beasts in his travels.

"Perhaps he might know what kind of creature attacked your cow," Ston suggested.

Sivino shrugged and continued walking.

The Andel ran heavy as the boys moved along its bank. Reflecting golden light from the sky, its smooth movement belied its speed. Salmon and shad swam against its mighty current, struggling to reach the spawning grounds that lay to the distant east where the Andel left the Cudgel Mountains. The river formed gently, running from the rocky region in numerous streams of rain and meltwater. Before long, however, these small brooks came together, combining their strength to create the beginnings of a river that would swell and intensify into a silver path of water and life that flowed to the sea.

The sounds of life reverberated within the Nucono. Small elk darted onto the path every so often, chasing each other in some unknown game. Overhead, swallows sang morning songs which served as the melodic heartbeat of the forest; This soft, constant song would go on to the ends of time with little concern for what happened outside its wooded boundary. The leaves were beginning to deepen in colour, the buds blossoming into rich shades of indigo and green. Summer had arrived in Embarria, and the land welcomed it with open arms.

Lomin Lailoken's hut lay silent. As the boys approached the humble abode, they found Torla Rallo instead. She was lying on the stone bench in front of the house, staring at the open sky. She held a hickory bow loosely in one hand. Her brother Kef sat nearby on a fallen tree, waving his walking stick idly through the air as he spoke. Torla was smiling, as most people did in Kef's presence. The boy possessed a wit sharper than most swords, and genially used the populace of Egim as his whetstone. He was a likeable lad, more common than his sister, holding none of her aspirations to see what lay beyond every hill and vale. His smile, like Torla's, was contagious, though used much more often, and his eyes were equally bright. He used all of these qualities to mask the pain that resided in his leg, damaged years ago in a foolish jump at the Falls. It had never fully healed. As Ston and Sivino approached, Torla spun, raising the bow and pointing an arrow directly at the pair.

"*Tor!*" shouted Ston. The knees of both boys buckled as they fell into a crouch. "Leave off, it's *us!*"

"I know," she said quietly, her eye still trained on Ston's forehead. "I guessed that lingering sleep must be the reason for your late arrival." She stood. "Hopefully, you're fully awake now." Traces of a smile played upon the corner of her lips. She pulled her sandy brown hair into a ponytail, and tied it with a small piece of twine. "Shall we?" She took a quiver of arrows from where they lay on the ground and returned the one she held, smoothing the yellow feathers of the arrow's fletching as she did so.

Kef took up a position between the boys as they composed themselves, an arm on each of their shoulders. "Early hours do not agree with these folk, Tor." He ruffled Sivino's hair. "Look at the head on this one. I feared you'd mistaken them for the northern bear."

"The other is equally dishevelled." She walked past them, adjusting her quiver as she shook her head. "But I could never make such a mistake.

"Bears smell better."

The trio followed Torla. She moved deftly over the rocky path, setting the pace as she did on most of their journeys.

"Have you heard from Lomin?" Sivino asked the Rallos. "Ston says he thought that smoke rose near here last night."

"Haven't heard a thing," Kef answered. "Though Torla said she saw smoke also." He raised his voice a little. "The smoke was further west, wasn't it, Tor?" His sister nodded without turning, and Kef continued. "It was late. Hard to tell. Did Lomin say when he planned to return?"

"No," Sivino replied. He breathed heavily through his nose. "Torla told you about the cow?"

Kef nodded.

"I just wish Lomin would hurry up and get back," Sivino said.

"You can't possibly be worried about Lomin," Kef scoffed. "The wolf could chew apart a brudog if he had to." Kef slowed his awkward pace, looking seriously at Sivino. "You know he has the magic, if need be. No harm will come to him."

"Keep your voice down, Kef." He shot a guarded glance to the trees. "You know it shouldn't be spoken of."

"You expecting company, Siv? There's no one around for miles."

"I'd guess Lomin assumed the same thing that morning," said Ston.

Kef smiled. Sivino assumed he was recalling that morning they'd crept up on the wolf, discovering his secret. "I don't know why he doesn't just share his gift with others."

"Because," Sivino replied, "he'd not have a moment's peace if he did. For years beyond counting magic has been lost. Egim's eldest cannot even recall *their* grandfolk speaking of its use. And one can only assume that it was lost for a reason. If not eternally pestered and questioned, Lomin would probably be exiled...though for him that would be a small price to pay. Regardless, his secret must be kept."

"What are you talking about back there? Pick it up a bit, the day is wasting." Torla spoke without looking back, as she usually did. Eye contact was not necessary, she believed. *When I'm talking to you,* she was fond of saying, *you'll know.*

The sun continued to rise above the peaks of the Cudgel Mountains and burned up all but the last remnants of the morning mist. Dew, however, still clung to the grass and bushes that bordered the trail along which the quartet walked, slightly south of the Westroad. It was a trail well worn, not wide enough for a cart, but well used by those upon foot or horseback. Separated from the Andel by only a spattering of trees, it meandered with the river.

"At this rate, we'll not reach Levebar 'til well past midday," Torla muttered.

Ston, growing frustrated with the girl's insistence on speed, spoke up. "What's the hurry, Torla? Levebar is pretty much Egim by a different name. Less people, a little more quaint, though not half as attractive as we Egimian folk." He pulled his wavy black hair to the side, winking at Sivino to evoke a smile. "So what's the draw? What do you hope to find there today?"

"A change, Ston," Torla replied. "My eyes grow weary of the same sights." She did not see Sivino flinch ever so slightly.

"You have itchy feet again," Kef said, watching the river. "By *Dahnu*, Tor, I go willingly, but if you lead us on one of your wild endeavours, *my* feet, sore as they might be, will itch as well. And when they do, I cannot control whose backside they kick."

Kef threw a sideways smirk at the boys, who were smiling at the idle threat he made toward his sister.

"Should your foot leave the ground headed in my direction, Kef Rallo, I assure you it would be returned more mangled than itchy. Now move."

The company continued on at a less than comfortable pace, but an uncomfortable walk was preferable to upsetting Torla. Whatever one could say about Torla Rallo, Sivino thought, you could not take from her the fact that she was driven.

As they reached an opening where the Andel met the trail, Ston began asking Torla when it would be time to stop and eat. The boys automatically deferred to her, this being ingrained in them after years of useless power struggles. Torla stopped at last and turned to the boys.

"Not long, understand? I'm looking at you, Tros."

Ston, who'd already sat upon the lush grass, looked up smiling.

"What did you bring to eat?" Torla asked. She had packed little, assuming that the boys would bring along more than enough for all.

"What we eat should come from the Andel," Sivino stated, removing his fishing line from his sack.

"You *cannot* be serious, Sivino Spallic. We don't have time to fish, let alone cook our catch. The sun moves like a jack-hare, and you wish to while away our time in the river?"

"I don't have a choice, Tor. When Father asked where we intended to go, I told him we'd be fishing. I have no intention of lying to him, so I'll fish, even if only for a short time."

Torla opened her mouth to protest, but she held her tongue as a look crossed her face. She knew Dels Spallic well enough to know how hard it would be to lie to him.

She'd lost her own father when she still toddled – a sickness that had seen him suffer for the better part of a year – and her respect for Dels grew with each passing year, so much so that she often felt the relationship was familial. She knew that he covertly helped her mother Dahlah whenever help was needed, and this knowledge endeared him to her greatly.

"Do it quickly," she replied, sitting on a rock lapped by the water.

Kef and Ston sat back amongst the tall ash trees, enjoying the shade as they ate a couple of apples.

Torla sat near the water as Sivino fished, sharpening a knife on a wet rock, her mind looking to be a thousand leagues away. Sivino stole quick glances in her direction to see if she was watching, evaluating his fishing technique. Likely, he thought, she was trying to clear her head, as she did so often when they sat by the river. *If you try hard enough,* she'd said on numerous occasions, *you can let the river wash the worries from your mind. You just have to be willing to open it a little.* He grew self-conscious as he tossed the bait into the water with the slender branch he'd cut. His father had shown him how to cut such a fishing pole. The ash tree, he'd told Sivino, is best, as its flexibility is ideal for long casts. But equally important, the ash heals. The removal of a branch will not permanently harm the tree. One can even plant the severed branch in the soil, and given time and the right conditions, it may blossom into a tree in its own right. *Remember this, son. All things broken may be made whole again.* His father's words played on Sivino's mind as he continued to cast his line, listening all the while to the boys laugh about the middle-aged woman from Levebar that Ston was certain had been making advances toward him on their last visit.

"Fancies himself quite the ladies' man," Sivino noted to Torla.

She looked back over her shoulder at the boys, shaking her head. "If he thinks depth of voice and width of shoulders are all that girls care for, he's got a few lessons to learn."

Sivino, who was lacking in both areas, smiled.

"A brudog?" She looked back at the river. "In this part of the realm?"

"We don't know that it was a brudog," Sivino said without thinking. This brought an inquisitive look from Torla, whose silence told Sivino to continue. "I just mean, we didn't see the brudog."

"What else could it be?" She turned toward him.

Sivino considered telling her what he thought he'd seen, but found he could not.

"I don't know." He shook his head. "Likely a brudog, I guess."

Eager to change the subject, and realizing that he was not destined to catch even the smallest shad, Sivino pulled in his baited hook, and removed the line from the ash branch. Torla, looking extremely relieved, quickly stood up and walked back to the path, telling the others to ready themselves. Kef, still laughing at Ston's story of unrequited love, struggled to rise. Ston extended a hand, and pulled the boy to his feet.

"Now, if there are no more delays?" Torla stood with a hand on her hip, an eyebrow raised.

"Just one more," Sivino replied, as he walked across

the path and back into the wooded area from which he had taken the sapling.

"Sivino." The tone of Torla's voice told the boy what she thought of his plan. "Are you really replanting that twisted twig?"

Sivino looked back with a smile. He knew that the others felt him foolish for his ritualistic replanting, but he told them time and again that a moment or two seemed a small price to pay to give a little life back to the forest. *It's a powerful thing,* he'd said, *to give life to something as great as the Nucono.*

"One moment, that's all," he said over his shoulder as he stepped through the thick underbrush that dominated the area closest to the path. Within, the space between trees widened, and Sivino could walk more easily. He could breathe more easily as well, feeling that the air was different here, though it was only a few paces from the path. It was a different world.

The voices of his companions were dulled, and the sounds of the forest became more acute. He looked up at the thin rays of sunshine that fought their way through the thick canopy to find the floor of the forest. Sivino glanced around, looking for the best spot to plant the branch that, though unable to catch him a fish, had spared him from a lie. For this, Sivino thought it deserved to become a tree, and a strong one at that.

"Come on, Siv! Torla's aiming arrows at Ston to amuse herself, and he's cowering like a trenoc in the rain. If you don't hurry, someone is apt to get hurt!" Sivino could hear the smile in Kef's distant voice, and was shocked at how far into the wood he'd wandered.

Despite this, he walked a little further and settled on an open location that seemed to get a decent amount of sunlight. On his hands and knees, he dug a deep but narrow hole and placed the torn end of the branch inside. It was almost second nature to him – he had planted saplings and small plants so often with his mother. After filling in the hole with the earth he'd removed, he patted the dirt firmly and poured out the contents of his water skin. Content with himself, he stood up and smiled. He gave himself a mental reminder to mark the location where he'd left the path so that on future trips he might check the progress of the young tree.

As he turned to walk back toward the others, a sudden burst of swallows flew from a nearby tree, flying so close that they almost struck him. Instinctively, he ducked. Looking skyward, he followed the flight of the birds, which circled around and reclaimed the same tree from which they had flown. Odd, he thought, shaking his head slightly. He began to leave again, and the birds repeated their circle, darting directly in front of him as he took the first step toward the path.

It was then that he heard it: a soft, low creak, followed by what sounded like the rasp of branches rustling in the wind.

Yet, there was no wind. Not even the slightest breeze.

He steadied himself, listening closely, his eyes scanning the landscape. The sound came again. It was a little further into the wood, over a small knoll to the north. He gave a quick glance over his shoulder towards the path. Two swallows jumped to a lower branch. He could no longer see the path, or his friends. He thought back to the old stories that Lomin had once read to him as a child; a story in which trees came to life and walked. Even spoke. Lomin had a small yet wonderful library and on many an afternoon, he'd take the young Egimians to places they couldn't have dreamed possible. Each page held them captive. He thought now of the sound the turning of the ancient, faded pages had made.

Not unlike the sound he was hearing.

He walked deeper into the wood, drawn to the source of the sound. The swallows, he noted, now sat silent. He took a few more cautious steps. His fingers lightly grazed the hilt of his shortsword as he walked around the trees and saw his friend.

Lomin lay upon the ground, his head resting on the base of an oak. His chest rose and fell at a disturbing rate. Blood covered his head, his face and hands. It soiled much of his clothing, which was ripped to rags in places. Off to the left, his beautiful grey horse, Sleipnir, lay dead, a dark arrow protruding from his broad chest. Sivino stood motionless, frozen as he watched Lomin's mouth work. From it came a heavy rasp that sounded like an old book, his tongue an ancient page, turning ever so slowly as Lomin sucked in what breath he could and muttered incomprehensible words. Sivino moved toward Lomin. The words that came from the old man were strange to Sivino, foreign and spoken with a tone uncharacteristic of his friend. Suddenly, he noticed Sivino.

"*Sivi?*" Lomin gasped. Fear and shock were palpable on his face. "*No*, Sivino. Go! Go…now! Run!"

The words did not register with Sivino, who continued to assess the gravity of the old man's wounds.

"Lomin, hold on." He knelt by the man. "The others are with me. We have to get you out of here. We ca–"

The words died on his tongue. From behind him came a deep, guttural growl that chilled him to his core. Turning, he saw in the distance a creature that embodied all that was dark and terrible in the world. Leaning heavily on a tree not twenty paces away, the beast stood and watched. It did not move. Sivino could discern that like Lomin, it had sustained great injuries. Yet though it faltered, it remained upright. Standing at a height of seven feet, the beast's head reached the lower branches of the amilliat, whose lower trunk grew no limbs. It had one muscular arm wrapped around the tree, and with the other it held its chest where Sivino thought he could see an open wound. It was near impossible to tell, as the creature was covered from head to foot in coarse, brown hair. Its face, unlike any Sivino had ever been unfortunate enough to dream, seemed some combination of humanfolk and dog, its mouth a giant maw that barely contained the jagged rack of teeth. Atop its head, jutting out through the matted fur, two horns shone red with blood. With horror, Sivino noted that similar horns jutted from just below the beast's jaw.

The world wavered. Panicked, he looked around, checking the trees for more of these– These what? *Creatures? Animals?* One word alone made sense to his racing mind. *Monsters. Damnation,* he thought to himself. *Have I walked into a faerae tale?* His memory pulled forth old stories told by the elders to keep the young ones in line. *You put away that saucy tongue, they'd say. Talk like that is sure to bring back the horned ones.*

The horned ones love tongues.

These were the stories – usually told to misbehaving youngsters – of creatures that had once wandered the land, spreading fear and death wherever they roamed. Whenever an elder was asked where these creatures now lived, the answer was always the same.

The shadows.

Sivino shuddered as he recalled the tales. Giant, hairy creatures that lumbered through the deep forests, eating the legs of anyone and anything that dared walk into their midst. The Shadow Beasts. The Horned Ones.

The *Nylacci*.

"Sivino, run…now!" Lomin said. "You stand no chance. You have…to save yourself." Painfully, he made a futile attempt to sit up. "Appeared…from nowhere. May be more. *Run!"*

In a swift motion, Sivino drew his shortsword and stepped between Lomin and the Nylac. With a deep, low growl that gurgled from its chest, the Nylac pushed itself from the tree and began to walk toward the boy.

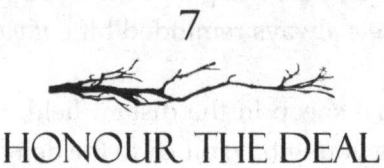

7

HONOUR THE DEAL

Not long after Drip's departure, Leath had been asked by his father to venture into Egim proper, a twenty minute walk to the northeast of the Spallic property. He enjoyed bartering with the townsfolk for needed supplies, which today consisted of a blade for a broken shovel.

For Leath, the measure of a day was the measure of work completed. Productivity was paramount. Days filled with skylarking amounted to shirked responsibility, and though Sivino indulged in this behaviour more often than not, Leath himself was entirely unconcerned with the *merriment of youth*. Dels, he thought, had always been a steadfast model of work ethic, and he in turn intended to be likewise for Sivino. He grunted to himself as he thought on this. He'd be an example, to be certain. But he'd also be the quick backhand the boy so sorely needed. Sivino was soft, and softness served little purpose when life demanded so much. The younger boy was Rhenna Spallic through and through, and though Leath had loved

Rhenna fiercely, he wanted nothing more than to grow into the very image of Dels.

Though the village was spread over a league of countryside, the most populated section of Egim, *Egim proper*, was the hub of the hamlet. As Leath crested the final hill, the village rose before him. As always, he stopped for a brief moment on the hilltop and surveyed the land. *Much can be seen*, Dels always reminded him, *if you take the time to see.*

He saw the sheep in the distant field, and noted the ram chasing a young boy, much to the delight of the lad's friends. The boy jumped the fence moments before the ram caught him. Must be birthing time, Leath surmised. He could hear the hammer and anvil, and knew that his uncle Lumb would be hard at work. To the west of the town he could see young women on the periphery of the forest, their bodies hunched to half their height. For weeks now the bushes of crimsonberry had been ripe for the picking, though their fullness would last only a few days more. The laughing women raced against rising temperatures and ravenous wildlife to maximize their yield.

Satisfied that he'd observed enough he turned and, for just a moment, looked to the east. In the distant field, a house once stood; a house once full of love and life, now little more than a memory under a field of wavering grass. He made a fist with his right hand and brought it to his chest. He quickly traced a waterdrop on his heart, twice, and set forth toward the village.

He had no desire to dwell on loss. What's done is done, he believed. However, the tightness in his jaw told him that letting go was never so easy. Talen and Jola Spallic had been stolen from him before he'd even been able to form a memory of their faces. He felt the bitterness rise like bile inside him. *Enough*, he told himself. With effort, he pushed the thoughts from his mind and continued on. He distracted himself with a mental list of the day's chores to be completed, which inevitably led to thoughts of Sivino.

Sivino. Was there anyone in Egim – man, woman or child – who might be considered such a lost cause? Such foolishness. Such forgetfulness. Sivino lived a life of fantasy, rather than one of practicality. Yet that wasn't entirely fair, he conceded. The boy did occasionally show promise: an ability to solve problems and think through various challenges – given sufficient time. And though Leath would never say it, the younger Spallic did demonstrate, time and again, the worth of his heart; the care he showed for wounded animals he'd found in the forest, and the foolish replanting of switches cut from trees. He thought of Sivino wandering up and down the Andel, such a dreamer, so far removed from the responsibility of his days. Sivino moved about as if deep in concentration, face and eyes lost in thought, so much so that the young boy often seemed to be wandering aimlessly. It was behaviour that infuriated Leath, like an itch just out of reach. Just thinking of it caused his heart rate to increase. He stopped walking, closed his eyes, and breathed deeply in an attempt to calm himself.

And he thought of Sianah.

His irritation subsided. He felt lighter. His father told him repeatedly that he seemed to carry the weight of the southern realms on his young shoulders. *The little plea-*

sures of life must be enjoyed as well, Leath, Dels had told him. And now, after eighteen years, Leath had found one such pleasure.

Sianah Pella.

He continued down the winding road to town, along the narrow strip of grass that ran between the dry, dusty ruts made by cattle and cartwheel. Thoughts of Sianah quickening his pace.

Egim was alive as he arrived. Hard working folk tended their gardens, joking with neighbours across the thin railed fences that separated the properties and kept the laying-birds from straying too far. Children ran from home to home, gathering others to join them in their games of fun and mischief. Two women at the village well cursed vehemently and swatted at a dokka that had perched on the well's roof, messily doing its business. Leath smiled with a raised brow as he passed the women, both of them flushing slightly as they nodded greeting to him before bursting into laughter. These things, the lively conversations, braying cattle being led through the outskirts of town, the squeals of children, even the complaints of the occasional trenoc; these things were Egim.

Townsfolk greeted Leath warmly as he walked through town. He complimented the success of Old Maddister's gardens, and agreed that, *Yes, the recent rainfalls have been a blessing. No, Father is not with me. Yes, he stays quite busy. No, I haven't seen the new arrival of lambs. No, Beauty is not pregnant with a foal yet. No, I haven't throttled Sivino today. Yet.*

By the time he arrived at Lumb Velto's blacksmith shop, the banging anvil was something of a relief.

"Leath! Come, my lad, I've not seen you in a week!" Lumb came around the corner of the counter and grabbed Leath in his rough hands. "How are you, my boy?"

Leath smiled widely. Lumb Velto had the most positive disposition in the land. His smile, firm handshake and joyous laugh were welcomed by all.

"Things are well, Uncle." The old smith was actually Dels' uncle, but Leath, and much of the village, referred to Lumb this way.

"Come in, my boy, come in." He laid an arm across Leath's shoulders as he led the young man through the shop. "What brings you to my dingy den today, my skills or my captivating company?"

Leath smiled. "Your wares, actually. I've split the blade on one of our shovels. Hoping to replace it."

"Ah, my boy, you have the strength of your forefathers." He grabbed Leath's arm as he laughed. "Breaking shovels! Good lad."

He turned and made his way to the back of the shop, talking to himself as he went. Leath took a seat on an overturned bucket, and smiled as a trenoc emerged from the back room, seating himself at the grinding bench in the far corner, his back to Leath.

"Good morning, Nihbo."

A grunt from the trenoc. Nihbo, the blacksmith's striker, took up a rough looking sword in one hand and with the other began to crank a large emery wheel. He soon had the wheel spinning swiftly, and any chance of further conversation was lost in the sharp scraping noise of the tool.

Rolling his eyes, Leath stood up and began to walk

the room. The nearest wall was lined with finished products, newly made or repaired. The coal forge had been lit, and in short time would make the heat of the shop almost unbearable. He ran his hand along the smooth horn of the anvil, which rested securely on a giant amilliat stump near the forge. When his uncle had cleared the land for his shop years ago, he'd left this massive stump right where it was, building his shop around it. He'd then sawed a flat surface on the wood and chiselled out the shape of the anvil's base to a depth of several inches. Once the anvil was placed and secured, friends had shaken their heads at his ingenuity. *Surely, it must be the only anvil block in the realm rooted to the very earth.*

He stopped at the countertop behind the grinding bench, and looked at the designs Lumb had sketched on the sanded amilliat. Since he was a small child, he'd always been fascinated by the supposed order of the chaotic writing. Words, measurements, and sketches regarding his many projects. Sivino had once commented that the countertop looked like a work of art, a comment that Leath could not disagree with. It almost pained him to think of how his uncle would regularly sand the sketches away whenever he ran out of room. Beautiful ideas, reduced to dust in the air.

The air, he now realized, was indeed growing increasingly warm, and he wandered to the large open doorway of the shop, watching as the townsfolk ran here and there, carrying babies, sacks of vegetables, buckets of milk, and stacks of wood.

Yet he did not see the one thing he sought most.

"She's picking berries," Lumb Velto said. His uncle's

warm smile was shining proudly. "On a morning like this, what would you expect?" Leath could not find the words to respond, so Lumb continued.

"It's hardly a secret that there is a special bond between yourself and Sianah. The question is why you have not yet spoken to Terstin Pella."

"It is not so simple, Uncle."

"Huh. Then…I'll make a deal with you. I will give you this *new* shovel blade – *free of charge* – if you can tell me why this situation is so complicated."

Leath smiled. He knew full well that Lumb Velto had never, nor would ever, charge his great-nephew or any family member for any tool or service rendered; however, the old man feigned a serious, questioning look, and withheld the blade.

"Alright." He glanced quickly at the door, to ensure that none were near its entrance, and sighed. "As you've said, there is a bond between myself and Sianah. Indeed I would marry her tomorrow if the situation allowed… with the blessing of Terstin, of course. But how can I turn my back on Father? And then there's Sivino! I couldn't make my own home with Sianah with any peace of mind, knowing that Sivino was the only help Father had with his crops."

"Do you consider Drip's contributions so insignificant?" Nihbo didn't turn around, but Leath could hear the scowl in his raspy words.

"Yes, there's Drip of course, but–"

"Could outperform two men, I'd wager."

"Yes, thank you, Nihbo," Lumb interjected. He turned back to his nephew. "Sivino's a good kid, Leath."

"Sivino…isn't able to carry the necessary responsibility."

"Are you so sure?"

"Uncle, you've seen him."

"I know that Sivi can scarcely make a move that's not criticized."

Leath stood motionless. There was hurt and anger on his face, as well as a hint of concession. Lumb smiled warmly, and passed the boy the shovel blade.

"You've honoured our deal," he said to Leath. He put a rough hand on the boy's shoulder, his voice a little lower. "Always honour the deal". He tapped a thick finger on the blade Leath held. "May this serve you well in all the manure you attempt to shovel, whatever its source." Leath, unable to help himself, laughed at this, and his eyes warmed.

"I apologize, Uncle. Seems these days I'm in a rut deeper than those of Rovil's roads. I just need something to pull me out."

The old man smiled. "My young fool. I told you she was picking berries. But…if you'd rather spend your day with a sweaty old man and a crotchety trenoc, suit yourself."

Nihbo muttered something about there being no blade sharp enough, as Leath shook his uncle's hand. "I'll talk to her father soon, Uncle."

"See that you do, lad. Time's tide waits for none."

8

THE PATROL

At the border of the Nucono, three riders made their way across the field, headed toward the path that would lead them west through the ancient forest. Since the onset of the conflict, the already scarce Ryndarra were in even shorter supply in the remote areas of Embarria, and regular citizens had been asked to volunteer to join local patrols – small groups of men and women that roamed the region to speak to the people and uncover any wrongdoings that warranted the attention of higher authority. They were men and women without formal training, common folk who saw fit to step up and help their tiny towns and villages. Each week, these patrols travelled to a centralized location to pass on reports from their respective regions. The Egimian patrol had started the day early, hoping to visit several of the outlying hamlets and homesteads before bringing their report to Stallion's Cross. From there, the information was brought to the city of Rovil.

The horses walked slowly along the edge of the forest,

enjoying the warmth that the rising sun offered. The riders spoke softly to each other of the improving weather and other trivialities as they took in the magnificence of the morning. The grass through which the horses trod shone; the animals' passage marked by three uniform paths that climbed a gentle hill leading to the forest. Tammet Yar, the lone male in the group, turned back and looked in the direction of Egim. Over the rolling hills, he could just barely discern a wisp of smoke that rose a short distance before being absorbed into the purple sky. Breakfast at the Spallic home, he surmised. He sighed, drawing the looks of his companions as he did so.

"How long must this continue?" he asked quietly. Young and full of life, he'd volunteered willingly, but there were mornings that he'd simply prefer the feel of his warm down-filled bed to that of his steed's sweaty flanks. He shook his head and removed a short length of string from his pocket. Holding the string in his mouth, he pulled his thick brown hair away from his face, muttering through the twine. "I'll admit, it's a lovely morning, though not half as lovely as my wife. I'm sure she'd take the chill from my bones more quickly than this slow-rising sun."

Myls Irrot smiled and turned to the young girl who rode to her left.

"Do you hear this, Hinna? The lucky lad rides with two of Egim's finest, and is still not satisfied."

"Likely still not sober," Hinna O'ilm added. She flashed Tammet a smile that, like her fiery red hair, had burned itself into the minds of many a young Egimian. "I hear one of the Harmino boys was celebrating a birthday last night. Did you happen by, Tammet?"

The young man reddened slightly, and finished tying his ponytail. "A meagre pint of mead," he smiled. Seeing the raised eyebrow of both women, the smile turned to a laugh. "Alright, three at the most. I swear. Don't mistake me, ladies; I know our task is necessary. I just wish the conflict would end so that we could get back to normal life. Talk of the war is all one hears. For the love of Dahnu, 'twas all I heard at Moppy Harmino's place last night. Fell deeds and fallen warriors. I tire of the accursed foolishness."

Myls spoke quietly. "As do we all." The fading smile showed her age; fifteen years beyond either of the young ones that rode beside her. Her husband Grenn, a proud Ryndarra, had been fighting in the south for three months now. She'd argued with him bitterly to stay in Embarria – for he'd been given that option – but his sense of duty, of honour, had led him south. Too often, she wondered if she'd ever see him again.

"Ah Myls, forgive my big mouth," Tammet apologized.

She shook her head and offered him a quick smile. "Don't give it a moment's thought." Before Tammet could respond, his horse began to whinny, huffing and stomping the soft earth with anxious hooves.

"Hano, easy now," said Tammet. He rubbed the head of his gelding and spoke encouragement to the animal. "Easy, my friend. Hold now, boy." With his free hand, he reached around Hano's head and gently rubbed the side of the steed's mouth, a useful tip Myls had offered a few weeks prior. He looked to Myls now, whose own animal was beginning to twist and step backwards, as was the mare of Hinna.

"Coyote?" he asked.

Myls glanced toward the forest, her hands firm on the reins. "Norix is not given to such fear." She dismounted and smoothed the animal's silky neck. "What is it, boy? Maybe we should–" It was then that she noticed the terror in the eyes of her companion's horse. "Hinna. Hinna, *hold her!*"

"I can't!" Panic choked Hinna's voice, her wavy hair falling over her face as she struggled with her horse, now braying an unmistakable cry of fear.

"Be firm, Hinna! Hold her," Myls urged.

"Nolire. Easy," the young girl pleaded. "Nolire, steady! Myls, *what's the matter with her?*"

Walking slowly, Myls made shushing sounds, holding out her palms in an effort to calm the horse, but her efforts were futile. The animal shook with fear, and then lost all control as a deep, pain-filled howl rose from the forest. They all spun. With a final look to the trees, Nolire turned and bolted, her hooves kicking dirt in every direction. She broke for the town, racing across the grassland with Hinna clinging desperately to the reins.

Myls swung herself back onto Norix, and turned toward Tammet, who was starting to give chase.

"No," she said. "Hinna will deal with Nolire. We must stay. That sound. It was–" She searched for a word, struggling as she looked to the trees. "It wasn't right, Tammet." Myls scanned the trees, in equal measure hoping and fearing the source of the sound would reveal itself. *That howl,* she thought. *What in the Goddess' creation could it have come from?* In short moments, the sound of branches being snapped reached the riders.

"Something approaches, Myls," Tammet's voice was almost a whisper, his eyes darting from Hinna to the trees of the Nucono, its fringes thick with towering amilliat and alder trees. He could see only a few paces into its depth before all turned to shadow.

"We can't be sure. Maybe just a wounded animal or–" Myls stopped. Voices rose suddenly, foreign and rough. *Half a dozen at least*, she noted silently. *Maybe more. And close.* They were soon joined by others, and Myls surmised from the tone that a dispute was occurring. The voices, many now, were then punctuated with the unmistakable clash of metal on metal, and a howl not unlike the first that had issued from the trees. The growing din, however, subsided when a singular voice, deep with authority and frustration, rose above the others. More branches cracked, and the faint sound of huffing, reminiscent of an afflicted horse, sent a shiver down her spine. Her hand went for her sword.

With a quick jerk of her head, she signalled for Tammet to follow her down the slight decline to the shelter of a small copse of trees. She turned, looking into the distance over her shoulder with squinting eyes. Hinna was nowhere to be seen.

"Ready yourself, Tammet. I don't know what's in those trees, but I've a feeling that Egim has not seen its like before." She looked at the quiver on his back. Tammet Yar, even while on patrol, was quite unable to resist the opportunity to hunt an occasional jack-hare. Myls' voice was nearly a whisper. "How many arrows have you brought?"

Tammet faced the Nucono, his face pale. "Not enough," he answered. The huffing and cracking within the forest had ceased.

The beasts had reached the clearing.

The Nylacci did not initially notice the two remaining members of the patrol who, while hiding behind the trees, struggled to keep their horses calm and quiet. The Nylacci emerged from the forest, their long muscular arms bending the alder trees which seemed to snap back into place as if recoiling in disgust.

"The horses won't hold," Tammet whispered. Only maturity, training and Myls' firm hand had kept them in place. Now the horses began to shake their heads, as if trying to rid themselves of fell thoughts. Their eyes grew ever wider as the Nylacci came into full, terrible view; their stench tainting the freshness of the morning air. Tammet looked again to the woman he'd grown to admire in recent months.

"What do we do, Myls?"

She looked around. Ahead and to the left the Nucono loomed. There was no telling how many of these creatures were hidden in its depths. To the immediate right and behind them, the land sloped gently away from the forest and was for the most part open, void of any shelter or refuge.

"We'll run, Tammet. We have no other choice. The village must be warned, and you and I are not able to fight such a foe."

She looked again at the beasts. Grotesque though they were, she found it difficult to look away. A dozen creatures now stood on the Nucono's fringe, their eyes on the smoke rising in the distance. Though they were foreign to this land, Myls could not help but feel there was something familiar about them. She knew with certainty that she had never been in the presence of creatures so vile. But still... Their facial features and limbs. Their height and horns. *The horns!* Myls drew a quick breath. A faint memory, hidden within the deepest regions of her mind, flew now to the forefront. An old man sitting before the fire; she at his side, and long shadows behind them both. In a flickering blaze that combats the darkness of a winter's night, he whispers to her tales that he himself heard as a young boy in Parrya; tales of creatures who weaken the strongest of hearts with their ferocity. Creatures of myth, supposedly once of Cahruia, but banished in the Forgotten Age by forces long since disappeared. To hear their growl was to hear hope fade, to sense the ruin of innocence and peace.

Such were the Nylacci.

"Nylacci," she whispered through fingers which rested trembling on her lips. The whisper sounded as it did when she'd uttered it years ago, as a child before the fire.

"What?" Tammet looked upon her now in disbelief. "Myls, Nylacci are creatures from tales of Fae, they..." Then he looked again upon the beasts, and Myls, knowing that Tammet knew the stories as well, heard realization fill his voice. "Oh Goddess Dahnu. Myls. They can't be!"

But she nodded sadly, for there was no question. These creatures, Nylacci, brought death wherever they wandered, if the old stories were true. They were beasts that were banished from the world long ago, in order to keep balance and be rid of the devastation they wrought. Myls looked to her companion, whose eyes had grown hard. "There will be a volley, Myls," said Tammet. He watched the hideous group before him with dread captivation. Breathlessly, he spoke. "Their bows. Creation, Myls. We cannot outrun such weapons." Fear constricted his chest. The horses grew even more uneasy, their neighing and stomping covered only by the noise of the beasts as they spoke in their deep, rough tongue. They had paused, standing about restlessly as they awaited the order to march. Myls and Tammet watched as the leader of the group pointed beyond the rolling knolls of grass and fields of shimmering wheat.

It pointed to Egim.

The beasts growled, and shook their hirsute heads in anticipation.

"I'll draw them away," Myls began. "I'll ride hard to the west, and hold their attention. When their focus is on me, you will ride with all speed to the village." Tammet shook his head throughout her words, but she raised a hand to silence his protest. "Ride to the stead of Dels Spallic. He is nearest. Tell him what comes, and go quickly to the town. Egim must be warned. They must be ready."

"Myls, I can't let—"

"You can and you will. I'll hear no more of it. Ride strong. Don't look back."

"Myls, I—" But she wasn't listening. With a quick smile that saddened Tammet's heart, she kicked Norix into full gallop.

At the very moment that the Nylacci began their march toward Egim, Myls burst from the brush. Tammet went cold as each and every beast bared its teeth in unison. Immediately, half the Nylacci drew their bows and let fly. Myls, who'd grown up on the backs of horses on the outskirts of Parrya, was not an easy target. Darting to and fro while still trying to maintain the shortest path to the forest, she struggled to escape the arrows that flew through the air. While the archers fired, other Nylacci began to run, pushing at each other as they went. To Tammet, it did not appear to be an attempt to catch the rider. Rather, it seemed the beasts each sought to be the first to reach the woman when she was eventually brought down.

As the first volley landed, Tammet broke for the village. He dared not look back and rode hard, a mirror reflection of his companion who fled in the opposite direction. Misfortune however, spat upon Tammet as a lone Nylac, apparently lame, emerged from the Nucono. While the others focused upon Myls, the lagging Nylac arrived just in time to see Tammet's effort of escape. Without thought, it drew an arrow and let loose the first shot that would find its mark that day. The back of Tammet's left leg exploded in fiery pain as the arrow struck him and his steed. The horse reared, shrieking as it fell to its side, partially crushing Tammet in the process.

For the next few moments, his vision came and went. He was lying on the ground, though it felt more like water. He struggled for his breath, fought against the feeling of drowning. Tammet could no longer feel his leg, or anything below his waist for that matter. He lifted his head slightly, gasping, struggling to break the water's surface.

And then he watched, across the sea of grass, as his friend was ravaged.

His mouth groaned open, his head bobbing as he wept. No tears spilled from his eyes. No sound came from his throat. He just lay there, one arm extended futilely as the beasts went to work on Myls' leg. It wasn't until he heard her cry that he realized she was still alive as she was eaten.

He screamed her name until his throat was hoarse.

Finally, when he'd exhausted his breath, he laid his head on the ground. He lifted his right hand and with his blood-smeared thumb he traced the waterdrop of the Goddess over his heart.

Horned shadows fell over him.

9

A CREATURE POSSESSED

Sivino's footing was unsteady. His vision was obscure, as if in a dark mist; all but the Nylac was washed away as his surroundings spun.

Upon taking its first steps from the tree, the beast had stumbled and almost fallen to its knees. Sivino could see that the creature had sustained great injuries, and could only assume that they had come from its encounter with the ragged man who lay on the tree roots. Snarling, the Nylac regained its balance, and through the blood and drool that ran upon its face, it huffed at Sivino. Red spittle sprayed the ground before it. Its eyes changed from narrow to insanely wide and back again. Sivino did not know if this was a result of the injury and pain it was suffering, or if this was natural behaviour for the creature. *Natural behaviour!* Sivino thought in disbelief. This creature was not supposed to exist!

"Sivi, please run," Lomin begged, tears running down his wizened face. "It's too strong." He struggled for breath.

"Magic is almost spent. You must run!"

Still shaking his head, Sivino turned in the direction of the river and screamed. "Ston! Get Kef and Torla away from here!" Gripping his short sword, he screamed again to his childhood companions: "Get away from here!"

The beast stumbled ahead, gaining speed down a slight decline on the forest floor. Lomin fumbled at the ground beneath him, and picked up a small branch.

Sivino could hear Lomin whispering unintelligible words, but he could not turn around. The Nylac struggled onward, both hands on its left hip, and then with sickly horror Sivino saw the cause of the struggle. From a scabbard concealed in rags and fur, the beast unsheathed a large black sword. Sivino could not think. He couldn't feel. All he saw was the glint of sunlight on the creature's weapon as he listened to the delirious mutterings of his friend behind him.

Lomin's voice rose for a moment, a whisper of muffled urgency, and what felt to Sivino like a small gust of wind whipped past his legs, rustling his thin clothing. Before him, the beast stopped as if struck, and growled with rage. It fell instantly to both knees and roared at the pair in pain and frustration.

Sivino spun to look at Lomin, whose arms now spread by his sides, his eyes closed, the branch still grasped in his right hand. With a quick glance over his shoulder, he saw the beast again struggling to its feet. Shaking off the effects of Lomin's attack, all thought bent on destroying the boy before it, the Nylac lunged for Sivino, who could only hold up his childlike sword and hope for a painless death.

Sivino cringed as something flew by his head, passing so closely he felt the air move. The Nylac stopped abruptly in its attack, and looked down with surprise at the arrow which now protruded from its midsection, the yellow feathers standing in stark contrast to the beast's utter darkness.

The Nylac looked from the arrow to Sivino, its face contorting into a grotesque visage. With a sound that made Sivino sick to his stomach, the creature ripped the arrow from its body and closed the distance between itself and the boy. Another arrow cut through the air, piercing the Nylac's shoulder, but it moved now with no thought of pain. It moved on pure need, the need to kill, and the hate which drove it would withstand any number of arrows.

Certain that it would be the last breath he'd ever take, Sivino Spallic drew it in deeply, and drew back his sword. The Nylac's black blade came up, seeming to steal the light from the sky. Behind him, Sivino heard his friends screaming, running with all the speed they possessed to come to his aid. Yet, it was too late. The Nylac's blade began its powerful downward swing and would surely have rent Sivino in two had the trenoc not flown from the trees, catching the beast's arm in mid-swing, using the momentum to swing himself up onto the back of the giant monstrosity with a scream unlike anything Sivino had ever heard.

Drip was a creature possessed. Shrieking at the Nylac, he clawed and bit, holding firm the Nylac's long arm, his teeth tearing to the beast's bone. The Nylac roared, reaching for its assailant, claws tracing down Drip's face. The two creatures screamed in rage, in pain, and determination. The black sword slipped from the beast's fingers. Grabbing Drip by the leg, it gave a violent twist and threw the smaller creature into the trees skirting the clearing. Sivino cried out as Drip hit an amilliat and fell behind a dense bush of redhollor.

The Nylac growled again at Sivino, though the growl now seemed to twist into a horrible smile. Glancing at the ground around its feet, the beast quickly found its sword. It moved with purpose. Stalking toward Sivino, it held its sword before it, the dark, stained tip pointed directly at Sivino's face which, in contrast to the weapon, had faded to the palest of whites. Entirely dismissing the injuries it had sustained, it lunged at Sivino and swung the sword with brutal strength. Sivino barely had time to raise his feeble weapon as the Nylac attacked. With a sharp, reverberating clang, the blade of the Nylac smashed into Sivino's sword. The force threw the boy to the forest floor, as the top part of his pathetic blade shattered and flew into the trees.

The Nylac roared, and with a hateful glare, moved toward the young Egimian to deliver a messy, gratifying end. So intent it was on Sivino that it failed to notice the bloodied trenoc emerge from the redhollor bush, firmly holding a large branch of amilliat. Eyes brimming with rage, Drip swung himself in a full circle to increase the momentum of his weapon, and with a thick thud brought the branch down upon the back of the Nylac. The beast roared, its shoulder dislocated. Not taking his eyes from the Nylac, Drip screamed at the boy, blood spraying from his mouth as he dealt the beast another devastating blow.

"Run, merrow! *Now!*" Drip jumped again onto the monster's back, reaching for the protruding arrows. But the strength of the Nylac was far from spent. With both hands it reached behind its head and grabbed Drip by the throat. The trenoc let go of the creature immediately, and fought to tear the hands from his neck. But it was useless – the power of the Nylac, even wounded, was too great. It climbed again to its feet, and tightened its grip on the trenoc. Drip gasped for breath, finding none. Tears ran from his eyes, blood from his cheeks.

Then the Nylac's hands loosened, and fell away from Drip's neck entirely. Dropping to the ground, the trenoc sucked air into his lungs, coughing and panting. The beast dismissed him and stared at the boy before it.

Ston stared back defiantly, both hands twisting his longknife, now buried deep in the chest of the Nylac.

10

A THOUSAND IMAGES

Alone at his homestead, Dels took a break from mending the fence and drank deeply from his waterskin. In the near silence of the land, he heard a horse approaching once more. He tightened the cap of his skin, and moved quickly in the direction of the hoofbeats.

One look told him the situation was dire – a horse tearing across the field; a rider holding the reins in desperation. She slid in her saddle, jerked by the erratic movement of the horse. Her attempts to calm the animal were lost in the mare's screams as they flew through the grass, following the dark tree line of the Nucono as they sped toward the Spallic home.

As in his military days, Dels' reaction was instantaneous. Before his eyes could narrow at the strange sight before him, his feet were moving and his hand instinctively went for his sword, which no longer hung on his hip.

Hinna. One of the patrol, thought Dels. *But where are the others?*

He glanced over his shoulder, looking for his horse Rumble. Spotting the steed, he jumped the fence and ran, mounting the tall animal in a fluid motion. With a quick cry from Dels the animal burst into motion, it being accustomed to the quick, demanding riding style of Dels' eldest son.

They raced across the field, Dels hoping to cut Hinna off before she and her mare entered the forest. A fool could see that Hinna was holding on for dear life, and at that speed, the branches of the Nucono would quickly turn deadly. He looked around, still wondering where the other patrol members might be. One would think that such a circumstance would have them chasing Hinna, attempting to help the poor girl.

Her mare, young and erratic, could not hope to outrun Dels' animal, and in short time, the steed had almost overtaken the panicked pair. Dels began shouting instructions, drawing up alongside the terrified animal.

"Hinna, try to relax! Don't jerk the reins!"

Hinna shook her head, her mouth open though no words came. Tears streaked her face, thin lines running from eye to ear.

"Calm, Hinna!" Dels tried not to shout too loud.

"Dels! I can't. I–"

"Hinna! Down!"

She spun and instantly ducked, only barely avoiding the amilliat branch that Nolire sped beneath. She screamed anew, her fear palpable.

"Dels, help me!"

"Pull the rein to the right, Hinna. Gently! Circle her around the field. Breathe. *You're* in control. Ride her in a circle."

Hinna attempted to pull the rein, but the horse jerked its head back. It slowed, twisting in a frenzy, and then the terrified animal gave an unnatural lunge. It bucked, a thrust that the strongest of riders could not have countered. The slender girl was thrown from the mare's back. Momentarily suspended upside down, a final cry escaped her lips as she fell, hitting the ground with a terrible cracking sound. Dels cursed and dismounted, knowing from the manner in which Hinna had landed that she would not recover. Nolire ran in the distance, violently shaking her long brown mane.

Dels knelt beside Hinna, speaking her name as he lay his fingers on the side of her neck, hoping against hope to feel a bloodbeat. There was none. Gently, he brushed Hinna's eyelids closed, and with his hand on her forehead he traced a waterdrop, whispering the words to wish her peaceful entry into the Land of Ever.

Dels jumped up on Rumble and with a kick and a shout that informed the animal that nothing but the greatest speed would be accepted, he raced across the wide, wavering meadow, mentally preparing himself for whatever lay ahead. As he rode, his thoughts simultaneously fixed on both of his boys. Sivino, wandering in what Dels now considered a dangerous, uncertain region. Leath, not so isolated but in no way safe from potential harm. Unable to go to both, he instinctively made the decision to ride in the direction from which Hinna had emerged. Whatever trouble lay there, he would do everything necessary to ensure it remained clear of his boys.

He knew in his rational mind that Drip would quickly

find Sivino; past experience had made the trenoc an expert in this area. However, the heart of a man who does not ride toward a son in danger, no matter the reason, does not understand rationality. He told himself, repeatedly, that he'd see them both soon. And again, his heart cast doubt's shadow on his mind. He told himself that he must take actions which would serve to protect everyone dear to him, but his inner voice, which so easily and eagerly succumbed to guilt and regret, chastised him for his inability to do more.

As it had on the day he'd lost Rhenna.

"*Enough,*" he growled to himself. Memory would serve only to distract at a time like this. He focused his thoughts on the forest to the northwest, and drove Rumble forth mercilessly. He'd first spotted Hinna near a dense copse of amilliat, and it was to this area that he raced. His trained eye noted the tracks of the horses in the morning grass; some of those Hinna's, but others besides, likely those of the patrol. Horses, he observed with some sense of relief, he could handle. Yet, he feared some beast fouler than any horse had driven Hinna's animal into the frenzy he'd observed. He tried not to imagine what manner of creature it may be. Harcole's warnings came rushing back; animals, dismembered on the doorsteps of farmers. He was a fool to have let the young ones venture out this day. He knew that they were children no longer; that their strength and understanding grew with each passing year. Yet he could not yet consider them adults, as close as they might be to reaching such status. They were the young ones. Egim's young ones.

His young ones.

Despite his efforts to focus on the present, he could not help but recall a young Sivino planting tiny shrubs in the yard. It was as he pictured his son, toddling in overalls much too big for his little body, that he heard the ruckus.

Cresting the knoll, he halted Rumble and took in the sight.

The creatures roamed the grass, walking through flowers that should never have been subjected to such filth. Outside the range of arrows, Dels took just a moment to gauge the threat. He noted the number of creatures, their weapons and their size. He saw the horns that jutted from their heads. He saw the two horses that lay on the ground, being torn apart next to what he soon surmised were the remains of Myls and Tammet.

One of the beasts turned and looked at him across the field.

"Dahnu save us," he whispered. Turning, he fled for Egim.

Without horses, the creatures would not progress as quickly as Dels, yet he wasted no time. He knew that the town would have to find some way to defend itself as it fled. There was surely no other option. Egim would have to empty, and quickly. *We'll have to head east,* Dels thought. *Take the Woodcutter Path into the forest.*

The sheer size of the Nylacci, and the fact that they were armed with both bow and sword, meant they were a force with which the tiny hamlet of Egim could not contend. Dels' mind raced with a speed equal to Rumble as he considered the possibilities. He would head to the Tros homestead and, with Stellen, organize some sort of defending party that could lend some time to the townsfolk as they fled.

But first, he needed to go home.

As they ran, Dels continued to look over his shoulder. No sign of the Nylacci could be seen as Rumble's hooves pounded through a shallow depression in the fields leading to the Spallic homestead. Yet he was no fool. The beasts had spotted him, and would soon be in pursuit. Weaving between the Whispering Leah, he rode up to the storage hut beside the house.

Dels dismounted before the steed had fully stopped, burst into the hut and headed straight for the old amilliat box, resting on the highest shelf. Not allowing himself even the slightest pause, he ripped it from the shelf and threw back the lid.

The sword rested upon the folded Ryndarra uniform, protected in the scabbard that had hung at his side for many years.

The sunshine that entered the storage hut danced on the hilt; the blade begging to be unsheathed. After he'd given up the life of a commander, there'd been times that he'd been tempted to return the sword. Surely a farmer would have no such use for a blade. Yet, he'd never been able. This morning, he was grateful he'd resisted the temptation.

He removed the sword and wrapped the scabbard belt around his waist. At the bottom of the box lay his uniform and the tough leather chest-garb, along with the chainmail that was worn just below the uniform's outer cloak. As he threw the leather and mail over his head and fastened it around his chest, his eye was drawn to a Whispering Leah swaying gently beside his home.

Rhenna had once knelt in the very spot where the fragrant tree now grew, a slender sapling in her hands. Two little boys ran around her, squealing with delight as they engaged in an imaginary battle to save the world. She had scooped the earth and gently placed the sprout within the hole. She turned to him and smiled, pointing to the little tree she had accepted into her care. *One more,* she mouthed to him from a distance. He'd told her so often that she'd planted enough of the Leah; that though they are beautiful, they would overrun the property as they grow. She'd smiled back each time, and said that there could never be too much beauty in the world. Dels Spallic looked at the spot where his dead wife no longer knelt. His breath caught in his throat. He ran to the house, struggling to keep his composure. Through the doorway, he saw a thousand images of her – of Leath and Sivino. His sons. He quickly grabbed Leath's bow and the longknives from where they hung by the door and turned to leave, but stopped as quickly as he started. From the doorway of the house he grabbed the mat that lay upon the threshold. *Let Sunshine Enter.* Whatever happened, he told himself, no foul beast would defy the determined wish of his wife. He ran back to his steed, and shoving the mat into the saddle sack, he mounted the animal. He rode quickly behind the house and untied Beauty, the quiet mare. Her superb training would see that she heeded Dels' command to follow. With a quick kick and no backward glance, he left for the home of Stellen Tros, praying there'd be time to do what must be done.

He urged the mare along beside him, shouting to her to stay close as they raced through the Whispering Leah.

The leaves shuddered in his wake.

11

THE STUFF OF FAERAE TALES

The trenoc spat loudly.

Sivino watched as Drip rinsed his mouth with river water to rid himself of the taste of Nylac, and tended to his wounds, cleaning them as best he could with a dampened piece of cloth. The group had quickly left the clearing to return to the trail, leaving the Nylac corpse behind. Torla tended to Lomin as Drip, loath to let anyone touch his own wounds, rapidly recounted the events leading to his arrival. When he finished, he turned, and spat blood into the Andel. No one had spoken while the trenoc had told of Harcole's warning; the silence palpable when the trenoc informed them that, from the trees, he had spotted other beasts akin to the one that lay dead behind them. Torla knelt beside Lomin, washing blood from his face. She didn't look at the trenoc as she worked, though she heard all – the restrained fear in Drip's voice, the restless shuffle of Ston's feet, and the almost imperceptible grunts that Kef emitted as he shifted his weight uncomfortably.

Her young brother leaned heavily on his walking stick, his face wrought with worry. Sivino looked Drip squarely in the face, as though he sought to read some hidden thought or find withheld information. Finally he spoke.

"They can't be Nylacci," the boy whispered. "They can't. That's the stuff of the old faerae tales. I don't know what that *thing* is...was, but there has to be an explanation." The more he spoke the more it sounded as though he were trying to convince himself. "Monsters that rise from the shadows, who stalk the doorsteps of children who misbehave? Nylacci? What next? Grongels? *Elves?* Whatever that thing was, it was real. From beyond the mountains maybe. Across the sea? I don't know. But this is *not* a faerae tale." He looked at each of them again, his voice even lower. "This is real."

Ston stormed past him. "We need to get back to Egim!" As he drew his longknife, it caught awkwardly on the scabbard's throat. With a venomous curse that caused even Drip to look up, he yanked it free. "We need to return. We need to go home and help!" He looked at each of his companions, surprised at their hesitation.

Looking to the forest, Drip replied, "No, Ston Tros. We won't be doing that. The beasts I spotted while I sought you were directly between us and Egim. Our path has been severed by the blackest of swords...so sheathe your own."

"Then what do we do?" Ston shoved his weapon into his scabbard, walking in rough circles. His hands trembled, fingers lost in his thick shock of tangled brown hair.

"We must first tend to the wolf," Drip said. "If we're to move in any direction, he must be carried in the swiftest manner. While you prepare him, I'll see what I can from above." The trenoc made three powerful strides, and leapt into the branches of the nearest tree. Sivino did not miss the pained grunt that came from the trenoc. He then sheathed his ruined sword and moved toward Lomin. Kef, leaning still upon his walking stick, followed close behind.

Torla had cleaned most of the blood from Lomin's hair and face. A damp cloth had been laid across his wrinkled forehead, and her cloak had been spread across his chest. He shivered despite the heat of midday, and his mouth, moving almost imperceptibly, emitted moans weighted with pain.

Sivino knelt at Torla's side, and touched Lomin's shoulder. He realized suddenly how thin and frail his friend had become. He looked more aged now than Sivino had ever seen him.

"Lomin," Sivino said softly, his face beside that of the man. "We can't stay here. Bear with us. We'll move as smoothly as possible."

He stood up, and quickly surveyed their surroundings and their materials. A stretch-bed of some sort would be required.

"The cloaks will serve well enough," he said. "We just need the support."

"Thin trees. Thin, *fallen* trees," stated Torla "We'll not risk giving up our location with loud, longknife chopping." She quickly pointed out a couple of suitable birch, and directed the boys in the making of the stretcher. Knowing her as well as they did, they knew better than to draw attention to the occasional tremor in her voice. As they completed the task, Drip fell from the tree to land amongst them. "We go west," he stated simply as he moved to check the handiwork of Sivino and the others.

Ston left the knot he was tying and stood quickly. "Egim lies *east*."

"Death lies east," the trenoc replied. He shouldered Ston aside, and set about retying the knot that the boy had apparently botched. "Dozens of beasts, *packs* of them, stalk the trails and meadows leading to the village."

Ston was furious. "Our people, our families will be attacked as we stand here and do nothing! I won't abandon Egim! We have to return. We have to help!" As he began to stalk away, Drip stepped in front of him and grabbed Ston's shoulders with his powerful hands.

"You'll die before you reach them," the trenoc hissed. "It's so easy to jump into the waiting arms of death in the name of valour. Aside from those as young and foolhardy as yourself, Egimians balance valour with *reason*. Do you think that your father and Dels will stand and fight this foe, risking the lives of the young? The feeble? They will flee, Ston Tros, for that is all that can be done. The able will slow the creatures with arrow and sword. Let us hope the creatures are as slow as yourselves, and led by one whose savagery pales in comparison to my own. I will lead you, Ston Tros. And you *will* follow." Drip punctuated his final words by jabbing Ston's chest with a long, thick finger.

Ston opened his mouth to retort, but closed it again as Drip tilted his head to the side, daring him to defy. Ston turned and looked back at the others, tears welling in his eyes. With a slight nudge, Drip pushed Ston back in the direction of the company, following close behind.

"Your heart is bold, Ston Tros, and your bravery will

be tested. Of that, we can be sure." He spat and muttered an unintelligible curse. "We are too few. We need weapons and we need the strength of numbers. We need protection. We're going to Levebar."

As they prepared to take up the trek to the nearby village, Sivino's hand moved slowly to his chest. Safe within his inner pocket, he held the small willow switch that Lomin had wielded as though it were the most threatening of weapons. He'd picked it up before they'd left the site of the attack, and placed it carefully within his tunic. He thought of placing it in Lomin's cloaks, but some inner voice told him to hold it for the time being. There was a security in its feel; a tingling of sorts, deep in his finger. He knew well that he could never yield it as Lomin had. After a moment's consideration, he pushed it deeper into his pocket, and hurried to catch up with the group.

12

MUCH LIKE LOVE

Sianah Pella's wooden pail was empty.

She had not set out with great motivation to collect berries that morning. Rather, she needed to walk, to set her mind straight, and to do that she needed the quiet cover of the Nucono.

For several seasons, she and Leath had shared their bond. Yet, she could not understand why he still refused to seek out Terstin's blessing and ask for her marriage hand. She knew that her father respected the Spallic family, and his answer would be one of enthusiastic approval. For long months, he'd excused his non-committal with rants about the shortcomings of his brother, the demands that would be placed on his father, and the need for the time to be right.

She laid the pail down, and sat heavily on the soft earth. Could she do this? Could she tell *Leath that she had waited long enough? That she grew weary of his refusal to publicly acknowledge their bond – refusing to hold her hand in the town, making excuses not to visit her home, limiting the amount of time they spent together?* Both had passed their seventeenth year, reaching an age deemed to be most appropriate to enter into wedded union; indeed, most of Egim's elders considered it strange for a man of eighteen to live still beneath the roof of his childhood home. Exhaling heavily, Sianah lay back on the soft ground, and tried to see the sun beyond the thick canopy of her troubled mind.

She turned her head to the side, grass tickling her ear, and through two swaying wildflowers, she saw him approach. Extending her hand, she plucked the flower on the right and placed it in her hair.

"A bit deep in the woods, aren't we?" Leath looked to his sides as he approached, as if checking to see that they were alone.

"How'd you find me?"

"Blyss Hanney and her sister. They were on the edge of the forest. Saw you a while ago."

Sianah rolled over, and propped herself up on her elbows. "Where's your bucket?"

Leath walked over and looked down at her pail. "Where's your berries?"

She sat up slowly, and pulled her knees tight to her chest. "I believe most of the berries that have grown in this region have found their way into the pies you've been enjoying these past weeks. It seems the Mother of Nature only has so much to give. Like all women, she has her limits." Sianah stood and moved through the trees, off the beaten path.

The words hung on the morning air as Leath searched for a response, but he found none. *Creation!* How was it she always found the words to wound him so? He sighed, and began to follow her, trying in vain to look unaffected by her comment.

"Sianah, wait." This type of aimless wandering bothered Leath more than he cared to admit. He was a young man who needed a destination, and meandering through the trees, following the girl before him, made him uncomfortable.

She stopped and turned on him suddenly. Her look of incredulity gave way to a sardonic laugh. "Oh, I can wait, Leath Spallic. I *have* waited. I've watched the *seasons* change, while your resolve to do nothing remains steadfast. How long must I wait? You know the custom, Leath. One year. One full year we must wait for Dahnu's Favour. A year, in addition to all the time I've waited already."

Leath rubbed the bridge of his nose with his right hand. He knew the custom all too well, as did all Egimians. When a young man and woman made their intentions known, and the blessing had been given by the woman's father, a planting ceremony took place. What was planted was chosen by the couple involved, but more important than the type of seed or sapling sown, the true importance lay in the initial growth of the plants. Three plants, representing the man, the woman and the Goddess, set into the earth with the utmost of care, and for the next year, it was the responsibility of the pair to oversee the plants' healthy growth. The strength of this growth represented the fate of their union. After a year's passage, the couple, and indeed the entire town, decided whether the Blessing of the Goddess had been given. If a decision was made in the affirmative, the wedding took place soon thereafter.

Conversely, a negative outcome could potentially lead the couple to part ways, fearing a union that might be fraught with hardship.

Leath shook his head, thinking of his parents who'd not partaken in the planting ritual. Rhenna had found herself so quickly with child that they'd deemed the ritual unnecessary. Whatever the outcome, they'd be together. Years later, several of the elders would blame Rhenna's illness on the fact that they'd forsaken the ritual. Leath had heard the whispers, and had silently cursed both the elders and a Goddess that could be so fickle.

"I don't put much stock in such silly traditions."

"You don't put much stock in me." She turned and strode off through the trees once more, ducking between branches, forcing her way through thick brush. Leath muttered at his own stupidity, and set to following her.

"Sianah! It's the ritual I find silly, not the thing between us."

"The *thing*, Leath?" She looked back, disgusted. "The *thing* between us is a redhollor bush. If you're talking about love, say as much."

He pushed his way through the foliage, somewhat surprised that he struggled so much more than Sianah. Though they pushed aside the same obstacles, she did so with lithe movements that made him appear all the more clumsy. She was soon far ahead once more, and he struggled to keep her in his sight.

"Damnation, Sianah. Where are you going? I can't even get my bearings in this mess."

"It's a difficult thing, not knowing where you're headed, no?" Her reply, from somewhere in the distance, was heavy with meaning.

For much longer than he preferred, Leath followed Si-anah through the forest. Occasionally he caught a glimpse of her through the thick branches. If he didn't know better, he would have thought she was enjoying this. He was soon ready to give up on this ridiculous pursuit, to yell to her that he was turning back and she could make her own bloody way out, when he happened upon her suddenly. He hadn't seen her, as she was kneeling in the soft undergrowth of the forest, an animal resting before her. As he approached, he saw that it was a young hare, its back leg wounded horribly, likely by the arrow of a hunter who'd been off his mark.

He knelt beside Sianah, and laid a hand on her leg. She looked at him, pained at the suffering of the small animal before them.

"It's an odd thing," she said. "If my father were to cook such an animal in a stew this evening, I'd enjoy it as fully as any. Yet, I'm kneeling here, tearing up like a fool as the creature dies." Slowly, she scooped up the young jack-hare – it being so weak it could not resist her strong hands – and nestled it to her chest. "Death should be death, no matter how it manifests itself."

"Much like love," Leath said.

She turned to him, and looked about to speak but did not. She turned her gaze back to the hare, and whispered to it words that he couldn't decipher. It was a moment he'd remember for all his days; a vision of a mother not yet a mother. A young woman, gently holding a forest creature as if it were her own infant, as the sun pierced the canopy and for the briefest moment enshrouded her in green and gold.

He knelt behind her, and placed his hands on her shoulders. Leaning close to her ear he whispered to her; quiet words that would forever bond them. She closed her eyes and let her head slowly fall back on his shoulder, smiling as the sun moved beyond and left them, as if to lend them privacy.

"The joke, Leath Spallic, is on you. *I would have waited forever…*"

They walked slowly through the forest. There was no need to hurry.

Indeed, such a weight had been lifted from Leath – much to his surprise – that he felt almost light as they weaved through the trees, their fingers entwined more tightly than the branches of the vennar overhead. He'd loved Sianah's smile for as long as he'd known her, but it was somehow different now. It shone from her face, and lit the dim forest around them. Leath smiled inwardly. To think that just a few words could do this. Not just the words, he corrected himself. It was the promise that went with them. He'd promised her himself entire, and he'd not made the promise lightly. No matter what hardships they faced, he would be there to meet them with her, and protect her, every step of the way.

They skirted the edge of the forest, staying slightly within its cool embrace. Leath, being who he was, almost made the mistake of suggesting a quicker return while there was still time to make the day one of productivity, but wisely, he kept his mouth shut and let Sianah lead him. She moved gracefully, almost pulling him along at times.

As they moved over a rock outcropping that afforded a decent view of the village, Leath stopped. Sianah did likewise.

"Have a look," he said.

Sianah stood beside him, standing on the tips of her toes as she followed his gaze.

"What?"

"There's a lot of movement."

"It's midmorning in Egim. Of course there's movement, Love."

Leath shook his head. "Seems like more than usual. People are moving to the eastern field."

Sianah smiled, wrapping her arm around his waist. "I'll bet the Harmino ewe birthed."

Leath smiled. Leave it to the girl to see things in the best possible light. A veritable ray of optimism, this one. He was more inclined to think darker thoughts.

"Tell you what," Sianah continued, rubbing Leath's back with one hand. "We'll make our way down through the maple path, head to the meadow and see what's happening. Deal?"

Leath looked to the eastern field, and nodded.

"But..." She took his face in her hands, and kissed him firmly on the lips. "...I can't promise I'll be in any particular hurry."

13

THE CERNUNNOS

He'd been following her for centuries.

Through fields and forests, across realms and worlds, he'd watched the faerae come and go as she continued her unknowable work. He knew much, surmised even more, and suspected a great deal. He was a creature of great magic, the Cernunnos: a creature whose power surpassed most of the Fae of Elysium. It was indeed this power that had allowed him to go undetected as he tracked the beautiful creature before him, for his power seemed to grow with the passing years.

And hers seemed to fail.

There was no mistaking it. He could see the difference in her once nimble gait, the hesitation that often preceded her use of the Paths. And perhaps most telling of all, he'd seen the way that she often slowed, her thin hand resting on her chest as she seemed to collect herself, gathering herself together before pushing forward once more. He suspected that this was why he was now so easily able to follow her, for in ages past, the need for caution had been tremendous. Too often she had sensed him, felt his presence, and he was forced to abandon his pursuit. On a few occasions, though not in recent years, he'd been discovered and had been forced to concoct a fast excuse to explain his presence. Yet this was little trouble for the Cernunnos, for his tongue was capable of weaving its own magic, his mind sharp beyond comparison.

Yet, despite this sharpness, his mind had changed. It was a fact that he seldom conceded to himself, but one that could not be ignored. A mind as brilliant as that of the Cernunnos could not help but be aware of the changing intricacies of his own headspace. A darkness grew in his thoughts. He knew this, and he accepted it. In recent years, it seemed, he'd even come to welcome it. It seemed that as his thoughts turned more and more toward fell deeds, he was able to think with more clarity and rationality, and while this would concern and perhaps disturb a more common faerae, the Cernunnos saw this as an asset. For Cehron Cen Kohr, it was a small price to pay for the power it brought him.

He watched the faerae move through the trees of the Nucono, returned once again to the land of Cahruia. *Niamh*. The daughter of Obaeron, king of the Fae, walked a narrow path through the forest, her gaze turning often to the trees above. She seemed more cautious than usual on this day, and for this reason, the Cernunnos kept well back. At one point she'd actually stopped and turned, as if she'd felt his presence. He'd slipped instantly behind a thick amilliat, waiting several moments before he ventured out once more. Though the distance from which he followed was great, the keen eyesight of a faerae made the distance less important than stealth.

Cahruia. The Cernunnos detested the place; a world that to him was void of wonder and magic, but held no shortage of common simpletons and mundanity. Yet, again and again, it was the land to which Niamh returned. The Cernunnos had followed her enough in recent years to know that there was a singular reason that she returned so often to this land.

The young one.

He'd been following her here since the boy was a babe. And though she'd never attempted to shift a child, he knew all too well that she'd done this to certain of their family members. He knew there must be intricate connections; connections he might use for his own amusement, or possibly, for his gain. Each time she visited, it was the youth of that pathetic little hamlet that she watched. The youth *and* the ragged man, he corrected himself. The one they called the *wolf*. While he did not understand the connection that the king's daughter could have to these little whelps or their families, he knew it had something to do with the prophecy.

The *prophecy*. Divination. Whispers. Prognostication. Whatever in the worlds one wanted to call it, it was vexing. It was the last message he'd received from the Faant, that unknowable, disconnected faction of Beings. *Demiurges*, some called them. Since the change had occurred in Cehron Cen Kohr's mind, he'd become apathetic when it came to all things enigmatic and unknowable. The Faant had been passing along their divine messages for millennia, carried forth by the Gods and Goddesses to inform and instruct the more powerful creatures of Fae. He was one of these creatures, and for many years had executed their requests. But times change. And, when given the significant lifespan of his kind, the Cernunnos believed that it was only fitting that the Faer folk be allowed to likewise change. Much of his change, he felt, was brought about by an increased awareness of what was right and rational, and what was not. Shifting people from one world to another – all in the name of fulfilling the Faant's will – was something he'd decided he'd do no more. In truth, he'd not done so for many years. This decision was in no small way influenced by the events of his past, events that saw men and women, and in rare cases children, moved to worlds where they truly did not belong. Yet, there were other, more personal reasons. He had seen those who had no place in his world steal what was his, enjoy the fruits of Fae labour without the slightest inkling of how truly blessed they were to even be able to walk the soil of Elysium. It was not right, he thought to himself. Things had not been right for centuries, since the shifting had increased and, despite being decreed by the Faant, had become more reckless. If one were to watch the Cernunnos think these thoughts, it would have been impossible to miss the way his mouth twitched. The curl of his lip was the shape of disgust. So hard he'd tried to convince the Council that this was not right; this moving of bodies from one world to another. Obaeron, he knew, was entertaining the idea. A seed had been planted. The king was aware of what the shifting was doing to his daughter. He was also aware of the unscrupulous behaviour that was being reported from various fronts. These days, it seemed the Paths led to damnation as often as salvation.

These magical waters of the Paths were but one method of ethereal transport. Cehron knew many a Faer folk who preferred the use of the Rings. Fae Rings, comprised of the whitest of mushrooms that bloomed under the fullest of moons, were a favoured choice of the beautiful Fae who lured humans in with their magical dance. Once one had fallen captive to the allure and danced within the ring, they'd often open their eyes to find themselves in another world entirely. And then, of course, there were the Gates. The Mist Gates, created only by the most powerful of magic, formed when a larger group of faeraes worked together, led by a true master of the ancient magic. Once created, this leader used the lyrical words of an almost forgotten language to create rifts within the brilliant fog. Through these openings, movement was possible.

And unnecessary, thought the Cernunnos. There was no doubt that his decision to ignore the wishes of the Faant had not gone unnoticed. Their messages, their insistence that he continue the shifting, had continued unabated, their intensity increasing. On occasion, their intensity had been such that they'd disabled him completely, and he'd awake from an unconscious state on some forest floor, confused and shaken. These events – attacks as he considered them – were deemed a personal affront, and his resolve to spit in the face of the deities further increased as he set his mind to denying their divine wishes. Some things, he thought silently, are not meant to be.

Cehron Cen Kohr was steadfast in his view that the shifting must end. With the passing years, his desire to see it ended had become an obsession. Such was the reason that he'd begun a course of events that he hoped would see the matter settled with some degree of finality. He'd devised a plan, one that he hoped would convince all that mattered that some worlds should be left alone, abandoned as it were to their own fate. He had tried diplomacy. Diplomacy had failed. Stronger action was needed, and the time was nigh to bring things to a head.

Fate. Prophecy. What did such things mean? He stepped silently over the gnarled tree roots of an ancient oak, as echoes of the last whisper twisted in his head.

Within the unnatural storm, a shepherd true and dark shall find his blood spilt on the sword of a boy. A lost soul shall know those bonds that dying blood reveals. In the shadow of loss the shepherd shall fade, for the sword of a boy shall cut through a power both great and terrible.

The Cernunnos tried to convince himself that the words did not disturb him.

A child with a sword.

The Cernunnos scowled, muttering silent words that he himself did not notice. In the trees around him, the birds watched him closely as he stalked through their midst. A thought crossed his mind then, and he stopped suddenly. Maybe another course of action was required. He considered this for a moment, and then slipped behind a tree, causing the birds to take flight. Maybe pursuing the faerae was not what was needed. Maybe he needed to bring the faerae to him. It would, however, need to be done in a way that provided him with an opportunity to learn a little more about this so-called prophecy, be it good or ill. And ill it would be, he was certain. Prophecies. *Ah, the foolishness of the Faant.* This could, he thought, be the opportunity he so desperately desired – a means of proving that the Faant are not in fact infallible, and that he, Cehron Cen Kohr may actually be able to twist the predestined situation into a debacle that set nothing right. It would, if all went according to plan, be a situation that punctuated the malice he had planned for this world for so long.

As he changed his course, the scowl subsided, and a slow smile grew upon his face. It was time, he decided, to pay a visit to the young ones.

14

ONE SHOT

The young ones moved west.

Sivino and Ston carried Lomin, aware of the need for haste yet sensitive to his fragile condition. Kef and Torla followed close behind, the young girl looking upon her brother with the same worried look that she'd exhibited whilst tending to Lomin. Drip, agitated and restless, scouted for danger ahead of the group.

"Could you fellows slow yourselves a little?" Torla asked.

"Tor, I'm fine," Kef replied, easily reading her motives. He pushed himself all the harder.

She grabbed him by the shoulder. "No, you aren't. Do you think the pain on your face is invisible? If you should become unable to walk, what shall we do? Ask Lomin to shift to the side and make room?"

Sivino told Ston to stop, knowing this was what Torla expected. He knew as well that the unexpected events of the day were surely the cause of Torla's heightened concern for her brother.

"Perhaps I should swing from the trees like Drip," Kef replied, his eyes hard. "Or, barring that, Torla, I might ride upon your back."

Torla closed her eyes, realizing that she had, as she did so often, unknowingly embarrassed her young brother.

"I would be more inclined to float you down the Andel," she said, gently ruffling his hair.

He accepted her apology.

"We *should* slow a little," Sivino said. "The quick pace is not good for Lomin."

The old man's moans had become whispers, barely strong enough to be heard.

Drip fell amongst the group with a soft thud, ending any further argument Kef might have made.

"The path appears clear to Levebar," he informed them. "I can see the smoke of their cookfires. We'll walk as far as the Falls, and rest there."

The Falls, in Sivino's mind, had long been associated with the purest fun that an endless summer day could offer. Hearing the roar, he let himself remember better times. Gasps of awe from onlookers as fearless young ones leapt from the peak, screams of challenge and bravado as others wrestled playfully in the pool below, shimmering rainbows in the mists that formed at the waterfall's base, adding to the magic of their childhood. It was a place of wonder, where escape might be found, furtive glances might be exchanged, and laughter always reigned supreme; at least it had been, until the fateful day that Kef had accepted an outrageous dare, and leapt into a world of pain and regret.

"Cursed place!" Drip muttered as they approached. "We'll rest quickly and move on. The roar of the water covers all other sound." Mumbling incoherently to himself, he strode off to resume his watch. The others followed close behind, though their progress was made slow by the burden of Lomin and the condition of Kef's leg.

Gradually they made their way down the winding path to the pool below and drank the cool water. All eyes fixed upon the dark trees around them. The sound of squealing laughter and innocence was a lifetime away now for Sivino, tainted in no small way by the memory of the Nylac's growl. As the others caught their breath, Torla turned her attention to redressing the bandages she'd applied to Lomin's wounds, and washed his head again with fresh water. She noted that though he shivered, his face gleamed with sweat. She closed her eyes and traced a waterdrop on his forehead. Even with Drip present, she felt the weight of the leadership role she'd held for so long in the little group. As she worked, she kept a keen eye on each of them.

Sivino sat on a rock by the pool's edge, removing his boots to shake them free of the pebbles that had gotten in during their descent. He looked up at the waterfall as he did so. Funny, he thought, that no child of Levebar would be about at such a time. The Falls were not too far from the settlement, and the day was warm and waning. There were several from Levebar with whom the Egimians had formed friendships; Brehn Pellet. The Janter Twins. Sandry Tilamin. And Tonnis. His boot stopped mid-shake as the boy crossed his mind. Tonnis Fernika. A boy content to linger on the periphery. A boy whose thoughts and feelings lay hidden from most everyone. A boy without voice or hearing. Sivino gave his boot a sharp smack on the rock where he was seated, and pulled it on roughly. Tonnis, he knew, was a decent fellow, but he struggled to concede this, for despite his silence and his mystery, Tonnis was the boy who seemed to have caught the eye of Torla Rallo.

He stood quickly and brushed the thought aside. Looking to the west, he thought he could discern the smoke of woodstoves and outdoor spits rising in the distance. He muttered something about losing time and indicated that they should get moving, causing Drip to raise a shaggy eyebrow.

They resumed, and walked for the better part of an hour, resting only when it was absolutely necessary. Each of them breathed relief when the edge of the bridge finally came into view.

A village slightly smaller than Egim, Levebar had grown on the southern edge of the Andel. A wooden bridge covered in ivy and built by the finest of Egimian and Levebaran carpenters ran from the small town to the Egimian side of the river. While no fancy carriages would ever cross the structure, it was just wide enough for a horse-drawn cart to traverse.

As the company approached the bridge, Drip emerged from the forest, muttering his thoughts on the neighbouring village. A wide-eyed squirrel watched him pass.

"...of fools – without the sense to build a town on the *proper* side of the river. No more sense than the Goddess gave a dokka."

"Drip seems excited about the crossing," Kef noted to

Sivino. He glanced across the river toward the path that left the riverbank and wound its way up a slight embankment and entered the Nucono. A couple of minutes walk within, the little village lay nestled in the oak and maple. "A rather quiet afternoon in Levebar," he added.

Sivino thought of noontime in Egim; he recalled that though his village was small, as a child he would walk through with a swivelling head which barely contained his darting eyes. Frequently his father would have to remind him (usually after bumping into an unsuspecting townsperson) to watch where he was going, rather than the goings-on. The movement, sound and energy, he felt, was the living breath of the village, and he had inhaled it with his entire being.

No air stirred as the group approached Levebar. The only sound to be heard was the steady flow of the river, and the occasional song of the birds of the Nucono.

"A meeting in the square, perhaps?" Sivino offered.

"The smoke is odd," Ston said. "*Wider* than you'd expect? Drip, is it not too early for a slash-and-burn of the old gardens?"

Drip grunted, and they moved on.

Crossing a bridge ranked with the most unpleasant of experiences for a trenoc. All the same, Drip went first. Behind him, Sivino and Ston carefully carried Lomin. The occasional creak of the boards caused Drip to seize up, a sudden intake of breath the only discernible sign of life in his frozen form. Kef came slowly behind, his stick tapping out each stride with a hollow thud. Through the planks, he could see the waters that raced below, deceptively deep and swift. Sweat caused his hair to cling to his forehead.

He wiped it away and looked back at his sister, who had stopped not ten paces onto the bridge. She looked to her side, to the trees beyond the river.

"Tor?"

"Something's not right," she muttered, as much to herself as her brother. By now, the others had slowed to see what was holding up their progress. She nodded toward the village, her eyes scanning the trees. "Look," she said. "Listen."

No child played on the banks of the river, splashing along the shore or casting line in the hope of a finny. No Levebaran hauled water from the Andel, nor knelt on its banks to wash the family clothing. The air should have been filled with the cries of laughter and play, and the sounds of anvil and hammer, even over the roar of the river.

The only disturbance of this tranquil scene was the strange, slow smoke that rose through the trees before them. Drip started noticeably, as realization slapped his face. He moved ahead of the others, a hand raised to keep them from following. His unease seemed to have little to do with the waters below him. Sivino watched as the trenoc continued on before coming to a sudden halt. He leaned forward, and touched a dark maroon stain on the wooden planks of the bridge. He brought his finger to his mouth, spat quickly and turned.

"Back. Now!"

Ston shot a quick, questioning glance at Sivino, who jerked his head toward the Nucono. It was the only choice. Sivino's heart, which had been racing since the encounter with the Nylac, now pounded even more heavily in his chest.

Heeding Drip's order, the group retreated to the edge of the bridge, and quickly crossed the open ground, up a slight incline, back into the menacingly welcoming arms of the Nucono. The forest was a world unto itself, and though the people of the villages were familiar with its fringe, all knew that the deeper wood held creatures that, while not as grotesque as the Nylac, posed threats worthy of consideration. *Shadows and secrets,* Lomin had told them on many occasions, *were an integral part of all things ancient.* Ston's wry response, comparing Lomin to the forest, had earned him a rap on the back of his head.

Standing in the shelter of the trees, they turned slowly, peering across to the far bank of the Andel. There was still no movement to be seen, no sound to be heard. No one spoke until Kef, groaning with the strain of his crouched position, commented on the smoke.

"It's too even. And all around the village." He paused. "If I didn't know better—"

"I do know better," Drip whispered. "Levebar has been razed."

Ston, who had been watching the riverbank with the rest of the group, turned quickly toward the trenoc. "Nylacci." His voice was hushed. "That's why we've seen no one. Those creatures you spotted, Drip! They must have done this last evening. Oh Goddess." He made a couple of steps toward the bridge, stopped suddenly, and turned back, adrenaline driving his body more quickly than his mind. He rubbed his hands through his hair. "We need to get back to Egim. If we can get around the beasts you saw, Drip, perhaps—"

"Shut up, Ston Tros. Let me think." The trenoc didn't even look at the boy.

"Stallion's Cross, maybe?" Ston continued. "It's but a day's journey beyond Levebar. We can follow the Andel. I know we carry Lomin, but we can make it. Surely the Cross stands intact. Its size is triple that of Levebar and Egim combined. There'll be riders. Horses. We'll bring them back to Egim."

From where she knelt beside Lomin, Torla's hands shot out and grabbed Ston, pulling him violently to the ground. His startled cry was covered by Torla's quick hand.

"*Quiet!*" she hissed without turning from the Andel. She inclined her head toward the river.

All eyes scanned the distant riverbank. The sun turned the water a deep orange, and the company squinted as they searched for the cause of Torla's distress.

And then it appeared. Emerging from the trees, the Nylac stopped and sniffed the air. From their location the group could not hear the beast, yet the sound of the deep huffing that the beast was surely emitting was as fresh in Sivino's memory as the stench was in his nose. He felt his hands begin to shake, saw the rest of the company sink even further into the underbrush. As if sensing anew the presence of evil, Lomin began to stir uncomfortably.

"Foulness," Drip hissed. "We must be away from here!" Slowly, he began to rise to his feet, his eyes not leaving the beast. The four horns that jutted from the creature's head shone in the sunlight. The beast appeared taller even than the one encountered in the Nucono, its long hair darker and danker. Looking around the river, the Nylac scratched at its tattered rags with claws that Drip could still feel within his fresh wounds.

Her gaze still set across the water, Torla laid a hand on his shoulder and gently pulled Drip back.

"We cannot go, Drip," she whispered. She reached over her shoulder and withdrew an arrow from her quiver.

"No," Sivino whispered, yet it wasn't to Torla that he spoke. He saw now what Torla had seen. "Oh Goddess Dahnu, no."

On the far side of the Andel, the Nylac tilted its head as it looked up the length of the mighty river. Walking with his back to the creature, not two hundred paces ahead of it, was a boy.

A boy who stumbled over rocks turned slick with the water of the Andel. A boy who walked as though in a dream, a dream which was about to turn into the most savage of nightmares.

Tonnis. The deaf boy.

Determined not to waste another moment, Torla stood and began to move toward the bridge. As she saw the others rise to follow, she gave them a look that caused even the trenoc to take heed. She raised a finger.

"I'll do this alone. I'll hold the first person to argue and delay me personally responsible for Tonnis' death." Quickly she turned, bent to almost half her height, and descended to the bridge.

Sivino cursed, and prayed that the angle at which the Nylac stood would prevent its seeing his friend. The space between the bridge railings, measured to prevent the loss of most dropped objects, now seemed to be terribly wide. She was exposed to the horrible eyes of the beast on the riverbank. But the Nylac's focus was on the boy entirely. The group watched as Torla moved with quick steps, her leather shoes tapping softly on the wood. All haste was required. The Nylac was closing in on the boy with its sword drawn. Should Tonnis not turn, the beast would walk right up behind him, its foul breath upon the boy's neck before he realized his own doom. The thought sickened Sivino. His eyes darted from the beast to the boy, and back to Torla. Scrambling over the riverbank with his left arm held before him, Tonnis' splayed fingers seemed to silently scream for help. His right arm was extended to the side. Neither caught him, however, when he slipped on a wet piece of driftwood and fell heavily onto the rocks.

The pace of the Nylac quickened.

Anguished groans escaped the company huddled amongst the trees. When Torla reached the end of the bridge, she began to run in full. Sivino saw her glancing into the trees as she ran, certainly wary of other creatures. He remembered how the beast they had encountered outside Egim had endured several arrows and still forged on to attack. *One shot,* Sivino thought. Should she miss her mark, the beast might reach Tonnis, or sound a call for others. Unless her shot was true, it was likely the boy would die.

Drip looked to be in physical pain, though it was an agony born solely of inaction. Sivino knew that to sit in the bushes as his charge chased down a monstrosity was more than Drip could bear.

"Should not have let her go," Drip muttered to no one

in particular. "What would my brethren say, to know that I sat by and let the young girl run into danger alone? What would they say? Shame, such shame they would bring down upon my head."

"There was no choice, Drip." Sivino watched as Torla ran along the riverside. For as long as he could remember, he'd been captivated by Torla Rallo. The young woman could walk into the midst of a maelstrom, her face void of fear, if it suited her unpredictable purposes. In similar situations, Sivino would question, debate, and worry about the outcome of his actions or inactions.

But hadn't he taken a stand before the Nylac just this morning? he now thought. *Hadn't he? Did that not count as courage?* The word itself seemed out of place in his head. He thought of his shattered sword. He'd not been able to protect Lomin. He would have succumbed to the Nylac in moments had it not been for Drip and Ston. He had needed Drip to save his life, and the lives of his friends. He had needed Ston to take the life of the Nylac.

He asked himself if he could do what Ston had done, should the need arise. He wondered if he'd ever be able to do what Torla now did. He watched as Torla began to run harder toward the Nylac. A spray of wet dirt flew behind her as she ran, an arrow held ready. Whether the creature heard her approach or smelled her with its horrible snout mattered not. With a snarl, it spun and faced her. Surprise further twisted with its hideous features, and it gave a savage shake of its head.

"Damnation!" hissed Drip. He burst from the bushes at a full run. Without a second thought, Sivino and Ston chased him.

The group watched, horrified as the beast reached back to draw an arrow. Its face twisted in an expression so foul that Sivino questioned how the Goddess could ever allow such horror to exist. Spittle dripped from its pointed teeth and dark lips, the fur on the lower half of its face hung dank and matted. As Torla nocked an arrow, it drew in a breath and roared at the girl. It was a sound that made Sivino's skin crawl, a sound that seemed to wrap itself around one's head, scratching and mauling its way into the ears. As the beast moved to nock its own weapon, Torla fired; a yellow fletched arrow that flew straight into the Nylac's mouth.

Like her resolve, her shot was true.

No sooner had the arrow struck the Nylac than Tonnis began to rise, turning back toward his ruined home. Immediately he saw the beast and Torla. He grabbed a piece of driftwood as he scrambled to his feet, and raced toward them.

Drip reached the girl as the Nylac fell to its knees. Torla watched, transfixed by the sight before her. The Nylac tried to cry out. It had dropped its arrow and with an empty hand was attempting to nock his long black bow. It worked its mouth, though each attempt to shut its hideous maw met the resistance of the arrow. With Drip now beside her, Torla watched in silence as the kneeling Nylac dropped its bow, raised one leg and made a feeble attempt to regain its feet. Drip darted behind the creature, picked up a rock and brought it down on the back of the beast's head.

The Nylac's arms, reaching for Torla, went limp. It fell on its side, dead before it hit the ground. Beside the creature, Tonnis collapsed as well.

15

A VILLAGE TO EMPTY

Fallette Tros had just finished hanging freshly washed clothing when Dels crested the hill above the Tros homestead. Turning, she smiled and raised her hand in welcome. Within a moment however, the smile vanished and her hand froze in the warm morning breeze. Her fingers fell together in a loose fist, which went to her mouth in mounting fear.

Dels Spallic rode like thunder, dressed in the garb of the Ryndarra.

Panicked, she turned and glanced around the property for her husband, still uncertain as to whether this was some trick of her eye. Stellen had only just returned from his visit with Dels an hour prior, and he had said nothing of the Ryndarra. Not seeing him, she began to walk back to the house, all the while glancing over her shoulder at the approaching rider. As Dels neared, she could see the look on his face; a look that caused her to utter a small cry of dread, and she began to run.

"Stellen!" Her voice cracked as she yelled. "Stellen! Come here!"

The big man burst through the doorway of their home, and from the gardens in the east end of the property, the trenoc Shyll came running. When Stellen saw Dels, he faltered and almost missed a step. He came to an abrupt halt as the trenoc raced up beside him.

"Stellen?" asked Shyll.

The big man knew simply from the way that Dels Spallic rode his horse there was cause for alarm. He'd never push Rumble such if the situation was not dire. Behind them, Beauty pushed herself relentlessly to keep up.

"Prepare the horses." Shyll heard the concern in his voice and raced to the stable.

"Fallette. I think something's happened." Taking her by the arm, he began to lead her toward Dels. "Come now, hurry." As his friend drew near, Stellen whispered a low curse when he saw the Ryndarran sword that Dels now wore – the one he'd sworn he'd never wear again.

The former Ryndarra reined in abruptly before his neighbours, the horse's hooves digging violently into the soft earth. The gravity of Dels' eyes tightened Stellen's grip on Fallette's arm as their neighbour quickly dismounted.

"Stellen. Fallette. We have to go. Now." He moved toward the Tros homestead, unwilling to pause for even a moment, his voice filled with urgency. As the shocked pair followed close behind, he continued. "Something's coming. A group of creatures. Thirty. Forty. I'm not certain. They're headed for the western end of my property." He stopped then, for he needed to look the pair straight in the eye to speak his next words. "I'm no fool, you both know this." A pause before he spoke again. "The creatures are Nylacci."

"Dels?" Stellen began, but Dels raised a hand to silence him.

"Don't question me on this. We're in danger. They move quickly."

"No, Dels," Fallette reached out and grabbed his arm. "No, it must be Isrorians surely. Or deserters of the war, dressed in animal furs, travelling in packs. Dels, it must–"

"Hinna O'ilm is dead." Dels said it simply. Bluntly. "Tammet Yar and Myls Irrot...I'm not sure, but I think they're dead as well. Fallette darling, these are not Isrorians."

"No." Fallette shook her head quickly, determined not to believe. "No, I just spoke with Hinna yesterday. She's to be married in a fortnight. She is to be *married*, Dels!" Stellen tried to comfort his wife, to no avail. "And Tammet! He was at the Harmino's party last night. He sang six verses of *I Know No Rovil Maid*." She began to sob. "They can't be dead!"

"Fallette, listen to me." Dels spoke for his friend, his mind a fraction more rational than Stellen's as he had had more time to process what was happening. "Fallette, we need your help now. We must all keep our wits about us if we are to escape." She began to interject, and he spoke quickly. "Listen to me now. We need you. *Ston* needs you." Her eyes went wide, and she sobbed anew. Dels instantly regretted mentioning the boy. He quickly put a hand on her forearm, and answered the question in her tear-filled eyes. "Drip is seeing the young ones to safety.

You needn't fear. Now, Shyll approaches with the horses. You must go into the house and retrieve any weapon that you may possess; any at all – knives, bows, an amilstaff. Stellen, we'll do likewise in the stable. Move quickly now, Fallette. *Quickly.*"

Dels could easily see that she wanted to despair, wanted to question and plead. Yet, the mention of her son had triggered something – that powerful maternal instinct to protect – and she held back all she wanted to ask. She closed her mouth, nodded, and ran for the house.

The two men turned and raced to the stable.

"Truly, Dels. Nylacci!?"

"In all honesty. Stellen, they're horrible." He reached the old wooden structure and turned to his friend. "We need to get the villagers into the trees, and as far up the Woodcutter Path as possible." He grabbed a pitchfork and several longknives. "Be sure of it friends, any who remain will be slaughtered like lambs.'"

In short time, Dels and the Troses crested the final hill before Egim, pausing on the very spot where Leath had recently stopped to survey the land and pay respect to his dead parents. Dels knew there was no spot that would serve as a better vantage point, and upon reaching the top of the hill, he turned, seeing what he feared most.

Smoke.

A lifetime of work and memory, love and growth, fallen to the fire of these beasts. His eyes couldn't be certain, but his heart knew that the distant smoke rose from his home. He thought of the stitchwork of Rhenna, the creations that adorned the walls of every room, and grimaced as he thought of the intricate threads being ravaged by hungry flames.

"Damnation," Stellen muttered as he watched the smoke rise.

"Let's not waste our breath on curses." Dels turned his horse quickly, his jaw set. "We've a village to empty."

The pounding of the hooves drew attention to the riders before they reached the first home. Curious folk moved out onto the narrow dirt street to see what the fuss was about, and Dels instantly pitied them. Innocent folk, he thought to himself as he saw their eyes filled with wonder and concern. Children, who stood in the garden with freshly pulled carrots hanging from their little hands, confusion on their faces as they turned to their parents. These were folk who, each of them, cared more for the well-being of their families and neighbours than for themselves. Men and women who gave freely of all they owned, asking nothing in return. And now, all that they owned, everyone they held dear, was in danger. With a few words, Dels was about to shatter the life of every man, woman and child in Egim. The thought made him sick.

He slowed momentarily and let the Troses flank him.

"Ride the perimeter," he said to the pair. "Stellen, go right. Fallette, left. Tell everyone to drop everything, and move to the square with all haste. *Command* them! I'll meet you there. Go!"

As his neighbours set to the task, he cut directly through the town, calling to all he passed to take their families and move to the square at the centre of the village. The trio rode with such haste, and commanded with such severity that none refused the order. Short time passed before all the citizens were aware of the situation, as word of mouth and shouts of urgency reached every home and workshop.

A few minutes later Dels pulled up at the town square, and stopped inside the circular benches that lined the whitewashed platform. The Egimians rushed forward to surround Dels, who twisted on his horse, looking for Stellen and Fallette, waiting to be sure the village had been encircled. When at last he saw them, he felt a firm hand grab him by the elbow.

"Dels? What in hell's creation is happening?"

Dels looked at his uncle, feeling the fear and uncertainty in the man's grip.

"Danger, Lumb," he said quietly. "Of the worst kind." He looked up and saw the Troses arrive, a few straggling residents close behind them. From the crowd gathered around him, he heard the murmurs. *The uniform*, they said. *The war. It's reached us. Goddess save us, it's Isrorians.* Throughout his people, he heard the speculation. Unfortunately, what approached was far more horrific than any southern enemy.

Dels stood in Rumble's stirrups, holding the reins firm in one hand, and centred himself before he spoke. He raised a large, scarred hand, and a hush fell over the crowd.

"Listen, and listen well." He did not shout, but the power and depth of his voice washed over all who surrounded him. He spoke quickly. "I beg that you'll keep your finest wits about you until I've finished. Hold firm to the bravery I know you possess, each and every one of you. A group of beasts march now for Egim. They are indeed a force which we cannot hope to resist. I have seen them as surely as I see each of you before me." People began to question and shout, but he drowned them out with the authority of his voice.

"Listen, I say! They come, and we cannot survive if we remain. Each of you will go to your homes, and you will retrieve your weapons. Every weapon! There is no time to gather keepsakes or precious items – none! Those without weapons will go to Lumb Velto's smithy. We'll use whatever we must to hold back this filth – crossbows and longbows especially!" He considered his words. "We do not want to engage these creatures in close combat. Do not mistake me, we do not prepare for battle, we prepare for flight! The bows will lend us time enough to stay ahead of the beasts."

"Did the patrol see any of this?" A thin man named Denn Corr called from the crowd.

Damnation, Dels thought. *This is going to be bad.*

He paused, and took a breath. "I believe they have fallen."

A wail of agony pierced the crowd, followed closely by the sobs of many others. The families and friends of the patrol riders were entirely unprepared for the news. Such things did not happen in Egim, Dels knew. People were not *murdered* in Egim.

Not until today.

"My heart is broken with yours," he continued. "Truly, it is. But we must move now to prevent further loss. Let us not have the patrol's sacrifice be in vain. We've little time. Go, get your weapons. Spread the word to all, find those who are not present. We'll meet on the eastern field.

Quick now! Go!"

The folk scattered, those in grief being essentially carried by those closest to them. The trenocs outran all, their powerful legs spraying dirt and dust from the street as they raced for the houses. The few who wore their only weapons upon their side remained in the square, preparing horses and carts for the elderly and immobile. Others closed in on Dels, eager to be better informed of the danger that moved toward their gentle village, but Lumb Velto brushed them all aside.

"Dels, where's Sivi?"

"Drip has gone to Sivino," Dels replied quickly, as if speaking of it caused him too great a pain. "I believe the young ones were some distance from the group that I observed. They were trekking near the Andel. Drip will find them, be sure." Lumb noted the pained look on the face of Stellen, and the look of absolute desperation on the face of Fallette. Dels' brow suddenly furrowed, and he looked behind Lumb, scanning the crowd. "Lumb, where's Leath?"

Lumb's eyes suddenly went wide with realization. "Ah Goddess! Damn it all!" He rubbed his filthy hands through his thinning grey hair, squeezing his eyes in anger and agony. "Dels, he went to find Sianah. She's picking berries."

Dels couldn't remember the last time he'd had the wind knocked out of him, but at that moment he remembered the feeling well.

"The twin oaks, near the crooked vennar tree," Blyss Hanney spoke up. Her sweet round face, usually graced with an innocent smile, was turned down in fear. Berry juice stained her long beige apron as she wrung her hands in its worn fabric. "They went into the forest."

Dels looked to the trees, judging the distance and the time it would take him to get to the forest, find the pair, and return. He started toward his steed. *Stellen could move the townsfo–* His thoughts were interrupted as a young rider moved forward. Lues Torgo, a friend of Leath, wasted no time.

"I'll go, Dels." He pushed past the former Ryndarra, but Dels grabbed his reins.

"I can't ask that of you," Dels said.

"You didn't," Lues replied. "Nor did Terstin Pella. I do this myself. I have family in Levebar. They need to be warned. I know I'm needed here, but we cannot have another town caught unaware. I'll find Leath and Sianah on the way. I'll have eyes out for Sivino and the others also. Once the warning is given, I'll return and help." He gave a quick nod to Dels' hand, which was still on the reins. "No time. I need to go."

Dels released the straps, and Lues kicked into a full run.

As the rider sped away, Dels looked at the forest. A light breeze blew in from the west, and the leaves trembled with its touch.

16

A CUP OF TEA

The boy lays upon the ground, a trickle of blood running down his cheek. He rolls onto his side, grimacing with the effort as his ribs scream in agony. The late autumn air causes him to shiver. Wiping blood from his upper lip, he slowly opens his eyes.

They fix upon a lavender flower, swaying softly beneath a magnificent oak. It grows in a thick patch of soft-rush weeds, whose attempt to choke and suppress the purple flower has failed. It leans toward him, petals shining proudly as it soaks in rays of sunshine. As his senses begin to return, he thinks not about what has happened to cause his pain, but why the flower should grow in such an unsuitable location. It shines with a brilliance that contrasts so severely, so beautifully with the surrounding foliage.

Though it is alone, surrounded by that which would steal its essence, it thrives.

His family had arrived from Slattenton only two seasons prior, and he was still considered something of an outsider.

Being unable to hear, he's grown quite accustomed to being on the periphery. He had been walking on the fringe of the forest, spending a quiet afternoon observing each and every creature that walked, crawled or flew in his vicinity. He vaguely recalls watching a pair of red dokka, their feathers colouring the sky as they flew from tree to tree. The dokka, a bird abhorred for its long, high-pitched squawk and scavenging tendencies, is wary of townsfolk. They are often the target of sticks and stones, flung to drive them away. Of course, he cannot hear their mournful cry. He sees the beauty that others dismiss, and the birds sense this. He carries dry crumbs on his walks, and the dokka now know him by sight. A few crumbs, his grandfather had taught him, could reap the most splendid of rewards. Just a few crumbs.

His world spins as he tries to gain his feet. He stops midway, leaning heavily upon one knee. He vaguely remembers an impact to the back of his head, and the way he was rough-handled as he lay dazed, helpless on the forest floor. He is still trying to retrieve wisps of elusive memory when strong hands grab him beneath his arms, and attempt to pull him to his feet.

He groans as he tries to turn, preparing himself for another beating. He reaches for a nearby branch, but his wrist is grasped in slender fingers. He looks up and gazes into the eyes of a striking young girl. Beautiful, in fact. Her eyes are green as late summer grass. He reads her lips, which he imagines are moving in a whisper.

"He's gone. It's alright now." He will never hear her voice.

She looks to the trees, still talking, and he cannot see what she has said. She turns, waiting in a silence that he knows follows a question. He shakes his head slowly, and points to his ear. He points then to his eye, and Torla's lips. She seems not to understand, and then her eyes widen a little. She thumps her forehead with the heel of her hand.

"Sorry, Tonnis Fernika." She takes his hand, and shakes it warmly. "My name is Torla."

The boy does not need to wonder how his name is known to her. There are very few in this part of the realm who live in a world of silence. She helps him to a fallen tree, and sits beside him. Her hand rests on his shoulder as she speaks, slowly and with many gestures of face and body, as she relays to him the details of what has transpired. A stranger to the area, an Isror-ian by his appearance, had struck him on the back of his head. Tonnis' pockets, empty though they were, had been searched. The dull thud of a yellow feathered arrow striking the tree be-side him seemed to be reason enough for the assailant to quickly move on.

Tonnis watches her lips intently, but most of his inner fo-cus is on the hand which rests upon his shoulder. He looks from her lips to her eyes, places a hand over his heart, and bows his head toward her.

She returns the gesture. "You're welcome," she replies with a smile. And for the first time in recent memory, he smiles as well.

With great care, the company helped Tonnis to his feet. Looking from the Nylac to the girl, he extended his hand urgently toward Torla. He pointed at her, question-ing her with his frantic eyes as he raised a thumb and pointed at her again.

She nodded. "Yes, I'm fine."

He pointed to the Nylac, and then splayed his hand

several times, opening and closing it. There had been many creatures. Tears streamed from his eyes as he turned again, and pointed to Levebar. He shook his head, and looked back at Torla. Extending the fingers of his left hand toward her, he wiggled them slowly, raising his hand in the air to indicate the flames that had ravaged the town. Shaking his head again, his body trembled with the agony of what he'd seen. He pointed to himself, made the gesture of casting a line. He'd been by the river, fishing, as his loved ones screamed screams that he could never have heard. Nor could he hear his own when he returned to the village, and saw all that had transpired behind his very back. He'd run and hidden, spending the night in a thick copse of trees outside the village.

"I'm sorry, Tonnis." She pats her heart twice as she speaks. *"I'm so sorry."* She hugged him to her as the others hurried up the riverbank, each of them staring at the Nylac in fascinated horror. Giving the beast a wide berth, they walked over to stand beside Drip. And then, because there was nothing else they could do, they watched as Torla held Tonnis, the boy's shoulders shaking as he silently wept.

Drip slowly wandered off to one side. Things had begun to spiral out of control. In addition to the cripple and the ragged man, they would now add a deaf boy to their fold, he thought. As he absently scratched the back of his shaggy head – a telling sign of his frustration – he thought again of what his fellow trenocs would say if they could see his failing attempt to lead the young ones.

"Such shame," he muttered under his breath.

He thought then of Dels. This man, this *friend*, he'd admit to himself. His respect for Dels was great, and he knew it was reciprocated. Dels had trusted him to find his youngest son, as he had on so many occasions. Yet this time, lives hung in the balance. He glanced toward Sivino, who knelt with a hand upon Lomin's shoulder, speaking words to the group that the trenoc could not distinguish. They had no set route and very little protection. He could see the anxiety on the faces of each of the companions. Sivino's hands were shaking as he looked between Lomin and Torla. Kef leaned on his stick with the weight of the sun leaning on the horizon.

Darkness would soon come.

Having waited for Tonnis to regain his composure, the company moved down the banks of the Andel. Some form of camp would need to be struck, and the further they moved from the site of recent carnage the better. Narrow eyes kept close watch on the forest, strained further by the sun that descended behind the behemoth that was the Nucono.

After walking half a league, Torla pointed out a spot below a group of particularly tall, dense maple, and Drip nodded silently. A soft wind had begun to blow, and the trees would offer shelter when the sun set. The boys lowered Lomin to the ground and stood fully, stretching their weary muscles. As their shoulders loosened, they began to make the necessary preparations.

Torla knelt beside Lomin, her face grave as she studied his wounds. Pus now drained from several of the more severe cuts. "He needs a yarrow poultice." She turned to

Drip, whose mouth turned down severely. She was not deterred. "It need only be a small fire, Drip. And brief. Enough to get a quick boil, then we'll put it out."

Drip turned away from the girl and put his hands on his hips. Even when Drip was in agreement, Torla knew he needed to act as if he knew better.

"Very small," he said. "And very quick. First, let me scout the area. Merrow, you and the brute gather some branches."

"Maple and ash," Torla said as she took a tiny cookpot from Sivino's backpack. "Less smoke."

Drip grunted. "Thank your Goddess that one of you had the sense to listen to the wolf's lessons." With that, he ran toward the nearest tree, swung himself up on a branch and disappeared.

Sivino and Ston gathered the branches. Kef sat on a rock beside Torla, Tonnis and Lomin, rubbing a bit more feeling into his tired leg. As his sister removed Lomin's cloak to expose a nasty gash on his upper arm, Kef cringed and chastised himself for thinking himself the most afflicted by their flight. He stood slowly, and offered to fetch the water from the Andel.

As he returned, Drip fell from the trees and brushed bark and twigs from his furry arms.

"No sign of danger. Set a flame quickly, Ston Tros. The fire cannot reach the night."

Kef moved to Drip's side, having filled the pot.

"One boil," Drip said as he pushed Ston aside and began to light the fire himself.

"Drip, one boil will be needed for the poultice," said Kef. "One more for a cup of greyleaf would do no harm,

I'm sure."

The trenoc, arranging the kindling, didn't look at the boy. "What *I'm* sure of, Kef Rallo, is that a small fire could burn us all. I'm in no mood for needless risk. Would you light a beacon for the creatures that may lurk yonder? I realize that the forest is dense, much like your thick skull, but like your skull, a little light can still get through. If they see us, a lack of tea will be the least of your worries. Boil the water."

"Fine," Kef shot back. "But if you crave a warm cup as the sun sets, don't come muttering to m–"

The pot of water fell from Kef's hands, its contents splashing across Drip's carefully arranged branches as the boy stepped backward.

"Fool!" the trenoc barked. The others turned quickly to see what had happened as Drip swore under his breath.

"We're surely doomed if you can't handle a task as simple as this. What are you–" The trenoc stopped when he saw the look on Kef's face. He knew without turning that they'd been found. Grabbing the nearest rock, he spun, teeth bared.

"Goddess protect us," Sivino whispered.

On the thickest branch of the nearest oak, the faerae sat. His cold eyes regarded them intently, malice hidden just below the surface. No one moved, nor spoke. So shocked were they by the unexpected presence that none noticed that the wind had ceased completely and a heavy stillness had fallen over the riverbank. The reverie was broken only when the faerae tilted his head, ever so slightly, and a smile grew on his pale, thin lips. He looked directly at Sivino as he spoke, his dark tone evoking a shiver that no winter wind could rival.

"The Goddess, Master Spallic, has far better things to do this afternoon, I'm certain."

Casually he leaned forward, slipping from the branch. Though he fell from a significant height, he landed lightly on the forest floor.

The Cernunnos walked toward the group, his focus directed entirely upon his left hand, at what seemed to be a troublesome fingernail. A splinter, perhaps. As he walked toward the company he looked up, and with tremendous hidden amusement noted their shocked, confused faces.

He smiled. It was, thought Sivino, one of the most disturbingly enchanting smiles he had ever seen. He appeared as a common man, save for the antlers that rose up from his head like those of a young stag. Unlike the Nylacci's horns, these were almost pleasant to gaze upon; their symmetry seemed sculpted, as did the sharp features of his face. He was dressed in a fine cloak that was the skin of some animal, smooth sienna that almost reached his knees. He stood well over six feet tall, and though the bottom portion of the cloak flowed loosely, gracefully behind him, the upper portion was snug enough to reveal the powerful physique of the creature's arms and torso. He brushed a couple of stray leaves from his arm, and removed one that had stuck in his long dark hair. He stopped directly in front of the group, who had come slowly and cautiously together upon his approach – and held their gaze. They had created a protective barrier between Lomin and the stranger, which was noted with amusement by the latter. After a moment, he looked down at the branches that the boys had collected, now soaked. He turned to Kef.

"A pity, Master Rallo." His voice possessed the rasp of the river, and all its power. "I should have liked a cup of tea…"

He made a slow circle around the group, his hands joined behind his back. The youths turned with him, never allowing their backs to be to him as he walked lithely, his eyes on the ground, as if searching for something.

"I've watched you for a while. Just a little while, mind you, but long enough to put some names to faces. In fact, I feel I've known you for quite some time." He stopped then, and smiled at some thought that crossed his mind. "I believe I may even have…dreamed of you. At least some of you." He rested his dark eyes on Sivino. "Yet, one can never be sure. Dreams are tangly things. Obscure faces and mixed messages. Whispered words in those hours of dark imagination. Harbingers, some would say. *Prophecy*, say others. Yes, I've met you before, in my head, and now, at long last, in the flesh." He extended a hand to the group, who instinctively drew back.

He lowered his hand, and continued with an easy laugh. "Yes, yes, you are right to be cautious, the stranger that I am. Please allow me to introduce myself." He looked to the racing waters of the Andel. "My names are many. They seem to change with each world I visit, dependent of course on the Age in which those visits occur." He spoke then to Ston, though his eyes never left the river.

"Lift your slackened jaw from the banks of this river, young Master Tros, for fear the waters will enter your body and drown your very soul." He turned to face the boy, his voice low. "Your shock, I'll grant you, is justified, for long ages have passed since the *true* creatures of Fae have felt the need to come once more to Cahruia." He took a breath, as if his patience grew short. "I digress, though I'm sure you'll forgive me. I've been known as Hob." He paused, thinking with eyes closed. "I was once Poake. Then Goodfellow. Ronson. Byrnt Tayle. Will O' the Wisp – many names, and many years of coming and going." He joined his hands behind his back again. "For our purposes, my young friends, you may call me–"

"*Cehron.*" The new voice trickled down from the Nucono like a small mountain stream, meandering between the trees. And though gentle like the smallest of streams, Sivino was somehow sure that this voice could cross leagues if it so desired. All heads turned, save that of the Cernunnos who bowed his and closed his eyes with a rueful smile.

The second faerae stepped around a tree, her thin hand lingering on the trunk of the maple as she came into sight. Her wavy brown hair and flowing white robe swayed slightly as she stopped on the forest's edge, waiting long moments before she moved forward. She seemed to be considering possible words, possible actions, or perhaps was allowing the other to consider what actions he would evoke as she walked towards him. She did not return the smile of the Cernunnos, and stopped only when she was close enough to feel the cool breath of the faerae before her.

"Cehron Cen Kohr. I had hoped ages would pass before I had to gaze again upon your handsome face. Time has been kind to you."

"Niamh," the Cernunnos replied, smiling with all the charm of the worlds. "Niamh, my dear... You've aged."

17

A WAVERING ARROW

The crying of a child was the only sound that Dels Spallic could hear.

Throughout his years, he'd dried a thousand tears; Sivino's more often than Leath's. To this day, his eldest son seemed to consider every shed tear to be a tiny loss of strength that one could never regain. As he adjusted his chainmail, Dels looked around at the townspeople. He could see the terror in their eyes through the dust that danced above Egim's dirt roads – a dust filled with panic and prayer.

For his part, he prayed to the Goddess that he had them all. Watching as the group came together in the eastern field, he quickly made note of the families, trying to confirm that all were present. Surely each individual family would be taking stock of its own. He looked toward Stellen, who nodded as though he knew what Dels was thinking.

The town was assembled. It was time to leave.

He was about to turn when a thin body collided with his own, and he spun to see the tear-streaked face of Dahlah Rallo.

"Dels, tell me you know where they are!"

The big man opened his mouth, and in that moment of hesitation where he sought the right words, Dahlah sobbed and fell into his chest.

"Dahlah, listen to me." He put a hand on each of her shoulders, gently separated himself and looked directly into her clover green eyes. *Torla and Kef have the same eyes,* he thought to himself. A voice whispered then in his head, *So did Kolle.* He shook the thought away. "Listen. I sent Drip to check on them earlier, before there was any sign of danger. There's no one who knows the area like that trenoc. I have complete faith that he found them, that he'll keep them safe." He rubbed her arm, knowing full well how useless the gesture was.

"Oh Goddess, Dels, I can't lose them." She looked up at him, her body trembling. "They're…" She tried to continue but could not, and one of the nearby women came over and wrapped an arm around her, leaning in and whispering assurances. She looked at Dels a final time as she was led away. Her eyes finished her sentence.

They're all I have left…

He heard again that voice, the whisper in the furthest reaches of his mind, provoking him, stirring up feelings of guilt and regret. *Leath,* it whispered. *Sivino.* He took a quick breath and joined the others as they made their way through the streets of Egim. Dels took up the rear, and couldn't help but notice how Egim fell silent in his wake. He saw the rugs hanging on the line, the brooms that had beaten them forgotten on the ground below. He saw the axe, leaning silently on a woodpile that awaited cleaving. Open windows, curtains hanging like veils over the life that had existed inside these homes. Silence everywhere. But this was not Egim. Egim moved toward the eastern field, preparing to make its way up the gentle hill that would take it into the Nucono and beyond.

What chance did such a group have against the strength and rage of Nylacci? Time, he realized, would be their only ally. The ability to fight, he knew, was less important than the ability to run. He kicked his animal into a trot and followed his flock, urging them forward. *The failed shepherd,* he thought. The old fable his grandfather had often recounted; *No matter how many you keep in your fold, your failure lies in the lamb you leave behind.*

Damn it, Dels thought. *No matter which way I go, someone is left behind.*

From the west, a late morning breeze began to blow. Overhead, a rusty wind vane that had sat unmoving as the town emptied now slowly began to turn.

Its arrow wavered.

Through the thick trunks of trees that had watched ages pass unnoticed, Leath and Sianah made their way toward the field.

The closer they came to emerging from the forest, the slower Sianah seemed to walk. She dragged her heels, a devilish smile on her face as Leath pulled her hand, trying to speed her up.

"Are you so anxious for my father's blessing, Leath Spallic?"

Leath let himself smile. "Giddy with anticipation."

She jumped on his back, a sudden move that caught him off-guard. He stumbled forward with a grunt.

"Sarcasm doesn't become you, dear." She wrapped one arm tightly around his neck.

"Being carried doesn't become you," Leath managed to rasp. "Is this how we'll walk across our threshold a year hence?"

She slid from his back with a sigh, her smile glowing. "Our own place, Leath. Just the two of us. The outskirts of Egim. A fence of white palings, and gardens and lambs. Summer parties, and we'll invite the entire village." She slowed, and looked at him as she spoke. "And children. I've envisioned it a thousand times. A beautiful life, that's what awaits us. We can–" She stopped, seeing the look on Leath's face. "Leath?" She turned and followed his gaze as they stepped from the Nucono.

The entire village was moving through the northern field. Men, women and children; even the horses. But it wasn't necessarily the movement that worried Leath. It was their haste.

The village was running.

The sound of hooves pulled his eyes from the north. A rider was coming toward them, pushing his horse entirely too hard.

"Hellfire," he whispered.

And with that he was running as well, dragging Sianah by her slender hand, leaving all thoughts of their future in the shadow of the indifferent forest.

"What's happening?" Leath shouted as soon as Lues

Torgo was in earshot.

"Attack from the southwest." There was true fear in Lues' voice, and Leath knew that if the threat could scare his friend, it was serious indeed. The rider's eyes kept darting to the distant western fields.

"Attack?" Sianah couldn't process the word. "What do you mean? Isrorians?"

Lues shook his head. "Dels was the only one to see them. From a distance, but close enough, he assured us." He looked at Leath. "The town flees. I'm going to warn Levebar. You have to be quick. Skirt the edge of the forest to the northeast fields. Your fa–" The word died in his mouth, and he looked past the pair. Leath and Sianah turned.

Dark stains had begun to seep from the thicket to the west. Too far away to hear, or see with any detail, the figures were still unmistakably wrong.

Lues swore. Sianah shook her head slowly. Leath recalled Sivino's words from the previous night. *Two legs*, he'd said. *The movement of no humanfolk, be sure of it.*

Was this what Sivino had seen? Leath jolted then, and spun to look toward the town, then the forest. Sivino. *Where was his brother!?*

"Go!" he shouted as he gave Lues' mare a smack on the flank. He pulled at Sianah's elbow and they tore away as if the creatures were on their very heels.

They ran, hard.

Leath desperately wanted to take Sianah's hand, to give her at least the assurance of his grip, and to pull her faster through the scrub bushes and high grass that

covered the upper field. He did neither. They ran without speaking, using every breath to fill their lungs as they
flew across the land, their eyes set on the mass of people
that hurried toward the trees at the top of the distant hill.

They were close enough now to see the townsfolk
more clearly. Despite their panting, their pounding feet
and the throbbing in their temples, they could hear the
cries of their people. From the rear of the group, a rider
separated and began to race toward them. Leath recognized his father immediately. What he didn't recognize
right away was the garb Dels wore, but he soon realized
what it was. And what it meant.

Dels reached them in moments. He reined in and dismounted. Rumble shook his head, his eyes wide. *Even
the animal is afraid,* Leath thought. Dels grabbed him in a
rough embrace, and turned to Sianah.

"Sianah, dear. Take Rumble to the top of the hill." He
put a hand on her back, urging her forward. "Hurry now.
We'll be right behind you."

She started to protest. Panting and bent to almost half
her height, she shook her head and gestured toward Dels,
but she was too winded to make her point. Dels gently but
quickly took her hand. "No arguments dear. Your parents
wait. Go."

She let herself be helped into the saddle, and Dels
gave Rumble a smack and a sharp cry that set the horse
to running. No sooner had the horse bolted than he began
to run behind it. Leath quickly caught up to him as they
followed Sianah.

"Father, what approaches?"

Dels spared his son one quick glance as he continued

to sprint toward the hill.

"Death," Dels replied. The answer wasn't meant to scare Leath. Dels could see that the young man was already sufficiently terrified. His answer, simply, was the most honest one that he could give. "We'll all die if we're caught." Dels' breath was short, but he continued. "We need to give the greatest chance of escape to as many as possible." He pushed himself harder then, knowing that despite his speed, his son slowed in order to stay with him. He would not leave his father behind.

They raced to the flock.

18

THE CREATURES OF FAE

"It was you."

It was not a question, and the smiling creature before her felt no need to respond. Niamh stood firm in the face of the Cernunnos. Long had it been since she'd seen him, since she'd listened to the superior tone in his voice, endured the poorly suppressed antipathy that in more recent years had become increasingly pervasive.

"I returned because I could feel that something was amiss," she continued. "That something dreadful was happening." She stopped, choosing her words carefully. "I care for these people. Deeply. I don't expect you to understand, Cehron, as I know that this is but one of the many issues on which we shall never see eye to eye. I came here to con-" She stopped suddenly, as behind Cehron, two beasts lumbered from the trees and moved toward them. The Cernunnos didn't turn, as he seemed to sense the approach of the Nylacci. He simply raised a hand when they were twenty paces away, and the creatures stopped. The raw, guttural growling however, continued. The Cernunnos smiled.

Though the group were shaken by the arrival of the creatures, Niamh was – though visibly disgusted by the Nylacci presence – the essence of composure.

"I came here to confirm the well-being of these young ones – and I find *this*." She tilted her head slightly toward the Nylacci, refusing even to look at them.

Cehron raised an eyebrow and turned to the creatures, as if silently asking if they were offended by her words, before turning back to Niamh. His feelings toward her were as complex as they were dark. One might not say so upon seeing the smile he presented in her presence, but if appearances were deceiving, then Cehron Cen Kohr was among the most deceitful creatures that had ever ventured from the world of Elysium.

Lifetimes of knowledge lay hidden behind his eyes, years and years of experience, observation, manipulation. In recent centuries, he had been more calculating, more devious than Niamh could ever know. He'd done terrible things, been the cause of many tragedies, but the blood on his hands always seemed to wash away so easily. He had changed.

She looked at him now, and realized that she was looking at a being that had grown empty, bitter, and dangerous. Such would not be seen by the untrained eye, but Niamh saw it all too well.

She also heard the ancient, whimsical tune he hummed, low and deep.

She looked from the Cernunnos to the others. They seemed entranced by the entire spectacle. For they *were* simple, she realized, in the kindest sense of the word. Innocent. Unprepared for the eternal drama of the Fae and the effect it so often had on the lives of unknowing populations. She could see that the subtle song of the faerae had captured them, their eyes had grown increasingly interested in him since he'd begun the quiet tune. She turned back to him, saw the dark smile on his lips, and spoke his name firmly.

The song ceased, but the smile did not.

Now that she stood before him, she saw that the rumours she'd heard whispered for years – rumours of the distance in his eyes, the strange behaviour and eccentric discourse – were indeed true. He was a creature without limits. How he'd dared to risk entrance into the world of Dreg she couldn't imagine. He had always been a solitary figure, a rebel of sorts, content to wander and work his usual mischief, with the intended targets usually being the only audience. But in recent times, it was said that his mischief had grown more cruel, tinged with an increasing bitterness; a taste that could never be spat away.

"Niamh." A tilt of his head. "With so many worlds, so many fools to convey hither and thither, I find it remarkable that we both find ourselves in the shadow of the very same oak." His arms were crossed over his chest, and a shadow not of the sun crossed his face, absorbing the smile. "You are the faerae that few can find. And here you stand. Terrible coincidence, no?"

"I'll be found where I am needed." Sivino did not miss the glance she cast in his own direction as she spoke those words. "For my part, Cehron, I remember a time when your smiles were true, and nothing more than music and a skin of wine were required to create them. I remember the Rebellion of the Harpies, when your song alone stayed chaos. You were always loved throughout Elysium. Your very presence, I'm sure, was the reason for a thousand celebrations throughout the ages. You were mischievous, yes, but *good*." Her voice lowered. "I've heard nothing of the sort for three hundred years. You've changed, young one."

"Spare me, Niamh. I have evolved, while you remain as stagnant as the Dren Marshes, and the halfwits that reside there. I've often wondered why you never settled in the Dren – hundreds of miles of pools and fools, tickling reeds and underwater villages that would surely satisfy your penchant for *swimming*. The great paradox, Niamh, is that the more you shift and the more you move, the more you stay the same." His eyes grew dark, and Sivino could see the menace that lurked just beneath the false surface. The Nylacci moved a step closer, their muscles taut with the possibility of violence.

Niamh shook her head, and when she spoke, her voice was barely more than a whisper. "The dreadful stories you told my father of mad, renegade faeraes up to fell deeds; those tales have trickled to my ear, Cehron. Beautiful damsels enticed with song, and led to watery graves. Babies, stolen from their mothers, to be replaced with changelings. Tell me Cehron, what's the going rate for a human child these days? A pocketful of gold? And innocent men and women shifted to unforgiving worlds, where survival was not possible and torture was certain. How pleasurable was it for you to watch them scrape and crawl through the hopeless void of those worlds? You warned my father that it was happening…and it was you. He *trusted* you, Cehron." She struggled to maintain the calm of her voice, but the realization that washed over her threatened to crash upon the still waters of her composure. "*You* did those things. Such…*evil* things, terrible things, so that my father and the Council would forbid shifting on the Paths?"

"It was necessary, Niamh. It *is* necessary. For ages I've watched this mingling, this disgusting merge of Fae and common folk. I've seen our rich blood *watered down*, I've seen steadfast traditions tarnished, and I've seen the sickness that spreads all too easily, from world to world, because of the shifting. I tried to warn the Council, but none were able to see that it was time for Elysium to end such reckless interaction. You would accuse *me* of fell deeds, yet the games you play with the lives of those you shift are truly pathetic." He folded his hands before him. "Do you still mourn the mortal?"

So still was Niamh's face, so steady her eye, that for a moment Sivino feared she'd lost consciousness. After a heavy silence, she turned and looked at the young ones, though it was to the other faerae that she spoke. "There is no damage, no malice in my actions. The effects are negligible. However, I see behind us banished creatures that *truly* have no place in Cahruia. *Creation*, Cehron! How desperate is your situation when you find yourself in Dreg?"

The Cernunnos shook his head, disgust now plain on his face. "Listen to yourself! *Creation?* You even begin to use the language of these imbeciles!" He gestured at the young ones. For Sivino, the look held more disgust than he could stand. He turned away, noticing that none but

Torla held the Cernunnos' gaze as the creature continued. "You may ask yourself – and I'm sure you have – how I come to be in the presence of these dear young ones. It may be that I'm trying to prove a point." He swept his hand in a slow arc, indicating the group that surrounded them. Sivino felt oddly disturbed by the whiteness of the creature's fingers, and the sensation they created as they passed over him. Even more disturbing was the quiet way the Nylacci circled round the group, cutting off any path of escape. "I've seen them before, Niamh; seen you watch over them like a doe behind her fawn. Oh, don't look so shocked – I *get around* too. But understand now, Niamh, the consequences of shifting – how even the most innocent of children, in this world and others, can find themselves at the mercy of such ravenous, insane monsters as a result."

A grunt from the closest Nylac.

All eyes turned in its direction. For several long moments there was silence. The young ones waited, helpless. There was no way to flee, and even if such an opportunity presented itself, they could not leave Lomin at the mercy of these creatures.

The second Nylac growled, inclining its head as it licked its black lips.

"Steady, *steady*." Cehron then turned from the Nylac to Niamh. "As you can see, my big friends grow impatient."

"Tell your *friends* to look upon the result of impatience," Torla interjected, nodding in the direction of the fallen Nylac and the arrow that protruded from its mouth. Her voice startled those around her. They looked at her with wide, incredulous eyes. Each held their breath as they turned from her to the Cernunnos and the Nylacci. The beasts growled, long jagged teeth gleaming in the late afternoon sun.

Beside them, Cehron Cen Kohr laughed.

"Well said, Lady Rallo! *Well said.*" He clapped his hands as he continued to smile widely, shaking his head at the courage of the girl. Turning to the side, he laid a hand upon the muscular arm of the closest Nylac. His smile faded slightly as he craned his neck to look up at the beast's hideous face, speaking in a voice that was lowered, but loud enough for all to hear.

"The girl amuses me. So few are able to achieve such a feat these days. And so–" he turned back toward Torla, his smile gone, his hand still upon the Nylac's arm as he spoke, "–you'll save her for last."

"Cehron Cen Kohr!" With a swift motion, Niamh moved between the Nylac and the others, hands held out to her sides, fingers splayed and ready. "If you think I'd let that happen, you're more insane than I thought. Call back your filth. *Now.*" Behind her, Sivino, Ston and Kef stood ready, holding rocks, longknives and a broken sword. Drip stood before Lomin, his teeth bared. Torla stood beside Tonnis, her face expressionless, her eyes locked upon the faerae.

"Niamh." Cehron raised a hand to settle the Nylacci. "Niamh, my dear. Can you not see the role you played in bringing about these events? An edict will be passed, you can be certain, that will see shifting come to an end. I'll see that your father makes it so. I'll *force his hand,* so to speak. All of the passages – the Paths, the Rings and Mist Gates – will be closed. You continue to move these folk about as if you owe them something. I've simply come to request that you stop." He showed too many teeth with the last couple of words.

"Your minions will *not* touch these children, Cehron. They are destined for things you couldn't understand, and they'll remain unscathed, I promise you." She paused, and almost smiled. "I'm sure you've seen what lurks in the trees."

Sivino saw the anger in the faerae's face, his eyes narrow and cool. He also saw the quick glance the Cernunnos made to the forest behind Niamh, and noted how his demeanour changed almost instantly. A look of warmth entered Cehron's eyes, and Sivino felt a chill. The creature could smile all he wanted. That warm look was a front, and covered the cold steel of his thoughts poorly.

"I must admit that my waning interest in this world has made something of a resurgence. You see, I dream too, *naiad*. The Faant still deem me worthy of their divine thoughts. I've had visions of late, and in these dark reveries, I've heard the quiet whispers. I too have been told of the child with the sword."

The group shifted uncomfortably. Sivino quickly glanced at his broken sword. The Cernunnos barked a rough laugh.

"Never you fear, little man. You'll have to wield a sword a little larger than that to fit the bill."

Niamh watched the Cernunnos, motionless, and for the first time Sivino saw a hint of real fear in her eyes. "I was under the impression that the Faant's whispers no longer meant anything to you."

"Nor do they. But give me some time, Niamh, and

I may satisfy my *morbid* curiosity. There is blood in this prophecy, and much uncertainty. Just remember what I've said. As beautiful as you may find the rivers of this world, our rich blood will *not* be watered down."

"No further blood need be shed today, Cehron. The hyters will tear your beasts to shreds if they make another move, and if you yourself attempt to hurt these children, your life will be forfeit."

He stopped for a moment, folded his arms and raised one hand to his mouth, his index finger resting upon his lip in feigned concentration. He smiled, and slowly bit a fingernail, the perfect whiteness of his teeth shone in the sinking sun as he passed his gaze over each of those gathered one final time. With a derisive shake of his head, he turned from the group and faced the Nylacci.

"We have much work ahead of us," he said to the beasts. "Let us attend to these matters. We shall deal with our new friends here in a matter of course." He raised a hand to silence the objections of the Nylacci, and gave them a look that caused them to lower their eyes. "Don't test me today," he whispered. "Besides, we have more pressing matters that beg our attention."

He turned to the company a final time. "Niamh. Children." He bowed as he addressed each. "I bid you a good evening. Tread carefully upon your chosen Path."

With that, he and the monsters of myth turned and retreated to the darkness of the Nucono. As they faded from sight within the limbs of the oak trees, the waning voice of the Cernunnos began to sing; traces of misguided magic that weaved through the trees to the ears of the company who stood captivated upon the edge of the Andel.

*"Her voice so enchanting, melodious
Left me quite unable to go,
My heart it was loaded with sorrow
For cailin deas cruite na mbo…"*

For several long moments, the company looked to the trees as they listened to the song of the Cernunnos. The voice was beautiful, dancing upon the limb of every tree and plant, slender leaves drawn to the source. Several of the company exhaled deeply, slow breaths with eyes closed, as after a long journey. The song seemed to tickle upon the eyelids, behind the ear, into the heart. It was not until Kef began to step slowly toward the Nucono that Niamh spoke, her voice firm and immediate.

"Listen not to the song. It will lead you to your doom."

Not until it had faded completely did they look away, as though by turning their backs upon the voice they might expose themselves to some unknown peril. When the voice had faded completely, Niamh turned, her eyes upon the sinking sun. She began to walk.

"Gather up Lomin," she said. She cast a glance in their direction, her eyes resting on Sivino.

"I would lead you to safety, if you'd follow."

19

A BLUR OF FEATHER AND SKIN

Dels Spallic should not have been able to run so fast, but on this particular day, there were far too many things which should not have been.

As he and Leath closed in on the townsfolk, he noted again how the people moved as one. *Not a flock of sheep,* he thought, *but birds. This was flight of the most desperate form.* A few of the riders broke from the group to come to the Spallics but Dels waved them away, gesturing vigorously toward the hilltop.

The elders, ill, mothers and young comprised the first group to crest the hill and enter the relative protection of the shadow of the trees as they made their way along the trail, known locally as the Woodcutter Path. Many rode horses or sat within the carts that were towed. Dels was relieved to see Stellen Tros at the forefront, ushering the vulnerable into the Nucono as he directed the archers to prepare the first defence.

It was Dels' plan to have a group of twenty or so archers position themselves just inside the fringe of the Nu-cono. From there, they would attempt to take down as many of the Nylacci as possible, while giving the towns-folk the needed time to escape. If luck was on their side, they might in fact turn the enemy away or defeat them entirely, but Dels knew the likelihood of such an outcome was slim. If and when the beasts came close enough to render the arrows useless, the archers would retreat to join the second line – the armed townsfolk who waited slightly deeper in the forest.

This second stand, if necessary, would be made with hand-to-hand combat.

There wouldn't be a third.

Less than half the townsfolk had horses, and these men and women had ensured that each of the vulnerable had a place on a horse or within the carts to which several of the animals were hitched. Dels and Leath reached the trees as the last of this group entered the forest. He saw Dahlah, her face pale, walking beside the cart that held her mother, Kitt. The shadow of the trees fell over them, and they disappeared into its depth.

The final Egimian to leave was Lumb Velto. He moved to Dels and gave his nephew a rough embrace. It had been decided that he would organize the second line of defend-ers when the time came. He drew back from Dels, and the younger man was surprised to see tears forming in the smith's eyes.

"We'll get through this, Uncle," said Dels.

Lumb smiled, and jerked his head toward the town. "Nihbo," he said quietly as he looked in the direction of the town. "He stayed back on the outskirts. Figured he might be able to lead those beasts off in the wrong direction. Blasted trenoc, wouldn't listen to a word I said."

Dels closed his eyes. "Damnation."

"I told him he was a cursed fool," Lumb said. "He told me he was sharper than any blade that ever met my shoddy filework." The old man took a breath and forced a smile. "He'll be careful, I know. Just...just watch your arrows if they all run this way." Dels put his hands on Lumb's shoulders, and put his forehead to the smith's. He gave him his assurances and Dahnu's blessing as he patted his shoulder. Lumb turned then and headed into the forest to help his people.

Dels and Stellen moved quickly to organize the archers. There were few Egimians who were truly skilled with the bow. While it was used occasionally for hunting bigger game, most of the townsfolk preferred to snare a hare or trap a slow-witted drummer grouse as it scavenged the forest floor for buds and broadleaves.

Dels turned, his sharp eyes searching for any vantage point that might assist both their offence and defence. He settled on a copse with thick oaks and a scattering of large boulders, not far from the beginning of the Woodcutter Path. He noticed the smoke that now rose in the vicinity of the town.

"Find a spot," he called to those gathered, gesturing to the trees. "Get out of the open. They'll arrive in short time."

He nodded to the men and women as they passed by him, giving each a quick, reassuring smack on the back and as much smile as he could muster. His smile faded when a young boy strode past. Karm Naphor. *Creation,* thought Dels, *how old is the lad? Three years younger than Sivi? Four, more likely.* He grabbed the boy by the elbow.

"Karm. This is not the place for you." His voice was low, serious. "How did you escape the eye of your mother?"

The boy took in his breath, attempting to broaden his lacking chest, and lifted his jaw as he pulled his elbow from Dels' grip. It was not a show of disrespect, but a childlike gesture that tried to give the false impression of manhood.

"I told Mother I would help see the elderly into the forest, and that I'd catch up with her. And I *will* catch up with her, Master Spallic…as soon as I've helped here."

"Karm," Dels took him again by the elbow and led him into the oak. "I've no doubt you're as brave as they come, but what's coming is like nothing we've ever seen. They're huge, and they're terrible."

The boy nodded as he tested the string of his bow. "Thank Dahnu for that. The bigger the target, the easier the shot. I don't intend to wrestle one, Sir." He looked from the bow to Dels. "You heard about the nickel ring?"

Dels sighed. It was a story that had made the rounds through the village earlier that year. He recalled Sivino recounting the story, breathless, that evening.

A group of the young ones had been watching the Harmino brothers make a bit of sport shooting acorns off the top of a stump. Being something akin to local heroes to the young ones, Moppy and Tapper Harmino took a bit of amusement from the wide-eyed audience. As the contest reached its final shots, the brothers were in a deadlock. The winner, in addition to taking home bragging rights, would also take a crendisc from the loser. Not a huge amount of coin, but worth ten nickel rings and enough to buy a batch of yeast for the next brew.

Moppy took the second to last shot, and grazed the acorn enough to send it over the side of the stump. He raised his hands in the air to the applause and hoots of the children. Then, he set another acorn on the stump and walked back toward his brother. As Tapper reached for the bow, Moppy made an act of passing it over, and with a quick flick of wrist, he snapped the bow toward his sibling and cracked him across the fingers of his right hand.

"Son of a brudog!" Tapper doubled over, cradling his afflicted hand and cursing more than he'd have normally done in front of young ears.

"Unfair!" cried a couple of the children, pointing accusations. Moppy gave them an innocent look, his palms raised upward. Tapper righted himself, gently shaking and flexing his fingers. He couldn't help but smile a little as he looked at his brother. Antics such as this were not uncommon with the Harminos.

"Well played, brother, but that crendisc is off the table…or stump, as it were. A pity too. I know your yeast supply is as lacking as your charm."

"There's nothing in the rules to account for injury, brother," Moppy replied. "If you need to forfeit, I'll give you a chance to win back your coin within a fortnight."

"How about I substitute?" The voice was low, but not weak. The Harminos, along with the others, turned to Karm Naphor with a look of shock.

"Come now, Little Karm…" Moppy spoke with bemusement, but his voice lacked any trace of condescension. "Your mother would rattle my head if she knew I let you play with the bow."

"He can use a bow," Sivino put in. "He's good, Moppy."

Moppy glanced at Tapper, and gave him a wink to indicate he'd play along. He turned back to Karm.

"You got a sharp eye, my boy?" Moppy asked.

Karm slowly put a hand in his pockets, and seemed to fumble for something. Then he extracted his hand, and held a nickel ring up to his eye. Through its centre, he squinted at Moppy Harmino.

"Sharper than some," he replied.

"Ooooh…" It was the universal sound of a group of children signalling that a challenge had been made, a gauntlet thrown down.

Moppy Harmino stepped aside, and with a restrained laugh and courteous bow, swept an arm toward the stump to indicate that the challenge was accepted.

Karm strode confidently toward the stump and, upon reaching it, flicked away the acorn that Moppy had placed there. He turned, held the nickel ring aloft for all to see, and then placed it on the rough bark on the face of the stump. Moppy threw up his arms in an incredulous gesture, laughing as Tapper smacked him on the back with his good hand. Karm then came back to the firing line – a branch on the ground fifteen paces away – and took his aim.

"Little Karm, do you–" but Karm fired before Moppy could finish his question. The arrow hit the stump with a thud.

Silence. For one second. Maybe two. Then the shrill

screams of elation.

"Yes, Karm," Dels said quietly. He glanced at Moppy and Tapper, who stood in the trees with no trace of their usual jovial spirit. "I heard about the nickel ring."

"You know, Master Spallic, that if you send me away, I'll only hide in the trees and fire on them anyway. Not that I don't respect you, Sir. It's just that I need to do this. I need to help protect our people."

Dels looked across the field, thinking that he could now hear the sounds of the approaching beasts. "Right through the centre, hey?" Dels looked at the boy.

Karm reached into his pocket, and pulled out the ring. It was nicked in several places, evidence that it was a target on no small number of occasions.

"It's something of a good luck charm, Sir."

Dels nodded, and inclined his head toward the others as he watched the smoke thicken. "Come then. Dahnu knows we'll need all the luck we can get."

They waited in silence. Its depth was terrible as it allowed them to hear the distant cries of animals, those fleeing and those tortured. Though every gate had been left open, there were many that had remained within the confines of the wooden fences. Dels tried not to envision the beasts that now crashed through the wooden rails upon which the young ones had so often walked in tests of balance. Yet, he had little choice when the enemy lumbered into sight. Smoke and flame rose in the air, animals ran in every direction, and amongst the madness, the Nylacci advanced. Many were preoccupied with the sheep and cattle, even the frantic hens, but the majority moved on-ward, seeking human prey.

The Egimians waited, eyes straining in an effort to get a true sense of this unknown enemy. They would not need to wait long, as the Nylacci wasted little time. A thunder seemed to rise from the ground. Dels heard sev-eral prayers whispered above the dreadful pounding and shouting as the creatures moved in on them.

"On my word," Dels said in a low voice. He sensed the bodies of those surrounding him tense instantly, strings of bows pulled taut. The deafening clamour intensified as the beasts noted the tracks of the carts and horses that converged into one on the hill below the Woodcutter Path. The dispersed monsters tightened their ranks and banged swords on their shields, bellowing as they sprinted toward the trees. Dels took an arrow from his quiver, pointed it at the clustered group of Nylacci, and after a quick plea to the Goddess for mercy, let fly.

"Fire!"

The Nylacci, Dels saw with no small amount of satis-faction, were shocked by the attack. As the arrows flew, their cries of rage turned to shock. Five fell, each pierced by an accurate – or possibly fortunate – shot. However, Dels' satisfaction receded when three of these five rose again, and drew their own massive arrows.

"Again!" he yelled. "Stop them!" He hated the futility he heard in his own voice.

Though the beasts took up their run once more, they moved more cautiously; hunched and with eyes scanning the trees. Their shields were raised. As they ran, several of them fired their own arrows. The long shafts ripped through the branches of the Nucono, causing the Egimians to fall flat upon the ground as leaves floated down around them.

The trenocs were the first to regain their feet, followed by Dels and Stellen.

"Let loose!" Dels screamed.

"Every single arrow! Now!" Stellen was frantic.

Again the Egimians fired upon the Nylacci, unprotected save for their shields and leather armor in the open field. With each passing shot, they grew more accurate. In short time, nine of the Nylacci had fallen. But there were too many. As an onslaught of arrows flew around him, Dels pressed himself against the thick oak. He turned his head to the left, waiting for a slight reprieve, and watched in horror as a black arrow tore through the chest of Egim's first victim. Jannie Joshule was nearly lifted from her feet, landing in a lifeless heap in the dirt, the arrow pinning her to the ground.

"No!" Dels screamed. "Fall back! Now!" It was an outcome that was inevitable. Dels had known the village would not escape unscathed, but knowing such did not keep the tears from his eyes as he forced himself to look away from his murdered friend.

The Egimians gained their feet, and with their final shots, they turned and fled into the Nucono, driven by the dread of the beasts which were ever closer to gaining the forest. As they began to run, another Nylacci arrow found its mark. Georon Hanney, Blyss' father, was taken in the back, impaled by the brutal force of the arrow. Dels screamed as he ran, hesitating for the slightest moment until an arrow hit the tree beside him. Dels looked quickly to his side, searching for Leath. Two had fallen for certain, perhaps more that he'd not seen. Among the scattering archers he saw Leath in the distance, running behind Karm, screaming at him to go faster. A quick surge of pride rose in Dels, as he watched Leath help the boy, rather than run past him. It was something Sivino would have done.

They ran amidst the screams, flying arrows and roaring monsters. Men and women stumbled, falling to the forest floor only to scramble to their feet and run again. The trenocs sought refuge in the height of the trees, swinging and loping among the solid limbs of the Nucono. It was not until a Nylacci arrow took the trenoc Kranet from the trees that they realized there was no safe place. With a sickening crash, she fell through the branches and hit the forest floor directly in front of Leath and Karm. Leath quickly grabbed the young boy and forced him to continue running. Cries of warning and terror flew between the Egimians, mingling with shouts of satisfaction from the Nylacci.

The beasts had caught their prey.

The rank creatures drew their blades as they released the final arrows. They were closing in on the Egimians and the close range, coupled with the thickening trees, made the arrows less effective. However, the path of misfortune is both cruel and random, and one of the final arrows fired followed a haphazard path as it deflected off a thin birch tree, changed course and struck a young boy who had put entirely too much faith in a nickel ring.

Karm went down hard, his body skidding through the leaves and soft earth. The arrow, slowed to an extent by the deflection, had pierced his upper arm. About a handspan of its spine had made its way through his arm, and it now clung to him by a small piece of soft, pale flesh. He lay on his side, unable to see the arrow for the dust in his face. He could hear nothing but screams and an internal roaring in his ears. *Mother will kill me,* was the first thought to make it through the pain. When the rough hands grabbed him, he lost all control and thrashed violently.

"Karm! Hold yourself!" Leath knelt beside the boy, one hand on his shoulder. Upon recognizing the voice Karm stopped struggling. He began to cry.

"Leath! They're everywhere. You have to go! You have—"

"Shut up," Leath said absently. His focus was on the arrow, and how best to remove it. The arrowhead, he saw, was damaged and loose, and he knew he had but one option. He took an unsteady breath. "Karm. This will hurt. Be still." Before the boy could respond, Leath snapped the arrowhead from the shaft and pulled the wooden spine from the boy's arm.

Karm screamed. It was the scream of a boy experiencing pain too severe for his meagre years. Tears spilled from his eyes. He sucked in a deep breath, and coughed it out roughly. As the blood gushed from the wound, he fought to remain conscious. The world spun. He rolled onto his back and in his tortuous state he thought he saw shapes flying above him. People. Women. With wings. *Creation,* he thought. *This is the end.* Were these the angels his mother had spoken of on occasion? Otherworldly creatures that guided the dead to the Land of Ever? Were they now come for him, waiting to deliver him to that eternal land of rest? The thought was cut short as an arrow thudded into the tree beside him.

Leath went down hard as another arrow whistled past.

He scrambled back to Karm's side despite the approaching Nylacci that pounded their way through the trees and brambles. Karm moaned deeply through clenched teeth, forcing himself to stifle the cry that begged to be let forth. Then, he took two quick gasps of breath and turned to look Leath in the eye.

"Run," he rasped. "For Dahnu's sake, run!"

Leath shook his head at the boy and attempted to pull him to his feet, but the approaching Nylac did not give him the opportunity. Taking a quick look over his shoulder, Leath cursed and drew his sword, standing protectively over Karm.

With speed that caused both boys to cringe, a blur of feather and skin streaked over their heads and flew into the Nylac, ripping away its left arm. Spinning, this newly arrived creature retracted its wings and with an ear-splitting shriek dropped to the forest floor, scanning the area for its next victim. A woman, Karm realized. This creature was a woman – with *wings*. With blinding speed she flew into the Nylac to the left of the Egimians. This Nylac was not caught off guard as was the first, yet it made little difference. With a look so venomous that Karm felt a bitterly cold shiver up his entire body, the creature flew directly into the face of the waiting Nylac. A second later, the Nylac's face was gone.

All through the forest, high pitched screeches filled the air. This creature, whatever she was, was joined by a throng of her companions. The Nylacci attempted to strike down the creatures, but could not land a single blow as the airborne assailants ripped into them from all sides. In short time they were retreating, their eyes never leaving the upper branches of the forest. And as they fled, they fell, each of them dying a gruesome death on the soft earth of the forest.

After the last beast had drawn its final ragged breath, the winged women gathered around the wounded boy and his companion. Leath looked from one creature to another, unable to process what he was seeing. The full body of a woman, but with wings whose span was as long and substantial as a woman's body itself. And talons, retracting slowly as the last drops of blood fell. Karm, so struck by the beauty of the vicious woman-bird, seemed to momentarily forget his pain. The creature nearest the two boys leaned forward to assess the boy's wound, but another creature at the rear of the group stepped forward suddenly and emitted two quick, sharp whistles that caused the Egimians to cringe. There was no doubting at whom the command was issued.

The closer creature who attempted to look at the wound stopped abruptly, and stood to a height that rivalled Leath's. Her wings stretched to a breathtaking span and with one powerful beat and thrust of her muscular legs, she tore upward through the canopy of the Nucono. Immediately, the others followed.

Only one remained.

The creature who'd whistled stood some distance away, unmoving, her dark face seeming of stone. She slowly scanned the area, as though assuring herself that the threat had been fully eradicated.

"Thank you," Leath whispered.

The eyes of the creature narrowed for an instant, its gaze hard and deep. Either she didn't understand his words of thanks or couldn't be bothered to hear them. Her head turned as Dels and several of the townsfolk cautiously approached.

"The young are safe," she said. "These..." she looked at Karm before turning to look west. "...and the others."

Dels moved forward. "Sivino? You've seen them."

"The young are safe," she repeated. "They move from here. South. You must go to Ras."

Leath shook his head. "No. Where are they? We need—"

"You will find them. But not by following them. Your path leads to Ras."

She gave a final look to the west, and with a great burst of her wings, she was gone.

Somewhere in the distance, a swallow sang.

20

TO TIP THE SCALES

The sun lingered on the distant hills. The air cooled with its descent, and just beneath the sheen of sweat that coated the faces of the company, a chill could be felt. It was, Sivino realized, a chill caused by much more than the day's ending.

They'd walked for several long hours. Though it was small consolation, Sivino thanked the Goddess that Lomin's weight was so insubstantial. Though he was of average height, he was thin as a garden rake, and proved to be a tolerable burden. On a couple of occasions, Torla and Tonnis had carried him for a spell, but only long enough for Sivino and Ston to rest their weary arms.

Niamh stopped frequently, allowing them to rest as she tended to Lomin. His wounds, cleaned with river water, were now dressed, but twice she removed the bandages and rubbed a thick green oil upon them. Despite the discomfort of being transported for so long a period, his breathing had seemed to steady.

Only when the last light of the sun flickered through the Nucono did Niamh call the group to a halt. She indicated a tussock of moss and grass where Lomin could be set down, and turned to the young ones.

"Now," she said quietly, "we'll have your fire and your tea."

She knelt again by Lomin as the others gathered branches and rooted through their backpacks. Drip's eyes never left the trees. It was a detail that Niamh did not miss, though her back was turned to the trenoc.

"We are safe here, Master Trenoc. Rest easy."

Drip scowled.

The fire was soon blazing, and the tea lent a comfort to the group as only tea can. As the young ones passed around the small metal cups of greyleaf, Niamh turned to face the fire, though she remained by Lomin's side.

She let long moments pass, as if she were reading the flames. Finally, she spoke.

"My name is Niamh, and I am of the land of Elysium." The faerae spoke quietly as she watched the small fire. Her face was impassive as she turned to look at each of those gathered before her, as if studying them. Though the trenoc and young ones felt uncomfortable to be looked at so intently, the faerae showed no such discomfort. "The land, like its inhabitants, is diverse, and has a multitude of names. Otherworld. Tir Na N'Og. Avalon." For each name she gave, she leaned forward and placed an additional branch on the flame, carefully rubbing her fingers along the length of each before placing it. None failed to notice the way the colour of the flames deepened as she crisscrossed the kindling. A moment later, the fire intensified, and took on subtle tones of lavender. The heat rose quickly, and enshrouded those before it in soft warmth.

"It is there that we reside, when our services are not required elsewhere. It is a world where the very air one breathes embraces the body, comforts, and pulls one in. It is a world without season, where warmth prevails, and grasses of the lushest green grow forever under a gentle breeze. Music may be heard almost anywhere you roam. Sweet. Enchanting. Melancholy. Eerie. *Enticing.* Gentle songs of pipe and flute float on the air, and voices meander through the trees, wrapping themselves like cord around those who would listen. It is something to behold." Her eyes rested briefly upon Kef. "It is something of which you must be wary. Too easily, you may be misled."

She quieted as she turned to Lomin, her hand on his chest. He was resting more easily, his breathing slow and deep. Sivino watched the faerae, studying her movements as he considered her power. *What did she do to those branches? How did she intimidate that other creature by the riverbank? And how in creation did she come to this world?* Niamh smiled at Lomin, though her mouth remained tight. Her hand moved from Lomin's chest, her pale slender fingers grazing lightly upon his cheek. She paused for a moment, then softly rubbed his bruised forehead again. Her touch left some remaining residue upon Lomin's skin; a thin, shining layer of moisture, not unlike sweat, which shone for the briefest moment before fading completely. She looked up.

"There are Fae who are beautiful, and those who are hideous. Some are both. We can be caring or cruel, visible or hidden. Indifferent or obsessive. We are many, many things, but there are some things, some traits which we all share. We all speak truth, and we are all of us clever. These characteristics do not vary, having been in our nature since our origin, in the time of the First Ones. There are many of our kind who have never, nor will ever, leave Elysium. The allure of different worlds simply cannot compete with the pure comfort of our own. And there are others, myself included, who wander." She looked through the fire, and despite its brilliance, a shadow seemed to fall over her face. "I've wandered far, and long. At times, I feel I'm no more substantial than the morning breeze, yet I do as I must. I move by means of Paths – conduits which may only be created by the most powerful of the Faer folk. Our motives may be different, as are our methods, but one can be assured that the creatures of Fae wander still in the forests and foothills of most worlds. It is not leisure travel, for our directives come from the Faant – a higher power that transcends both magic and meaning – and are meant to set right things which have become complicated. You have a question, Master Trenoc."

The group turned quickly toward Drip, who'd been sitting on the periphery of the loose circle around the flame, well out of Niamh's line of sight. The trenoc was taken aback by the comment, but recovered quickly, masking his surprise. Though all expected a question regarding these Faant that Niamh had just mentioned, this was not the cause of Drip's concern.

"What roams the trees, Mistress?" he asked quietly, but in a rough quick tone that showed neither his fear nor the disconcertion of being seen through so easily. His eyes fixed on the trees above, silhouetted against the pale white glow of Silvenna, the largest of Cahruia's moons. The smaller, darker moon Artemis lay low in the sky, hidden from sight in the black Nucono.

"Hyter sprites," Niamh replied without hesitation. "Winged women. They are kin to the dryads…nymphs which dwell in the deepest forests. They followed me to Cahruia. They may only travel upon Paths made by another, and will return the same way before the Path fades. The hyters find their way to the places where they're needed." She looked at the young ones. "Hyters will not tolerate the mistreatment of children. They are generally severe, but when they witness cruelty directed at the young, their wrath is beyond reckoning."

"How did you know where to find us?" Sivino spoke up. "*Why* did you come to us?" Sivino immediately regretted speaking so harshly, worrying that he might have offended the faerae. Yet her face remained calm as she considered his questions in silence.

"For years, I have loved the tranquility of Embarria and her surrounding lands. With her people, I hold a special bond. It is one that goes back generations, and one that the Faant would have me protect. Though I travel widely, it is to Embarria that I continually return. My connection to the place is complicated. I travel the Paths, do the Faant's will, and see that balance is maintained to the greatest extent possible. I protect those who need protecting, whenever I can." Sivino noted the sadness that hid just below the surface of Niamh's words. "Cehron now works to tip the scales toward chaos. I work to right them."

They talked for some time. Niamh gave the young

ones as much information as she felt they needed and deserved. They were confused, she knew, and scared. Separated from their loved ones, they'd faced dangers and creatures they'd not known existed, and had been forced to carry the unconscious and battered body of the one friend who could have lent them strength and reassurance. When they raised their concerns surrounding their families, she assured them that the town had fled the Nylacci and made their way east. Without delving into the darker details, she informed them that the Nylacci who'd pursued the Egimians had been defeated.

"So, the faeraes are to blame for this." Torla looked from the fire to Niamh as she spoke, the raging flames reflected in her eyes. "Your kind brought this on us."

An uncomfortable silence fell on the group, broken only by the crackling of burning hawthorn. Niamh looked to Torla, her face unmoving. As much as Sivino tried, he could not accept the reality of this creature in their presence. Her pale gown glowed in the firelight, and her wavy brown hair shimmered as though it were flowing from her head, crashing like a waterfall on her shoulders to spill about her. Sivino watched as Torla, to her credit, held the faerae's gaze.

"Too often, other worlds bear the burden of our work. Yet Cehron's actions are not the will of the Faant."

Torla shook her head, her disgusted smile showing that she did not consider this an acceptable answer. She was about to tell the faerae so, when a rough cough rattled the evening air.

"Lomin!" Sivino scrambled to the ragged man's side, smiling so widely upon seeing his open eyes that Lomin emitted a quiet, weak laugh that warmed their hearts more than any fire. Sivino grasped Lomin's hand in his own. The sharp eyes of the wolf looked around the fire.

"My young friends," he said softly. "I should say, you are a sight for eyes – and bones – wrought with soreness." He smiled at each, though the smile faded slightly as he turned to his left and noticed the faerae. "And old friends also." He drew in a deep breath, which seemed to cause a pain within his chest.

"Niamh – to what madness do we owe the pleasure of your presence?"

They spoke through the evening. Sivino and his companions described in detail the events of the day. Drip interjected where he saw fit, spitting upon the ground each time he mentioned the Nylacci. Lomin noted that he had indeed heard whispers of a threat while he was away, and it was for this reason that he'd cut short his western sojourn and returned to Egim. The faerae let them tell their story uninterrupted. As they discussed the razing of Levebar, Lomin watched Tonnis closely. The boy was making little effort to keep up with the conversation. Sivino assumed that the images in his head were enough with which to contend. Upon hearing of the fate of the neighbouring town, Lomin shuffled slowly toward Tonnis. When the boy looked up, Lomin patted him twice on the arm, and traced the sign of the waterdrop on Tonnis' heart. After a moment, the boy placed his fingertips on his chin and nodded his thanks to the ragged man as Lomin pulled him into a rough embrace. The faerae let them continue to speak even as they described the appearance of Cehron, and Niamh's subsequent intervention. Her face remained expressionless as Kef explained how she had driven Cehron back to the trees, his voice adding dramatic effect.

"Master Rallo gives me too much credit. Cehron knew fully that the hyters watched from the trees." She paused and looked at her friend. "Lomin, my powers are not great, but your wounds should feel much better when the sun rises." She passed him a water skin, cool and brimming. "This will help you sleep peacefully, and will aid in your convalescence."

When Lomin had swallowed several mouthfuls, she took the water skin and turned to the others. "Water of Elysium." As she passed the water skin to Ston, her face reflected a fatigue equal to the others. "Each of you should drink of this. It will help the memory of the day fade as morning mist, and will restore some peace to your hearts." Ston raised an eyebrow in question, and Niamh nodded her assurance. Each of the companions drank; they settled into the soft grass and breathed slowly. Heavily. Niamh made simple gestures to Tonnis that suggested the water would help bring sleep, and he drank deeply.

At last the skin came to Torla. She held it for several long moments, until she grew conscious of the faerae watching her. She looked up, and saw the sadness in her eyes.

"Have faith," Niamh whispered.

Sivino, lying close beside Lomin, heard him murmur softly from beneath the warmth of the cloaks upon him. "We shall need it."

As he considered Lomin's words, his eyes fell shut and he slept deeply.

21

ONLY A HOUSE

The smell of smoke wafted into the forest, carrying with it the burnt memories of Egim. In the wake of the slaughter and the flight of the hyter sprites, the Egimians came together in confusion and grief. The second line of defence had escaped the need to engage the beasts, and now joined the archers. Dels' heart was lifted to see the trenoc Nihbo among them, the firm hand of Lumb squeezing the trenoc's shoulder. The smithy hushed the trenoc as Nihbo commented incessantly on his own failure to mislead the Nylacci.

The bodies of those passed were carried from the Nucono and laid with the greatest of respect on the edge of the golden field. The injured were seen to as best as could be expected, their wounds wrapped quickly but with much care. Water and food, though in short supply, were shared among the survivors.

They left the Nylacci corpses to rot beneath the trees.

Georon Hanney, Denn Cor, Jannie Joshule, and the

trenoc Kranet lay still, their eyes staring lifelessly into a clear sky marred only by the smoke that drifted from the ruined village below. Denn's wife Patua sobbed uncontrollably in the arms of her sister. Dels knelt by each of the deceased in turn, letting each of them feel the final touch of the sun. He traced a waterdrop on the forehead of each, and with Dahnu's blessing completed, he gently passed his hand over their faces. His heartrending smile to each would be the last image to appear before their open, empty eyes. Behind him, the other townsfolk looked on silently.

"We have to move quickly." Dels stood, unable to look away from the bodies. "Our friends will be buried, for their sacrifice was the greatest. When this respect is shown, we shall join the others, and head toward Ras." There was a murmur among the people. Dels raised his hand. "I know. I *know*. But we *must* assume that these creatures know best. They saved our lives. There is no telling how many bands of beast wander these lands. Our kin will not be too far ahead, but danger may lurk around any corner."

Before Dels needed to ask, Nihbo stepped forward. "I'll go."

"Thank you, Nihbo. Halt them, tell them only what you must. We'll catch up with you shortly." Without a nod or a word, the trenoc began to run.

All moved to help in the effort to wrap the deceased in the protective embrace of the Embarrian earth, under the shadow of the eternal forest. More than once, the company stole glances to the burning village, though none could look for long. The planked roofs of the homes had burned with ferocity. The solid wooden frames were consumed more slowly, but with more intensity; glowing red skeletons that fought to stay upright. One by one, they fell to the ground, and with them the hearts of their former inhabitants crumbled likewise.

Dels and Leath looked to the west. Thin wisps of grey smoke hung still over the land upon which their home had stood. Dels saw his own pain mirrored in the eyes of his son.

"It's only a house," he said.

Leath nodded slowly, his gaze held by the distant smoke. After a moment, he turned to his father. His jaw was set, his lips tight as he nodded again. He looked over at the dead, and the loved ones that sat beside them. Beside Kranet, a man cried silently. Hadric Bell, the town cobbler, rested a hand on the trenoc's chest. His other held the grass as if to secure him to the earth. His eyes were empty.

"Shovels in the gardens yonder," Leath said quietly as he began to move down the hill. "Let's be done with this."

The Harmino boys moved toward Dels. "The road to Ras is long," Tapper said quietly. "Me and Moppy are gonna go gather a few things that our folk will need – some blankets, bread maybe. A few potatoes." Dels was shaking his head, but Tapper continued. "Only essential stuff. And only from the nearest homes. Denn's place is just down the h–" He stopped, and took an anguished look at Denn Cor's body. He cursed, and turned away. "The old ones will need blankets. Dels, we'll run at the first sign of danger. The house is visible from here. We'll be but minutes."

Dels sighed. There was no time to argue.

"Minutes," he said, and the boys set to running.

Upon burying the bodies and marking the final resting place, the group hastily gathered their scant belongings, including those retrieved by the Harminos. Stellen had led a group to the upper gardens to collect what vegetables they could carry. Once they'd gathered what they could, they turned once more to the Nucono, giving the grounds of carnage a wide berth.

Leath walked beside Karm, whose wound had been bandaged neatly by Pann Leuko, a woman of some skill in the healing arts. Having quickly but skillfully tended to Karm, Pann now focussed upon her younger sister Patua, who wept silently as she leaned on her sister. There was no art, healing or otherwise, that would stay the grief that flowed from Patua's broken heart. An arm's length of earth and a lifetime of memory now separated her from her husband Denn. The women walked just ahead of Leath and Karm, neither of whom could block out Patua's slow, deep breaths or the shaking of her hands. Leath watched her with a heavy heart, realizing how easily it could have been him, or any of them, that had had their love ripped from their lives. The Irrots were numb still, having learned of Myls' fate only that morning, and now having to say goodbye to Jannie, a close cousin of the family – all this on top of not knowing Grenn's fate in the conflict to the south. Leath quickened his pace, as if trying to outpace the grief that surrounded them all.

They'd only begun their trek through the forest when

Lues Torgo returned. Dels and the others heard the approach of a rider and readied their weapons before they saw that it was one of their own. Lues slowed a little when he saw the group, seeming relieved that he'd found them alive. As he neared, Dels could see the redness of his eyes, and the tears on his face that were likely caused by more than the swift ride.

He dismounted, and stood before them. He could make no eye contact.

"Gone," he said. "The entire town. Slaughtered."

There were curses, and faces that turned away. The blood bonds that connected Egim and Levebar were as numerous as the many trails that ran between the towns. Lues shared what he'd seen, leaving out the more gruesome details. He'd found no survivors. He surmised that the Nylacci had surrounded the small hamlet, and when the first group attacked, the beasts on the periphery fell on any that attempted to flee.

"Dahnu have mercy on their souls," Terstin whispered.

They spoke quietly for a few moments. Dels filled Lues in on what had transpired in the forest. The younger man's grief was such that even the description of the hyter sprites did not evoke wonder or shock. After this morning, he had little interest in strange races of any kind.

They walked on for half a league, and spotted the villagers resting near a bend in the Andel. Dels watched the river, which appeared to turn purposefully, as if trying to circumvent the ragged group as it flowed toward the fire-ravaged town to the south. He looked from the river to the people. They'd travelled with great speed, and must have been ready to drop when Nihbo had brought them the news that the Nylacci had been slaughtered.

Cries of relief and gratitude filled the forest as the two groups merged. Tears of joyful reunion mixed with tears of grief as the family and friends of the fallen learned of their loved ones' fate, and that of their homes. Dels shook the hands of several of the citizens, and accepted embraces of thanks from others. Quickly, he sought out Dahlah and taking her aside quietly recounted the arrival of their winged saviours. He avoided the details of the slaughter, focussing on the short conversation that they'd shared with the creature. When he spoke of how they were told the young ones were safe, Dahlah let her face fall into his chest, and she wept. He brought a hand up, and rested it on the back of her head. Slowly, she regained her composure, and laying a hand on his chest, she looked up at him and nodded, before moving back to tend to her mother.

He watched her walk away, her shoulders held a little higher. Then he turned as Kayl Naphor raced toward Karm; the young boy raising his arms to prepare for either a crushing embrace or a thorough boxing of the ears. Dels was sure he'd get both. Next, he saw the tear-streaked face of Sianah Pella run through the crowd as she found Leath. The young man took her in a strong embrace and kissed her gently. Behind Sianah, her father followed.

Terstin Pella was a bear of a man, with a heart to match. As he approached the couple, he laid his large hand on Leath's shoulder. Dels could see respect in his eyes as the big man stood by his daughter and spoke quietly to Leath. He continued to tap the young man's shoulder softly, nodding as he spoke words that Dels could not hear. Dels understood the nature of the exchange, and knew all too well that in countless ways, life beyond this day would never be the same. He folded his arms, and allowed himself a little pride as he saw the emotional enthusiasm with which Terstin accepted Leath. Yet, he couldn't help but acknowledge the selfish pang of loss that the union would mean. Leath and Sianah would soon strike out on their own, forging their own path, sowing the seeds of a new life. He glanced back over his shoulder, considering the way their world had changed in the last few hours. The pair's courtship would be far from traditional. In place of Dahnu's Favour, an entire village would need to be raised from the ground. Yet, watching them now, seeing the way they looked at each other, Dels realized that there were few, if any, who possessed half the determination and drive as the pair before him.

After slapping Leath's shoulder a final time, Terstin turned and embraced his daughter once more. As he did so, Leath folded his arms, a gesture that reflected but one of the many ways that he was his father's son. He turned and spotted Dels, who smiled and nodded at the boy. Leath nodded back in likewise fashion.

The blessing, it seemed, had been given.

Kitt Rallo was tended to by her daughter. Dahlah Rallo looked older than her forty years, and felt older still as she rubbed a wet cloth over her mother's forehead. While Kitt was in dire condition, Dels noted that Dahlah struggled as well. The toll on her, he surmised, was likely more emotional than physical. Uncertain of her children's safety,

Dahlah had doubled her efforts to help her townsfolk, to both provide a distraction and compensate for the care she could not give those she loved most.

As she moved to the river to moisten the cloth once again, Dels walked over to her to where she knelt. "Do you need any help?"

She jumped as he spoke, then smiled for a brief moment.

"No, my thanks, Dels – for everything. You've already done so much."

Dels shrugged it off, and smiled at the woman. Having lost her husband Mytan a decade ago and her eldest son Kolle much more recently, Dahlah had struggled to keep herself from falling apart. It had been her mother and children, and the compassion of friends that had kept her as near to whole as possible. Dels had done everything he could to ensure that the Rallos never did without. While they were a resourceful and independent lot, Dels knew that an occasional basket of crop never went astray in a dry season.

"How is Kitt?" he asked.

"She's hanging on, but I fear the stresses of the day have sapped her of her energy. I don't know how she can possibly continue. She refuses to ride a horse, saying that it's both uncomfortable and unladylike. She's past her seventy-fifth year, Dels, and I hear the cough that rattles her chest each night." Dahlah shook her head in frustration as she wrung water from the cloth. "She's so headstrong...so determined."

"She's like her daughter," Dels said with a small grin.

Dahlah paused as she twisted the thin cloth, and

turned to look at Dels. She gave a little laugh, and sighed. She stood slowly, and looked downstream to where the river disappeared behind the trees. Her face fell, her smile snatched up by the afternoon breeze, and she wrapped her arms around herself. "They'll be alright, won't they Dels?" He did not have to ask about whom she inquired. The Rallo children were ever present in the bright green eyes of their mother.

"I believe that they will be, yes," he said. "As soon as we reach the realm of the Drales, myself and several others will go to them. We will find them, Dahlah, and we'll bring them home."

As they walked back to the group, he considered the meaning of the word.

Kitt sat with several of the townswomen, struggling to present an appearance of strength and resiliency. She sat stiffly on a large rock while others milled about around her, asking her questions which she answered repeatedly with a smile and a shake of her head. The women glanced at each other whenever Kitt grimaced silently or shifted her position. As he reached her, Dels lowered himself to one knee, resting his elbow on the other as he regarded the aged woman. Her eyes warmed as she looked upon him.

"Good day, Kitt," Dels said softly. "How are you feeling?"

She looked around, gauging their distance from the nearest women. When she spoke, it was in a hurried whisper. "I am feeling like a child, young Dels. That is how I am feeling. Doted upon as though I were a sick babe, unable to take steps on my own. I have told these women that I'm quite capable of continuing on to the front gate of those big bloody Drales. I don't need extra water, or dried apples or blankets or whatever else they'd offer." She coughed with the exertion of her speech, and shook her head when he reached for her. "I'm a little winded is all, but who here is not?" She made to stand, but needed a second attempt to do so. She reached out and took his hand. "It is time to leave, Dels. Let us go now. I would like us to be on our way."

"I see," he responded. "Well, let us allow the others to catch their breath, and when they are as rested and able as you and I, we shall set out once more."

She gave him a wry look. "Dels Spallic, are you jesting with me?"

"Yes, I am." He smiled. However, the smile disappeared as quickly as it had come. "Yet, do not mistake me. This situation is grave, Kitt. I am certain that you can appreciate this. We need to move on, and do so with haste, but we will need you to ride for a time." He saw the beginnings of protest, and raised his hand. "Just beyond the bend, there's a terribly rocky hill. We'll need to climb it, Kitt. It will be most difficult for *any* of us to cross, and the carts will need to be emptied. I am offering you my steed, Rumble. He's as sure footed and stable as any animal, and both he and I would be greatly offended should you refuse this offer. He is trained in the Ryndarran way, and will carry you smoothly." Dels gave a low, quick whistle and the big animal walked briskly to his side. "To refuse him now, Kitt, would be the greatest of insults." He extended both hands before her and nodded reassuringly. "Come."

"Dels Spallic," she sighed, as if uncertain how to continue. "I'm seventy-five years old, Dels. I've not ridden in decades." A sad smile tugged at her mouth. "Now, back in the day, I could ride with the best of them, you'd best believe."

Dels laid a hand on her shoulder. "I do." He looked around at the townsfolk, at their resilience and courage. "And I believe you ride with the best of them still."

Dahlah stepped forward and with Dels helped her mother on to the back of the horse. The younger woman looked quickly to Dels, and nodded her gratitude.

As the sun descended in the western sky, Egim's oldest citizen led her people east, toward the land of the Drales on the ever changing banks of the winding river.

22

A VERY GOOD QUESTION

The boy rights himself, and surveys his surroundings.

He stands upon a mountain of sand.

There is no foothold to be found, only the shifting support of the soft world beneath him. For each step he makes, his progress is but half. He wipes his brow, reaffirms his resolve, and continues his climb. There is no means of orienting oneself, no signpost or marker to measure the distance travelled, or the distance remaining. His heart alone tells him how far he's come, and it's never far enough.

Heat radiates from this shifting slope, manifesting itself into invisible hands that push down upon his shoulders; shoulders which have not yet broadened to those of a man. It consumes the air he tries to breathe, steals the moisture from his body, and distorts his nearly blinded vision. The sun, having risen to its apex, assaults him with intent fury. Waves rise from the surface of the slope, waves that dry rather than invigorate. His thoughts touch upon the river, and for a moment all is clear.

The well…

It is a whisper in his ear, a reminder that every journey, even this one, has a reason. A purpose. The thought encourages him. His eyes — nearly shut with the brilliance of the sun — close briefly, and his head turns just a shade down and to the left. His jaw, instinctively, has set. He gives a quick shake of his head to rid himself of sweat, sand and confusion.

The well…

He assures himself that he has reached the halfway point; that the worst of this ordeal must now be behind him. Looking back, he is unable to see the origin of his ascent. The effort of turning, looking downward, causes his head to spin despite his newfound determination. He falters momentarily, reaching out to steady himself. He takes only the slightest comfort in realizing the height he has achieved, which must be significant for he can no longer see the ground below.

He focuses on putting one foot before the other…above the other. The incline seems to have increased. He laughs a soft laugh that would sadden the heart of any who might hear it, and tries to rush onward. Faster now. Patience is discarded like bothersome clothing, thrown by the wayside, covered by shifting sands. He pushes himself faster, and faster still, but the exertion soon brings him to his knees. Magic is almost spent. He turns his face skyward, slowly, and uses the opportunity to pray for mercy, but looking for divine intervention, he finds nothing. His mind is beginning to falter; the intensity of the sun unbearable. Magic is almost spent. Where has he heard those words before? Who has spoken them? The image of a man he cannot presently remember flashes in his mind. The man is then replaced by a woman, beautiful yet sad. She steps away from him, walking slowly backward as she sings, her voice barely discernible above the sound of distant, crashing waves.

> *Fancy brings a thought to mind*
> *Of a flower that's bright and fair,*
> *Its grace and beauty both combine*
> *To make the thought more rare*
> *Just like a maiden that I know*
> *Who shared my happy lot*
> *Where we parted, when she whispered*
> *You'll forget me not.*

Her voice fades, as does the vision of her. The boy screams to her. Why am I here? What does this mean? I don't understand! *But she does not hear him. He screams for her to come back, just for a moment.* One moment! I don't understand...

But she is beyond him.

He looks up again and is surprised at how close the well now seems. His sadness, his frustration is replaced once more with hope. He can discover what this means. A sudden smile causes the skin of his lips to crack, and he soon tastes salty blood. Just a little further. He continues with his eyes closed, his head spinning, but there is no fear of losing the well now; it's so close.

A small breeze caresses his skin as he forges on. His smile deepens. He will make it. The warm wind seems to encircle the hill, spinning in an effort to intensify. Loose sand grains move upon the surface of the slope, sliding downward past his bare ankles. In short moments the wind has gained an intensity that he would not have thought possible, and it causes him to waver. His wet hair, which had clung to his face with sweat, has now begun to wave. Soon, it is whipping his cheeks.

I won't be stopped, *he screams, but his voice is lost in the mounting gale, a shimmering wave of power that he is not able to cut through. He is close enough now to see the individual bricks which make up the well, the cracks that show its age, and the bucket, hanging on an ancient rope that would draw to him salvation from within. Grains of sand now enter his mouth, and he emits an utterance that is part moan, part weeping.*

The sand has begun to blow down the hill. Flow down the hill. His feet and lower legs are now entirely covered, and he struggles to draw them out. With a great effort, he pulls his left leg free, and he falls. He cannot see, lying upon the sand as it whips past his face. If he can just reach the shelter of the well, hide in its lull until the winds die...but he knows he'll not make it.

Again, he won't make it.

With the acceptance of his failure, he begins to slide, then rolls down the hill. The sand enters his mouth and he coughs, gasps for air. His throat is afire. His eyes fill with the sand's hatred, the wind's indifference.

For a time, all is lost to him. There is movement and there is pain. Nothing seems to exist but the suffering, the burning, and the loss of what he had come so close to attaining. To achieving. And then, silence.

The world has stopped. He lies on his back, afraid to move; to open his eyes. In the distance a bell tolls, echoing in his head. He sits up and performs the excruciating task of blinking his eyes clear, his tears assisting only minimally.

The mountain is gone. The sand has been completely blown away. There is horror as he takes in the scene. Before him stands a tower, cold, grey and impenetrable, stretching toward the darkening sky. He stumbles to its base, reaching out to touch it yet at the same time dreading its feel. He recognizes the bricks, and the cracks that show its age.

There is no door.

Emptiness engulfs him as he looks skyward, and in the late glow of the setting sun, sees the ancient rope. Upon it a bell swings, echoing...

He has lost his chance. Eternities will pass before the sands gather again. The process must begin anew. The boy collapses.

The sands of time have moved again, Sivino.

He hears this whisper in his head.

This, and a tolling bell.

Sivino opened his eyes, and looked directly into the face of a swallow.

The small bird stood within arm's reach of him, twitching its head in a quick, curious manner. The two looked at each other for some time in the dull morning light, the bird hopping to and fro as it ate small morsels of food from the ground. Sivino pushed himself up onto one elbow and watched as the bird bounded around him and jumped into Tonnis' open hand. Sivino's tired eyes opened widely, and he smiled as the bird ate from the boy's palm.

Only a few crumbs, but the swallow ate of them eagerly. With quick jerks of its head, the bird pecked the bread from the boy's hand. Then, suddenly, it turned its head and chirped to its brethren in the trees. A little group of birds flew down, and the first swallow stepped aside, allowing the others to enjoy the meagre feast.

A tilt of its tiny head, and one could not help but think that the bird thanked Tonnis for the gift of food. Its beak opened then, and it brought forth its song, a beautiful melody of warbles and whirrs that gently awoke those who slept nearby.

As if beckoned, the sun broke above the wooded hills.

As the company rose, Niamh stepped from the trees. Sivino wondered if she was returning from an early walk, or whether she had slept at all. He knew next to nothing of the Fae, and there was so much he wanted to know. *Needed* to know. She seemed to be their protector, though he still wasn't sure about her motivations. What little he knew of this race came from old folk who sometimes shared these ancient tales. Most of these he dismissed as forgotten fantasies. He looked toward Lomin, who rose with Kef's help. He marvelled at the boy, who grimaced not with the effort of helping the old man, but with the pain it caused his own leg. His determination was formidable, as was the concern of his sister who pushed him aside to help Lomin to his feet. Kef made an offhand remark that Sivino couldn't hear, though he guessed the gist of it when Torla smacked the back of his head as Lomin restrained a chuckle.

Lomin. If there was anyone who might be able to share the secrets of the Fae, it would be him. He had called her 'old friend'. Sivino wondered how much information, if any, he might be willing to divulge.

They ate a hasty meal of berries and fruit, though Torla insisted that Lomin eat some of the dried meat that Kef carried in his satchel. Ston fetched his older friend a suitable walking stick, and Lomin nodded his thanks. Torla watched him as closely as she did Kef and Tonnis. She fretted over her brother as her grandmother did, though the similarities, in Torla's mind, ended there. Kitt Rallo was entirely content in her life; at least she had been until the day prior. She would often say that if one day of her life could be painted, she'd be satisfied to live in it forever. Torla could not imagine such an outlook. She often complained about her grandmother's ramblings to Sivino, insisting that life necessitated change, that change was evolution, and evolution was the betterment of all things. Sivino would shake his head and tell her that things which were not broken need not be pieced together. *One day Sivino*, she would reply, *you will see things as I do. You will see that perspectives change. They must.*

Niamh did not rush the group, but her actions informed them that the time to leave had come. She stood, watching the frolicking swallows as the company rolled their cloaks and bound them with Sivino's fishing line. The morning was warm, and promised to grow increasingly so as it passed.

"The east is fraught with danger, as you know," Niamh said. "Swift travel will lead us out of the forest by day's end tomorrow. We need to go west to the plains, and then, we will need to take a southerly route." Whether she saw Torla's head twist toward her with eyes widened or not, she did not acknowledge the gesture. "There are people to meet, and perhaps, some questions to pose. These people, these answers lie in that direction." She could see the looks of confusion and concern on the faces of all, but her own remained impassive. Sivino was entranced by her lack of movement, how nothing – her hair, her eyes, her garments – moved in the slightest as she looked westward. If not for the parting of her pale lips, one would have sworn she was sculpted.

Like the others, he desperately wished for reunion with his family. But unlike his friends, he did not feel that this was the only option. There was a need in him to follow this faerae. He could not explain it, but he somehow felt that his path had merged with hers for a reason, and it was a path meant to be followed. Even as he considered these feelings, the group voiced their objections to travelling south – Torla most vehemently. Her seething resentment of the faerae was evident on her face as she informed Niamh that they would find their own way without her assistance, *so thanks but no thanks*. Niamh listened to their protestations, though Sivino could see that her mind was set, and she would not be dissuaded. This creature, small and lithe, was as immovable as a mountain. She was driven by a purpose and a power, and Sivino intended to learn much more about each.

"We need to follow her," he said. The group turned to look at him, and he felt an inward stab of insecurity. The looks were much like those he received from Leath on so many occasions; looks that suggested he was speaking of things which he was incapable of understanding. He could almost see Leath among them, dismissing him with a shake of his head as he usually did, telling him to leave the thinking to the adults. He stood a little taller, and asserted himself more fully. "Egim moves east, *away* from us. Certain death lies between us and them, in the form of creatures I've no desire to see again anytime soon. It seems clear to me – the only good thing to happen since all of this began, the only hope we've been given–" he pointed to Niamh, "–is her."

His friends struggled for words, looking for flaws in his reasoning. When none of either could be found, Sivino spoke again. Turning to the faerae he lowered his voice. "I don't know you, but for some reason, I trust you. I trust you to lead us in the right direction." For just a moment, her pale face softened, and she nodded. Sivino turned back to the others. "I will follow her. I hope you'll do the same."

They walked west in near silence. The sounds of the forest and the sun which shone through the trees in sharp rays made the troubles of their minds a little easier to bear. Sivino wished to speak with Lomin in private, to ask him the questions which burned upon his mind. How had the wolf come to meet the faerae? Did he trust her fully? Did she serve only her own purpose, or did she truly consider the welfare of others? He'd have to wait for these answers, as Lomin walked close beside the faerae, their hushed voices covered by the sounds of the company's footsteps.

"Secrets and shadows, indeed," Drip mumbled beside Sivino. His scowl, a permanent fixture on his face, had deepened, and his narrow eyes viewed Lomin and the faerae with undisguised contempt. "I knew that the wolf was not what he appeared to be. Always I told your father that there were things about Lomin that were... unnatural. Friend of faeraes! Friend or fiend? Can't be too careful. Motives, hidden plans – we're but pawns in their games. You may not understand, little merrow, but we trenoc remember the tales well. We brought old tales over the mountains from Jhora, and we will never forget. Faeraes are evil, malicious and, despite what you think, not to be trusted. They lead innocent creatures to their doom, for their own pleasure and gain. Yes, they possess majdic, but does this mean they deserve our respect? It may elevate them in the eyes of others, but not in those of trenocs, who are sharp enough to see them for what they are." Sivino walked on, refusing to enter into an argument with Drip. He realized that he possessed no information to support his stance, nor any to refute the trenoc's claims. The only tales he'd ever heard shone the Faer folk in an ambiguous light, depicting them as mischievous and elusive, enigmatic and yes, a little dangerous. He was following his heart, and he knew it for the risky path it was. "And what do they speak of now," Drip continued, "with heads bowed and voices lowered? Nothing good comes from whispered words."

"Drip," Sivino interjected. The trenoc's voice had grown in correlation with his agitation. Sivino, fearing that the faerae would overhear, attempted to quiet the trenoc. "Were it not for Niamh, you would likely be a bloody carcass, left to rot or be chewed upon on the banks of the Andel. We all would."

"You do not know that," the trenoc rasped. "Did the Nylac we met last morning not meet his end at our hands?" He extended his long slender finger toward Sivino. "Do not make hero-folk of those who've not earned it. It is not a title to be given lightly."

As Drip stormed off, Sivino thought, just for an instant, that the agitation he saw on the trenoc's face looked very much like concern. For the first time, Sivino took the time to fully consider the actions of the trenoc. Drip had jumped into the waiting arms of death, had done battle with a monstrous creature, a battle he'd likely known he couldn't have won. But this had not stopped him. He'd come at the Nylac again and again, giving Sivino the chance to escape.

He'd been willing to sacrifice his life for the boy.

As he attempted to catch up with his companions, he thought on the words Torla had spoken: *You will see that perspectives change.* He had always associated hero-folk with warriors, tall and proud upon steeds of pure-bred power. Looking at the trenoc, he saw that this title might also apply to furry, foul-tempered creatures that hated the rain.

As they walked, Sivino noticed how frequently Torla looked back in Kef's direction. The boy, tired of the un-wanted attention, began to exaggerate exhaustion, hoping to irritate his sister enough that she'd stop fretting over him. Hands upon Sivino's shoulders, he feigned being dragged along, his mouth hanging open. Shaking her head, Torla turned back to the path, muttering that the Nylacci would enjoy legs so tender.

The group sat to rest and eat near a trickling brook. The sound of the stream soothed them, and each drank deeply, feeling refreshed afterwards. Throughout the day, they could often hear the Andel's consistent roar, yet the faerae continued to lead them upon a path that meandered some distance from the river. She seemed more comfort-able surrounded by trees, as though their embrace might protect them from harm.

Near midday, their path brought them out of the trees and into a wide clearing. The sunlight, so brilliant after the gloom of the forest, caused all but Niamh to squint.

Her eyes were fixed, and her face was grave. Slowly, as their eyes adjusted to the light, the others saw it as well.

A house.

Niamh moved toward it slowly, the fringe of her gown gliding across the tips of the grass blades. The property was well maintained, the gardens tended and the grass short. Sivino looked around. There were quite a few dwellings such as this throughout the western Nucono, though many were well hidden. In most cases, this was done purposefully by folk who desired a life of seclusion and simplicity. He looked to the right of the house and saw the trail that likely led to the Westroad. While he was unfamiliar with the area, he wondered if his father might know the people who dwelt inside. Dels knew so many people from far-reaching locations. As the group rounded the corner of the house, he realized that he'd not get an opportunity to ask.

The bodies were strewn across the flowerbed.

They all stopped short of the appalling sight. Torla's hand went to her mouth as Lomin placed a hand on her shoulder, his eyes fixed on the elderly couple that lay in the midst of the blooming snapdragons. Niamh alone moved forward, her face depicting none of the horror that the others so obviously felt. She knelt beside the pair, whose hands, Sivino noticed, were still entwined. How they managed to do this while their other arms were ripped off was beyond his reckoning.

"Secrets," Niamh whispered. "Secrets of the future and the past, kept deep inside until set free by a touch." As she reached out, Sivino moved closer. Torla led Tonnis and Kef from the sight, while Ston moved in beside Lomin and listened to what Niamh had to say. "Some say they can speak, revealing quiet words of what has been and what is to come. It is a magic, of sorts." Slowly, she leaned in as the Egimians held their breath. But it was not the people she touched. She reached between the pair, grasping a snapdragon that had not been crushed in the altercation. Gently, she squeezed the silky blossom of the flower, opening its delicate mouth with her touch. A moment later, Sivino could smell its whisper, a sweet scent that reminded him of cinnamon and summer evenings. The faerae released the flower, and turned her gaze down to the deceased woman. She looked about seventy, Sivino thought. Deep wrinkles meandered across her face and from her eyes. Though it was hard to envision with the blood on her face, Sivino was sure that these wrinkles had once lent warmth to the woman's smile. "Secrets," Niamh said again, and with one hand covering the eyes of the woman, she ran the other along the stranger's throat, squeezing slightly as she did so. The faerae bowed her head, her fingers sliding gracefully along the woman's neck. The silence of the garden was palpable. By now, Torla and the others had turned to see what was happening. After what seemed to Sivino to be an eternity, the faerae's head jerked to the side, and she stood quickly.

"What did you see?" Sivino asked. He flushed as the others turned quickly toward him, but said nothing. He did not know why he'd asked the question. Indeed there was no way of knowing if Niamh actually saw anything. His question was spontaneous, and confused all but Niamh who looked at him thoughtfully.

"Nylacci," she said. "A group of five." She looked from the group to the man who lay in the dirt. "He tried valiantly to save her, right up to the end." She crossed her arms, and turned away.

"We should be away from here. This attack is fresh, and came from the north. We must continue west."

She was beginning to walk away when Sivino spoke. "Wait," he said. He turned and ran toward the humble cottage, and the shovel that leaned on its faded planks. Working quickly with Ston, the two dug a shallow grave and laid the pair within, ensuring that the couple's aged hands were joined once more before the earth covered them entirely.

There was very little to say after the burial, as each of them tried to make sense of the situation they found themselves in. Niamh led them west, though she now did so at a distance; a distance that was as emotional as it was physical, to Sivino's mind. As she widened the gap between them, the company formed a rough horseshoe around Lomin. Torla was the first to speak.

"We'd hear your story now, old wolf."

Lomin nodded, warmed a little by the term of endearment they so often used during their discussions. They waited in silence as he collected his thoughts like the herbs and wild berries he gathered in the forest surrounding his home. How often they had gone to see him, only to find his house deserted and him wandering hunched among the Leah and the rowan. He gathered knowledge as he did berries, and created a preserve of information that satisfied those who had need of such things. He devoured information, so immense was his hunger to know. *Questions are the path to knowledge,* he'd always told them. *Each question is a sapling, which will take root in one's mind when asked, and the knowledge we seek, the knowledge we attain, will grow as the forest.* He'd continue to gather his wild plants as he spoke to Sivino and the others, his voice warm and present. *A wise man once asked me if we should judge wisdom by the answers a person may give, or by the questions a person may ask.*

And what did you say? Kef had asked.

The old wolf had smiled. *I told him that it was a very good question.*

"You have questions for me," Lomin said simply.

"There is so much that you've not told us," Torla said.

"There is so much you did not need to know. However, you are children no more, and while I hope you bear me no ill will for my secrecy, you should know that certain information is not meant for all." His eyes lowered, as did his voice. "There is still much that I do not know. Some things, I presume, I'm not meant to know.

"I've known Niamh for many, many years. She is as old as the Nucono, and has spent much time in Cahruia throughout her long life. She has strong ties to this land and, over time, she has guided countless individuals between worlds."

He saw the heads turn in his direction, and nodded slowly. "You are curious about the Paths. I know little of them, but I'll share what I know. The reasons for their use are varied. Some are complex, some are quite simple. Niamh has shifted many upon the Paths. Some shifts are due to sickness...and some shifting may *cause* sickness. Some shifts are voluntary, but all are necessary. Some are difficult, while others are seamless."

"Were you shifted, Lomin?"

All eyes turned to Sivino.

"Sivi. I would have suspected that the question would come from you." The lines in his face deepened. "No, no I have never been shifted, though it was not for lack of trying. I often asked Niamh to take me with her – temporarily of course, just for a short time. I would have been satisfied with just a few moments in another world to smell the air, see the people and their societies, to hear their languages. But she would not take me. It wasn't necessary, she told me. Her actions are guided by powers beyond our comprehension, but while so many of her kind execute these instructions with an automatic indifference, she balances her dedication to duty with a care that ensures as little harm as possible to any involved. So you see, my young friends, the actions of Niamh are indeed thoughtful, and necessary, and *never* done upon a whim.

"You speak the truth as always, my friend," the faerae said. The group were shocked to discover her beside them. Being so caught up in the words of Lomin, they'd failed to notice how she had stopped, waiting for them to catch up. "I do the will of the Faant. They guide my actions deftly, and I've found no reason, in my long years, to question their judgement. For me to shift you, Lomin, would have been fruitless, and ultimately harmful." Lomin nodded respectfully, his eyes closed with understanding. "If a shift is not needed, it is not needed. My work does not satisfy curiosities or the need for entertainment. It is done because it needs to be done."

"And the work you do now," Torla replied. "Guiding us west. Does this need to be done? Is this part of a bigger plan?"

Niamh seemed to consider this for a moment before

responding. "There is no plan that is not significant, for plans necessitate choice. Every choice has a ripple effect that influences everything." Sivino's head tilted as he struggled with her meaning. There was wisdom in the faerae; of this he had no doubt. But so often, the wisdom was shrouded in riddles.

"But to answer your question, Torla Rallo, yes. Leading you west *is* a part of the bigger plan. I am indeed guided by powers that see much more than I. Also, as I've said, there are people who will lend us assistance on our journey. People we are *meant* to meet." She looked to Sivino. "We do what is necessary, and our journey, you can be certain, is indeed necessary." She looked toward the sky, and the dark clouds that slowly rolled in from the west. "This sun will not last," she said, and started walking once more.

One by one, the group fell in behind the faerae. With many questions, and very few options, they let themselves be led.

23

THE SENSATION OF THE IMPOSSIBLE

"Forgive me," she whispers, *as thin hands burst from the water and pull her below.*

And she sinks. For a moment, she feels nothing. She is void of all life and all emotion as she is pulled through a vortex that she does not care to understand. The pool, waist-deep but moments before, now reaches depths that defy all physical laws. She knows however that she is no longer in the pool.

She knows there never was a pool.

She is carried along the torrent. She cannot breathe, does not even try. She knows that this is more than water, more fluid, more tangible to the mind than to skin.

This is magic.

This is the Path.

She has travelled this Path before. Though her last journey was many years ago, the distant memories flood into and through her mind, helpless passengers on an internal voyage of their own.

She opens her eyes and absorbs the colours. Hints of blue

and green fade into silver, then darkness, then back again. The lights manifest themselves in streaks, their ebb and flow further heightening the sensation of waves and speed, of flowing and floating. Flying.

She hears the fluid around her. It ranges from a constant, rushing hiss to a determined roar that threatens to pull her very soul from her body. She thinks of swimming upward through a powerful waterfall. The sensation of the impossible.

She feels the hand. The hand that has been her salvation and her sorrow. She is held tightly. This hand would never let her go. She tries to look at the woman who pulls her along, who has guided and protected her, kept watch and kept returning. This hand that has attempted to offer her happiness. Her thoughts return to the man on the beach, and she is again overcome with a surge of regret. She recalls the advice of her mother: Regret is what was *not* done, or what was *not* avoided. Both are the past. Neither should be indulged. Learn from your mistakes. Regret none of them.

She regrets that she cannot heed this advice as they burst through the surface of the water.

She is instantly warm. The chill of the pool lingers upon the Path, but it is washed away in the evening air that she now breathes deeply, greedily. She opens her eyes slowly, and smiles at the beauty she has forgotten; the scent of redhollor, the Whispering Leah, the sky of brilliant orange. As they step from the river, she stops suddenly. Sorrow rises again in her heart. She looks at the faerae beside her, as tears join the last trickles of river water that run from her face. Slowly, she releases the faerae's slender hand.

"He will never taste the air of Embarria."

"We do what is necessary." *A slight pause as she looks to*

the forest, the limbs of the amilliat swaying their welcome. "Be proud."

The setting sun of Cahruia turns all to gold.

The faerae sighs, her eyes unreadable as she looks at the woman by her side.

"Welcome home."

24

WORLDS APART

Doran Dunarrk stood on the precipice of his realm.

From his vantage point atop the Keep, he watched as the people of Orshos conducted their business. The fishmongers, merchants and traders were hurrying about as a flotilla of schooners made their way ashore. A thick fog rolled in over the ocean, driving the fishers ahead as it threatened to engulf the Rentorrian capital. It was well known that such a fog – *the curtain*, locals called it – was a harbinger of poor weather. Soon the waters would roil, white caps dancing on the angry waves like the drunken sailors in the taverns by the waterfront. The weathered white sails of the fishing vessels begrudgingly pulled the men and women ashore. Some of the vessels brimmed with a fortunate catch, while for others, their nets had hauled little more than bitter disappointment.

The king of Rentorria leaned on the westernmost parapet of the Keep. Disappointment was a daily affliction of Doran Dunarrk. The city needed to be fed, but a great number of its boats lay tied to the wharves below, abandoned by men and women who'd had no desire to leave the familiar decks. It was a harsh reality, one with which every citizen of Orshos, and indeed Rentorria, had struggled.

While the need to feed the city was great, the need to *defend* it was greater still.

For years, Doran Dunarrk and the people of Rentorria had viewed their relationship with the realm of Isror as a necessary, if not sometimes bothersome, partnership. Their coastal efforts had been primarily bent upon extracting a living from the harsh environment which was their homeland. Western Rentorria, and the city of Orshos in particular, focused upon harvesting the sea, and the living of many was made upon the waves. But it was an unsteady subsistence, as many species in the Sinking Sea were in recent years depleted by the *harga*, a deep water predator from the Far West. Some years saw the shelves of the Sinking Sea virtually empty of the schools of fish the people so heavily relied upon. In such times, fisherfolk were forced to travel greater distances to find suitable fishing grounds. Often, they were forced to venture beyond Solla, to harvest the waters that surrounded the distant Isles of Lamirtia. And so it was that in this land and on the sea, hardship and hunger were deemed more important than the small Isrorian settlements that sprouted in their realm like the wild Rentorrian Rose.

All this had changed however, when an Isrorian envoy had arrived at the Keep one foggy morning, relaying a message that would change the realm forever.

The conflict, in many ways, had developed like an oak. Its seed was said to have been sown in the form of a dream, and a steady rain of desire and greed fostered its rapid growth, impatient limbs spreading, stretching ever outward.

Below the ground, the roots stretched even further.

In the realm of Isror, King Idach Garron stood as firm as this oak. Tall and foreboding, he led his realm with an intimidation that was as powerful as his physical stature. Raised in royal privilege, he'd never entered the mines, save for the times he and his father Ikron, the former king, made brief visits to assess security and productivity. Walking through the mines, his father had told him frequently that any of those workers could easily crush his skull with their bare hands. *You'll not work in the mines,* his father had said, *but neither will you grow to be a soft man.* Idach had been trained vigorously, to fight as well as strategize. His muscled chest and massive arms, coupled with a mind that could untie the most knotted of dilemmas, made him a king to be reckoned with. And in the five years since his father's passing, he'd transformed the governance of Isror. Laws were made by which all would abide, or face brutal consequences. Mine production had increased significantly, as had the death rate of those who worked within. It was to be a land of uncompromised order and purpose, Idach believed. And consequently, it would be a land of unsurpassed wealth.

The mines of Isror, vast and deep, had for centuries provided the realm with the metals necessary to forge the finest of weaponry and machinery. Throughout the lands of western Cahruia and beyond, Isrorian metal was a highly valued commodity. As production increased, wealth indeed followed. To accommodate the heavy traffic created by trade and the influx of those seeking opportunity, new roadways were created, dusty veins that brought fresh blood to the vibrant city of Iskall, which lay beside the largest nickel and iron ore deposits in the realm, at the southern base of the formidable Cudgel Mountains. It seemed that Idach's coronation signified the rebirth of Iskall, and he was determined to see that it grew according to his desires. He ordered the garment factories to quadruple the production of black robes – his colour of choice. He stated that when a realm dressed like their king, they were more inclined to act like their king. There was a unity in such trends, he declared. None but those closest to Idach knew of the advisor who'd been beheaded for questioning whether the trend might be viewed as a notion of vanity.

This advisor was not the only Isrorian to suddenly find himself significantly lighter. As the wealth of the realm increased, so too did the rate of crime, as will happen in any thriving society. Priding himself on the order of his land, Idach saw each and every criminal act as a personal affront. Those arrested were tried before a group selected by Idach himself, and the fate of each was invariably messy.

And so it was that Idach forged his realm. He maintained order, attracted the masses, and sent forth a staggering amount of steel. It was jested that on a clear day, the gleam from the metal of Isror could be seen from the mountain peaks of Ahrasis. Realms near and far paid very well for the precious metal and the products it generated.

More than ever before, Isrorian products spread across the lands.

And so too did its borders.

Flanked by Embarria to the north and Rentorria to the west, Idach felt like a constrained oak, eager to grow, to expand to the far reaching sky if not for the limitations imposed upon it by its surrounding brethren. To feel the sun, to be the first touched by the cool rain and soft breeze off the ocean, he would need to force himself beyond the limbs of those around it and realize his true potential – *Isror's* true potential.

In recent years the Isrorian border had crept to the west like a weasel winding through tall grass to reach forbidden crops. With the surge in population that came as a result of Isror's increasing wealth, it was not surprising that homes sprouted like weeds across the realm. It was Idach's assertion that Isror should expand to the furthest shores of the lake it shared with Rentorria – the Madimest. He maintained that this aspiration was not born of greed. Rather, he assured his people that it was the wish of Dahnu, who'd told him in a dream that the realm of Isror had once been entirely covered by water; an inland sea that stretched over the vast region. This water, over many millennia, had receded to its current form, Lake Madimest. While most of the lake was situated in the realm of Rentorria, Idach claimed to have been told by Dahnu that this lake had once been the lifeblood of Isror. As such it should be reclaimed, slowly and steadily, by the land from which it was born, to which it had given life. This reclamation, Idach said, should include the lands to the north and south of the lake, lands once covered by this great Isrorian water source, lands that should rightfully still be the claim of Isror, though the waters had long since receded.

The fact that cities had grown in the region that was to be reclaimed was a matter that Idach said could not be helped. The fact that his people had discovered great deposits of ore outside these cities – deposits that might supplement the rapidly depleting Isrorian mines – was a matter that Idach did not feel needed to be shared beyond his inner circle.

Doran had listened intently to the envoy, resisting the urge to smile. He'd always been truly amazed at the credence given to the Goddess by the other realms. Dahnu, Doran felt, had long since lost interest in the people, and so he was mystified by how firmly a realm could base much of their thought, behaviour and lifestyle on an entity that had supposedly left this world in a time long forgotten.

The ambition of the Isrorian people was rivalled only by their fear and respect of the Goddess – a fact that Idach knew all too well. It was believed by some that Dahnu spoke through the ruler, whoever he may be. Therefore, Idach was seen as the vessel, and the message he conveyed was deemed sacred, and not to be dismissed. It was from these supposed messages that Idach based many of his edicts.

On that day however, Doran's impending smile had faded when the Isrorian envoy had told him that Idach intended to take control of Ronec, on the northeastern shores of the Madimest, before the passing of the following summer. Three seasons, Idach had assumed, should be sufficient time to transfer the rightful rule of Ronec to the Isrorians.

A year later, the blood born of a dream still stained the cobbled streets of the city.

Ronec. Being the largest settlement near the border, it was a hub of trade and business. Its location on the northeast shores of the Madimest made it accessible to riverboats from as far away as Orshos, and the many villages in between. Like Nahcin, its sister city on the Madimest's western shore, it was gated on three sides. Its magnificent waterfront was its doorway to the world. It was from here that most travel was initiated, and from here that most travellers entered into Ronec's welcoming embrace. It was said that this city – which could rely on crops, crafts and trade as opposed to the sea – did not bear the necessary hardship of Orshos. The people were friendly to a fault, and found time for music, drama and other forms of recreation that those of Orshos simply could not. Yet, rather than resenting this fact, Orshos – and the entirety of Rentorria – viewed the city with pride, a jewel in the crown of the rugged realm.

The Isrorian army had moved forth when all attempts at diplomacy had failed. The Rentorrians would not suffer the takeover of the city they held so dear, so the decision was made – not lightly, Idach would maintain – to take the city by force. Their initial strategy had been to cut off Ronec's ties to the outside world. River routes to the city were the first severed, and soon after, camps of black-clad soldiers surrounded the remaining sides. The crop fields to the north of the city were overtaken – their determined, yet innocent farmers being driven from their home. The people of Ronec had watched, helpless, as this black ink stain had flowed around their city and into their lake, forever rewriting its destiny.

Short weeks later, the first true attacks would be mounted. Under cover of night, the Isrorians had infiltrated the city in small groups, and had strategically set fires throughout. They targeted the vital organs of Ronec; the merchant shops, trade districts, even the theatres. Food was in short supply, as was the confidence once felt by the Ronec men and women.

It was at this time that a larger company of the Rentorrian Guard had arrived, cresting the western hills at sunrise, coming to the defence of their beloved city. The Guard already residing within Ronec were lent hope, and their first true assault was mounted. Over fields of blood and fallen soldiers, the black-clad invaders were temporarily beaten back. Doran had called his generals to his tent. They'd strategized, cursed, called for more troops, and cursed some more. *In the morning,* Doran had sworn, *the Madimest will shine red with Isrorian blood.*

For long months blood ran. The tide of the battle shifted continuously. At times, it would seem victory was at hand, as the Rentorrians pushed the enemy back far enough to get food and supplies to the citizens of the city. Yet, just as quickly, the tides of war would shift again, and the city would be surrounded, its gates and waterfront assaulted relentlessly. Outlying hamlets and farms were ravaged. Men and women died by the hundreds, and for every person that met their end on the field, another rose up to take their place. Hope faded in the once vibrant city, and survival became the order of the day. Death, hunger and despair drifted through the city like a fetid wind. The cobbled streets fell into disrepair. Shutters covered windows from which lively music once flowed. Laughter stopped entirely.

And the war raged on.

On the edge of the world, Doran Dunarrk stood and looked to the east. *A year of blood,* he thought as he shook his head slowly. His gaze moved over the city and the plains beyond. His mind's eye moved over the cities that yet stood – Orshos, Nahcin, and Ronec, which now stood on its last legs. Beyond the Madimest, the rocky landscape of western Isror, and the mines that continued to spew forth fuel for this bitter struggle. His gaze fell, finally, to the city of Iskall, nestled in the foothills of the Cudgel Mountains. Though it was of course too far away to be seen, it was here that Doran looked – through space and time, through blood and death – to a day when he would encounter the King of Isror, and serve justice as only a true king could.

Many leagues away, Idach Garron stood on a precipice of his own. He looked west, smiling at the fortune that had recently come his way, bringing him a force that was as formidable as it was hideous; a force that would change the face of this war as savagely as a landslide from the mighty Cudgels that rose around him.

He looked west with a smile that bared his teeth, and returned the gaze of Doran Dunarrk.

25

THE FATE OF THOUSANDS

Inlonia Talchol placed her feather in the silver quill before her, and twisted her tired wrists.

They cracked with the sound of seashells being trampled on a cobbled street. With a sigh, she leaned back in her chair, gripping its mahogany arms as she adjusted herself to assuage the parts of her that had grown numb.

She had never wanted to rule the realm.

It was not that she didn't love the land and peoples of Embarria. In truth, there were few who were as concerned with its welfare and prosperity. For years, she'd worked tirelessly beside her father to ensure that Embarria continued to be a realm in which people felt secure and prospered. In her continual travels throughout the land, she'd come to know the people better than any royalty that preceded her. She saw firsthand their hard work and hardships, their struggles and their triumphs. While she was in no way *common* in the Levebulan sense of the word, she tried her best to be *among* the people, in order to see more clearly the people that she would one day lead. Her father, Intraal the Sure, had warned her on numerous occasions that her actions put her in serious danger. Too often she would sneak away without informing the King's Guard – the division of the Ryndarra assigned specifically to the protection of the royalty – as to where she was going.

You are asking for trouble, Loni, her father would say quietly upon her return. She would always feel bad when she saw the stress she'd caused him, but in her mind, her hands were tied. When she rode out of Levebule with even a couple of the Guard, the nature of her conversations with the villagers was invariably more stifled. She recalled the time that she'd been accompanied by a particularly zealous guard on a trip to a southern town. She'd been speaking to an elderly man who'd spent the day turning hay for his cattle, and when the poor fellow had innocently used his pitchfork to indicate the fields he had left to scythe, the guard had whipped his sword from the scabbard, startling the farmer so greatly that he'd almost fallen over. From then on, she'd preferred to travel alone, so her conversations were not impeded by the imposing faces of those meant to protect her.

Long had it been since she'd been able to make such a journey. Standing wearily, she moved around the desk and crossed the room to look out the window. Her dress flowed behind her, a deep burgundy to match the three wine-coloured locks which ran through her long black hair. The fading sunlight caressed the dark skin of her face. She sat on the sill, pulling her hair back and tying it with a silver ribbon. Below her, her father looked out over the city. His stoic face, set forever in marble, watched as the men and women of Levebule went about their daily affairs. It was a city, Inlonia had long realized, that was proud to a fault. The war that raged to the south – a war that could quite possibly make its way north in the coming months – was the furthest thing from the minds of most that dwelt within the fabled walls of Levebule. Even though a significant number of the Ryndarra who'd ridden south had been from the city, the people still did not seem to grasp the severity of the situation. As a city whose population had recently crested thirty thousand, the general consensus of Levebulans was that they were untouchable.

It was not a notion shared by their queen.

When Inlonia had made the decision to send soldiers of the Ryndarra south, she had tried to explain her reasoning as clearly as possible. Letters written by her hand and stamped with her seal were distributed to all corners of the city. Those who could read, which constituted a considerable percentage of the population, pored over the words and shared the message with those who could not. Inlonia outlined the injustice of the Isrorian attack and the devastation that such a conflict would inflict on the realm of Rentorria. She also noted that if greed could motivate the Isrorians to attack the west, there was no reason to dismiss the possibility that they could also turn north.

One month later, the first company of Ryndarra soldiers were sent forth to lend assistance to the realm of Rentorria. Slowly but steadily, further companies were sent to join them – most across the land by horse, but many upon the Sinking Sea. It was Inlonia's hope that

Isror's king, Idach Garron, would see that Embarria was fully committed to the defence of Rentorria, and turn his army back. But Idach had done no such thing. For every battalion that arrived from the north, another was sent from the east. In the realm of Rentorria, these waves of soldiers crashed, leaving the plains strewn with the dead as they receded.

A quiet knock on the door turned her from thoughts of death.

"Come," she said, as she moved to her desk.

Gilsanna Sliccol, one of the more *intense* members of the Queen's Guard, moved silently into the room, her eyes instinctively darting to the dim corners. Ennis Tinod'atu, the queen's most trusted advisor and childhood friend, followed close behind, shutting the door as he entered. Inlonia nodded to both, and made a mental note to ensure that more females like Gilsanna were added to the Guard when the time came. It was important, the queen thought, for the realm to see that women were every bit as capable as men when it came to protection and power. The Council had been aghast when she'd accepted Gil into the ranks, she remembered with a smile. Their doubts had been quickly lessened when they'd seen her dispatch a would-be assassin from a distance of twenty feet. The image of the knife hilt protruding from the back of the man's head was one that none present that day would soon forget.

Gilsanna stepped to the window and peered out as Inlonia beckoned Ennis to take a seat beside her.

"You've not changed your mind?" the big man asked.

Inlonia shook her head and tried to read his face. It

remained unchanged, as she'd assumed it would. Ennis was a man who spoke his mind and did not rely on what he considered to be the false weight that emotion lent to arguments. He did not yell or beat a fist on the table when he was adamant to make his point. He let his words, heavy with resolve, break down the stubborn doors that barred out reason.

"I feel that you're wrong," he said calmly. "If you were merely my friend, I'd shake a bit of sense into you. But you're my queen as well, so I must respect your wishes."

"Thank you." Inlonia looked from Ennis to the window. "And what do you think, Gil?"

"It's wrong, as Ennis said." She spoke without turning. "But noble. The Ryndarra will be lent inspiration by your presence."

The queen nodded, and gestured toward the stacks of papers on her desk. "I've made preparations for Viggen to oversee things here while we're gone. None will know that I've left. The Ryndarra remaining in Levebule will be sufficient to keep order, and a respectable number still patrol the outlying regions. It is the force in the south whose need is most dire."

As Ennis looked over the papers on the desk, Inlonia moved to the window. Beside it, a falcon sat unmoving on its perch. *Wyncor*. Long had the bird been the queen's companion, and indeed, her most trusted guard. To every member of the royal family, one of these majestic birds were assigned, forging a bond that lasted until death. Forged as well were the silver rings of Embarria; one of which was worn on the right hand of the queen, the other on the leg of the proud falcon.

The city of Levebule enjoyed the last of the day's fading light. To the west, The Sinking Sea glowed as if afire, a million embers of light dancing on its surface, and to east, Inlonia knew, Lake Samah would be likewise alight. An orange hue coated the tall marble towers that rose above the capital. They rose in a circle, at the very heart of Levebule, and their creation was one of purpose. Centuries ago, King Jahms had ordered that seven great towers be erected around his palace to form a crown truly befitting the king of Embarria. The construction had taken decades, and when they were completed, it was Jahms' grandson Terric that held the throne. It was Terric Talchol that was responsible for the creation of the Ryndarra. For long years, nobility had been guarded by a select group of warriors; men who'd proven themselves skilled with the sword, and loyal beyond measure. Terric, a king of great compassion and wisdom, felt that this group should be grown to great numbers and trained to not only protect the king, but the king's people as well. It was his dream to create a host of valiant warriors who would keep order in the land and see that every citizen in the realm of Embarria was allowed to live and prosper in freedom.

Inlonia clasped her hands behind her back. Absently, she twirled the ring on the middle finger of her right hand. The Ryndarra had naturally evolved over the years, as they took on new responsibilities with the changing times. Yet, their original mandate was the same as it had been in the time of Terric – the protection of the people. It was why they were created, and why, after hundreds of years they continued to sacrifice their lives. For the good of the realm.

The realm, Inlonia realized, was now in her hands. She held the fate of thousands, in what was possibly the most threatening time the city had ever faced. While Embarria was large, its population was significantly less than that of Isror. There was no reason to believe that Idach Garron would not turn his army north, should he succeed in destroying Rentorria. Idach was a chauvinist to his core, refusing even to send Inlonia the standard Letter of Royal Recognition two years prior; the acknowledgement of coronation that the kings of the neighbouring realms had always presented to a new ruler. It was evident that he did not consider a woman able to rule a realm. From her sources, she'd learned that Idach considered the Council to be in charge since the death of Intraal, calling Embarria the 'leaderless land'.

The shadows grew as Inlonia considered what she was about to do. The first female ruler in the history of the Three Realms, and she was at war. If ever there was a time to prove one's mettle, she thought, it was now. All around the property below, she saw the statues of former kings. Cast in rock that was unshakable, they stood over fifteen feet tall and faced time and the elements with a look of fierce determination. Even from this height, the queen felt herself to be below them. She'd not been prepared for her father's death, even though she'd watched Intraal battle his disease for several years before he'd finally succumbed. The king had died without a male heir, Inlonia being the only child of him and his wife Casan, who'd died before Inlonia saw her tenth year. Inlonia's acceptance of the crown at the tender age of twenty-six had shaken the realm, leaving all to wonder at the fate of

Embarria.

It was a fate she considered daily.

"Are you ready for this?" Ennis stood beside her, his thick arms folded over his chest.

Inlonia felt the cool shadow of the sinking sun. She looked behind her as Gilsanna set to lighting the candles, and then turned back to the window, which slowly filled with dusk. Far to the south, a star twinkled to life, eager to be a part of the approaching night.

"I am," Inlonia replied. "Have the stables ready the horses. We leave at sunrise."

26

SEEDS ACROSS THE WORLD

Torla Rallo didn't like to be led.

Walking behind the faerae, she continually adjusted the quiver of arrows she carried over her shoulder. Her left hand clenched her bow, tightly. She was not in control, she knew, nor would she be for quite some time. She stayed back from the faerae, but far enough ahead of the others that she'd not need to join their conversation. They knew to leave her alone.

Not having control was difficult enough, she thought, but passing control over to someone she didn't know was unbearable. Who knew where this faerae would lead them, and what dangers they'd encounter? She listened to Kef behind her, speaking lightly with Ston. She needed to be in control, she thought, in order to protect her younger brother. Kef was the brother she could actually protect.

She thought on Kolle every day; many times each day, in fact, but the wound was still as raw as it had been on that fateful day that the messenger had arrived at their home.

As the sun had set on that distant evening, a hand had knocked upon the door of the Rallo homestead. Its sound was as deep and empty as a night sky with no stars. Kef had looked up from the fire he stoked in the large room at the back of the home, and called for Torla to answer the door. Torla, intent on mending a small tear in her shirt, had called back to her brother, asking him in a warm voice if his other leg was now lame as well.

"About as lame as the hand that mended my trousers last week!" he'd replied.

His mother, walking past her youngest child toward the door, stopped suddenly and looked down at the boy.

"Kef! I did the mending last week!" Dahlah Rallo's face brightened with a smile that glowed like the cheeks of her son.

"Mother, I didn't mean – I mean..."

His mother's smile broke into a heartwarming laugh, and she playfully ruffled Kef's hair before moving from the room.

"Ah Kef," Torla said, a smile heard easily in her voice. "I apologize. No one with two lame legs could ever put his foot in his mouth with such ease."

"True. True," Kef replied, as he approached her at the table. "But you should realize, the foot in one's mouth tastes much better than the worn sock which covers it." In one fluid motion, Kef belied the limitations of his leg, and whipped his sock from his foot. With surprising quickness, he lunged with a laugh, thrusting the sock at Torla's face.

Torla sprang to her feet and grasped Kef's wrist as he

pushed the sock toward her. She tried to pull it away but only succeeded in stretching it to twice its length.

"*Careful* Torla! Careful!" Kef feigned concern through a laugh. "If you rip my sock, who could I possibly find to properly mend it?"

The laughter that came from them was pure. It was innocent and joyful, and filled the room like firelight. It was laughter that would not be heard for some time afterward in the Rallo home.

From the doorway in the adjacent room, Kef and Torla heard the heart wrenching sob of their mother.

Torla looked over at Sivino, who walked with a new determination of late. She saw how he cast furtive glances at the faerae, saw how his brow was increasingly creased with thought. Aside from her family, he was her constant, she realized. She recalled how present he'd been for her following Kolle's death. He was there whenever needed, the constant that gave her comfort, and said nothing more than needed to be said. She stole another quick look at her friend, and recalled the day of her brother's funeral.

She had heard him coming above the roar of the waterfall.

"Do you believe in destiny?"

Sivino, not surprised that she had sensed his presence, had sat beside her on an ancient oak log. A stone's throw from the brink of the Falls, they'd watched the water disappear from sight.

"I don't know what to believe."

"I can see why people would believe in destiny," Torla

had begun, a forced calmness in her voice. "It must make things easier to accept." She'd slipped her feet from her thin leather sandals, and let them rest on the wet earth. "But I think it's a fool's reasoning. To go through life, feeling that we have absolutely no control of things; that everything that happens in our lives is predetermined. If this is truly the case, then what is the point? If we believe that destiny will lead us to our final purpose, whatever it may be, then could we all not just sit back and do nothing! We could just be dragged along according to the whim of Fate!"

She'd stopped. Her breathing had grown more quick. Sivino had placed a comforting hand on her shoulder as she tugged nervously at the hem of her new tan dress. She looked down, conscious of how odd she must look in such garb. The occasions on which she'd worn such a garment could be counted on her hands. Dresses were impractical, she thought. They were also foolish-looking and quite uncomfortable. However, they were also the only option for a girl who had just buried her brother.

She'd stood, taken a deep breath, and closed her eyes. It was her way of regulating emotions. Never would she let them get the better of her, for Torla Rallo felt a loss of control of oneself was the truest sign of weakness.

She walked to the river's edge, and stood above one of the small pools of water which gathered on the edge of the Andel following stormy weather. Her bare feet left footprints in the wet earth. She lowered herself to the water, sitting on her heels, her arms upon her knees. She stared into the pool, its shallowness mocking the depth of her eyes, and the thoughts behind them.

Behind her, Sivino had removed his own shoes and moved to her side. "I want to say it was a nice ceremony," he said, lowering himself to her level, "but it wasn't. It couldn't be."

Torla appreciated his honesty, and nodded her agreement.

Time seemed to slow as she looked into the pool, at a reflection rippling with confusion. She did not move until a tear fell from her face and landed on the shimmering cheek of the girl below her.

She rose and readjusted her dress with awkward tugs. As she turned, her eyes fixed on a mound of rock under the limbs of another oak, piled as part of some game by the young ones who sought adventure at the Falls. Bending, she picked up an acorn that had fallen into the crevasses between the stones. Turning it slowly over in her hands, she considered the acorn.

"Destiny. *Fate,*" she whispered through her tears. "These are just kinder words for helplessness."

She turned, walked to the Andel and dropped the acorn in the clear water. It swirled as if confused about its direction, mesmerizing her already grief-stricken thoughts. Images appeared in the water as the acorn moved in a slow cycle. The face of her father. The face of her brother. The face of her mother as she clung to the messenger's shoulder and wept. Kolle had been her rock since her father passed several years prior. It was Kolle that Torla tried to emulate, Kolle that she sought out whenever she needed advice. Yes, she loved and respected her mother, but Dahlah had had so much to deal with in recent years, and Kolle had worked so hard to relieve the burden placed on his mother by the physical and emotional care of the younger Rallos.

She continued to watch the water, and the acorn that slowly spun. After several long moments she turned to Sivino, and falling into his arms she wept. The acorn completed one final cycle before it was pulled into the powerful current of the river and carried over the brink to the crashing waters below.

As the day waned, Torla let the group catch up with her. Niamh had, as she often did, wandered into the forest. The faerae would turn on these occasions, point in the direction she expected them to travel, and then slip into the trees in a completely different direction. Torla was keen enough to realize that appreciated the time that they were free of the faerae.

"Lomin," she said, as the group stopped to drink from their depleting skins, "you know what I think of this war. *You know.* Is there nothing else you would suggest?"

"There is not." His reply was immediate, but soft. "Niamh has told us that this journey must take place, and there are none I trust more. Her words reveal what is, and what must be." The group looked at him, confused. "You must understand that Niamh and her kind are able to communicate with beings with whom we cannot. Divine beings that have been explained to me, to an extent, but which I still do not fully understand."

"None can fully understand such beings." Niamh stood a stone's throw from them, stepping out of the forest. Stray leaves clung to the hem of her gown, looking so symmetrical they might have been sown there. Sivino was about to question her quick return, but she spoke before he could do so. "The Faant," she began, "have existed since time out of mind. They are the Creators, the demiurges that brought into being the first world and all worlds since; they are beings whose infinite wisdom and power surpass any and all living creatures. From whence they came, I could not say. I presume that none can.

"The Faant created the world of Pange; the only world. It existed for a time that our narrow perspectives are truly unable to grasp. Pange, like many worlds since, expired. When it did so, it was rent apart, cast into time and space in myriad directions. The Faant did not try to prevent this, for it is the way of things. Everything expires. Yet, so intricately had the Faant spun elements of themselves into the fibres of this world that even in its breaking it seemed to try to hold itself together, like the hands of lovers pulled toward different fates. These deific connections remained even as Pange separated. They remain still: the *fingers of the Faant*, connecting all the worlds of this universe, binding them together. More commonly, they are known as *the Paths*.

"Over many eons, the countless pieces of Pange spun themselves into worlds of their own; worlds that could sustain life, and over which the Faant would continue to keep watch. For indeed, they keep watch over our worlds. All worlds. They oversee their universe, as they oversaw Pange; to ensure that a balance is struck, and life continues to thrive.

"As the space between worlds grew, and more effort was required to maintain their intricate bond, the Faant shared a collective thought. They agreed that a group of carefully chosen beings, destined to become deities in their own right, would be selected to help oversee the matters of these worlds. These beings were selected from the very first race to rise in awareness and understanding – the First Ones. The original *Fae*.

"To protect the connection that the Faant wished to maintain between the separated worlds, they gave my ancestors what we have long considered to be our first and most important gift – the ability to move on the Paths. To shift. The Paths are a manifestation of this Pangean connection, and as the Fae were the original race born of the early worlds, they became an integral part of this connection."

Lomin moved forward, seeing that the group struggled to fully grasp the relationship. "So, the Faant oversaw the birth of the worlds, and then from the first race they created Gods and Goddesses that would oversee the maintenance of these worlds. They then used these deities to convey their messages to the faeraes, so that their will might be followed, and order maintained."

Ston turned to Niamh. "So, our Goddess was once a faerae?"

For the first time since her return, Niamh turned from the forest. "There was, amongst the First Ones, an ethereal creature by the name of Dahnu – The Flowing One. A strikingly beautiful creature, she was observed by the Faant as she flowed within the waters of this ancient land. From a trickle upon the mountain, to the raging rivers and the expansive lakes, she moved as the water – and within it – gentle yet powerful, able to command such change. As she flowed, her form was said to fade, to blend with the current, so that her body became one with the waters and her being ran across the lands like a joyous vein, to join with the great waters of the oceans before returning to the land once more as rainfall. It was while she was gathered as rain that she was spoken to by the Faant, that her destiny was laid before her, and she forsook her physical, albeit fluid form, and accepted the charge to watch over this wonderful world. She accepted the charge to be its Goddess."

Sivino felt shivers upon his skin as he considered this. If Niamh spoke true, they were now led by a faerae creature who had been spoken to by the Goddess, and possibly, beings even more powerful. The forest itself seemed to grow silent, intent on Niamh and the divine mysteries she attempted to explain. As had happened several times since their meeting the faerae, Sivino could not help but think they were part of something bigger, something that could indeed have a lasting impact.

Torla could keep silent no longer. "So, it is the will of the Faant, these all-powerful, all-knowing beings, to have a little company such as ours follow their will?" Her tone revealed her thoughts on the situation. "For that is what we're doing is it not? You, Niamh, are following the will of the Faant, and we in turn are following you."

Lomin spoke before Niamh could respond. "We must trust in Niamh, Torla. I know you find this difficult, but she is leading us where we need to go."

"That's your opinion, Lomin." Torla was unflinching. "Why does a faerae creature need a group like us to accompany her on this shadowed path?" She refused to look at the faerae, even when Niamh responded.

"Because you belong on this path, Torla Rallo. All of you. I do all I can to execute the wishes of the Faant, and their wish is that you join."

"I tire of this *path* talk! What path? This blasted trail to the west, or your magical routes to the ends of the universe?"

"Whichever is necessary."

"That's the problem. I'm not sure any of this is necessary." Torla moved away from the group, her hands shaking on her hips as she looked east.

"Ultimately," said Niamh, "the Faant do not command. Many people in many lands feel that it is the nature and intention of the Faant and the Gods and Goddesses to assert their dominance and exert their will. The people of Isror fear offending the Goddess above all else. In Rentorria, the opposite is quite true, as Dahnu is believed to be a distant observer, far removed from the situations and circumstances which shape their lives. I need you to remember that I attempt to guide you, not command you." She looked to the trees from which she'd recently emerged, and let several moments of silence settle over them all. "Yet, though I guide you, I must leave you for a time. There is someone I must see." She turned to Lomin. "You know the way."

The ragged man nodded.

Niamh returned the nod. Without another word, she slipped into the forest as silently as she'd emerged from it.

A weathered limb caught Lomin's eye, and he quietly retrieved it from the bushes to his side. He held it up, studying its form, length and stability, before giving it a satisfied look. He moved back to the group, eyeing Kef, who stood with some discomfort. He passed the boy the walking stick. "We need to help each other," he said quietly as Kef nodded his thanks and discarded the shorter stick he'd been using. Seeing Lomin scrutinize the limb suddenly reminded Sivino that he still carried his friend's willow stick in his inner pocket. He withdrew it and slowly handed it over. For just an instant, the old wolf's eyes went wide, but he quickly composed himself. Sivino could see relief and gratitude on his face, but pain as well. Lomin smiled, placed a hand on Sivino's shoulder and patted him gently. He exhaled as he took the stick, breathing as though he were whole once more, and addressed his young friends. "We need to work as one, even in the face of such confusion and doubt.

"Many years ago, as I sat with Niamh in an open field of golden grasses, she attempted to explain the will of the Faant. I was a young man...young and naïve. Yet, she endeavoured to explain the Faant in a manner that I could comprehend. The messages they share, she told me, and the possibilities they might set into motion are like seeds, scattered wildly upon the winds of change."

Lomin knelt then, a slight grimace on his face as Sivino helped him to the ground. He laid his own walking stick by his side, and from the ground plucked a small dandelion. Past its flowering stage, its sphere was now ready for dispersal. Lomin smiled. *"Dahnu's lion,* we'd call this in Forachia." He held it to his lips, and gently blew forth the seeds which were picked up by the forest breeze and carried in all directions.

"These messages of the Faant, these possibilities of potential futures are spread as seeds across all worlds. The good earth, the earth that sees us flourish, is the earth that accepts the seeds, and never gives up the hope for rain and trust in the sun. Like the lands surrounding our home, we need to trust that they will see us through the dry times; times wrought with doubt and difficulty. This earth sustains the seeds, nourishes them, and allows unlimited growth. In this earth, the possibilities are limitless."

The young people surrounding Lomin considered this silently. Sivino, Tonnis, Ston and Kef watched the old man, waiting to see if he would continue. Torla moved about anxiously, a few paces away from the others. Drip sat on a low tree branch, facing the descending sun. For long moments, none of the company spoke. The silence of the Nucono was disrupted only by the far off song of a swallow. Sivino looked from Lomin to his friends, from his friends to the trees. He looked for direction. Guidance.

Was it possible to defy the wishes of the Faant? And what was their wish exactly? They were to follow the faerae, but to what end? And why them? Again, his inner voice spoke of the need to follow Niamh and trust her. He felt a connection to her that seemed to be absent in the others. He bent slowly and grasped a handful of the soft soil beneath his feet. *What was needed from him?* Squeezing his hand into a fist, he felt the soil compact itself, tighten into a clump. He opened his hand and observed the soil, its edges outlined by the impression of his fingers. The shape of the space inside a fist. His prints were barely discernible in the red-brown edges. He closed his hand again and broke the soil, which spilled from his fingers to the ground below.

"We need to move on." Torla spoke quickly, startling Kef, who sat by her side. "There is nothing to be gained by standing here, idle as stones. We can speak as we walk. As long as I'm not commanded, I'm willing to see where this road leads us."

She moved toward Lomin and extended her hand. Taking it, he gained his feet and adjusted his grip on his staff.

"Torla." Lomin smiled as he placed a hand on her shoulder. "I should not be surprised that you'd need to take time to flesh this out more fully." He paused, and she saw that the smile on his face faltered as he spoke. He leaned in toward her, his voice lowered. "But please, do not take too much time.

"The seeds have already been cast."

27

HOME

The faerae walked through the forest, conscious of the coolness of the ground beneath her bare feet. She moved lightly and swiftly, her thin clothing swaying about her body. She could move more quickly, of course; such was the power of her kind. Movements that called upon the most basic, elemental magic would bring her to her destination in short time. Yet time was what she needed. Time to think. To consider her options carefully, and do what must be done.

She needed to speak with her father. Obaeron, king of the Fae, needed to be informed of what was happening. It was news that would hurt him deeply. One of his own, especially one as trusted as Cehron had always been, having manipulated him so greatly would be a mighty blow to the ancient faerae.

Obaeron, some would say, was the most foreboding of the creatures of Fae. He stood impressively tall for one of his kind, with thick locks of red hair that fell to his shoulders. Though aged, his face still held the rugged features of his youth. For long millennia, he had overseen the governance of the Council, and none could argue that he was indeed a leader both wise and powerful.

There were in Elysium Fae creatures that were entirely indifferent to the doings of the Council. It was, after all, a relatively recent establishment when compared to the inestimable history of the faerae world. There were creatures within the otherworld that held no concern or respect for the edicts of the group, for good or ill. They were simply uninterested in the actions and decisions of the thirteen members. These diverse, detached populations located throughout Elysium simply lived as they always had; in peace and pleasure, voluntary isolation and, at times, selfish indulgence. The affairs of the faerae world, let aside other worlds, concerned them not. With these populations, Niamh knew, her father had no great issue. As long as their actions did no harm, there was no need to interfere. In recent years, more pressing issues plagued this ruling body.

As she reached the river, she tried to recall how many years had passed since they'd last spoken. And now, after such time and distance, pain is what she would bring him. As she stepped into the cool waters of the Andel, she let herself be pulled in by its deceptive depth; a depth rivalled only by her troubled thoughts.

Emerging from the water, Niamh breathed deeply the air of Elysium. As she stepped from the waters of the River Faer, the rays of the sun exploded through the trees and the waters of the river shone as a rainbow. The sound and movement of the water was music. The tiny waves that flowed so smoothly down the river's expanse were as the keys of a piano, the sun and gentle breeze tracing their delicate fingers along these keys in a duet of rippling wonder, each colour of the fluid rainbow a gentle note of its own.

The air hummed with the sound, a late evening air which hung so heavy on all it surrounded. The scent and taste of the air was intoxicating, for unlike the air of any other world, the scent of the growth, the beauty and lushness of this land could be tasted. As Niamh stepped from the edge of the river into the forest, she closed her eyes.

In the distance, a harp was lightly strummed.

She was home.

The softness of the forest floor so greatly exceeded that of any other world in both texture and richness that Niamh, as she had done on countless previous occasions, wished that all could experience the sensation of walking barefoot within its hold, if only once. No rock or errant root would stub the toe, or cause one to fall. Within the forest, only grass, moss and fallen leaves, perpetually being replaced by new growth, varied the deep brown-red consistency of this earth.

Niamh had always loved the orange firmament of Cahruia, especially when leaves of similar hue fell from the trees above. It gave the appearance that the sky itself floated to the earth. Yet it could not compare to the light purple shades that gleamed overhead in her homeland. Streaks of dazzling light could be seen throughout the sky, day or night; undulations that reflected the subtle waves of the river. In Elysium, the shimmering sight brought no sense of awe and wonder to the creatures of Fae, as it so often did in other worlds. It was simply the sky.

As she walked through the forest, she raised her hand to catch a long purple leaf that fell before her. As it landed in her open palm, she looked upward to the limb from which it had fallen. A moment later, at the very spot from which the leaf had detached, a slender new leaf unfurled, slowly, slowly until, in full bloom it replaced its fallen predecessor. Niamh watched with pleasure as the new leaf, initially the palest of green, darkened to deep emerald before showing in its veins the first traces of brilliant purple.

A purple to match the sky.

She walked through the forest on a winding path that meandered between silver maples. To her left and right, traces of music wafted through the air, seeming to surround her. Her anxiety was diminished by the pure joy that she felt as she walked through her native world.

She hummed along with the song.

"At long last..."

She did not need to turn, for she had seen the faerae Tryn walking among the trees beside her for several minutes. His blond hair, streaked with occasional locks of olive green, shone in the sun.

"Tryn." She smiled cordially. "Is it mere coincidence that you'd be the first whom I should meet upon my return?"

"Would you believe that it was by chance I happened to stroll into the Silver Wood this morning?"

"Ah. And I thought you left nothing to chance."

The faerae did not look at her. "I am pleased that you

have returned. Your father, I am certain, will be likewise pleased." For the past several years, Tryn had continually sought out Niamh, begging her on behalf of her father to return to Elysium and join him in his rule. She'd always maintained that there was too much to be done; the Faant's requests were constant, and Elysium, she'd asserted, would be fine in her absence.

"Then let us not keep him," she responded, and without another word the two creatures of Fae strolled down a long worn path and emerged before the home of the king.

Niamh stopped and gazed upon the great towering structure before her; a structure made of wood and music, stone and sunlight.

The home of Obaeron was truly that of legend. Niamh stood for several moments and gazed upon the castle in which she had spent so many of her youthful years. Most of the rooms to which her fondest memories clung could not be seen, however. While several levels of the home rose above the ground, an even greater number lay beneath the surface.

So much beneath the surface, Niamh mused. Truly fitting for her kind.

"Welcome home," Tryn said from behind her. When she turned to respond, he was gone.

As she stood before the home of her father, the air seemed to reverberate with life. She noted the birds that flew through the lavender sky. As they passed above the home of Obaeron, the fowl seemed to be drawn to the structure and its surrounding grounds, swooping and gliding close to the shining towers and parapets, their song all the more urgent, intense and wonderful. For several minutes they circled longingly before rising once more to soar upon the warm breeze.

The grasses to each side of the path were trimmed to perfection by the grazing herd of Lolissi that wandered the properties at their leisure. Long, skinny creatures in spite of their insatiable appetite, the Lolissi breathed a soft, constant whistle through their narrow nostrils. Their songs were melancholy when the beasts hungered, but uplifting and joyous when they had feasted on the rich grasses.

Niamh walked past a young Lolissi foal, grazing her hand along its silky coat as she approached the slow winding path to her former home. She noted how time seemed to stand still. So accustomed to time's swift passage in other worlds, it was with great pleasure she remembered time's actual length in Elysium. Days, each of them glorious and alive, seemed to last forever.

And for the first time since her return to Elysium, Niamh felt the faint pang of heartache. It brought back distant memories of a young man; so young for what seemed to be so very long. The words of the Cernunnos rang in her ear. *Do you still mourn the mortal?*

Niamh stopped and wrung her hands gently as she watched the reflection of the sky in the shallow pools to each side of the path. Within, graceful birds flew, gliding effortlessly beneath the soft earth between the still waters.

She gazed into the pool, remembering the firm set of his jaw, and the blue eyes that had pierced her soul.

Oisin.

Niamh jerked sideways as a hand grasped her shoulder. It was rare for anyone to approach her without her knowing. Whether this lack of awareness was a product of her increasingly troubled mind or the magic of the faerae that stood beside her, she didn't know.

"Welcome, Daughter," Obaeron whispered as he glanced into the small pool of water at Niamh's feet. Within, the faint image of a young man with blue eyes quickly faded.

"Father." Placing her hand upon his she inhaled deeply, and turned to look at the man who towered above her.

"We have much to discuss."

28

NOTHING THAT I SEEK

Niamh walked with her father beneath the branches of the Silver Wood.

Though years had passed since they'd last spoken, they walked in silence for a time; each content to quietly share the leafy path which led to Niamh's childhood home.

Thoughts of Oisin lingered. Niamh's memories of their time spent together were triggered by her surroundings. He had loved Elysium, which was reminiscent of his homeland; only *richer*, he'd often said. Richer in colour; in sound, scent and beauty.

It had initially surprised Niamh to hear him speak in such a manner. He was, after all, a fighter. With his father Finn, he'd helped lead the Fenian warriors in many bloody campaigns. He was a man who drove a sharp, cold fear into the heart of his adversaries. Over fields and through valleys, his battle cry blended seamlessly with his joyous laugh. He'd lived a life without boundaries. He'd not been bound by material possessions, and he'd cared little for the comforts that lured so many. *Life is simple enough,* he'd said so often. *It's only fools that complicate it.*

Yet, this former life had not been enough for him, he'd told Niamh.

With each passing year of his youth, his restlessness had grown. Solitary weeks spent hunting grew to months, and by the time he reached the age of twenty five, these months spent away from his father's home had grown beyond a year. Not even the conflicts of the Fenians could draw him back to his homeland. He'd lost himself.

She had found him sitting upon the shore of a still pond, humming a quiet song at sunset. He'd been looking beyond his reflection in the waters, following the erratic movement of small fish that swam so close they were almost within his reach. A slow rain had begun to fall. He'd closed his eyes and, tilting his face skyward, smiled as the first drops struck his cheek.

When he opened his eyes a moment later, she stood before him. Her slender form was covered in a loose white dress that clung to the water's surface. Though she stood to her knees in the pond, no ripple stirred the water about her legs.

He'd blinked the rain from his lashes with a look of such innocence that she'd very nearly smiled.

"You have been sitting by these waters for many evenings," she whispered quietly. "Are you waiting? Or is there something for which you search?"

He'd smiled at her, causing her face to soften ever so slightly.

"There is nothing that I seek, and as a result there is

much that I find." His eyes held hers firmly. "I am content to wander. I find more peace in strange forests and distant fields than any home I've ever had." In the days that she had watched Oisin, Niamh had not heard him speak. She had wondered at his wisdom, his thoughts and desires, and the tone of his voice.

She was not disappointed.

Though her affection for the young stranger had come as something of a shock, the quiet request that slipped so gently from her mouth had been well-considered.

"Come then," she had said, "and I will show you the strangest forests, and fields so distant and beautiful that you may never wish to leave."

She extended her hand to Oisin, knowing that her request would not be denied. Oisin had looked upon her for a long moment – not in consideration of whether he'd accept her offer, he later told her, but rather in wonder of how fate could deliver such fortune into his unsuspecting hands.

The brief shower ended as Oisin stood, and a swallow sang from a branch overhead. He had taken her delicate hand and let himself be led into the still waters.

In the land of Elysium, the young man indeed found the free life of wonder that he'd sought for so long. From the very first moment, he'd said that it felt as though he were one with the lands and waters. Niamh took no small amount of satisfaction as she watched him revel in the sensations of the Fae world. She saw something in him that moved her so deeply that she required his presence, for a time at least, in spite of the edicts that forbade all but the Faer folk from residing in this world. She meant to know the man by her side; this man who gazed so thoughtfully upon a world he knew nothing of, but loved all the same.

Days dawned and faded with gentle certainty, and each had been filled with happiness and pleasure. Through the forests they wandered, the faerae and the man. Niamh was indeed true to her word, for Oisin beheld sights that surpassed even his unbound imagination. Creatures of all manner wandered into the periphery of his vision, and more still lurked out of sight completely. Music, which seemed a constant in Elysium, accompanied them everywhere. In the hills and valleys, the whimsy of the pipe and whistle swept through the wheat like an errant breeze. Upon the mountainside, the sylphs sang their heart-wrenching songs. In the deep of the wood, the distant reverberation of drum and horn enshrouded the forest and its inhabitants alike. Near the water, the fluid sound of the harp held sway, washing itself over all, cleansing those who would listen.

For the first time in his life, Oisin had felt himself at complete peace. He'd felt truly alive, he'd said.

He felt he was home.

Time passed, and a love both deep and intense grew between them. Niamh felt no fear for Oisin when he ventured out on his own. He'd grown familiar with the meadows and forests, the mountains and lakes, and understood the creatures that lived upon and within. His familiarity with these areas, she'd said with a soft smile, seemed to grow as quickly as Elysium thyme. He knew the rivers and gullies inhabited by creatures best left alone, and those to avoid entirely. He knew the forest trails most perilous, and those most beautiful. And so, on a morning as beautiful as every other in Elysium, Niamh had smiled as Oisin rose with the sun and set out for an early walk on a path which led to the River Faer.

   She could not have known that a creature consumed by dark hatred would await him upon this path, its mind bent solely upon ensuring that the young man suffered a death both slow and unimaginably painful.

29

ALL THE WAY TO THE RIVER

Dels watched as Karm Naphor cringed and stifled a cry of pain.

"Sorry, sorry," Karm's mother Kayl whispered as she tended to his arm under the watchful eye of Pann Leuko. Despite days of their ministrations, Karm's wound continued to fester. Dels had seen the growing concern in both the women's eyes as they washed his wound, which had taken on a troubling shade of red. The flesh surrounding the gash had begun to swell, and Dels noticed that each time the wrapping was removed, a yellowish fluid stained the cloth. Karm looked around the camp, seeking to distract himself from his mother's efforts. As he turned his head, he saw that Leath and Sianah stood nearby, watching with concern. He attempted a smile.

Three days after the attack, the Egimians still wandered through dark trees on a path to Ras. The day after next, Dels had assured them, the city should be in sight. He and Stellen had chosen camp locations a considerable distance from the Andel and away from the more regularly travelled paths. A group of lookouts, which included most of the trenocs, were set to watch in regular shifts. As Karm watched the first shift move to their vantage points, he gritted his teeth, both at the pain and the fact that he now considered himself a burden more than anything else.

"Don't worry yourself, Mother. It seems to be healing. Right as rain in no time." Her face had aged tremendously in the days since they'd left their home. She didn't breathe as she finished wrapping his wound. At times, she grimaced more than her son, as if she felt the pain herself. She pulled the ends of the cloth tight and breathed again with closed eyes.

"It's my job to worry. It is yours to allow me." She put her hand on his good shoulder, which he tapped in thanks. Rubbing his shoulder, she raised her head and looked toward Dels.

He stood on the periphery, watching over them all. The Egimians were quiet, as they usually were. They spoke in hushed tones as they tended to each other, none among them as concerned for their own well being as they were for that of their neighbour. Such was the nature of these people. Each life was inextricably connected to the others, a collective character and subconscious that lent great strength to each individual. Simply razing homes and gardens could not destroy the village of Egim. The heart of Egim could not be undone by flame or sword.

None knew this better than Dels Spallic.

He hadn't allowed a fire during the first two nights for fear of being discovered. His people had understood this; they appreciated the care and caution that so defined him. However, as the arduous journey took its toll on the weakest of the company, Dels saw that he had little choice. They'd fled with so little warning; essentials such as blankets and heavy cloaks were scarce. The very young and very old needed heat, and warm food and drink. As well, a number of jack-hare and even a young elk had been caught as they travelled, and the meat needed to be cooked. Dels tended the flame. It was a contained fire, calm yet intense in spite of its size. He thought of Sivino. Sitting alone, he watched the sparks rise, their light glowing fiercely before they winked out of existence. He watched as some rose to great heights before fading, while others barely rose above the flames no matter how brightly they shone.

He saw the deterioration of the older Egimians: for Kitt Rallo and the other elders this journey was just short of impossible. He watched the young tend to the aged and saw Kayl Naphor move between her injured son to her ailing aunt, Eselin. He watched Karm for several moments, and the way the boy hid the pain. The boy was not well.

Again, he thought of Sivino.

How quickly things change, he thought. He was, for most parts, a traditional man who appreciated the constants in life, the predictable and controllable. He knew that things must change, and that change often brought with it benefits and wonder both. Had his great grandfather not demonstrated this when he accepted the friendship of a trenoc? Yet now, as he stared absently through the weakening flames of the fire, the face of Dahlah told him that the sharpest edges of change could in fact undo the very fabric which held one's mind, one's heart, together.

She looked back at him. They held each other's eyes for long moments until a loud crack from the burning wood caused her to jump. She took a deep breath and pulled her woollen shawl closer around her shoulders, thankful for the added warmth it provided. She looked to Kitt, who now attempted to get herself comfortable on a grassy patch of earth. Dahlah helped her settle, but when she tried to place the shawl over the older woman, she would not hear of it.

"My leathery skin is all the protection I need," Kitt grunted as Dahlah knelt beside her. "It is you – the soft young – that I worry about." Dahlah gave Dels an exasperated smile. He returned the smile, knowing that she'd simply wait for the old woman to fall asleep, and cover her then.

Sleep was the furthest thing from Dahlah's mind. Her delicate face was drawn, and darkness marred the edges of her green eyes as she attempted to help some of the women settle their little ones. It pained Dels to see her so.

He rose, and walked around the fire to sit by the woman. He laid his hand upon her knee. Dahlah's head now nodded with the heavy fatigue that hung upon her like wet clothing.

"Go, lay down with your mother. She needs your warmth, and you need the rest."

"I'm alright, Dels. I just—"

"You just need to sleep."

"Dels, I'm…" but she didn't have the words to finish. Her mind was as weary as her body.

"A stubborn Rallo woman is what you are." Dels extended his hand. Taking it, Dahlah got to her feet and walked slowly to Kitt. Lying down beside the old woman, Dahlah removed her shawl and wrapped it snugly around the shoulders of her mother.

As she let herself fall into the elusive arms of sleep, Dels removed his cloak and spread it gently over both of the weary women.

Dew forming in the morning brought the company to its feet. Parents urged the young ones to eat an unappealing meal of tough, cold jack-hare and elk put aside from last evening. They sighed, chewing with little enthusiasm.

As the last of the watch returned from the final shift, the Egimians collected their meagre belongings and continued the trek to Ras. Two days, under normal conditions, would bring a swift rider from Egim to the Drale city, but there were not enough horses to carry the weak, injured and young, and Dels knew that the progress of the group was half that of an unhindered rider. At their current rate, they'd likely reach the East Bridge in a couple of days. Then, having crossed the Andel, they'd need another day to reach Ras. He had considered sending one of the stronger horsemen ahead to the Drales to request help, and discussed the idea with those around him. The options, the group had agreed, were limited. To send a strong rider to Ras was to lose a valued fighter should they be attacked again. As well, the rider would have to travel alone, would have to make camp alone, and the Nucono was not a place in which anyone should currently travel or sleep while Nylacci roamed. It was Stellen Tros who raised the concern that plagued the minds of many, a fear that none had yet mentioned.

"Suppose," he said just loud enough for the others to hear, "suppose the Drales refuse to help us. Suppose they turn us away."

"Wouldn't surprise me," Lumb Velto mumbled as he put on the sword belt he'd removed the night before.

"They're not the most social creatures," Leath offered. "But, given the circumstances, I can't imagine they'd turn us away. Would they?"

There were grunts from several of those gathered.

"Not the most social, and hardly sympathetic," said Stellen. "Old Harb Crondo was once injured on a hunting trip, showed up on their doorstep bleeding like a stuck pig. The Drales looked at him with blank faces until Harb's hunting party finally gave up and carried the poor bugger home. Almost died, he did. It's quite possible we'll get the same reception."

"There is that possibility," Dels said. "We must remain hopeful that help will be provided. If the Drales can be made to see that their lands are in as much danger as ours, then we may have a chance. We must maintain hope, thin as it may be."

Stellen shook his head. Apparently his doubts were great regarding the outcome of their arrival in Ras. He folded his arms, and walked away with his shoulders slumped. Dels looked around the camp, making a final check of the preparations and, in particular, the ailing.

He did not particularly enjoy leading others. Egim had always been led by a carefully chosen pillar of the village who would resolve and serve matters that were not of a severity to necessitate Ryndarra involvement. Cision Jamaroh had done remarkable work, enhancing the town's relationship with neighbouring villages and providing sage advice on various plans to promote the town's growth and prosperity. Most importantly, she took care of her people. She settled the occasional disputes with gentle authority, be it a fence encroaching on a neighbour's property, or a flower garden eaten by a neighbour's ewe. She had been greatly respected, loved, and humble in her accomplishments. A few years prior during a visit by one Feirl Shauven – head pillar of the Rovil Council – the sweaty bald man had guffawed and turned to the gathered group comprised of a dozen men and women, including Cision Jamaroh. *I'm most curious,* he'd said. *Does* Egim *have no* men *capable of leading the township?* Dels had smiled and stepped up to the fool. Laying a hand on the man's shoulder – and squeezing perhaps a little tighter than was necessary – he turned to Cision. *Of course we do*, he'd replied. *But none could dream of being half as effective as this woman.* Shauven smiled awkwardly and began to step away, but Dels held his shoulder a moment longer. *But now, you tell me,* he'd continued. *Because* I'm *most curious. Does Rovil have no men capable of progressive thinking?*

No further guffaws were heard that evening.

Dels would later learn that in addition to being an effective leader, Cision had also been quite adept at hiding the deadly sickness that grew within her for more than a year. She died suddenly one morning. According to her family, as the sun rose above the hills that embraced her town, Cision extended her hands to grasp its warmth, its light, as she smiled and entered the Land of Ever. No one had offered to succeed Cision in the four years since her passing, and the town had continued to implore Dels to fill the role. He dodged the requests deftly, though he and several other men and women of the town stepped in when required. He had always said he must give it more thought; he never made decisions lightly.

And then Rhenna got sick.

Satisfied that the camp was sufficiently broken, he moved on. Walking through his people to once more take the lead on their trek, he assessed their condition. By the time he reached the front of the group, he realized something that had become more apparent than ever since the attack.

Some decisions were not his to make.

"It won't be long." Rhenna's cool, sweaty hands clasp those of Dels, which in total contrast is warm and dry. He has worked so hard to create for them a life that is filled with comfort and peace. But while these hard, caring hands have succeeded in creating such a life, there is one he cannot save.

He shakes his head, not in denial, but in an unwillingness to let go. Then he stops, fearful that his actions may upset her. His wife smiles. She can read him so well. Every movement, every word, every thought in his mind has only her best interest at heart. He lives a proud life of integrity, hard work, and love. But he lives it for her. Her and the boys.

Sivino and Leath enter the room. They've been back and forth to see her throughout the day, knowing she is quickly losing the battle that rages against her weakened body. Leath sits beside her bed and lays a small gift on her lap, watching as she traces her thin fingers over his handiwork: a wooden plaque, carved with a meticulousness that even Dels hadn't thought Leath capable of. He has shaved and sanded the frame to create small waves upon each of the four sides. Written on the plaque is a single word – Forever. A sunrise breaking behind the word brings a tear to Dels' eye; every magnificent ray duplicated from her woven welcome mat. Rhenna catches her shallow breath, and a tear falls upon the plaque. It lands on the sun, splashing outward, sparkling in the golden rays that shine through her window.

"And always," she whispers, and hugs Leath with all the strength she possesses.

Sivino sits beside her as Leath steps outside to regain his composure. He stares at the plaque that his mother holds to her chest. "I'm not good with woodwork," he says. She reaches to take his hand. "I know," she replies. "Remember that birdhouse you made?" His mother laughs, and though no sound comes from her mouth, her thin shoulders are shaking, and her smile is deeper than it has been in days. Dels laughs as well, though his cheeks are damp with tears. He recalls Sivino's failed attempt at carpentry. The boards had been so poorly fitted that the evening sun shone through entirely. Some gaps were actually wider than the hole through which the birds were supposed to enter. When Leath had chided Sivino about his handiwork, his mother had laughed and said that the birds would appreciate the variety of exits and entrances and the wonderful sunshine that the little house allowed.

Sivino smiles. "It lasted quite a while though."

"That it did," she replies. "That it did. It was a wonderful job, Sivi."

"I knew that Leath was – that he'd made this for you," Sivino says, gesturing toward the plaque. "But I knew that I

couldn't do anything nearly as good."

"Sivi." She reaches out and takes his hand. "Everything you do is good. Your heart is good. It is bigger than any heart I've ever known...even his." She tilts her head toward Dels with a smile, whose hand goes to his heart with a feigned look of shock and a smile. Sivino looks at Dels, and then back at his mother. His father moves to the window and sits upon the sill, looking at the garden just below. It explodes with life; colourful plants and flowers fill every available space around their humble home. Dels looks at the flowers for long moments, thinking of how severely they contrast with the pale white of Rhenna's face. They all know that she is dying. For long months, Dels has prepared himself for this. Yet, as he gazes more deeply into the garden, the lilies stand out against all the other flowers, and he realizes that he is not ready. He has tried to be resilient, but he cannot. All he can do is sit, watching her, willing her to live.

After some time, Sivino rises and kisses her forehead. She pats his hand and closes her eyes to rest. Yet, when Sivino leaves the room her eyes open again, and the look she gives Dels is serious. Almost apologetic. She asks him to sit beside her.

"He is special." With great effort, she turns so that she can face her husband. He tries to stop her, but she smiles and shrugs him off. "It's alright," she says. She breathes slowly for a few moments, and then speaks again. "He is special, Dels. Leath is as well, but in a different way. I love them both so dearly."

Dels nods, and looks to the door to ensure that Sivino is not present. "He did something for you," the big man whispers. "He watched as Leath worked on his carving, and he told me he wanted to create something for you." Dels folds his hands, and leans forward to rest his chin upon them. "I saw him, near the Whispering Leah on the far end of the property. This was a couple of months ago. Late in the afternoon he was digging, removing tiny new saplings from the base of your Leah. He took them, so many of them, and set off toward the forest. On that beaten path to the Andel, he planted those trees. All of them. He stopped every thirty paces or so, and planted a Whispering Leah. How closely he must have watched you at your garden. I swear to Dahnu, every movement of his hands, every gesture – it was just like you. All the way to the river, Rhenna, he planted your trees. There's not a step he'll take on his walk to the Andel that you'll not be in his sight."

Rhenna's lips are tight as she fights to not cry openly. She closes her eyes for a moment, and steadies herself. When she opens them, they are calm. "I don't have much longer, love." She places a hand on his knee. "There is something I need to tell you...about Sivino." A look of slight confusion, almost concern, comes to Dels' face, and he nods slowly.

When she has finished, he is silent. The evening air is heavy, and the setting sun casts long shadows throughout the room. Slowly, Dels goes to one knee, and embraces her. She whispers to him, and he nods.

He finds Leath and Sivino sitting on the front step. Bending, he puts a hand on each boy's shoulder. They rise to follow him back into the house. The three sit around Rhenna, and in the fading light they cry, laugh, and speak of times that have been filled with joy. When the lanterns have been lit, she tries to sing. Her voice is dry; weak like the light of the lantern, and she cannot get the words out. She smiles apologetically. Seeing this heartbreaking smile, Dels does something that, in all their years together, he's never done before. He takes her hand and he sings to her; a song he's heard her sing a thousand times. She closes her eyes and listens.

Fancy brings a thought to mind
Of a flower that's bright and fair,
Its grace and beauty both combine
To make the thought more rare
Just like a maiden that I know
Who shared my happy lot
Where we parted, when she whispered
You'll forget me not.

She's graceful and she's charming
Like the lily in the pond
Time is flying swiftly by
Of her I am so fond
The roses and the daisies
Are blooming 'round the spot
Where we parted, when she whispered
You'll forget me not

And then there came a happy day
When something that I said
Cause her lips to mumble 'Yes'
And shortly we were wed.
Now there's a cottage by a lane
With a little garden spot,
Where grows a flower, I know it well,
It's a sweet forget me not...

She opens her eyes one final time; eyes which smile as deeply and beautifully as her graceful lips. She looks at each of them as they gently hold her hands.

"Forever," she whispers, as her eyes fall shut, her smile eternal.

30

THE ERRATICS

Angry waves crashed far below the king of Rentorria.

Doran Dunarrk had risen early, as was usual, and left the Keep to walk the grounds. Minutes later, he was joined by a friend whose counsel he held above all. Kellert Sentero, his most trusted advisor and head of the Rentorrian Council, accompanied him through the dissipating fog with a scowl that would repel sea waves as surely as the sheerest of cliff faces. His energy seemed without limit, and his insight and skill were sought by many. Standing just above five feet, his stature did little to reduce the respect he commanded. He was as fierce as any when the need arose, and oversaw the defence of his homeland with fervent passion. Isror had swept into the land and with relentless blades sought to rip Rentorrian roots from the ground; roots that had held firm for many generations. Roots that belonged. Kellert had sworn to Doran at the onset of the conflict that they would beat this foe, but as time passed, doubt had crept into the deepest crevasses of his mind.

Doran sighed, and for the first time spoke the realization that had weighed upon his mind for days. "Ronec will fall."

"The defences are holding, barely." Kellert hesitated as he considered his words. "They will not continue to do so. Yes, Highness, Ronec will fall in short days."

Doran measured the eyes of his friend, eyes filled with pain and guilt. He stopped walking, and with a slow nod he folded his arms over his broad chest.

"Nahcin?"

"Those defences have been steadily reinforced. Most of the soldiers fight in Ronec of course, but Nahcin readies itself. Many citizens have left the city limits, as they did in Ronec. More will come to the coast. But yes, Nahcin is next. The Isrorian forces at Ronec will move swiftly onward, their eyes set on Orshos."

Doran's teeth clenched. "Any new information on numbers?"

"Not yet. We hope that our intelligence from Isror will…fill some gaps."

Doran turned to Kellert, his eyes asking the unspoken question.

"They are four days overdue, Highness."

Doran rubbed his right eye with the heel of his hand. Walking past his friend, the king stopped and faced the stone gargoyle that kept silent watch over the cliffs. He rested his hands on the statue's curved horns, feeling the age and wear in the bones of the ancient creature.

These days, it was a feeling to which he could easily relate.

***

The trader, though overdue, was not concerned about punctuality at the moment. He was preoccupied by more pressing issues.

Slowly, he crawled over the dead Isrorian, put his back to the nearest boulder and listened intently.

Nothing.

At least not in his immediate vicinity. The battle raged on, but it sounded as though it had shifted once more to the northern edge of the Erratics. Hoping he was right, the Rentorrian quickly uncorked the cap of his waterskin, never releasing the grip on his sword. He drank deeply, then splashed a little over his face to clean the blood that had caked around his eyes. He didn't know if the blood was his or that of his enemy. Staid Dyrro didn't care.

How quickly life changed, he reflected.

He'd been returning from a reconnaissance mission in Isror with two companions. It was a land with which he was somewhat familiar. Through the years, his occupation of trade had carried to all corners of the Three Realms, and he'd spent significant time in both Isror and Embarria. The number of active traders had been abridged by the need for men and women to bear arms, as many put aside one livelihood to replace it with another. Staid's knowledge of foreign lands was a valuable asset. It was for this reason that he had agreed to the request made by Doran Dunarrk. A small group, the king had said, was needed to assess the situation within Isror. Intelligence was essential. If a group could infiltrate the city, observe preparations, and gain a sense of the size and plan of the army, such knowledge would be invaluable. But it needed to be done by individuals who knew the city, its streets and local customs, and could blend in seamlessly with its population in order to overhear talk on the streets.

With the group selected, a plan was set in place and three Rentorrians set out on the uncertain journey. Staid Dyrro was joined by two others; Recker Lorr, a lean yet fierce fighter, and Basha Noan, a former Isrorian who had fled her homeland years prior. Her husband, the only family she'd had in the city of Iskall, had served Idach Garron, and had been summarily executed when he'd expressed a strong opinion contrary to that of the king. Noan was a risk, Doran Dunarrk had conceded, but many trusted Rentorrians, including Kellert Sentero, had vouched for her, assuring the king that her hatred for Idach Garron was intense and pure. She knew the city well, and was hungry for revenge.

A nearby cry shook Staid Dyrro back to reality. Slowly, he leaned around the boulder, his sword held firm. The midday heat exacerbated the intensity of the battle, which had now entered its second hour. It was almost impossible to see with the blinding sun, which reflected horribly on the off-white clay that covered this cursed place. *The Erratics*. A vast plain devoid of vegetation, the land appeared as if massive bolts of stone had rained down over the region. Some stood erect, while others lay on their side. All were weathered by the elements of millennia, their surfaces both smooth and porous. It was, he thought, like the ancient ruins of a stone city such as Ras.

Between his boulder and the one adjacent, two soldiers suddenly discovered each other and clashed with a ferocity that shook them both. Staid jumped as the swords met with a sharp clang. Flattening himself against the boulder, he carefully moved around to check the sparring fighters. A quick look and he identified which was the enemy. With no hesitation, he lunged and drove his sword between the shoulders of the unsuspecting man.

"Thanks," the other rasped. He spoke without looking at Staid, as every rock in this place hid a potential enemy. One moment of distraction could cost a soldier their life.

Many had attempted to gain perspective from the tops of the boulders, but they discovered all too quickly that this made them an easy target for archers that waited on the periphery of the battlefield. And so, the battle raged within the hundreds of rocks, as neither side was willing to expose themselves to the open plain that lay without.

Staid fell in behind the man he'd just assisted. *Crake. Was that his name?* It was hard to recall, as they'd only joined this regiment the day prior. He, Lorr and Noan had been returning from their mission, eager to share their intelligence with Doran Dunarrk and his advisors. He shook his head. Lorr and Noan now lay dead on the periphery of the Erratics, killed in an ambush as the Rentorrian force had entered the plain. The Isrorians had been hiding within the stones, waiting for an opportune moment to strike. It happened quickly. In an instant, the air was filled with arrows, the roar of several hundred soldiers, and the blinding light of swords. Short time passed before both sides found themselves within the veritable maze of the Erratics, seeking some form of advantage, or shelter from the slaughter.

Staid glanced around. *How many remained?* After more

than an hour of relentless battle, the numbers were clearly decimated – perhaps a hundred soldiers still lurking within the stones, he'd guess. Maybe less. Around every corner, the bodies were strewn; piled up in many cases. The pale clay face of the Erratics was stained with the blood of both sides.

Staid and Crake crept between the rocks, one looking left, the other right. As they traversed a long alley within the maze, Staid caught movement to his left. A Ryndarran soldier moved toward them, stepping over a dead body as he approached. Seeing Staid, he raised a hand, silently gesturing for the pair to wait for him. Three comrades could watch three different directions. As he moved toward them, however, the apparent dead body that he stepped over suddenly surged upward, driving his sword into the man's midsection. Staid burst forward, intent on reaching the Isrorian before he could get to his feet. As the man gained his knees, Staid threw his small boot knife with what strength he could muster, catching the man in his shoulder.

He rushed forward to finish the job, but the big Isrorian deflected the blow, and grabbing his wrist, pulled him to the ground. Staid's sword landed just beyond his reach as he gripped the black uniform of the enemy. Teeth bared, Staid rolled in the clay with the Isrorian who was at least a foot taller, and more solidly built. Despite the wound, the Isrorian used his weight advantage to roll Staid, pinning him to the ground. Fortunately, it appeared the big man had lost his own weapon as well, which was the sole reason Staid was still alive. He glanced to his left, wondering where Crake had gone. All around him, the newly arisen clash of swords and the screams of the dying filled the air. The Isrorian shifted slightly, released Staid's wrists and grabbed him by the throat. Exhausted and pinned to the ground, there was no way to remove the man's grip. He swatted at the black-clad enemy with no more strength than a child. The Isrorian adjusted himself once more, moved his hands further behind Staid's neck, and in one quick motion lifted Staid's head and smashed it back against the clay ground.

His vision began to fade. Stars both beautiful and terrible appeared before his eyes. *Moments*, Staid thought, *and I'm done.* His eyes felt as though they were bulging from his head, so tight was the man's grip. As if to emphasize this, the Isrorian squeezed harder, leaning so close their faces nearly touched.

"Just. Die," the brute grunted, as a thin line of drool ran from his mouth to fall on Staid's cheek. But before Staid could comply with the command, a body fell from the rocks above. It landed with a crash beside the pair, an arrow through the chestplate.

The distraction was enough. The hands of the Isrorian relaxed for just a moment, long enough for Staid to pull them from his neck and take hold of the man's wrists. He gave a quick twist toward the body, and despite his agony, could not help but notice the size of the arrow that protruded from the dead man's chest. Huge and black, with coarse dark feathers, it was unlike any he'd ever seen. Staid then noticed the knife that resided still in his attacker's shoulder. Just within his reach, if only he could release the Isrorians wrists momentarily. He was contemplating how to do this when the horse walked though his line of vision. Through two arm spans of space between boulders, a cloaked figure rode past atop a massive black steed. The figure turned his head, slowly, and though his eyes were hidden beneath a black hood, Staid was certain that the man looked directly at him. *What in Creation?* Staid faltered a moment. The man could not have been a combatant in the battle. Though he'd only been visible for a moment, it was long enough to see that he carried no weapon as he moved leisurely through the horror of the Erratics. Hands casually holding the reins, he'd looked over at Staid and the Isrorian without the slightest hint of interest before disappearing behind the rocks. There was no effort to hide or defend himself, no concern for his well being. He was, Staid thought, the picture of indifference.

The beast that followed the rider was far from indifferent. Through the same space between the boulders, it lumbered. It was, Staid thought, a monster that only a child could dream up. Seven feet tall and covered in mangy fur, the beast walked past without looking toward them. Staid couldn't be sure, but short pointed horns seemed to protrude from the beast's head and jaw. In one hand, it carried a long dark sword. In the other, it held the severed arm of a man. As the beast was about to pass out of sight, it raised the arm and took a rough bite. Staid instantly felt the Isrorian's hands relax. He too was looking at the nightmare that had just walked by. Seizing what was likely to be his only opportunity, Staid released one of the man's wrists, and yanked the knife from his shoulder. In a fluid motion, he buried it in the Isrorian's throat.

Pushing the writhing man off of him, Staid crawled behind the nearest boulder and tried to breathe. As he did so, sounds filled the air that raised the hairs on his neck. Screams, but unlike those of rage and pain, these were the sounds of terror. They were screams of a higher pitch, sounds that were made when all hope is lost. More terrifying than the screams were the roars that followed. Deep and rough, it was like the sound of thunder from some great rabid bear.

Staid got to his feet and moved around the rock. The rider and the monster seemed to have headed east, so Staid, grabbing his sword once more, moved west. After several minutes, the screaming subsided. Staid, ever the loyal warrior, knew that he'd never be able to desert his comrades on the field of battle. Finding a suitable rock, he lay flat and slowly crawled to the top, his head just visible over its peak.

What he saw made him sick. It appeared that every soldier, friend or foe, had fallen. There was no shouting, no clashing of metal or cries of pain. There were only monsters. Staid could see them everywhere in spaces between the boulders. He looked closely at the nearest beasts. The size. The matted fur. But most frightening of all were the horns: two rose from the beasts' heads and two from the base of their jaws. Memories of his grandfather's stories rushed to mind. The old tales of monsters long since banished from Cahruia. He whispered a curse, and sank down from the rock. This news, he knew, must be carried back to camp, and then to the king. There was nothing else left for him to do. The battle, it appeared, was over.

The feast had begun.

31

THE MOST GENTLE NAME FOR FEAR

Sivino and his companions stood at a crossroad.

The course they'd followed through the Nucono ran roughly adjacent to the Westroad. As they emerged from the thick of the forest, the path upon which they tread curved sharply to the south, keeping to the shelter of the trees. The Westroad, should they take it, ran due west, widening as it crossed through open terrain and larger settlements until it finally reached the city of Salkor on the coast. It was on the border of the forest that the company now stood; each acutely aware of the decision which needed to be made, none wanting to make it. Niamh had still not returned. Indeed, her wanderings had grown so frequent that none but Sivino and Lomin noticed most of her departures. She'd left no directive on what way they would venture at this point, and rather than wait, Lomin had determined that they should make the decision themselves.

Dark clouds overhead made this decision seem all the

more urgent. Sivino knew Lomin was eager to turn south. He had told his young companions that, upon emerging from the Nucono, they should change their course. Niamh had noted that they were destined to take a southern route. Yet, destiny, Sivino knew, had never had to contend with the will of Torla Rallo. And Lomin, for his part, would never force the young ones upon a path they did not wish to pursue. He would wait, and use his words to gently nudge them in the direction he saw as most appropriate.

The old wolf stood silently, leaning heavily upon his walking staff. He was tired, and rightly so. The company had made tremendous progress throughout the day, stopping only twice to quickly eat and rest. Though Lomin had strength that they did not fully grasp, he was aging nonetheless. Used to travelling upon Sleipnir, Lomin was unaccustomed to covering so much distance on foot.

After long moments, Lomin quietly cleared his throat and looked to the sky. "The sun will set more quickly this evening." Sivino saw Torla close her eyes upon hearing these words. Sivino was fully aware that she, along with Kef, was more torn than either had ever been. It was the south that had stolen their brother. He knew that Torla especially would always view the south with anger and no small amount of grief.

Ston was standing with his hands on his hips, walking in rough circles as he kicked aside loose rocks. Drip, as usual, stood a distance from the others, quietly cursing the change in the weather. And then there was Tonnis, who Sivino kept reminding himself had literally had his entire world destroyed before his very eyes; wiped away in a maelstrom of blood. He stood beside Kef, taking some small comfort in the other's presence. Standing like sentinels, Sivino realized that staying together was quite possibly the only thing that prevented each of them from falling apart.

Torla turned to Lomin, and watched him with the saddest eyes Sivino had ever seen. As, one after another, the company sat to rest, she walked toward the old man, and stopped when she reached his side. They stood arm to arm, facing opposite directions, each looking at a different sky. The first drops of rain began to fall.

"South?" she asked simply.

He rested his chin upon his staff. Though they spoke low, all could hear the conversation in the heavy silence of twilight.

"I understand your hesitation, Torla."

"Do you, Lomin?" she asked, not unkindly. "Do you?" She stood her bow on the ground before her, and folded her hands at its tip. "Kolle always told me that I should trust my instincts. He said that it was the deepest, keenest part of a person, and rarely led one astray. Of course, his instinct led him south, and look how that turned out. Mine tells me to run, to take Kef and just go back home and find my family."

Lomin nodded. "There is a part of me that wants nothing more than to do the same."

Torla looked at her bow, and picked at a splinter of wood on its edge. "I've always been the first to look for adventure. You know that. I think I get that from Kolle. Journeys to new places, different experiences, the thrill of uncertainty." She paused. "But not like this."

Lomin placed a hand over hers. At his touch, tears began to spill down her face. She cried silently. Of the group behind her, only Sivino noticed. She wiped her cheeks. "I just miss him so much."

"I know you do," Lomin said. He put an arm around her shoulder, and she rested her head on his chest. She took a breath to compose herself, and then looked at him.

"My instinct tells me to run." She lowered her voice, so none but the ragged man could hear. "But my heart is telling me to follow Sivino." They both looked toward the group. The boys were exhausted. Drip busied himself with fixing the strap of Sivino's fishing sack, which he'd pulled from the boy's shoulder with a mutter. "Kef has told me he'll follow me wherever I go, and I've got to take that into account," Torla continued. "I don't trust the faer-ae. Not yet. But, I believe her when she says that Sivino has an important role to play in this."

Lomin nodded. "Trust should never be given lightly. I would hope that you trust me, Torla, and know that I'd never allow any of you to venture down a dangerous road unless I thought it was absolutely the right thing to do. Or the only option. I've said before that the decision is yours to make. Sivino will go where Niamh guides him, I believe. Where you go, essentially, is up to you. You know all too well what my hope is."

She wiped any residue of tears from her face as she spoke. "I don't understand what's to happen, and that makes me uncomfortable. But whatever happens, we'll face it together." She allowed herself a wry grin. "I've always wanted to see the coastal capital."

She walked over to the group. "Have a quick bite and

catch your breath," she said. "The road south is not likely to be any easier."

"South?" Ston asked, his eyes narrow. "You sure about that, Tor?"

"No. But the faerae seems pretty certain that Sivino needs to get there." She looked at Sivino. "Let's be clear. It's not the faerae that I'm following. It's you." She gave his head a shove that was only partly playful. "Don't disappoint me."

They were gathering their belongings to set out once more when Drip's head twisted to the north. An instant later he was on his feet, snarling.

Three riders stood at the edge of the forest.

As the two groups regarded each other, the rain began to fall in earnest.

None moved. None spoke. Sivino saw the sword and longknife that hung upon the side of each rider. Bows hung on their backs. He noted that underneath their heavy cloaks, the riders were dressed in the burgundy garb of the Ryndarra. The leather and mail they wore appeared well made. Upon seeing this, he relaxed slightly. However, he thought, it was easy for anyone to steal the garb of a dead enemy in order to deceive.

The closest of the trio, a tall man with broad shoulders, nudged his horse forward and indicated that the other two follow. When he pulled back his hood, bright eyes shone out beneath a shock of long brown hair, lightly streaked with grey. He had a face used to conflict, Sivino thought. Thin scars traced across the left side of his face like tributaries, crossing the bridge of his nose before fading into his right cheek. Aside from the scars, he had quite a pleasant face. His eyes smiled with his lips, crows feet deepening as they did so. It was a smile that was likely meant to disarm the group and assure them he posed no threat. *There is much to be read in a face*, Dels had always told him. *Each movement of the mouth, the eye, is the turning of a page, and should be read carefully.*

"Where do you lead the young ones?" said the man as he dismounted. The voice was deep and rough, though not unkind.

"You'll forgive me," Lomin began, raising his voice to be heard over the rain. "But perhaps an introduction is a more appropriate way to begin our discourse." He tried to speak cordially, not wanting to offend the other.

"You are right to be cautious, friend." As he spoke, the other riders removed their hoods as well. Both were men, and while not as large as their apparent leader, they appeared to have been equally exposed to hard conflict. The big man extended his hand to Lomin. "The name is Ennis. Ennis Tinod'atu." Lomin accepted his hand, hesitating, as if the name were somewhat familiar.

"My name is Lomin."

Ennis Tinod'atu smiled knowingly as he shook Lomin's hand. "Lomin Lailoken, no?"

Lomin frowned, and looked from Tinod'atu to the others.

"Be at ease, Master Lailoken. We are friends, you may be certain. We've been expecting – hoping to find you for some time now. We were told that we'd find you upon this path, though we did not expect you so soon."

"Our journey was hastened by the foul beasts that

snapped at our heels between meals and the occasional break to water the bushes." Kef stood as tall as he possibly could.

Ennis smiled. He turned to the forest then, and made a beckoning gesture. From the trees, three more riders came forth. Despite the assurances of Ennis, the group tensed visibly, and Drip moved closer to the young ones.

The riders of the approaching group seemed almost protective of the one between them, upon whose shoulder perched a sleek peregrine falcon. As they approached, they too pulled back their hoods, exposing themselves to the elements as well as to those that regarded them cautiously. Sivino's eyes were drawn to the middle rider, whose thick dark hair fell in waves about her shoulders. She was looking at her falcon, which was making an ordeal of having to readjust itself around her hood, and whispered to it with a smile. Sivino was taken in entirely by that smile. The rider then moved ahead of the others, who branched out to each side. They had all, Sivino noticed, formed a rough circle around the woman, who dismounted gracefully in front of the group.

To Sivino's side, Lomin cursed aloud as he was struck with the sudden realization. No sooner had he done so than his hand flew to his mouth, his cheeks flushing. "Please, forgive my language, Highness. It's... just the shock... I was–"

"Highness?" Ston spun toward Lomin, his eyes wide with confusion.

"Lomin?" Kef continued to stare at the woman before him, whose beauty suddenly seemed to glow all the brighter. "Is that...?"

The Queen of Embarria stepped closer, and extended her hand to Kef. "Inlonia Talchol," she smiled. She spoke in a voice that was as smooth as it was regal. "I'm honoured to finally meet each of you.

"Niamh said you'd be along."

After shaking Kef's hand, she turned to the others, and one by one the introductions and handshakes were exchanged. Ston stood awkwardly before the queen, choking a little as he spoke his name. Her smile widened at this as she squeezed his hand and turned to Torla. The young Egimian stood the same height as Inlonia, and Sivino was struck by the similarities between the two. Torla, beautiful and confident, stepped toward Inlonia rather than waiting to be approached. She smiled and bowed her head slightly as she spoke her name. "A strong name," Sivino heard Inlonia whisper to the girl. A hint of red rose to Torla's cheek, and she turned quickly toward Tonnis, placing a hand on his shoulder.

"This is Tonnis," Torla said as the Levebaran slowly moved forward. Inlonia moved toward him, and extended her slender hand. Tonnis accepted it, though his head remained bowed, his eyes upon the ground. Gently, Inlonia placed a hand below Tonnis' chin, and slowly raised his gaze to her own. It was not until his eyes found her face that she spoke.

"Tonnis Fernika... You've suffered much." The sadness in her voice further deepened the silence of the group. "Niamh informed me of what befell your village. Your people." She corrected herself in an instant. *"Our* people. Know that my support will be yours." She spoke slowly, clearly, so that he could read every word that her lips formed. Yet, it was the tear on the queen's cheek that communicated most truly. He squeezed his lips tight, trying to maintain his composure as he nodded, but the tears spilled down his face. The queen placed her hands on his face, and with her thumbs, pushed his tears away. "The healing will be hard," she said, "but I see strength in you. And I see the love of your friends." She wiped a final tear from his face, and smiled. "When the foolishness of this war is over, know that I will be there as we rebuild every corner of this realm."

She turned, and stood before Sivino. It happened so quickly, he was a little startled. She looked at him, smiling expectantly. "Sivino Spallic," he whispered. She seemed to linger just a moment longer as she gripped Sivino's hand, the look in her eye changing ever so slightly as she heard his name. "Sivino," she repeated. There was a knowing in her voice, as though she was privy to information that she chose to keep hidden, a knowledge that escaped for the briefest instant before being locked away again by the blink of her eye. She nodded, and smiled softly.

And then, she turned to Drip.

The trenoc had been watching the introductions from the side, observing the ritual with little more than an occasional sideways glance. It was common knowledge that interactions between trenocs and rulers had never existed. In generations past, the trenocs had forged their own path in the land, and the rulers had stood by indifferently. As the introductions were being made, Sivino had noted how Drip had moved slowly to the side, his eyes alternating between the shaking hands and the puddles which formed around the group. When Inlonia turned to the trenoc, Sivino had expected her to give nothing more than a quick glance before she turned her attention to the matters at hand.

"Master Trenoc?"

The words hung in the silence.

Drip's head tilted, his brow low in confusion. He truly had no idea how he should respond.

Inlonia Talchol extended her right hand, palm upward. Drip stared at her hand for long moments; a hand of calluses and small scars that marked a history of less-than-regal behaviour. Sivino realized that this may be a ruler unlike any that had ever overseen the realm of Embarria. Drip looked up at her, and seeing her raised eyebrows and restrained smile, must have realized with a hint of embarrassment that he was meant to take this hand. Slowly, he brought up his own, and it was grasped in the firm grip of the queen.

Words failed him.

"Highness, this is the trenoc Drip," Lomin spoke after a few moments. Sivino could hear the emotion in his voice. It was an emotion that Sivino could not readily identify, though *pride* came to the forefront of his mind.

Inlonia turned then to her companions. They formed a protective crescent around her, each with their hands joined before them.

"Ennis Tinod'atu you have met. Ennis is a former Captain of the Ryndarra, and now serves as one of my lead guards, as well as my advisor." The big man smiled at them warmly as he stepped forward and bowed with a flat left hand placed on his sword hilt. "My other lead,"

Inlonia continued, "is Gilsanna Sliccol. Gil has long been a trusted friend and a voice of reason when I most desperately need it. But don't let her timid appearance fool you. I've seen her impale a jack-hare from thirty paces with that knife she holds so dear." Gilsanna looked down quickly, not realizing that she'd been rubbing the hilt of her long-knife throughout the introduction. She smiled, somewhat defiantly, and joined her hands behind her back.

"Beside him are Raid Smillo, Hargen Fint, and Tregg Denstead." She gestured with her hand as she spoke each name aloud. "Valiant Embarrians, skilled fighters, dear friends." Each nodded briefly, and repeated the action of Ennis.

"And this," Inlonia said as she gestured toward a nearby branch, "is Wyncor." At the sound of his name the graceful bird swooped down to land upon Inlonia's extended hand. The peregrine opened its curved beak slightly, as if to speak, and adjusted himself on Inlonia's wrist. The black feathers of his head ran down to blend into his pointed wings, making the top half of his body seem almost invisible if not for the piercing eyes that scanned the group, one by one. "He is reliable, strong and ensures that the path ahead is free of danger." Her face darkened. "It likely won't stay so safe. I met with Niamh yesterday. She told us that the Nylacci continued to make their way throughout the realm. Yet, it seems that there is now some organization to their movement. They're travelling in groups of thirty to forty, and are headed south. According to Niamh, the beasts are converging in Isror, just outside of Iskall. The number of Nylacci that have amassed is staggering. The forces of Rentorria, even combined with our Embarrian fighters, will be hard pressed to hold back this force when it combines with the soldiers of Isror." She shook her head then, her face stern as she seemed to inwardly chastise herself. "You should remind me of my manners, Ennis." The big man raised an eyebrow as the queen continued. "Here I am speaking of war and doom while our friends quietly soak up the rain." She gestured toward the forest. "Our camp is near. Come, let us find some shelter before we speak further."

The camp was clean and organized, but to Sivino's eye, entirely unbefitting a queen. An arrangement of tarps kept a modest portion of the clearing dry, and a small fire pit had been built to one side. Large rucksacks stood beside a line of oak trees, to which were tethered half a dozen horses.

Sivino gave Inlonia a questioning look.

"Niamh," said the queen. "She arranged for our meeting, and knew that the journey south would be slow and arduous for you on foot. She found the horses at a farmstead several leagues away. She found a family as well." Her eyes lowered. "They'll have no more need of horses."

Lomin sighed, and shook his head. "So much unnecessary death."

Ennis stepped through the group with an armful of kindling, and set to lighting a fire. "And more to come, if Idach is not stopped."

"Will he be stopped?" Kef asked quietly.

Inlonia looked to the companions, struggling with an answer. She clasped her hands atop her head, looking beyond the company to the distant southern hills. "I believe he will," she said. She turned to the Egimians and Tonnis.

"We must all believe this. We must keep hope."

Sivino watched Ennis construct a small pyramid of split wood and placed strips of birch bark within. Then he turned to Inlonia. "I once heard a wise man speak of hope. He said it's the most gentle name for fear, but it matters not what we call it, as long as it keeps us moving forward."

Inlonia nodded. "He sounds wise indeed."

Sivino smiled gently. "He's alright, for an old wolf."

Lomin muttered a *hmph*, and moved deeper beneath the tarp.

"Our plan," Inlonia continued, "is to assess how things progress in the south. I want Doran Dunarrk and the Rentorrians to know that they have our support. I want to see for myself how this war fares." She paused, and glanced at her guard. "If things are dire, we may need to send word for more Ryndarra to join us."

"How many remain north?" Ston asked.

"Enough to tip the scale several degrees, I imagine. While I may deplete the defenders of Embarria, I must leave enough to prevent the realm from falling into chaos. War does not stay the criminals. Gangs in Levebule need to be controlled. I cannot have the Ryndarra abandon our people entirely." Inlonia sighed, and moved to pass Ennis more kindling to add to the fire which was slowly catching. "Perhaps if I took all the Ryndarra south, it would be enough to win this war. But if I took that gamble and failed, I would leave my people defenceless as the Isrorians moved north across the realm." Inlonia coughed and rubbed her eyes, which burned from the rising smoke. She stepped away from the fire, and stood with the group "These options have been debated for some time. We could come to no resolution, so I decided to come south, and get a better sense of the appropriate path." Tregg moved among the group, distributing dried meat and water skins which all accepted gratefully.

"In the meantime," Inlonia continued, "I've sent diplomats to Ashira. I'm hoping that they can convince the Ashirans that this war could potentially spread beyond the Three Realms. I did the same with the Jhorans."

To the side, Drip spat loudly. Inlonia nodded.

"I understand," she said to the trenoc. "They are a different breed. As greedy as the Isrorians, and even more arrogant. Likely, it would take a sizable amount of Embarrian silver to convince the easterners to cross through the Jhoran Pass and lend assistance. The same could likely be true of the Ashirans." Her teeth appeared to grit as she considered the realms beyond the mountains. "But I'll do what I must. The realm will be defended. If I have to personally cast a valley full of silver drops, I'll see Embarria defended. I'll buy, beg and barter for my remaining years, if I must." She wiped her eyes again, but this time, Sivino did not believe the smoke was to blame.

Lomin moved to the queen's side. "You do us all proud, Highness. Let us hope that the battles end in the south."

Inlonia laid a gentle hand on Lomin's arm. She smiled as she spoke. "I once heard a wise man speak of hope."

Lomin smiled through pursed lips and narrow eyes. The young ones laughed softly, and Ston's chuckle turned slowly into a yawn.

"Come," said Inlonia. "Let us eat a warm meal and find some sleep. Tomorrow, we enter the realms of the south."

32

THE TRADER'S REPORT

"For the love of the Goddess, *eat something.*"

Solstia Dunarrk sat beside her husband, watching as his evening meal went cold once more. He'd sat for half an hour, idly pushing the roasted pork around his plate as he stared down the length of the table, his conflicted thoughts fixed on war.

"What good is a king so weakened by hunger that he's not able to mount a horse?" she asked.

"Perhaps that's the problem," Doran replied as he dropped his fork on the plate. "Perhaps if I mounted a horse and got involved in this cursed fray, I'd feel some life return to me."

"It's not your place right now, Doran." Kellert Sentero let himself into the room, closing the door behind him. While his official title did not give him the right to speak in such a forthright manner to his king, the friendship they'd shared for the past forty years more than allowed such behaviour. The king looked up anxiously. He was on edge most of the time, but these days, he took on a panicked look every time Kellert unexpectedly sought his audience.

"News?" he asked quickly.

His friend nodded.

The king was on his feet. "Come." He beckoned Kellert to the door.

"Doran!" While Kellert was able to speak frankly to his leader, Solstia was not above barking an occasional order at the man she loved. "Sit down. Eat. If Kellert has news, he can share it here and now." She gestured to the room. "There's none here but the three of us. Do you need more privacy than this? Do you suspect me a spy?"

Doran looked at his wife. Under her anger was a love as solid as the rocks upon which Orshos Keep stood. While he was the ruler of the realm, and worked tirelessly to see that its future was secure and peaceful, Solstia was the queen of the people. While they toiled and sweat over policy and strategy, it was she that ensured that the crown was amongst the citizens. She was a presence in their daily life and, while she took no foolish chances, she descended the capital hill more often than any that had ever ruled from its high stone walls. She spoke with the people, shared with them. She lived their lives, as much as possible.

And they loved her for it.

He sighed, smiling for the first time in recent days, and kissed the top of her head. "Sorry, my flower." With that, he sat beside her once more.

"Actually," Kellert continued, "that is precisely the matter we need to discuss. Dyrro has returned."

Doran was back on his feet immediately. "When? Where is he?"

"They're bringing him here now. I just got word myself. He's ridden ceaselessly for many leagues, I'm told, eager to bring you word of his findings. "

"And the others?"

Kellert shook his head.

"Damnation." Doran circled the table, his hands on the back of his neck. "Dyrro," he said under his breath. "I knew the trader would come through."

In recent years, no one had moved goods like Staid Dyrro. He was renowned throughout Rentorria for the speed with which he travelled, and the quality of the goods he delivered. If a product did not meet his standards, it didn't go into his carts. While Rentorria and Embarria were his preferred destinations, he'd been known to venture into Isror from time to time. He knew his way around most cities, and was acutely aware of all that happened around him. His charisma, along with his courage and smooth tongue had quickly gotten him noticed by the upper ranks of the Rentorrian Guard. *Could sell stones to a Drale, that one*, a commander had quipped after Dyrro had left a particularly lengthy interview. Dyrro, thought by the man to be entirely out of earshot, had remarked over his shoulder as he left, *And get top coin too*. His work had also forced him to hone his skills as a swordsman, as traders were recognized in all regions as potentially lucrative targets. He was quick with a sword, and required his small crew to demonstrate no small amount of deftness with a blade.

After several long minutes, a knock came on the door.

Kellert opened it and a guard stepped in with the trader, both giving a slight bow to the king and his wife. Dyrro was hardly recognizable since Doran had last seen him. Taking no chances on his mission, he'd completely shaved his lengthy beard and dyed his hair from brown to black. He'd had both ears pierced with small silver loops, as was common in Isror. Though he was now garbed in unremarkable brown pants and a tan-coloured shirt, while travelling east he and his companions had worn the plain black tunic that Idach had insisted upon in his realm. Looking fully the part of common Isrorians, he and the others had made their way to Iskall, to see and learn all they could. Standing before Doran Dunarrk, the trader wished his companions were beside him now.

"My king," he greeted as Doran shook his hand. "It is good to lay eyes upon you again."

"And you doubly so, Staid Dyrro." He gestured toward a chair by the hearth. The guard departed, and Staid seated himself with a wince.

"Your travel has been difficult," Solstia noted.

"Yes, Highness. I wished to share my news as soon as possible." He took one slow breath and began. "Ronec has been taken. The defence was heroic, but with the number of soldiers that Idach threw at our walls, it was not possible to repel them. The reinforcements you sent engaged the Isrorians, but there were simply too many." He looked from Doran to Kellert. "The Guard was forced to retreat, taking with them any civilians they could. But the city was sacked. Our people move to Nahcin."

At this the queen stood slowly from her seat at the table, and moved to the window. Below, the moon lit the flowerbeds that had been so terribly neglected in the absence of skilled gardeners. *If a man can wield a hoe,* Doran had said, *he can learn to wield a sword.*

The king looked deep into the hearth, the flames flickering on his unmoving eyes. Ronec, a small city by most standards – perhaps six thousand citizens when times were good – now sat in Idach's greedy hands. Doran tried to push thoughts of his scattered, murdered people from his mind. There would be the long, sleepless hours of the night to brood on such dark thoughts. "What did you learn in Iskall?" he asked.

Staid's eyes fell shut. "Iskall," he whispered. As if reminded by the city's name, he put a hand to each earlobe and removed the rings that hung there. He tossed them into the hearth. "A city of intolerable pride. Men and women, flowing through the streets like a black river, singing the praises of a king who sheds blood in the name of the Goddess. They are murderers, though they sing their prayers out loud. Self-righteous bastards who will never–" He stopped suddenly, his face stricken. "Apologies for my foul mouth, Lady." The queen brushed it off with a wave, not turning from the window. "They are fools," Staid continued, "who will never see the greed of Idach, or if they do, will not care. They will never acknowledge the evil of their actions." Pausing, he collected himself for a moment, gathering his thoughts.

"Upon leaving Iskall, we travelled back to Ronec, where we found it overtaken. The Isrorians that remained were finishing the slaughter. With the Guard defeated, there was no one to defend the common–" He shook his head. "I later heard talk from the retreating soldiers of what had happened inside those walls; details I wouldn't repeat in front of my Lady." Doran looked toward his wife. One slender arm was folded over her breast. The other raised a hand to her mouth. "I knew that we needed to get around Ronec, and bring our news west." He grunted and shook his head. "Basha and Recker – by the Goddess, I'm sure they would have attempted to take the city back if I'd given the go-ahead." He paused, before continuing in a whisper. "Damnation. They were two fine people. Recker could have convinced his own mother he was an Isrorian. And Basha…" He smiled ruefully, and rubbed an earlobe where a little blood trickled. "Basha was masterful. She led us without error, through the outskirts, the market-places, and along the very steps of the palace. She took us places we'd never have found, and she likely could have taken us further, but we realized that we were well over-due. The knowledge we gained, the things we saw…" He paused, and Doran noticed the way his hand shook as he pushed his hair back from his face.

"Please," Kellert said to the spy. "Go on."

"We skirted the edges of Ronec, intent on getting to Nahcin as soon as possible. They needed to know." He looked up at the king. "Highness, you need to know." The light from the hearth was dim on his face as he lowered his voice to a whisper. *"Beasts,"* he said. "To the south of Iskall, we first heard of their presence. Though we saw none while in the city, there was much talk of a host of savages stationed in the southern plains. We heard talk of small bands of creatures roaming the countryside as well, though none penetrated the city walls. The beasts seemed to be popping up throughout Isror, even as far north as Embarria, we heard. At first, we thought the Isrorians were referring to the Kourg, those great bloody savages beyond the mountains. But this...this was something else entirely. In the Erratics, Highness, I witnessed them myself." At this point, Staid sat forward, and leaned his elbows heavily on his knees. Doran and Kellert shared an uneasy look as Solstia glanced over from her corner. "We'd found a regiment of the Guard near there a day prior, and travelled with them as they made for Nahcin. As we passed the Erratics, they fell upon us."

Staid Dyrro recounted the pertinent information of the battle. As he spoke of the blood and the bravery, he noted how Solstia's shoulders shook as she cried silently, still at the window. It was not until he spoke of the beasts and their unspeakable appetite that she turned and walked from the room. She rubbed Staid's arm quickly as she walked past him, not able to look upon his face. As the door thudded shut behind her, Doran stepped back and leaned against the solid oak table as if steadying himself. *"Damnation, Staid."*

Staid continued. "Within Iskall, there were hushed whispers of a leader of this host; some hooded warrior who is responsible for shepherding them around. He's said to possess weapons and power that even these beasts fall before immediately. I saw him myself in the Erratics, riding unharmed within their midst. What his purpose is, I cannot say. I know only that he seems to have allied himself with Idach Garron, and this, my lord, is ill news for us."

"We need to consider Nahcin," Doran looked at the fire, which had lost much of its strength throughout

Staid's tale. His regal face could not hide the panic that lurked beneath the surface. "With Ronec taken, Nahcin will be next. How many Isrorians march on the city at present, Dyrro."

"Three thousand, at least. More are to be sent from Iskall to join them. Nahcin is larger than Ronec. Idach will send a considerable force to ensure that it falls."

"We'll have to send what we can to Nahcin, immediately."

"I stopped at Nahcin, briefly, on my way," Dyrro informed the pair. "I told the commanders what I knew, and what was coming." He paused. "They'll be expecting reinforcements."

Doran nodded, silently working the math. Approximately two thousand soldiers stood at Nahcin. Granted, when the time came, every able bodied man and woman who remained would become such. With Idach's force headed its way, the king could not help but allow the dreadful shadow of doubt to enter his heart.

He moved to the window, placing his hands on the sill where his wife had just stood. His shoulders rose as he breathed the evening air. When he turned back to the men, he seemed changed. Gone was the anxious unease that had hung upon his face; a disquiet caused by tremendous uncertainty. It was replaced by a look of determination.

"Come," he said, as he sped by the men. "Those murderous wretches have advanced far enough. When the reinforcements move out tomorrow, I intend to be with them."

33

DAMN AND BLASTED FAIRIES

Cehron Cen Kohr lay in the cool grass, a young fox brushing against his outstretched legs.

He had lingered in this part of Elysium for some time now. How long, he could not recall. Days, weeks…it was all the same. Time was irrelevant here. He thought of the places he'd been, the worlds he'd entered where time itself dictated people's actions, movements, and sleep. He'd seen fools who actually wore time tellers on their wrists. Some things happened sooner, and some later. That was the true way of things. In the world of the Fae, this was a beautifully slow process.

And so he lay by the river. He'd been there since sunrise of the previous morning. In that time, various manner of beasts had roamed by, lingering, enjoying his presence. It was not his nature to remain in one particular area for long. Yet in present days, there was a purpose, a particular goal that was to be realized, and the loss of a day, in all the days given him, was a small price to pay indeed.

When he heard the young man approach, he sat up slowly, casually, and gestured for the fox to move along. The fox, like most animals who found themselves in his presence, was hesitant to do so.

"Be off, Vulpes," he mumbled lowly as he climbed to his feet. "I shall see you again soon."

He stepped from the path into the Silver Wood. The early sun had not yet penetrated far, and he walked in the cool shade of the birch. Within moments, he was walking next to the young man he'd heard approach, separated only by a few scattered trees and thoughts.

Oisin MacComhal, oblivious to the Cernunnos, sang quietly.

> *It was on a fine summer's morning*
> *The birds sweetly tune on each bough*
> *And as I walked out for my pleasure*
> *I saw a maid milking a cow*
>
> *Her voice so enchanting, melodious*
> *Left me quite unable to go*
> *My heart, it was loaded with sorrow*
> *For the pretty maid milking her cow.*

It was a sound that sickened Cehron Cen Kohr. Sharp and disastrously out of tune to the keen ear of the faerae, he cringed as he listened to the man mutter his melancholy song. How was it that Niamh could keep the company of this man? So rough and crass, so base and *unfae*. He sighed and continued to watch as Oisin strolled along. The young man looked all around him, taking in the sights and sounds of the morning, but did not notice the faerae who walked so silently but ten paces away, blending with the colour and the gentle movement of the forest. Cehron watched him leisurely, noting Oisin's uneven gait and the scars on his cheek. His disgust grew as he watched the man, yet still, there was a great sense of joy and anticipation. He smiled through his disgust, for there was one thing about this man that caused an excitement to grow in the heart of Cehron Cen Kohr.

Oisin was alone.

The Cernunnos moved further up the path, and lay in wait.

Oisin was almost upon the faerae before he heard him speak.

"You seem to have much on your mind, friend."

The young man's hand twitched with the instinct to unsheathe his sword, which still hung upon his side.

Cehron Cen Kohr sat beside a wide maple, plucking the petals from a bright yellow flower that grew beside him. A small, fresh petal grew gently in the place of every one that he removed. He smiled pleasantly as he considered the blossom. "So easily replaced," he whispered. "So easily replaced." He raised his eyes to Oisin, and with a small grunt, he climbed to his feet.

He walked over to the young man, and held out his hand. "The name is Cehron," he said cordially. He shook Oisin's hand, cringing imperceptibly as the man took it. The scent of Niamh was still on the man's skin.

A calm hatred roiled within the faerae, unseen by the man before him. Cehron was, even by Fae standards, masterful in the art of manipulation. Years of practicing this art – sometimes out of necessity, sometimes for the sheer enjoyment – had honed these skills. It would be impossible for Oisin to see that hatred behind his charming smile. The fool was blinded by love.

Love, thought Cehron. For just an instant, his hand grew tighter around that of Oisin. He thought with pleasure about how easily he could crush it, and how easily he could crush the heart that beat so joyously in the fool's chest. His own heart had once beat with the same vitality. Yes, he was capable of love as well – complicated as it might be. Over many years, Cehron Cen Kohr had been content to let it grow and intensify, let it mature fully before acting upon it. He'd guarded the secret possessively, waiting for the opportune time to make his intentions known.

But he'd waited too long. She'd fallen for the warrior.

And now, he thought with no small sense of satisfaction, it was the warrior's turn to fall. Niamh was a fool to involve herself with the human, and Cehron was determined to set things right. Love might be beyond the control of any, but there were certain things over which the faerae could hold sway.

Oisin was one of them.

"I couldn't help but notice how that lovely song faded so quickly, to be replaced by a most melancholy countenance." The faerae's face was a picture of concern.

"I was thinking–" Oisin replied. He was a little taken aback by the approach of the faerae. In all the time he'd been in Elysium he had never seen a faerae so forthcoming, so friendly.

"You are wary of me, I know," Cehron said, as if reading his mind. "I should guess that in all the time you've spent in our fair land, you've seldom been approached by one of our kind."

"Never."

"It's not surprising. In this world, there are few indeed that would openly welcome an outsider, even one with a past as storied as yourself, Oisin"

Oisin's head jerked at the mention of his name, his eyes narrow.

Cehron saw the concern, and waved it aside with a chuckle. "Though the realms of Elysium are vast, they do not stretch so far that the name of a humanfolk, living with the daughter of Obaeron, would not be common knowledge to many. A most lovely faerae, Niamh. And daughter to the King. You have done quite well for yourself, young Oisin. You are known even in the distant realm of Nalh'ia, where I first heard your name spoken. Curious creature that I am, I couldn't help but ask a few questions of those who spoke of you. I know of your past life, and your many accomplishments on the field of battle. You might say you're now something of a legend in these realms." He spoke with a tone of admiration as the concern on Oisin's face dripped away slowly. "I know too of your homeland."

The smile that had begun to grow on Oisin's face vanished, and a look of sadness filled his eyes. *There it is,* thought Cehron. *Yes, you love her, but she didn't get all those roots when she plucked you from your home, did she?*

"What do you know of my homeland?" Oisin stepped forward, interested.

"I know of many lands, in many worlds, including yours. I've always marvelled at its beauty, its diversity and character. And the people. Such wonderful people." Cehron looked skyward as an eagle soared above them, its cry one of longing. "You must miss them."

"I do."

"Has Niamh never brought you back, even for a short time?"

"She said that circumstances wouldn't allow it, that I was meant for this world, destined to live here." He hesitated. "She said something about an illness that would come over me if I were to return, a dark sickness, or some such thing."

The Cernunnos' eyes widened in shock, and he laughed a laugh filled with disbelief as he approached the other and laid a hand on his shoulder. "Ah, she's protective, that one. Listen lad, anything is possible in this magical land of *Tir Na N'Og*." His smile faltered then, and was replaced by a look of genuine concern and confusion. "Niamh, I am sure, must have her reasons for telling you this, but—" He shook his head, as if he struggled to understand Niamh's motives.

He watched Oisin frown slightly as he considered this. Likely, Niamh had shared with him that their race was one incapable of lies. There was mischief and manipulation, but the telling of a lie, a direct lie, was not possible.

"No," Oisin said immediately, as much to himself as to the faerae. "She could not have lied. She told me that if my feet were ever to touch the ground of my homeland, I would meet with certain death. Is this not true, Cehron?"

Damning boy! The faerae was careful not to let his frustration show. He needed to keep his wits about him and choose his words very, very carefully. He was so close. The scales could be tipped. He just needed to add a few grains of sand; a dusting of charm and conviction to the weight of his argument.

"Listen to me well, and know that what I speak is, *must* be, truth. There are ways – easy ways – to avoid such an unfortunate end." He let joy fill his eyes, and though it was the joy of deceit, Oisin could not help but feel that the creature had his best interest at heart. "If you ride upon the back of an Elysian steed, if you *remain* upon its back and keep your feet from the ground, then you may race the winds of your world once again.

"If you ride a creature of Fae, you will remain unaffected. Upon its back, no harm will befall you. And let me tell you: you've never experienced the speed and power of an Elysian steed."

Oisin could not help himself. He beamed at the thought, so long had it been since he'd ridden. Then, a thought struck him and he turned to the faerae, his face grave. "I have no such horse."

Cehron smiled, and turning to the forest gave a sharp whistle. It was answered by a whinny, eager and immediate. From the trees, a grey horse walked. Flecks of black ran through his shiny grey coat, and a mane of brilliant white fell from the animal's poll.

"This is Énbar. A magnificent animal. There are quicker ways to travel, but few are as pleasant." He saw the delight that filled Oisin's eyes, and patted him upon the shoulder. "Fortune, it seems, has smiled on you this day, young friend." He turned Oisin around to face him then, and spoke with a little more urgency. "It was fortunate that you happened upon us as we rested, but unfortunately, I have many leagues left to cross on my journey. If you wish to borrow Énbar, if you wish me to shift you to your homeland, then I have only two requests. Firstly, you must give her *back* to me when we return to Elysium, as hard as that might be."

Oisin laughed softly, stroking the animal's mane.

"And the second?" he asked.

"We must leave right away."

Oisin turned quickly to the faerae. "But I must tell Niamh." Cehron could see the desperation in the man's face. "I must. She'll worry, and—" But Cehron was shaking his head.

"I guarantee you will not see a look of disapproval in Niamh's eyes. She will understand your longing to visit your native land, just this once. In truth, I am surprised she has never made an offer such as mine. Now, what will it be? Time is fleeting."

After several moments Cehron sighed, then smiled sadly as he turned to Énbar, appearing to leave. "Unfortunate that you were not able to avail yourself of the opportunity. It will likely be your last—"

"I am ready," Oisin said quickly. "Please, I am ready." He rushed to the side of the faerae steed, his smile deepening as the horse turned its great head to appraise the young man.

"I've no doubt you are," Cehron said quietly.

As he mounted, the feel of the steed's back and the strength of the animal dispelled any doubt, and he looked expectantly at Cehron. "Let us not waste another moment," the faerae said, and taking the reins of the big animal, he led them to the rippling waters of the river.

It had felt like ages had passed since Oisin had last been shifted through the faerae waters that connected the worlds. He'd swum, bathed and drank from the River Faer on many occasions, but as they approached the water that day, it appeared different to him. Not exactly cold but...less warm. It did little to lessen his enthusiasm as they splashed into the magical river. Cehron forged ahead quickly, his eagerness rivalling Oisin's.

When they reached a depth that engulfed Cehron's chest, the faerae turned and looked up at the young man atop the steed. "Off we go," he said quietly and he and the great animal both slackened their legs and fell beneath the surface. Because he was atop the horse, Oisin's head did not immediately submerge, and below the water's surface, he could see what appeared to be a colourful whirlpool spinning below the faerae. It approached with incredible speed from an impossible depth. As it reached Cehron and Énbar, Oisin was jolted by the powerful force as it pulled all three onto the Path.

Again, he marvelled at the sensation of the Path. He could see Cehron, holding the horse's reins firm and the animal's beautiful mane spread about as if blown by a vibrant wind. He was weightless for a moment, and then the tremendous energy of the Path pulled him with such strength that, over his shoulder, he saw a blurred image of himself, stretched and fading, behind him.

And then they emerged. Oisin had feared for a moment that the Path might throw him from the back of Énbar as they arrived in his homeland; however, the steed stepped from the small lake tall and sure-footed, the water beginning to dry almost instantly in the heat of the sun. As they walked from the water, the faerae waited waist-deep in the lake.

"Time is a little different in your world. Ride through the afternoon, if you wish. Niamh will not miss you. A day spent here will not amount to more than moments in Elysium." He smiled, and inclined his head toward the forest. "Safe journey, my friend."

"Thank you," said Oisin. He turned Énbar and with a shout they broke into a gallop, racing through the trees, toward the sun and distant rolling fields.

"The pleasure is all mine," Cehron muttered as they disappeared from sight. A twisted smile grew on his face, and he stepped from the water and entered the forest. "All mine."

Oisin laughed as he rode.

He could not recall when last he'd ridden a horse. And never had he ridden one such as this. It was a horse that possessed such power and grandeur that he felt almost giddy. It felt as if he was floating, a similar sensation to shifting through the Path, though rather than colour and light, he was surrounded by tall grass and memory.

As they ran, Oisin remembered his days fighting on these fields. He remembered the weight of the sword in his hand, the screaming of horses and men, and the setting sun that made even the blood on the fallen seem beautiful. He thought of the Fenian warriors and wondered how they fared in his absence. He thought of his father and his mother.

He looked around, trying to orient himself. Little looked as he remembered it. There seemed to be more trees than in the days of his youth. He passed several cottages that were in a horrible state of disrepair, the gardens untended and wild. He tried not to let these thoughts upset him, but they resurfaced nonetheless. A return home, he thought, might bring more heartache to his family than joy. He'd wished to tell them that he was well, that they needn't worry, but to go to them only to leave again would possibly renew the pain and sorrow they'd felt when he'd left so long ago.

"I meant to return." And though it was lost in the air that rushed past his face, he whispered again. "I meant to return."

He was nearly atop the old man before he saw him.

The hunched figure, his clothing the colour of dust, blended almost seamlessly with the landscape. He pulled a cart containing a meagre load of potatoes. As the cart clattered along the rough path, potatoes bounced over its low side rails, but the man seemed not to notice. Oisin pulled on Énbar's reins and slowed the steed beside the startled old-timer.

"Aye, good day there! Good day!" The old man paused as he looked at Énbar. "Well, that's a magnificent beast y'ave there, young one!"

"He is that indeed. I'm sorry to have frightened you, friend."

"Bah, never ye mind. 'Tis grand to see someone on this lonely path. Many a day passes that I – my word, boy, but that *is* a fine animal. Wherever did ye come across such a horse?"

"Borrowed from a friend." He bent low on Énbar's back, and extended a hand to the man. "Oisin."

The old fellow paused as he extended his hand, a confused look crossing his face. Then he took Oisin's hand, and shook it. His mouth contained more gaps than teeth; the ones which remained were dark and crooked.

"*Oisin?* A real warrior, eh?"

Oisin smiled, and shook his head. "That was a distant past, my friend."

"Indeed. A distant past. Me name is Toby."

"A pleasure." He scanned the fringes of the field. "I'm struggling with my bearings, Toby. I wonder, could you point me in the direction of the MacComhal homestead?"

Toby looked up at him, a bushy eyebrow raised. After a long moment he spoke. "But ye must know, certainly: the MacComhals are no more."

Oisin's head was instantly light. *Finn.* Had he finally succumbed to some foe in battle? He could scarcely believe it. And his mother Sabd? What force under heaven could have brought about her end? His family, dead while he wandered grassy meadows in a far off world! Guilt threatened to overtake even his grief, and he struggled to catch his lost breath.

"What happened? Finn and Sabd MacComhal!" He resisted the urge to reach down and grab the man by his tattered garb. "The Fenian warriors? What happened to them, old man?"

"Gone. All are gone," Toby replied with a casual wave of his hand.

"How?" he pressed. "The warriors! Finn? How were

they overcome?"

"Same way we're all overcome," Toby replied. He knelt beside the cart, and gently shook one of the wheel spokes that appeared to have come loose. "The cold fingers of time, young one. They rise from the ground and pull us all in eventually." He gave a little chuckle as he used the cart's rail to pull himself up with a grunt. "As to the details, I'm afraid they're lost on me. 'Twas over a hundred years ago, lad. I scarcely recall me breakfast this morning."

Oisin's world spun. *No! This makes no sense! How could this* – and then the face, the smile, flashed to the forefront of his mind. *Cehron.* The faerae must have known that this world would have changed. This was why Niamh had never made the offer to return. She'd known that his home would not be as he remembered it. She'd known the pain it would have caused, and the risk associated. He looked at the ground, knowing that he could never again set foot upon this land. What possible motive could Cen Kohr have for leading him on such a journey? As he opened his eyes, he saw Toby meandering back and forth on the path behind the rickety cart, hunched over as he picked up the fallen potatoes.

"Agh! Dirty rascals! Pluckin' potatoes from me cart. They always said this path was cursed! And here be I, too much a fool to find another route. 'Never use the old paths of the fairies,' they say. Damn and blasted fairies!"

With a scream from Énbar, Oisin swung the horse around and tore back across the grassy field, leaving the confused old man to pick up his potatoes.

He found the faerae as he had hours before, beneath a tree. A long blade of grass extended from his mouth as he observed the sky. With narrow eyes and an ever present smile, Cehron sat up as Oisin approached.

"You knew!" Oisin's gritted teeth were bared, and he was once more a Fenian warrior. The last of them. "You put me through this misery. You knew they'd be dead, and still you let me go. Why?"

The faerae inclined his head, considering what he was about to say. "Some would call it retribution."

"Retribution? What have I *ever* done to you?"

The faerae rose slowly. "I've watched you. You live and love in the land of Fae as if it were your own. You hold the body of a faerae as if she were your own! The time came for me to show you what happens when we walk the paths of a world in which we don't belong." He looked at Oisin, not as a thorn in his side, but as a winding bramble that wound its way around his heart. A bramble that needed to be ripped free.

"Niamh?"

The Cernunnos smiled. Oisin shivered. "Niamh," the faerae whispered.

For long moments they looked at each other. The faerae did not move. His long hair swayed slightly, as if the breeze were trying to cover the horrible eyes that bore into the doomed rider.

Oisin looked around, desperate for an escape. There was no way for him to open a Path to Elysium, and Niamh had no idea where he was. She would not be coming for him. He looked back at the Cernunnos. The faerae was revelling in the misery he'd caused; the hearts he'd broken, both his and Niamh's.

Cehron's face was stone as he spoke. "You've lost her, boy."

With a roar, Oisin threw his leg over the steed, unsheathing his sword as he landed on the ground. As he did so, a sharp, agonizing pain ripped its way up through both of his legs. *The ground!* He gasped, sucking in air that now burned his lungs. As he exhaled, it was as if his very soul sought escape, clawing and ripping its way up from the depths of his body to free itself through his gaping mouth. The sword fell from his hands, which began to tremble uncontrollably. His knees buckled and he fell. He reached out to the faerae, though it was not for assistance. The dying warrior sought only to grip his enemy once more before he succumbed to his fate. Cehron stepped back, shaking his head in sympathy, restraining the smile that threatened to overtake his mouth. Time ravaged Oisin. The young man looked down, and saw that he was young no more. His arms, which just this morning were lean and muscular, were now spotted, gaunt and wrinkling. His hair faded from black to grey to snowy white, a long wintry beard growing slowly, painfully upon his aching face.

The Path. Niamh. Oisin turned to the lake, but a few paces away. Perhaps he could escape if only he could reach it. With an effort that impressed even the contemptuous faerae, Oisin pulled himself slowly to the water's edge. The faerae allowed this, entertained by the man's dying efforts. With a final, mournful groan, he pulled himself up onto his elbows and looked with horror at the reflection the calm waters held.

As Oisin saw himself and accepted his life's ending, Cehron Cen Kohr approached him, bending low to scrutinize the destroyed human who lay at his feet. The last image Oisin MacComhal would see, in his world or any, was the reflected face of the faerae appearing above his shoulder, gazing up at him from the still waters.

"Oisin..." the faerae whispered, feigned concern dripping from his voice. "Oisin, my dear... *You've aged."*

34

HOPE SPRINGS ETERNAL

Sivino reined in his mare.

For two days, the company had been riding south under dark skies and relentless drizzle. The journey had been uncomfortable but uneventful, as Drip and alternating members of Inlonia's company continued to scout the area for danger. Only one group of Nylacci had been spotted; these by the trenoc from high atop the trees on the previous day. The beasts, perhaps fifteen in total, marched to the southeast away from the Embarrians. By the time Ennis found a high clearing from which he might see them, they'd disappeared into the trees.

Sivino eased himself from the saddle of his palomino and rubbed the soreness from his legs. While thankful that he didn't have to make the journey on foot, he was not used to such extended periods on the back of a horse. His clothing, like that of his companions, was soaked through. However, he didn't complain as he knew that his discomfort was minor compared to that of others.

Kef gripped the cantle of his saddle as he braced himself to dismount. Such was his pain that he didn't put up the slightest argument when Torla reached up to help ease him to the ground. His legs trembled as he stood beside the horse, holding its saddle until greater feeling returned to his muscles. The journey, first on foot and now on horseback, was taking its toll on his leg. With each passing day, the pained look on his face deepened and he seemed a dull image of his former self. Lomin did what he could for the boy, finding wild herbs and leaves that helped alleviate the pain. But their effect was minimal, and Kef bore his burden in aching silence.

As Torla and Tonnis tethered the horses, Sivino watched Inlonia and her group prepare a quick meal. As if feeling partly responsible for Kef's discomfort, the queen ensured that he was fed often and well. Yet his appetite, like his spirits, had faltered and he picked at his food mostly to stop the worried looks of his companions.

Sivino walked toward Ennis Tinod'atu. He took comfort in the man, in no small part because the tall advisor reminded him of his father.

"How do you fare, Sivi?" Ennis asked as he approached.

Sivino could not help but smile. Since Ennis had first heard Lomin speak the name, it was the only one he'd use to address the boy.

"I'm well," he replied. He looked across the field to the hills and beyond. "How far have we come?"

"Tersh lies half a day's ride west. We're making good time."

It amazed Sivino how familiar Ennis seemed to be

with the land. It was as though he possessed some inner compass; some means of knowing exactly where they were, and exactly what landmarks would be found over each hill. "I should love to visit the city, to see some old friends. I spent many of my younger years travelling these lands. Growing up in Rovil, I preferred to be anywhere but there." He smiled as he assembled the kindling. "Tregg should return soon."

Tregg, the queen's most skilled scout, had been sent to Tersh, an isolated inland city, the day prior, charged with bringing news to the city, purchasing necessary supplies and gaining what information might be had. Before the fire had grown to cooking strength, the scout was spotted cresting a hill.

"The city fares well," he said quietly as he reached them a few minutes later. "Lord Stathen accepted my warning with more indifference than I'd have liked. He informed me that he'd received your messages and has made some preparations. He said he's received reports of wild animals attacking livestock, and said that two of the residents of an outlying village had been killed recently." He removed his rucksack from his horse. "Commander Rolt was a little more receptive. He's overseeing the city defences, and sees the potential for conflict to come their way. I told him he was wise to think such, and that he'd have the queen's thanks for taking every precaution."

Inlonia nodded. "He'll have my thanks, Tregg, as do you."

The scout's head bowed slightly, and he began to unpack the supplies as the queen returned to the fire.

Drip was nowhere to be seen, but the others were

nearby, resting in the grass at the edge of the field. Torla began removing food from her satchel, keeping a close eye on her sibling.

"Master Spallic," Kef noted with a forced smile as Sivino approached. "Do my eyes deceive, or are you moving about on an invisible horse?" Smiles came to the faces of the others and Sivino glanced down, realizing that he did indeed walk with a terribly bowed gait. He returned the smile, colour rising in his cheeks. "Don't be embarrassed," Kef continued, grunting as he adjusted his crotch unselfconsciously. "We'll all be riding such ghostly steeds for a time."

"My walk is far less noble, Kef, and far too unsteady. I look to be atop the shoulders of an unimpressed trenoc." So tiresome were the past days that they sought any opportunity to joke; to feel happy, to feel normal.

They all laughed. Even Tonnis seemed to catch the meaning of the last words on Sivino's lips. Sivino however, saw Kef use the laugh to disguise his grimace of pain. The only one who failed to see the humour in Sivino's words was Drip who, unbeknownst to the others, had been watching from the branch of a nearby tree. He spat loudly upon hearing Sivino's joke and with a heavy grunt, he fell from the tree and stormed off into the forest.

"Ah, hellfire." Sivino sighed as he watched the trenoc stalk away. "Drip, hold on." As he began to follow the furry creature into the woods, he looked back over his shoulder. "Give me a moment," he said. "And Ston, you glutton, save some of that bread for me."

Ston, who'd been shoving a generous portion of the loaf into his mouth, nodded absently. "Certainly," he said through bulging cheeks, "but I warn you, it's as crusty as your heart." Crumbs fell from his mouth as he laughed.

Torla, watching Sivino race through the trees after the offended trenoc, gave Ston's head a playful shove. "Be thankful you have it, brute. And besides, it's soft inside."

"What? The bread? Or Sivi's heart?" Kef asked.

The smack Kef received was slightly less playful. He continued to smile regardless.

Running in the direction he'd last seen Drip, Sivino shouted to the trenoc. "Drip! Come on! I'm sorry. It was a joke; a bad one I'll admit." He knew the trenoc well enough to know that he'd likely taken to the trees, and would refuse to accept even the most genuine of apologies.

Sivino couldn't help but remember the first Nylac encounter. He stopped, and looked back in the direction of his company. They were easily within shouting distance, though this brought him little comfort. Standing still within the birch and amilliat, he recalled how the forest around his home had once given him a sense of comfort and security. Much like the river, it was the forest he went to when his mind was troubled and he needed a sense of peace. He now realized that since he'd left Egim, the forest no longer held this serenity. What it held now was fear.

He looked around quickly, telling himself that he'd wander no further than a few more paces. The sparseness of the trees placated him slightly, and he realized that he could almost discern the movement of his friends if he peered closely enough. Just a few more paces. He called to Drip again, and looked to the higher reaches of the trees. There was no sign of the trenoc.

He was about to give up when he heard what sounded like the trickle of a stream. Its sound was so soothing, so safe and familiar that he immediately moved toward it. For an instant, he considered whether he should return and ask someone to come with him, but he dismissed this thought as foolishment. Doing so would make him look cowardly, to be sure. As he squinted through the trees, he saw what appeared to be a clearing. Climbing a nearby rock, he tried to see more clearly. He looked back in the direction of his friends, then once more to the clearing. Shaking his head, he walked toward the open space.

It was in fact water that he'd heard. As he edged his way down a slope of loose earth and exposed roots, he found its source. A spring in the ground brought forth a small but steady stream of clear water. While springs were not unheard of in Embarria and her surrounding lands, they were far from common. Sivino's eyes followed the meagre flow, until, halfway down the decline, the flow increased. He strained to see where it led, and thought for a moment that he saw a small lake in the distance. *A valuable find*, he thought. *Tregg and Ennis were always in search of a decent water source.*

Kneeling by the spring, Sivino reached down and felt the cool flow. As he did so, the water that glided across and through his fingers seemed to change before his very eyes. No longer clear, the trickle seemed to take on the colours of its surroundings. At first, Sivino mistook the orange hue for discolouration caused by the soil, or some underground substance. Yet, the orange fluid remained perfectly transparent until the faint orange became yellow, and then the yellow green. On his hands and knees,

Sivino watched the transformation in confusion and wonder. As the green faded to blue, he suddenly noticed his thirst. His tongue scratched the rough roof of his mouth. The spring glowed. The light blue water sparkled, and he knew immediately that he would not be able to resist.

He looked around and realized that he'd forgotten both Drip and the potential dangers that might lurk behind any tree. The water washed away his worry. He looked down at the stream again with what Leath would have called the smile of a fool, and pulled a great gulp of the springwater to his mouth.

Words could not describe the feeling, for it was more feeling than taste that characterized the water. It was alive in his mouth, and as he swallowed, this life permeated his entire body, soaking tension from his muscles and his mind. He cupped another mouthful, greedily almost, then another. He drank until he could drink no more, and lay down on the leaf-strewn forest floor. He lay peacefully, thinking he'd rest a few minutes before returning. But the gentle sound of the spring was so soothing. It trickled upon his senses, mingling with the faint sound of bells; distant bells which beckoned with some unknown purpose. The smile still played on his lips as he closed his eyes, and a faint vision of his brother's face came to mind. It was a look of disapproval. Disappointment. It was a look to which Sivino had grown quite accustomed.

By the eerily musical waters of the stream, he fell asleep with this image in his mind. Even as the tall, silent creature picked him up and carried his limp body to the lake, even as the water enveloped him, he slept on.

35

QUESTION ME

Dels could hear the riders approaching.

Lues Torgo and the Harmino boys had set out an hour prior to scout the area between their current location and the East Bridge. While he assumed that it was the Egimians that were returning and not some other threat, Dels feared the news would not be good. They were riding too hard, he thought. They've seen something.

With Leath by his side, he rode ahead of the townsfolk to meet the returning men. He gave a quick look and a nod to Stellen. *Be prepared*, the look said. Stellen nodded his understanding.

Minutes later, Dels and Leath spotted the riders moving through a meadow fringed with heavy rock. The Cudgel Mountains grew nearer with each passing day, and outcroppings of chalky stone became more common. As Lues and the Harminos saw Dels and Leath, they pushed their horses all the harder. In moments, they reigned in beside the men.

"What it is?" Dels asked as he turned his horse and began moving back to the townsfolk.

"Nylacci." Tapper Harmino's voice belied his fear. "But they're dead, Dels."

Dels and Leath both turned.

"The ones we *saw* were dead, but that's not to say there aren't others around." Moppy had moved up beside his brother as they followed the Spallics. "They were dead, Dels, but it was recent. Really recent. The blood had hardly dried. If I were to guess, I'd say they died this morning."

Dels continued riding. "How many?"

"Two," Lues replied. "Killed at the bridge. Or, at least hung there. They could have been killed anywhere, I suppose."

"Hung?" Leath turned.

Lues nodded. "We didn't get too close. We didn't know if there were more around. But we could see that their death was recent. We feared there were more about. Or…something worse, possibly."

"Worse than Nylacci," Tapper muttered. "What could possibly be worse?"

"Our people falling into their midst," Dels muttered. "Come. We need a plan."

Dels could not see the harm in sharing what little information they had with the townsfolk, if for no reason than to convince them that now was a time for caution and quiet. Two dead Nylacci, killed recently and hung by the bridge. The first complication was that whatever did the killing would in all likelihood still be in the vicinity.

The second was that this bridge was one that the Egimians needed to cross.

"What are your thoughts, Dels?" Lumb Velto asked quietly.

Dels scratched behind his ear, turning to his uncle. "There's little to be done for it. Turning back is not an option. Nor is remaining here. The danger could come from any direction, no matter which we choose. So we follow our given path."

Several mutters from the citizens.

Dels raised a gentle hand. "I know. There truly is no safe place. All that's left for us is to move with caution to the bridge and beyond."

"Caution is key," Stellen added. "We need to distribute our weapons and fighters as evenly as possible – equal numbers of archers on each side, and front and back. Best to keep the town tight, and ensure quiet movement, especially whe–" Stellen stopped, and his face flushed. "My apologies, Dels," he said, turning to the big man. "Listen to me here, assuming command of the whole outfit." He shook his head, and gave an embarrassed smile. "These were ideas only, Dels. Certainly, tell us how you'd see fit to prepare our folk."

"I would see fit to follow your wise suggestions, Commander," he replied. The corner of his mouth lifted. It was all the smile Dels could muster. "Also, I'd recommend we set out quickly. The noon hour is past, and we've several slow leagues to go before we reach the bridge." Dels soon delegated duties to the others. Lumb Velto and several trenocs went to the rear of the line. Stellen and Leath organized the front. Lues and the Harminos saw to the flanks. Where defences were poor, people and weapons were rearranged. Granted, Dels knew as he oversaw the preparations that they'd not be able to create an impenetrable barrier to attackers. What they were creating was the best possible chance at survival.

He'd gone up and down the length of his people several times, making quick suggestions, answering questions, and selecting scouts. Two riders would go ahead of the company, and he doubled the number of trenocs who would survey the area from the trees above. Having completed these tasks, he prepared to set out. Dahlah Rallo caught his eye, and gave him a grateful smile that could not hide her fear. He returned the smile, and moved to the head of his people, just behind the two riders that would soon disappear further up the path. He whispered a prayer to Dahnu that no dark beasts would fall upon them as they made their way to the bridge.

The East Bridge – the furthest bridge from the Embarrian capital whose upkeep was still deemed the responsibility of the Crown – was aged, but not in a terrible state of disrepair. It had been well-built, wide enough for two horse-drawn carts to pass each other unhindered, and even boasted a rounded roof that ran its entire length. Upon its initial completion, Dels supposed, it might have been deemed beautiful. Yet today, as two slabs of flesh, fur and blood swung gently from the roof at the entranceway, the structure's grandeur was decidedly marred.

The riders stood back a safe distance, waiting for Dels and the others to catch up. All eyes watched for movement within the trees, which in places were thick and close. It was certainly a sight better than looking at the corpses, each of whom were being pecked and prodded by a ravenous group of crows. The main body of the townsfolk was kept back from the scene, though none let their guard down. Every squawk from the black birds that circled overhead caused a child to jump or cry out.

"A murder of crows..." Moppy remarked.

"Never saw a crow that could tie a hangman's collar," Tapper replied, his eyes fixed on the beast closest to him.

Moppy rolled his eyes. "It's the *word* for a group of crows, dimwitter. I know the crows didn't do this. I thought it clever...given the circumstances."

Dels was aware that the boys, in true Harmino fashion, were trying to lighten the mood and lessen the fear that hung over all. He knew as well how futile such efforts would be.

"What does it mean?" Dels whispered almost to himself.

"A warning?" Leath offered.

"Maybe." Stellen shook his head. "Or maybe a punishment. Perhaps these savages have their own horrific code of law, and this was a consequence inflicted by their own kin."

Dels stepped closer, his eyes on the Nylac who'd recently lost his own to the pecking of the birds. "I'm more inclined to think as Leath does. It's a warning, set here to deter other Nylacci from crossing this bridge."

Stellen stepped back from the Nylac; the smell beginning to bother him. "What kind of savage beast could do this to Nylacci? What kind of sick monsters are we dealing wi–"

The steel tip of the blade resting on the soft flesh of his neck precluded his next words. He uttered a small, urgent gasp.

Everyone spun. Chaos ensued in the moments that followed. Cries of warning, which reached the ears of the townsfolk and set off a chain reaction in that group as well. Weapons were drawn, and the Egimians came together, shoulder to shoulder as they faced Stellen and the creature that held his life in his chalky, white hands. More of the creatures materialized from the trees; silent, weapons held ready. Warning cries had turned to screams, threats and more pointed blades and arrows. Just as the situation seemed about to explode into a bloody melee, Dels Spallic stepped between the two opposing sides, his empty hands raised.

"Stand down, now!" he yelled at the Egimians. When only a couple of arrows seemed to lower at his command, he issued another that held no room for delay. *"STAND. DOWN!"* he roared. The weapons of his kin came down, but not those of the newcomers. Dels remained between the groups, breathing slowly to regain composure, his hands still raised. Once his breath had been caught, he looked at the creature before him. His pale hands still held the blade firm. His face was both rigid and indifferent. He towered over Stellen, perhaps by a couple of feet. Though his hood was partially up, Dels could see his smooth, pasty skin and bald head.

Dels stepped forward. Slow steps. Small steps. "You are the Drales, are you not?"

The big Drale beside Stellen leaned forward, huge beside Stellen's large body. When his long face was next to

Stellen's, he turned it slowly to face the terrified Egim-ian. *"Are* we Drales?" he asked, his deep reverberating voice ended in a rasp. "Or are we…savage beasts?" Angry sounds from the other Drales. The one beside Stellen continued. "Or are we…sick monsters?"

"No." Stellen's voice was as weak as Dels had ever heard it. "No, I didn't mean that about…about you." He swallowed, impeded by the blade that still poked at his neck. "I, I just meant that anything so powerful to kill these Nylacci must be…"

"Savage?" the Drale asked again. "Then perhaps we must show you how we–"

"Skauro." Another voice, this one even more deep and powerful than the one beside Stellen. The newcomer walked up beside Dels, facing the one called Skauro. "You take things too far, young-son. Save your blade for those who would destroy you, not wound you with petty insults." This Drale was, if possible, even taller than Skauro. His skin, pale like the milk of white oleander shone as though almost translucent. Like all the others, he too was bald, but seemed to possess a brute strength beyond any around him. Skauro's lips grew tight, as did his eyes, but he lowered the blade. "May the Just Father absolve me, Daurr."

Dels perked at the name. Daurr. He'd heard it on rare occasions. Daurr was said to be the leader of the Drales. He regretted that they'd gotten off to such an unfortunate start, but was relieved that they had found the inhabitants of Ras, those whom they'd been told to seek out.

Dels attempted to move the conversation in a direction that might allay perceived insults.

"I commend you for your defeat of these creatures, Master Daurr. I can–"

"Daurr," the Drale interjected. "Only Daurr." Apparently, he had little use for titles or propriety.

Dels nodded. "We have had an unfortunate encounter with these…Nylacci as well." He was careful to avoid either of the previously offending words. "It seems that these lands are no longer–"

"How many?" Daurr looked over Dels' shoulder in the direction from which the Egimians had come.

"Dozens," Dels answered. "They razed our village and–"

"Not the horned ones." Daurr's voice was gruff. "Your people, small man. How many do you bring?"

Confusion furrowed Dels' brow for a moment. "Ah… A little more than a hundred. A hundred and twenty, perhaps."

Daurr grunted. "If they are crossing, let them cross. The bridge is about to burn." He turned away, exchanging words with the one he'd called Skauro.

Burn? Dels exchanged a look with Stellen, who'd hurried over to his friends, still rubbing his neck. It made sense, he supposed. This bridge must have allowed a number of Nylacci access to the lands south of the river.

"Thank the Goddess for good fortune," he said quietly. "It seems we arrived just in time."

Daurr turned his large head slightly, eyes narrow. "You did not. You arrived late. You can thank your Goddess that we saw fit to wait for you."

His words shocked the Egimians, who simply stared for several moments.

"Wait for us?" Dels asked. He glanced back in the distance towards the townspeople, then at Daurr. "How could you know we were coming?"

Daurr grunted as he walked to the bridge, signalling to those on the far side to come to him. "The Child."

"Child?" Dels was confused. "A child told you this?"

Daurr shook his head. "A *Child*. First Child… Fae."

"A *faerae?*" Dels asked, his tone suggesting disbelief. It was the wrong reaction. Daurr turned on the Egimian, closing the distance between them in seconds. Leath's hand twitched and went to his scabbard. "Question me, small man." Daurr leaned in, his face mere inches from that of Dels. *"Question me."*

Dels shook his head, his hands raised in apology. For the first time since their meeting, he felt true fear of the creature. "Forgive me. I trust you. I do. It's not so hard to believe, given all we've seen in recent days." Worried that he'd hurt the Egimians' chances of aid, he tried to assuage Daurr. "We cannot thank you enough for waiting for us, Daurr. Please, give us but moments and we'll have our grateful people across the bridge."

Silence surrounded them. A whimper from a distant child. Daurr waited a moment, his eyes hard. Then he grunted and moved away.

Dels made sure the crossing of the bridge happened quickly. He gave no time to coaxing or assurance. He had a job to do, and he did it efficiently. The townsfolk sensed his urgency and did not question him. As they approached the bridge, mothers covered the eyes of the younger children; the Nylacci bodies swaying silently as a macabre gateway above them.

They were soon across the bridge, and Dels watched as two Drales produced pails of some liquid that they spread down the length of the wooden planks. Some kind of animal fat, he assumed. Daurr pointed to the path beyond, ordering Egimians and Drales alike to begin the trek.

As Dels passed Daurr, he began to thank him again, but was abruptly cut off.

"You are weak," he said. Dels moved to speak but the Drale raised a hand to silence him. "The weak need assistance. The Child said it would be so." His hard eyes held those of Dels before glancing at a Drale who leaned against an oak in obvious pain. The Drale seemed young, standing at a height of six feet; short compared to his kin. His leg was badly hurt, broken likely. Deep cuts were evident as well – injuries Dels assumed were sustained in the Nylacci encounter. Daurr turned back to Dels.

"If you intend to reach Ras, keep up."

The Drales set out. Dels looked from the injured Drale to the creature's kin and back again, incredulous. It seemed they were going to leave the wounded fellow to his own devices. Whether he survived or not would depend on his resolve. Slowly, the townspeople filed past the injured Drale as well until the final cart had lumbered by. It had not gotten ten feet past the lame creature when a quick, forceful shout was issued.

"Stop!"

Daurr, who was watching the procession, turned his head as the Egimians came to an abrupt halt. On the bridge, small flames began to rise.

Kitt Rallo removed herself from the final cart and went

to the side of the Drale.

"You won't get far on that leg, in that condition. Get on the cart."

The creature stared at her for a second, and then moved to limp past her, paying no heed to her words. He took one feeble step and nearly fell. She stepped in front of him.

"You can't walk. Get on the cart."

At this, Daurr moved back to the exchange, impatience writ upon his face.

"Ghaur was injured in the fight. The Just Father has deemed he did not fight valiantly. This is his consequence. Step aside, small one."

"I will *not!*" Kitt turned to Daurr. "We've room on that cart for this young one. I'll not see him suffer when we can help."

Daurr opened his mouth to speak but Kitt cut in. "The alternative," she said, her voice sharper, "is that *I* will choose to walk as well. Beside *you*." She pointed a thin, crooked finger at Daurr. "I can make small talk all the way to Ras, *Son*. And don't doubt that I'll keep up."

Again, Daurr began to speak, but Kitt moved her finger up to within inches of the Drale's big face.

"Question *me*," she said.

No sound could be heard but the crackling of the fire as it took hold of the wood. After a moment, Daurr looked at the injured Drale. He tilted his head to indicate the back of the cart.

Kitt stole a glance at Dels, and gave him a wry smile and a wink.

Question me, she mouthed.

Dels allowed himself the smallest smile. They would reach Ras, he thought, and the relative safety it would provide his people. *Well, most of his people.* He took a breath and whispered a small prayer for Sivino. *I'll find you,* he thought. *I'll reach you.* He would take things one step at a time, but if required, he'd turn this world upside down to see that no harm befell those he loved.

He glanced behind the group once more, this part of the journey complete. With a new resolve, he hardened his eyes and began to walk.

There were leagues yet to cross.

Behind them all, flames licked the sky as the bridge was engulfed.

36

THE SWORD OF A BOY

Sivino Spallic awoke beside a lake.

He'd slept deeply. For several moments he mistook the low, swirling mist surrounding him for the clouded vision of waking. He looked around, knowing immediately that something was amiss. There was an unfamiliar feel to this place; a feeling of isolation. He turned around several times, trying to gain a sense of this wrongness. It was only when he looked up that he realized the gravity of the situation.

The sky was alive.

Never in his life had he seen something so strange, and yet so beautiful. His eyes focused on the wondrous hue beyond the mist, and his mind fought to make sense of a sight that made none. A wild purple firmament, bright as any noonday sky in Egim, shone above him. Though he knew it to be daylight, a plethora of the brightest stars twinkled throughout. Colour seemed to swirl around the stars, which shot across the horizon every few seconds.

The sky, he knew, was not his own. From the bright blues that greeted him each morning to the flushed redness that coloured the sky's cheeks as it relinquished its hold on the day, Egim's sky was predictable. Though dark clouds might occasionally block it out, its beauty never vanished.

And it was never alive.

He looked around more closely now, curious but cautious of potential hidden dangers. He wondered if he'd been shifted to another world. A thought came to him, which instantly tightened his chest. He looked around quickly, considering if he had been taken to the place from which the Nylacci had come. Dreg, Niamh had called it. *Was this the sky of Dreg?* Were Nylacci or creatures even worse hidden within the mists surrounding him?

No, he told himself. Though he knew almost nothing of Dreg, he doubted that such an awe-inspiring sky would cover so forbidding a world. He imagined Dreg to be dark and dirty in every conceivable way. Slowly, he sat back down on the sandy ground, straining his eyes to find anything that gave him a sense of orientation. Just a few paces before him, the waters of a lake met the shore. A variety of plant life grew within the thick forest that lay behind him. He recognized the lilies immediately, those being a favourite of his mother. Beside the lilies was a flower completely foreign to him. The plants stood to his knee and displayed blossoms of red, pink and white. In all his wandering, he'd never seen this variety of flower.

He looked down to check that his sword, or what remained of it, was still on his side. He withdrew it slowly, feeling that it would be wise to take no chances. He looked

at his reflection in the dull blade, his image barely percep-
tible in the weak metal. He lowered the sword and turned
to the lake, watching as the mist slowly burned away.

An incredible thirst was building within him. In
a matter of moments, he was almost overcome with its
intensity. He stood, and took a step toward the lake before stopping abruptly. The spring – he recalled how he'd
drunk deeply from it but remembered nothing afterward.
His eyes returned to the sky. Was it possible that he was
still in Cahruia? That the water that satisfied his thirst had
altered his perceptions, creating illusions in the sky and
foliage? He considered the possibility that his friends
could be within shouting distance, and thought of yell-
ing for them. He dismissed the thought as quickly as it
had come. He could not be certain of where he was, and a
foolish mistake could be deadly. He tightened his grip on
his broken sword, and turned from the lake. Though his
thirst burned, he would not risk drinking again. Slowly,
he took a few steps toward the forest and stopped again,
reconsidering. He sighed, uncertain of how to proceed.
He knew that he could not just sit in one location, waiting
indefinitely for Goddess knew what. He scanned the low
mist to his left and right, seeing very little.

It was what he heard that caught his attention.

To the right he heard flowing water, a sound that had
always and would forever draw his attention. Without
thinking he began to walk toward the sound. A few moments later, he stood before a meandering stream that
emerged from the forest to be swallowed up by the waiting lake. Cautiously, he dipped a foot in the water and
was surprised by its coolness. For the first time since he'd

regained consciousness, he allowed himself to smile. His lips cracked with dryness. He knelt, and leaned forward to drink, realizing what he was doing only moments before his face reached the river. He jerked back quickly, shaking his head. He'd need to keep his senses about him, he reminded himself. He could picture Leath turning away from him, grunting a comment about his weakness. He looked at his distorted reflection in the slow moving water, and shook his head as he was sure his brother would have. He knew that his brother was right. Too often, he was so easily taken in.

"Sivino Spallic." A voice from the mist.

He gasped and scrambled backward toward the forest, away from the voice which had floated over the lake. Moments later, the embodiment of that voice came into view.

She emerged from the mist, walking effortlessly through the waist-deep water, Sivino's body felt as though it was paralyzed. Gone were his thoughts of Leath, his thirst, and the dangers of the forest. He was entirely transfixed. The way he'd felt when he'd met Niamh did not compare to this encounter, perhaps because he was now alone, but more likely it was the sound of the woman's voice, which seemed to enter his mind and his heart rather than his ears. He felt a sense of peace descend upon him, though not enough to put him entirely at ease.

Slowly, he got to his feet. As he did so, the woman stopped and considered him. He felt entirely vulnerable, as though she was looking into his very soul. Her expression did not change. It was impossible to read her face.

For long moments, they stared at each other. The waters around the woman were completely still, as if her movement had no effect on the element. She moved forward again, and brought her hands – which had to this point been held below the surface – to her chest, her left hand wrapping itself around the right. She looked at him through slightly narrowed eyes.

"You have no need to be afraid." She spoke clearly, her voice as sure as an oak, though her lips didn't move. Sivino heard her voice within his mind. *"Do you know who I am?"* she asked.

The boy shook his head slowly, though he was not aware he was doing so. He looked down at his hands, turning them over. They seemed real. He looked back at the woman. Her face was like stone. *Dreaming,* he thought. *That's the only explanation. Dreaming, or I was knocked unconscious. Or that water did something to my head.*

She began to move, her loose clothing so thin and transparent that Sivino felt his cheeks flush. She scarcely stirred the water as she moved toward the shore. As she stepped from the lake, the water on her dress sparkled before disappearing, leaving the cloth dry. Sivino held his breath as the lady approached him.

"You know who I am." It wasn't a question.

He took a step back, his face stricken. The Flowing One. The Goddess.

She moved closer, her face impassive as Sivino shook his head. *"I would have you speak to me, Sivino Spallic. To me. Not to a name or a title."*

Struggling to steady himself, Sivino sat down heavily. His hands were shaking. "Dahnu," he whispered. He'd said the name a thousand times, it being a common, mild profanity within the Three Realms, but to actually speak the name to the being Herself was beyond comprehension. "I–" He took a breath, and composed himself as he looked at the strange sky again. "I seem to be...lost."

Dahnu shook her head. *"Not lost,"* she whispered as she stopped before him. Slowly, she took the sword from his tattered scabbard. *"Not lost, but...broken perhaps."* She slid a finger unharmed along the edge of the blade, and turned back to the lake.

"You seem to understand water as we do, Sivino Spallic. You see its beauty, its ability to give life, take life, and change. It is constant, much like the Fae. Taking many forms, the smallest trickle changes the face of the world over time. In it, you see a reflection of yourself, though depending on the wind and sky, the reflection may be quite distorted." She stopped for a moment, and then turned toward him. *"For you are a reflection of us. Though the waters are disturbed and deceptively deep, the reflection within is clear."*

She turned to the river, and stepped into the gentle flow. Again, Sivino saw the brilliant sparkle where the water met the cloth of her dress. Dahnu turned to face the current, and slowly began to walk up the river, her legs gracefully parting the water. Within moments, Sivino realized that like the creature before him and like the sky above, this was an unnatural stream, unlike any in which he'd ever dabbled his feet. As the deity walked through the water – the remains of Sivino's sword in her hand – she began to sink. It was as though some invisible staircase ran below the flowing water. In short moments, she disappeared. Sivino moved closer to the water and went to one knee, hoping to see some of what lay beneath. He looked closely at the spot where Dahnu had disappeared, but saw nothing. The water which appeared so clear and transparent reflected the deep purple of the sky, and all that existed below the water remained unseen. Leaning closer, he saw himself, reflected in the water.

Sivino reached out and touched the reflection. The current appeared to be flowing rather quickly, though it felt quite slow to his hand. He kept himself steady, his hand submerged, and could not help but feel that his touch was slowing the current of the entire river. It felt this way, though to his eye, the water continued to flow by unhindered.

Does she intend that I follow? He leaned closer still, until his face nearly touched the water's surface. Still he could see nothing.

For what seemed like an eternity, he waited. He studied the water, searching for any change in its appearance. Occasionally, he'd turn his gaze to the sky, or glance at the forest when a sound arose. At one point, a swallow landed in a tree quite close to him, and tilted its head repeatedly as if questioning the presence of a strange young boy. It was a tiny thing, with a snow-white chest and bluish grey wings and head. After careful consideration, the bird opened its bill and made a series of quick, consecutive whistles. Following each set, it would tilt its head before repeating the pattern, keeping up this cheerful conversation for several moments. Then, it began to sing in earnest, and the song was so pleasant to hear that Sivino suddenly realized he was smiling.

The bird then stopped, and tilted its head a final time.

"Thank you," Sivino said with a slight nod.

The bird ruffled its feathers and flew away.

Sivino shifted his attention back to the water. How long had it been since Dahnu had left him? Looking at the river, he was suddenly drawn to thoughts of his mother. How long had it been since *she* had left him? How many prayers had he whispered to the Goddess in the darkness of his room, pleading with her to save Rhenna? He closed his eyes, resting several fingers upon his forehead. The prayers, of course, had not been answered. In the year of Rhenna's sickness, he'd made the sign of the waterdrop over his heart enough times to have engraved it on his chest. If what Niamh said was true, perhaps prayers were as futile as trying to stop a stream with one's bare hands. Fate had a way of slipping through the fingers, following its own course with little care of the hearts it drowned in sorrow along the way.

"Something troubles you, Sivino Spallic."

Sivino jumped and his eyes snapped open. Dahnu had emerged from the stream so silently that Sivino hadn't heard her approach. The water ran from her body and loose clothing, which again dried instantly. Even her hair was dry, swaying slightly as she faced him. He stood without realizing he'd done so, and his gaze lowered to the sword she now held.

"It is believed," she whispered softly, *"that you need this."*

She raised the sword slowly. His eyes grew wide for just an instant, before incredulity turned to doubt. It was a blade unlike any that Sivino had ever seen. Long and slender, the edges looked as though they could cut through stone. The ebony hilt gleamed. Sivino looked at his empty scabbard, which he knew could never hold a blade such as this.

He felt the same about his hands.

Dahnu looked at the longblade with unknowable thoughts. Its smooth metal reflected the light of the sun along its entire length as she slowly turned it. Her slender hand gently gripped the hilt, her smallest finger tracing along the curve of the shiny black pommel. Her other hand held the blade just above the guard, where the metal was kept dull. She did not smile, but Sivino could see the pride in her eyes.

"It is ancient," she whispered. *"It is legend."*

"It looks as if it were forged moments ago," Sivino replied.

Dahnu looked from the sword to the boy, her face serious. Sivino waited, sure that she was about to say something, but she did not. Instead, she took a step toward him and lifted the sword once more, extending her arms. He hesitated in taking it; intimidated by the sheer size and potential of the blade, and fearful that even its weight might expose his weakness.

"Do not be afraid. Long have we waited for the moment that we could give this to you." If she noticed the shock on his face, she did not acknowledge it. *"Fell deeds threaten your world – many worlds – and you hold the light that is needed to find the way through. The mad faerae will wreak havoc through the worlds if you do not stop him."*

"No," Sivino said, shaking his head. "You're mistaken. I can't be the one you've waited for."

She raised an eyebrow, almost imperceptibly, but Sivino saw it and realized he'd just told the Goddess that she was mistaken. The Goddess.

"I'm sorry," he stammered. "I didn't... I...I never..."

"*I am more ancient than the blade itself, Sivino Spallic. From the birth of your race, there have been humanfolk who consider themselves heroes for the smallest of deeds...and there have been those who consider themselves too small to accomplish the deeds of a hero.*" She extended the blade once more, and he took it. It was lighter than he'd imagined, and though he held it awkwardly, his heart swelled at its mere touch. He turned the blade over in his hands, his eyes tricked by the strange metal as he seemed to be able to look deep beyond the surface to the very core of the sword. He couldn't help but smile. It was magnificent, from the pointed tip to the polished hilt. Perfectly crafted. And then he stopped. The smile vanished, replaced by shock and confusion. He looked at Dahnu, who already knew the cause of his astonishment.

Upon the hilt of the sword, beneath the brilliant, shining finish, there was an etching. A rough yet beautiful representation of a rising sun.

"This blade..." Sivino began.

"*Is your own.*" Dahnu took a step toward the boy, and tilted her head in an attempt to better see the carving. Somehow, Sivino knew that it was an unnecessary gesture. The Goddess was quite familiar with the blade, and likely many other aspects of his life.

"How?" he whispered.

"*You of all people should know, Sivino Spallic, that all things broken may be made whole again. This is the will of the Faant. This blade has been graced with their touch. Its power is immense. The strength you need has been forged within, though the courage to draw it must come from you alone. The blade has been passed down through generations and through worlds. Its history is a legend you've never heard. Broken. Reforged. Over and over. The sword has lived more lives than any blade in existence. And each time it is reforged, its strength grows. The Faant have...perfected it. This weapon will serve you against the darkest of foes."*

"Can you not help us?" Sivino interjected. "Do you not have the power to stop such evil?" He felt his voice grow thick in his throat, but he forged on. "People pray for the end of this war... People pray for *many* reasons. For...for the lives of those they love." He blinked away the tears that began to form. "Every day, people beg for your help and guidance. Is it ever given?"

The words were bold, but the memory of Rhenna's pain lent him the courage to speak in such a manner. Dahnu was unmoving, save for the gentle sway of her thin dress. The trickle of the river's water was the only sound between them.

"It is given every day," she replied. There was no anger in her voice, no indication that she'd taken offence. Her eyes looked to the sky and she continued. *"There are those who believe that Gods and Goddesses live beyond the clouds, in a far-removed place that can only be imagined. There are those who believe that a whispered prayer on a stormy night can traverse the distance and call me to action, beckon me from some imagined throne of gold and glory."* She looked back at Sivino. *"Such is not the way of things. I was given the charge to watch over this world, and guide its inhabitants to the best of my ability."* Her eyes held Sivino's firmly. *"To do this, I walk amongst you."* Sivino's eyes narrowed, his head tilt-

ing ever so slightly. "*I have walked the road to Rovil, Sivino Spallic. I have spent days in the darkest alleys of Torg, and the tallest ships on the Sinking Sea. In the city of Levebule, I was once chastised by the High Priestess herself for the thoughts I shared.*"

"The High Priestess?" Sivino's mouth hung open a little, his eyes narrow. "The High Priestess...of *Dahnu's* Order?"

"*Of Dahnu's Order.*" The Goddess almost smiled. "*I do all that is in my power to guide my people. I share my ideas, and perhaps more importantly, I listen to those who need to be listened to; those who have no one to listen. I walk all paths, Sivino Spallic. I may be the kind stranger who offers a word of advice to a farmer in the field, or the unfamiliar old lady who notes a likely remedy to the mother of a sick babe.*" She folded her hands before her, and glanced at the trees. "*I may be the swallow that watches the children at play, or cheers a grieving widow with a joyful melody.*" She blinked, and Sivino again saw that familiar shadow of a smile. "*There are few indeed who thank me for my song.*"

Sivino's eyes widened, but Dahnu continued, her tone growing serious. "*But I cannot prevent death, Sivino Spallic. I cannot interfere with the course of nature. I can only lend my assistance when the occasion arises, and offer a hand in setting things right.*"

She looked over the boy's shoulder, at the grey clouds that billowed in from the west, swallowing the purple sky as it approached.

"*I am connected to the Faant, and I pass their Whispers to the creatures of Fae.*" She looked him in the eye. "*I do not know what you will do with this blade, Sivino Spallic, but I'm well versed in prophecy, as you would call it."* For the first time, Dahnu's smile shone through, though a touch of sadness marred its brilliance. She moved closer to him, and laid a hand on each of his shoulders. *"And it is said that within the unnatural storm, a shepherd true and dark shall find his blood spilt on the sword of a boy. A lost soul shall know those bonds that dying blood reveals. In the shadow of loss the shepherd shall fade, for the strength of a boy shall cut through a power both great and terrible."*

Slowly, she traced a waterdrop over his heart. *"It flows within you, this strength,"* she whispered. Before he could begin to question her words, she traced the same shape over his forehead. He noticed the coolness of her fingers, the tingle of her residual touch.

"Go now, child, and do those things which must be done."

"But I…" And then he stopped, of a sudden, before another word could be uttered. He stopped not because he couldn't find the right words, but because the time for those words had passed. The time for excuses had passed. For the first time in his life, he stepped through and beyond the childish rationalizations, the shirking of responsibility, and the feeble justification of inaction. He pushed them aside, these imagined brambles and branches that had ever stayed his progress.

He looked to the sky, and thought he felt the slightest chill in that breeze which seemed to have come from no-where. *Perhaps*, he thought, *it came with those clouds.* The grey curtain drew itself ever closer, but today Sivino did not look away. Would not. He would not turn and seek clearer skies on a far horizon. And he would not look to the dirt.

It is time, he thought to himself.

Leath. *Ah, how Leath would laugh at him now, at these words and thoughts, at a boy who–* Sivino stopped. *No.* He would *not* go down that path, for as the Goddess herself had said, it was time to do those things which must be done. Rumination, he knew, did not fall into this category.

Sure, Leath might laugh at him.

But then, he conceded as he considered all things, *perhaps he might not.*

Sivino Spallic took the hand of the Goddess. He did so with no discomfort as he turned and looked to the waters of the lake. The path lay before him. Paths both great and small would now lead him where they would.

He accepted this.

"Come," the Goddess whispered as she stepped into the lake, toward a path that would carry him to a world no longer familiar, a future no longer certain.

"Come," she said once more.

"It is time."

HERE ENDS BOOK ONE
OF
THE EGIMIAN CHRONICLES

GLOSSARY

Cen Kohr, Cehron *(SEN-COOR, SEAR-un)*: An ancient faerae (see *Cernunnos*) from the world of Elysium. Once friend to the faerae Niamh and confidant to the faerae king Obaeron. In recent years, his behaviour has grown unpredictable and dangerous.

Cernunnos *(KER-NOON-ous)*: The Cernunnos has the appearance of a human, though he possesses the antlers of a stag. A faerae with deep connections to nature, the Cernunnos will often appear in the company of animals.

Dahnu *(DAH-new)*: Known as the *Flowing One*. Once a faerae, she was long ago elevated to the status of Goddess by the beings known as the Faant. Having been made a deity, it was the role of Dahnu, as a Goddess, to convey the messages of the Faant to the *Fae*, the first race trusted to hear and act upon the wishes of the Faant in order to protect and maintain balance between and within worlds. She has been known to take the form of a swallow.

Drales *(d-RAILs)*: An enigmatic, reclusive race that lives in Ras, a city carved into the rock of the Cudgel Mountains. Much taller than humans, they possess pale skin and sharp, muscular features. Most Drales maintain a bald head. They practice the polytheistic religion of An-trohkism, which holds divine two deities, the *Just Father* and the *Good Mother*.

Drip: A trenoc whose predecessors formed a partner-ship with the Spallic family in a previous generation. He lives on the Spallic property, and is generally considered a part of the family.

Faant (FAH-nt): Demiurges, or Beings responsible for the creation of the universe. Of incalculable age, the Faant is thought to have been comprised of three distinct yet connected entities. They created the First world of Pange, and subsequently, all worlds that were created following its destruction. Their connection to each other and to all worlds of the universe remains intact, in no small mea-sure due to the Paths, the *Fingers of the Faant*, which still maintain the connection between worlds known and un-known. Serving still as caretakers of these worlds, they relay their wishes and requests in the form of *visions*; mes-sages relayed to Gods, Goddesses and Fae who might see their wishes made manifest.

Fae (FAY): The term given to the race of faerae, the *First Ones*, also known as the *First Children*. From this race, a select few are chosen to receive the wishes and requests of the creators, known collectively as the Faant, in order to influence and regulate the balance of life upon the worlds. The Fae live primarily in the world of Elysium (known also as Avalon, Otherworld, and Tir Na N'Og). Many of their race have an inherent command of magic that allows them to exert a natural influence upon others, though the extent of the power wielded varies amongst the race. They are known to live exceedingly long lives, seeming immortal to other races. They are unable to tell a lie, but are known to mislead and create mischief when interacting with other races, quite often through the use of their song and music which can have an enchanting effect on any who listen.

First Ones, or First Children: *See Fae.*

Lailoken, Lomin *(LIE-LOW-Kihn, LOW-min):* A reclusive man of sixty years, who lives on the outskirts of Egim. Sometimes referred to as the *old wolf,* he is a friend of Sivino and his peers, and plays a protective role in their lives. He has a small command of magic.

Niamh (NEEV): The daughter of Obaeron, king of the Fae. She fell in love with the mortal man, Oisin, and brought him to Elysium. Once friend of Cehron Cen Kohr.

Nylacci (NYE-Lock-EE): A race of violent creatures who, in an age long passed, roamed the world of Cahruia. They were removed from this world, banished to the world of Dreg, by the Fae, at the behest of the Faant.

Obaeron *(O-BER-on):* The king of the Fae. He has ruled Elysium, and influenced other worlds, for most of his three thousand years.

Oisin (O-SHEEN) – Mortal man and former warrior who falls in love with the faerae Niamh and travels with her to the land of Elysium. Son of Sabd (Mother) and Finn (Father) MacComhal. Finn is the leader of the Fenian warriors.

The Paths: *The Fingers of the Faant* (See Faant). Powerful, ethereal passages that connect worlds, and places within worlds, created by the breaking of the First world, Pange. Travel upon these Paths (most commonly formed within bodies of water, mist gates, and Fae Rings) may only be initiated by the Fae, though mortal beings are sometimes conveyed by faerae creatures.

Rallo, Kef (RAH-low, KEF): A young man of fourteen years, close friend of Sivino Spallic, and brother of Torla.

Rallo, Torla (RAH-low, TORE-la): A young woman of sixteen years, close friend of Sivino, and sister of Kef.

Ryndarra (Rin-DARR-ah): A militarized organization responsible for the maintenance of peace, law and order in the realm of Embarria. In times of war, the Ryndarra comprise the greater part Embarria's force, in addition to those recruited/conscripted.

Spallic, Sivino (Suh-VEE-No): A young man of sixteen years, from the small farming village of Egim.

Spallic, Dels: A farmer and widower from the village of Egim. A former respected member of the *Ryndarra*. Father of Sivino and adoptive father of Leath. Respected as a leader in his village.

Spallic, Leath (LEE-th): Eighteen year old nephew/adopted son of Dels Spallic, and cousin/step-brother of Sivino.

Talchol, Inlonia (TAL-kole, In-LOW-NEE-a): The current queen of Embarria.

Trenocs (Tren-OCKs): A race originally from the eastern realm of Jhora. Forty years ago, they were driven from the land following an edict of the Jhoran king meant to cleanse the lands of the trenoc presence. Short in stature, covered in fur, and foul-tempered, they are hard workers, and loyal to those who have earned their respect.

Tros, Ston (TROWEs, STONN): A young man of fifteen years, best friend of Sivino Spallic.

Tryn (Trinn): Faithful advisor to Obaeron, he also serves as the king's confidante and messenger.

ACKNOWLEDGEMENTS

The story of Sivino Spallic and his companions has been with me since 2006. Through years of rewriting and reimagining this tale, there have been numerous people who have lent needed advice and encouragement along the way.

My parents, Jim and Mary. The writer Emilie Buchwald said that 'children are made readers on the laps of their parents.' This was the case with me, and the love of the written word that began in my childhood home has grown like wildfire in the years that have since passed. I'm incredibly lucky to have parents that provide the kindling for this fire, and fanned the flames with their belief that a dream might be realized.

To all members of the Lynch, Boland, Kavanagh, Farrell, Stone, Hefferan, Gibbons and Selst families, know that your interest in and support of my writing continues to be greatly appreciated.

Few aspiring authors are given the opportunity to have a *New York Times* bestselling author read their work and share thoughts on the story. Karen Lynch, your work continues to inspire me, and I'm grateful for the feedback you provided on this novel.

Deep gratitude is extended to my sister Marie Hefferan, Bonnie and Jeff Birmingham, Rachel Tessier, Dylan Matthias, Rosalind and Jim Pinsent, Andrew Lynch, Michelle Brazil, Gerard Brazil, Mark O'Neill, Jeff Chard, Jon Dobbin, Sheri-Lynn Singleton, Mark Snow, the Lanark crew (past and present), the incredible staff of the Writers Alliance of Newfoundland and Labrador, the beautiful members of Genre Writers of Atlantic Canada, the entire school community of Roncalli Elementary and supportive colleagues throughout the Newfoundland Labrador English School District.

Thank you to the entire team at Engen Books - Erin Vance, Amanda Labonté, Matthew Daniels, and especially, Matthew LeDrew and Ellen Curtis. In 2019 I registered for Matthew's writing course, and brought with me a rough draft of my manuscript which at the time was titled The Egimian. Throughout the course and in the time that followed, The Egimian was shaped into *All Things Broken*. Thank you for believing in this book Matthew. And thank you Ellen for the wonderful cover design and for inviting me to be a small part of the process. Your creativity and collaborative approach are greatly appreciated.

Great editors have the ability to look beyond and behind the words, and ask the writer to reach in and extract those hidden but necessary elements. Ali House, a big thank you for your work on editing the manuscript.

Finally, thank you to my wife Tara, and our kids Norah and James. Tara, not only do you allow me the time to write and encourage all my creative efforts, but you continually inspire me to follow the dream. Norah and James, it's a great feeling to write a story and put it out in the world, but it can't compare to the joy of watching how your stories are unfolding each and every day. Every chapter is better than the last...

ABOUT THE AUTHOR

David James Lynch is an award-winning author who has spent the last two decades working as an educator and school counsellor.

He grew up in the small town of Bellevue Beach, and currently lives in Paradise, Newfoundland and Labrador with his wife Tara, and their children, Norah and James.

His short fiction won both the 2022 and 2021 WritersNL Nightmare Writing Contests.

He has a habit of purchasing more books than he'll ever be able to read, believing a home always has room for one more bookcase.

All Things Broken is his first novel.